Bring Me
Sunshine

LAURA KEMP

ORION

An Orion paperback

First published in Great Britain in 2019
by Orion Books
an imprint of The Orion Publishing Group Ltd
Carmelite House, 50 Victoria Embankment
London EC4Y 0DZ

An Hachette UK Company

1 3 5 7 9 10 8 6 4 2

A CIP catalogue record for this book
is available from the British Library.

ISBN 978 1 4091 7485 1

Typeset by Deltatype Ltd, Birkenhead, Merseyside

Printed in Great Britain by Clays Ltd, Elcograf S.p.A.

www.orionbooks.co.uk

For Sufia, in memory of our Machers,
who brought so much sunshine.

Prologue

A Friday in February

'It's all backing up between junctions six and five anti-clockwise at Clacket Lane services. Avoid it if you can because no one's going anywhere anytime soon – just like our Charlie Traffic! Next up, it's Chris Rea with *The Road to Hell* ...'

～

Charlie Bold placed her meal deal on her desk and declared it was officially lunchtime. Her announcement was not made to the vast and shiny industrial-style open-plan office but to herself, in her head. If no one expected you to speak, no one would be listening. And even if she did talk out loud, she'd never be heard above the banter and egos at Orbital FM, the only radio station dedicated to the M25 motorway.

Besides, for most of the millennials here, their bento boxes and baguettes, salads and wraps were demolished by mid-morning: they were either feeding hangovers, unfamiliar with the concept of delayed gratification or too 'mad and crazy' to stick to convention.

Charlie, though, always waited until she was back from

the studio's 1 p.m. bulletin when she handed a script of the latest travel information to the DJ, who'd read it out before the news and weather. With a full stomach she'd be sluggish – when she came anywhere near a bright red 'on air' sign, she needed to be alert so she could react to any possible rug-pulling. She knew only too well how tears of bitter disappointment played havoc with the fader button on a broadcasting desk.

Not that she told anyone that was why she stuck to her ritual. Not that anyone really mentioned it any more – it was old gossip. Apart from Zoe, who occasionally dared to make hopeful noises about Charlie possibly going out with her for a bite or deviating from her same daily choice from Boots. But why would Charlie risk having something else and not liking it? She knew where she was with her Simply Ham sandwich, which she now liberated from the cardboard by the nine-times-out-of-ten reliable top left-hand corner.

Next, she perfectly pinched apart a packet of Walkers ready salted crisps and unscrewed a no-bits orange juice, leaving the cap on in case of spillages.

She checked the time on the huge green-figured digital clock on the news desk wall at the far end of the room, noting it was 13.07. As it was every day when she sat down to eat. But she felt neither pleasure nor boredom, just relief. She had been able to do her job satisfactorily minus any unexpected curveballs which would've thrown her out of her comfort zone and into danger. Some craved the spotlight but she would rather stay in the safety of the shadows. And that was fine, she told herself as she tucked into the adequate wholemeal sarnie, totally fine, because there was a place for everyone. Even here in competitive dog-savage-dog London. Because while Orbital FM's award-winning cheeky chatter and bouncy beats – 'keeping you moving even when your wheels aren't' – was the filling, their half a million listeners also tuned in for the four-times-an-hour bread and butter updates of junction closures and tailbacks, accidents and speed restrictions. And that was down to Charlie leading its coverage of all 117 miles of the circular road across 5 counties and 31 junctions.

A slurping sound approached and Charlie saw Zoe wiggling towards her from The Service Station, the kitchen area made up of retro booths, American fridge, posh coffee machine and a NutriBullet. Her scarlet lips were puckered on a straw of just-whizzed murky-brown liquid, signalling a new phase of cleanse that would last as long as the Big Mac she'd wolf down tomorrow.

'Let me guess, babe,' Zoe said, her eyebrows disappearing under the bangs of her sleek black shoulder-length bob, 'Mediterranean roasted eel with pig trotter hummus today, is it?'

Charlie offered her uniform sweet smile. 'Oh, do piss off,' she said in a low voice which only her friend could hear.

Zoe cackled more than generously as she slid onto her chair. She understood Charlie wouldn't dream of talking like that, or of even talking, to anyone else. But then having worked together for eight years, she knew how high Charlie's rising star had soared, when she was full of life, and how far she had fallen two years ago, how introverted she had become. To the rest, the dynamic twenty-somethings, she was a shy and quiet has-been on the road to nowhere, not to mention 'ancient' at thirty-three. She was pitied too for her career collapse, the memory of which still made her toes, legs, in fact her entire body curl with humiliation. If only there was a serum she could apply to her brain like the one she doused on her corkscrew blonde hair before she tied it into a straitjacket of a plait. Mind you, being tucked away in the corner next to media sales, monitoring the jams and crashes, diversions and dropped loads was quite good for that.

She was known as 'Charlie Traffic' – a jolly term of affection originally coined by her boyfriend Jonny Kay, the breakfast DJ, which among the go-getters caused hilarity: she was stuck in a rut with the lights permanently on red. And what kind of a freak worked in radio when she was mute in front of a microphone? How had she got away with it for so long? The listeners were in on it too – thanks to the 'wacky' jockeys who'd trail her arrival for the traffic news with an oh-so-funny horn-beeping sound effect, which mocked her self-imposed muzzle.

She'd sucked up the ridicule, lucky to still have a job, glad she hadn't had the shame of having to leave – unlike some people. Sometimes, but no longer, Charlie had thought she should have walked after her meltdown but then what else would she have done? Where would she have gone? Born and bred in Watford, at uni in London where she'd now lived for a decade, she'd never been outside the metropolitan area for longer than a holiday or to see friends. At least she could convince herself she was still in the thick of things and played a vital role. And with Zoe beside her, who'd chosen Charlie's side when everything had gone so disastrously wrong, she had someone to talk to and joke with. Although sometimes, like now, as Zoe thrust her *Psychologies* magazine at her, it got a bit much.

'No, ta,' Charlie said, sliding it back to her. 'Personal development isn't really my thing, is it?'

'I know,' Zoe said, arching a groomed eyebrow, 'that's why you should try it, babe. I remember when—'

'Not today, thank you.' Charlie put her fingers in her ears.

Zoe held up her hands. 'Suit yourself but I know there's some fight left in you ...'

Charlie shook her head, crunching on her crisps. Nope. Zoe was wrong. Fighting meant you faced up to your fears, which meant you admitted they existed. Denial was much better: it kept anxiety at bay and that was how Charlie wanted to live. She was ... happy with that? Happy was the wrong word; she was comfortable with the hand she'd been dealt. Predictable was good enough. End of. Zoe sighed then got up and put on her suit jacket.

'Right, laters,' she said. 'I've got to see a man about some tyres. And then I'm on the road all next week visiting M25 attractions in the vain hope someone will cough up for some airtime. Have a good weekend, my darling, I'm on the phone if you need me ... Oh, by the way, I might need to call you tomorrow. That guy who I thought was really into me, he's being coy about tonight after my fat thumbs incident. It doesn't bode well, does it?'

*

It didn't – no matter how much you liked someone, you'd be put off if they'd stalked your Facebook and accidentally 'liked' a semi-naked baby photo you'd been tagged in. But she'd wait until Zoe wanted to hear it. 'Just remember if he isn't making you feel good then he's not right for you,' she said tactfully instead.

Then with a wave goodbye, Charlie sipped her luke-warm OJ, musing at the ridiculous position she was in as chief romantic adviser to not just Zoe but Charlie's broken-hearted best friend and flatmate, Libby, who'd finished with her boyfriend because he had baulked at the idea of moving in.

Charlie's love life hadn't exactly been straightfor-ward – things had got off to a bumpy start with Jonny through a silly but still painful misunderstanding. It'd been over within three months the first time but she had locked that away in a file marked Jonny Come Lately. When they rekindled their relationship, the gear changes didn't crunch, they were smooth and effortless. Before him, she'd had a few flings with unsuitables – that made her certain Jonny was The One. In nine months they hadn't had a single argument, they had too many shared interests. She knew people wondered what on earth they had in common: in public he was the party dude with the high-energy personality, his golden boy act matching his hair. In private though he was totally different, less confident and more vulnerable, that was the real him, the twenty-one-hours-a-day Jonny who withdrew when he wasn't presenting. People thought breakfast DJs were still like the 1990s Chris Evans, turning up drunk to work on no sleep after hanging out with rock stars and supermodels. Some of the big ones perhaps still were, but

6

Jonny was the opposite: uber-professional, his chillaxed exterior built upon the foundations of being bright-eyed and bushy-tailed, well researched, and a bit of acting. Thrilled that he had chosen her, she would blossom when his misted silver-mirror eyes focused on her, letting her have her say when no one else allowed her to finish a sentence. He even developed some of her ideas for his show: the Going The Extra Mile Gongs for everyday hero drivers, Van Man Says talking heads and the Morning Fry-Up showbiz segment which awarded crispy bacon status to cool celebs and cold toast to Z-listers. She was really proud of that, and of him – he was a natural in the limelight, far more so than she had ever been and his success was hers.

While she had grafted away for her success, he'd climbed the ranks quickly; there was no bitterness, she felt she'd passed the baton on to him. Things between them were flawless – they'd got over what had happened on their previous go, the mistakes that had been made, and it felt like a grown-up relationship.

Maybe that was why her friends held her in high agony aunt esteem. As if she was better at being an adult. She had the experience of good following bad and intuitively she could see the grey in black and white situations. And by being a listener rather than a talker, she was certainly good at observing people. Whatever, it at least made her feel useful. She finished her lunch and then let her eyes relax, blocking out the roars from the 'playground' area where the lads were racing Grand Prix circuits on the Xbox. Her breathing slowed as she rolled her neck and stared at the reflection of her face in the computer screen. As her vision glazed, she saw herself become two and her mind began to wander – there was the Charlie who she was and the Charlie who she had been: adventurous and perky, going with the flow and letting it roll, from school to uni, from hospital radio to here, where she began as a runner and then worked her way up within a few years to be offered a shift behind the microphone, destined to become the nation's favourite DJ ... the Radio Personality of the Year Charlie Bold ... Charlie ... CHARLIE!

Her boss, Stig Costello, was calling her. Not ratings-puller Charlie Bold. But the Charlie Bold who'd crumpled when the pressure got too much, who'd been found out, and who did a good line in radio silence. There was no disappointment at her daydream bubble bursting – she had accepted her lot long ago.

'Got a sec?' he said from his metal door, where his bald head shone beneath a trendy exposed pipe.

She headed over, her trainers squeaking on the con-crete floor, not worried about being summoned to the station manager's see-through cubicle: he'd just joined on Monday and was in the process of meeting and greet-ing every member of staff. He'd obviously read her notes and picked her on a Friday afternoon because she'd be amenable and brief. He gave her a solid handshake and pointed at one of the posh white leather sofas before he shut them in, offering her a bottle of sparkling water from his fridge. She refused, out of habit, because fizzy gave her the hiccups – they were the enemy of live broadcasting.

'So, Charlie ...' he said, sitting down, crossing his legs and poking his heavy square-framed black specs up his nose, '... how are things going?'

'Fine ... good.' She kept it short because she was due to handover to Jessa, her second in command who covered the afternoon and evening shift, plus she had to do a write-up for Billy, who was in the hot seat overnight.

'Excellent, excellent.' He arched his fingers in a steeple like a caring, sharing corporate cliché and then leaned forwards to impart his wisdom. 'Charlie, I'm refreshing the brand to bring it even closer to our audience.'

New station managers – of which there'd been a few in her time – spouted this kind of thing: they wanted to make their mark. Increase listeners and advertising: profits, in other words. So she nodded and thought of her list: her ever-present mental compilation of what she had to do, which kept her focused and gave her a sense of achievement. Parmesan, she'd get that on the way home; it was change-the-sheets night; she'd do her nails afterwards ... Meanwhile Stig was droning on about his plan and she caught a few words. 'RAJAR figures ...' Would she go light or dark? '... market trend ...' Plum? Dark grey? '... digital share ...' Dark grey, actually, because she had nearly finished the varnish. '... changes to personnel ...' She could buy a new polish on Monday when she got her meal deal. '... which will affect you.'

'Sorry?' Me? What was he talking about? She headed up traffic. Orbital FM was all about traffic.

'Traffic is going to be incorporated into broadcast roles.'

Oh my God, what? Her stomach lurched. Traffic wasn't an add-on for amateurs! What if they got their clockwises mixed up with their anti-clockwises? Their northbounds with their southbounds? It was a matter in its own right, not to be bandied about with lining-up guests and collating responses to the phone-in on 'what's

9

the most embarrassing thing that's ever happened to you on the M25?'.

'We want to make it more human … we're going to have personalities presenting the traffic.'

She heard a car engine splutter, cough and die. Everyone knew she didn't go on the airwaves.

'I'm afraid your position and the department is being made redundant.'

Charlie felt the blood draining from her face and her stomach dropping to her bowels. She tried to slam on the brakes but panic, her old foe, hit the gas pedal. Her heart was racing and the dizziness, oh shit, she felt sick and that took her right back … She blinked hard and swallowed back the bitter taste of ready salted crisps, ham and orange juice. Nine years she had made the position her own – updating the website, the Twitter feed, the Facebook page … she had the Highways Agency and AA on speed dial and she could tell by the way vehicles bunched up on the bank of traffic cameras how long a delay would be. She *was* the traffic. She'd never complained, not in public anyway, and she was thorough, dedicated, hard-working, all of those things which had been in her annual appraisals. But then her balloon of pride was pricked by the one thing she couldn't offer. Personality. She shut her eyes and sank, her shoulders dropping as the truth hit her: they didn't care if she knew her Potters Bar from her Dartford Crossing or her junction 1a from her 15. They wanted a traffic geezer or gal to crack a few gags with the DJ. They wanted her out.

'You are very welcome to apply for a role and—'

'No.' She wasn't going to put herself through that. Not a chance. 'What are my options?'

'Redundancy or a transfer to a sister station.'

He didn't even try to convince her to rethink. He pushed on, prepared, reaching for a piece of paper on his desk. His eyes ran down the page as he cited a credit controller in Reading, software developer in Glasgow, sound engineer in Chelmsford, sales in Bristol ... then he stopped. 'What about this? Presenter assistant in Swansea. Sunshine FM. Smaller than here, a bit less money, a sideways move but it's in your field. There are very few openings for your level, I'm afraid. Cuts everywhere. They'll need to know Monday morning. I can deal with it.'

Stig looked at his watch. Her time was up. It was that simple. It was Wales or nothing.

'OK,' she said, beaten.

'Is the correct answer,' Stig smiled. 'You've had a good run here.'

By which he meant her lack of charisma had caught up with her. She couldn't argue back – hadn't she always expected that?

She got to her feet, her head trailing behind as if she was going the wrong way on a roundabout. Tears filled her eyes and she walked through a kaleidoscope of faces to her desk, where she spent the rest of her shift in shock. No one noticed any difference from her normal behaviour. When she left on jellied legs, her brain was so numb she barely registered the icy blast of the February afternoon at the bus stop and she spent the journey in an anaesthetised state, her head resting against the greasy window of the bus from Hayes to Fulham. She managed a shaky text to Jonny – he was so sorry and he'd cancel Pilates if she'd like ... But no, she just wanted to be alone. Charlie made it on autopilot to her front step where she scrambled with her keys, unable to recognise the right one. Libby must've heard her because the door of the grand Georgian two-bed ground-floor flat opened. Thank God she'd made it home to her sanctuary – to their apartment which they'd shared for ten years, having been friends since their media studies degree days. This was her cocoon, a safe haven that would hold her tight for as long as she needed. Charlie felt guilty for a moment because she was only thinking of herself, knowing she wouldn't be kicked out because Libby was single again. It was too early to consider living with Jonny: they had all the time in the world together. And she hadn't farted in front of him yet.

'Libby,' she croaked. Then she saw James behind her, his upright civil servant figure in the hallway. Libby's ex. And they were both beaming. A hand went up in front of her eyes – Libby was wearing a ring. A diamond.

'He came to his senses! He's proposed! He's moving in!' she said, leaping onto Charlie, oblivious to her distress. 'If it wasn't for you telling me to let him stew! We're going to the pub to celebrate. Coming?'

'Brilliant! Amazing!' she tried. 'But I can't.' In a robotic voice, she explained into Libby's tumbling red hair, 'I've got defrosted spaghetti bolognese. It has to be eaten tonight.'

Libby burst out laughing and Charlie was being lifted off the floor in a hug which James joined. This was hell – she was in an engagement sandwich of ecstasy and she couldn't breathe.

'You are funny!' Libby said, letting her go, only now seeing Charlie's blotchy face. 'Shit, are you OK?'

'I've lost my job.' And by the looks of it, her home too. Then, the horrible realisation: the geographical distance could also threaten things with Jonny. This was the most terrifying moment of her life yet: her foundations had crumbled and the fluffy duck-down duvet of her comfort zone had been ripped off, exposing her to the elements.

'Oh, mate, oh no, what happened? Come and tell me in the pub,' Libby said, grabbing a coat off the peg then threading her arm through Charlie's. 'Come on.'

But Charlie couldn't move. 'My spag bol. If I don't eat it tonight I'll have to throw it away.'

'What?' Libby took a step back and looked at her. Then she guffawed. A second later she realised Charlie wasn't joining in. 'Are you being serious? You are being serious.' Her voice softened as concern took over. 'Charlie, it's not important.'

'It is,' she said, allowing herself to be led into the lounge. 'That's what I've planned.'

Libby guided her to the sofa and crouched to her knees so they were at eye level. 'Plans can change, you know,' she said with kindness.

Charlie said nothing, even though inside she was roaring; she didn't want the plans to change, she didn't want life to happen to her. She wanted things to stay the same, to remain in control. Spontaneity was the enemy: it made the horizon dip and rise and she wanted it to be flat and true. Navigable and constant.

'Look, listen, you'll be OK. I know you're scared. But … maybe this is what you need? Things can't go on like this forever.'

'Why not?' she sobbed, breaking down.

'Because they can't. Because that's life. And good

things can happen if you let them. Charlie, you can't tell me you're happy living like this? You've been like this for too long.'

Libby rubbed her back and folded her into her arms, letting Charlie cry until her weeping became a shaky whimper.

'I've lost everything. In one day,' she sniffed, wiping her nose on the cuff of her waterproof sleeve. 'It's either reapply for a new role but I'd have to go on the radio, redundancy or a transfer to Swansea. I don't know anything about Swansea ... only that it's at junctions forty-four and forty-five on the M4.' Christ, I'm so dull even in the midst of chaos, Charlie thought. 'If I take the pay-off, how long will that last? I can't afford not to work.'

'I can ask around,' Libby said. 'But the BBC isn't exactly expanding.'

'I'm going to be miles from everyone, from you, from Jonny.'

'We'll still be here! And if you're meant to be, you two will survive the long-distance thing. Or,' she said, biting her lip so Charlie knew what was coming, 'you could tackle your demons? Reapply at Orbital. Could be less of an upheaval. Easier than going to Wales?'

'Absolutely not,' she said, violently. 'No way.'

'It's just confidence. Because you never shut up at home, you've got to conquer this at some point or—'

Charlie ignored her. 'This is hopeless. This is my worst nightmare. How did this happen?'

Suddenly, Libby's jaw dropped open. 'Oh my God, do you remember when we did those lists?'

Ten years ago when Charlie had flown the nest, got

herself a waitress job and was volunteering at hospital radio, before moving into Libby's flat, bought thanks to the bank of her mum and dad, they'd been different people.

'The things we said we'd do by the time we were thirty. You said you were going to live abroad! You could tick that off if you went to Wales!'

'I also said I'd be a breakfast DJ, I'd own my own place and be planning my barefoot beach wedding.'

'Yeah, well, I said I'd be a foreign correspondent in some war-torn region. The closest I get is introducing the news at ten,' she said in perfect Home Counties received pronunciation. 'There's not much call for continuity announcers in flak jackets. But my point is, you need a new list. Not a shopping list or one of your to-do lists. One with new goals. Because you can do this. You can take a chance. You can seize the day if you want to.'

'In Swansea?' Charlie buried her face in her hands.

'Why don't you go and then while you're there look for something else back here? Try it. I know you like to be the one giving out the advice but perhaps it's time you took some instead?'

There it was: the often-mentioned hint that Charlie was blind only to her own dilemmas, which was absolutely not true: she knew what she had to do.

'Look ... you two go to the pub, I'll get myself sorted here. I'm so chuffed for you, really, it's brilliant and I'm so sorry I've brought you down ... I'll pop along later, maybe. Or call Jonny.' She would do neither.

After ten minutes of convincing Libby, Charlie was trying to come to terms with the future as an unknown quantity. She'd had it all mapped out, her days time-tabled precisely so she could avoid anything which would cause her uncertainty. Choir on a Monday night, Jonny over on a Wednesday and Saturday, drinks with Libby on a Thursday, brunch at The Brasserie and housework on Sundays. Of course, it had been pointed out to her that by planning everything to the exact second meant she wasn't planning for the long term at all: what about going for promotion, buying a place? Especially at her age ... But that involved risk and thinking on her feet – and look what had happened when she'd done that. Order and self-regulation had saved her. Or at least, she thought it had. The only guarantee she had now was a bowl of reheated pasta. Beyond that, she was no longer in the driving seat but a passenger of anxiety. In her room, she pulled the curtains, got into her tartan fleece pyjamas, changed the sheets – it was Friday after all – and crawled into bed to feel the weight of her covers and switched on *Friends*. And as the light fell, she saw there was only one way of coping. She'd get through this blip – which it would be, because there was no way she was going to leave London for good – by considering Wales as more of the same. More proof she was a failure. At least she knew how to do that.

A month later ...

I

'Keep those brollies handy because it's raining cats and Welsh corgis. But as long as you stay with Sunshine FM, the sun will always be shining!'

～

The number 2A bus leaving Swansea's concrete city centre was destined for Mumbles.

If ever there was a bad omen, this was it. On the bright side though, being barely audible, Charlie would fit right in, she thought as she went halfway up to an aisle seat.

The air onboard smelt of wet dog, courtesy of the torrential downpour which hadn't let up since she'd arrived last night. She buried her nose into her scarf that she'd sprinkled with lavender oil for keeping-calm reasons. Of which there were many: top of her list were first-day nerves at Sunshine FM. Meeting new people, not knowing where the loo was, getting to grips with her job, finding somewhere to buy a ham sandwich, the prospect of getting lost ... all that and a wealth of uncharted variables which could reduce her to a quivering mess. Beneath that was the underlying bottomless terror of the unknown which had tormented her over the last four weeks. She was exhausted from the fight or flight reflex which made sleep so difficult. She'd tried warm milk and hot baths, placing the junctions of the M25 in alphabetical order and doing it backwards, but it was usually 2 a.m. before she dozed off. And then she'd wake herself up with a jerk at five, suddenly remembering her crisis. Because she'd looked and looked for jobs in London, but there was nothing suitable. Something wouldn't 'turn up', not in time to pay the rent anyway: Swansea was all there was. At work, she'd struggled through, barely touching her meal deal, her adrenalin spiking and biting every time someone gave her a look of sympathy or a smirk. Her duties fell away from her as she retrained the three bullish replacements who began to turn to her colleagues, Jessa and Billy, who'd decided they wanted to be part of the revolution.

On her last day, she cleared her desk with trembling fingers, then told Zoe she was nipping to the loo before the inevitable presentation of a farewell present – and slipped out. Just as painful was packing up her possessions and storing them at Mum and Dad's, having to face their barely concealed concern over what the hell was going to happen to her. The pressure of two pairs of hopeful eyes on her was immense: she was an only child and felt she had to succeed for them, not just herself. 'You'll be back before you know it, love!' Mum had said as Dad chipped in unhelpfully, 'Think of it as an adventure!'

Charlie didn't do adventure though. Nor temporary. And therein was another worry: she wasn't used to living out of a holdall and forging superficial relationships. Pep talks from Libby and Zoe, God love them, were filled with Facebook clichés – feel the fear and do it anyway – of which she had an interminable loathing.

Both of them had offered to wave her off from Paddington yesterday but she'd refused – she'd had to pretend she'd taken their motivational quotes on board because she didn't want them worrying. And she'd pooped enough all over Libby's party. She'd been re-assured there'd always be a bed for her but she'd heard them discussing turning Charlie's hideaway into 'the spare room'. As for Zoe, she was back on Tinder and had two dates lined up that afternoon.

It was Jonny she'd needed to get her on board. He understood she could never put herself in front of a microphone again. He had agreed emphatically that she had to go to Wales – a blank CV would ruin her chances of ever coming back to London. Swansea would be the means to an end and their relationship would endure. They'd have weekends: he'd swap his Friday Pilates for a week night so they could be together. And then once this blip was over, they could plan their future of homemade toasted granola and weekend walks in the park. She was so grateful he hadn't reacted with a wild 'move in with me' pledge. Jonny understood the practicalities of life: his flat was too small for two and she needed to earn her own money. Equals in everything, from their height of five foot six to their age, even down to the same month of December, they should do it properly when the time came ... And so it was bittersweet staring into his gentle eyes before kissing him goodbye, inhaling his talcum-powdered smell and touching the soft blond nape of his neck. As much as he wanted to run alongside her as she leaned out of the carriage until the platform ran out, he didn't want her to get her head chopped off.

On the train, she'd realised she knew nothing beyond

where she was going to be living and working. It was out of character – she knew the M25 better than the back of her own hand. It was denial. Swansea would be a place to live and a place to work. That was all. She would function within them and escape as soon as she could. As far as her role was concerned, she could do assistant to the presenter with her eyes closed – planning and researching for radio shows had been where she'd learnt the ropes, as simple as generating ideas, booking guests, writing scripts and general admin.

The third chopped off her salary was a worry but what would she need to spend in Wales? And she was surprised to find this shutting down, this wearing of blinkers helped to contain the spasms of fear, which peaked when she stepped out onto the grubby pavement outside Swansea Station where the words 'Ambition is critical ...' were engraved in a red font. Ambition? Here? This was a dead end, surely? Well, it would be for her – she'd be using it as a place to perform a three-point-turn as soon as she could.

Home was a short walk away in an even shorter-lease room found on Airbnb, miles from the high ceilings, airy space, original features and bijou decked garden she was used to in bustling Fulham. The squat pebble-dashed Victorian terrace was tucked away in a drab side street which stank of the chippy opposite. Her live-in landlady Genevieve 'but call me Gen' answered the door with pins in her mouth and a tape measure round her shoulders. Willowy and as slim as a needle, she had piled her thick silver hair into a chignon held in place by a pencil and her bewitching deep-blue eyes matched the colour of her denim shirt dress. In her elegant Scottish accent, she offered tea, telly and extra pillows – plus an apology for her framed sweary cross stitch creations which decorated the hall with 'f' words. But Charlie shut herself away in her cosy bedroom burrowing herself under the throws and cushions, where she allowed herself a dollop of self-pity, another fruitless job search on her phone and the rest of the ham sandwich she hadn't eaten on the train.

Their paths didn't cross in the morning – Charlie was up and out before Gen, eating her breakfast in silence without the usual company of Jonny's show on the radio. She didn't want to wake her up and be forced to make conversation with someone who would one day be a fleeting memory. When Charlie rang Sunshine FM last week to check her hours, the woman, Tina some-one-or-other, said she should come in around nine-ish. But because Charlie didn't do 'ish', it was a little after 8 a.m. when she caught the bus from the central terminal. It weaved its way through the city before pulling in at the boxy university, Soviet Bloc-style hospital and then chugged along a boring A-road running parallel to the silent grey sea, which was metres out, leaving a yawn of muddy sand.

She couldn't help it and she knew she sounded like one of those London types but Charlie was looking down her nose at the place. It looked cheap and nasty, beige-bricked and characterless. Like a graveyard. It failed on every level compared to her beloved capital – there was no buzz, no bustle, just a depressed deflated air of a so-called city. Where was the edge? Where was the romance?

'Terrible this traffic, awful,' said the old lady beside her in the window seat. Charlie ignored the mad woman.

No one spoke to anyone on public transport, did they?

'I said,' she repeated louder, 'this traffic, it's awful terrible.'

A hand touched her arm. Charlie looked at the wrinkly face poking out of a transparent rain bonnet which was tied with a neat bow at her hairy chin. She was waiting expectantly for Charlie to answer. This was not terrible traffic whatsoever. They were moving and there were no roadworks. It wasn't bumper-to-bumper M25, the biggest car park in the world, was it?

'Mmm,' she replied, turning her head away.

'Although I can't moan. I've got buses to thank for my family. I met my husband on one in a traffic jam.'

Here we go, Charlie thought, the crazy lady's off on one.

'We were next to each other, like you and me are now, started off strangers and by the time we got to Sketty he'd asked me to go to the pictures with him!'

What a letch.

'I said no, but he came into Kristy's, the bakery where I worked, for a cream bun every day until I said yes.'

An elbow in her ribs demanded a response.

'Nice,' Charlie said reluctantly.

'Sixteen grandchildren, we had. He missed the seventeenth.'

'Oh, dear,' Charlie said, doing a sympathy face.

'Oh, dear?' she said, getting up as the bus driver announced 'BLACKPILL!'. 'The old bastard collapsed when he was knocking off her next door. Served him right.'

Where *was* the romance, indeed? The guy in the shiny suit with a footballer's gelled quiff was having a shot, she noticed, with a girl across from him, giving her a smile and a wink. She was interested, Charlie could tell by the way she flicked her hair. Back home, you'd do anything to avoid eye contact – that was the point of reading a book, wasn't it, so you could focus on that rather than other people, who were nutters until proven otherwise.

Charlie put her ear buds in to switch off, not to listen to anything, because she needed to hear when it was her stop, but to prevent anyone else talking to her. She wished she could tune out though – the driver had the radio on and it was a total dirge. Some miserable old git was moaning about the weather and now he was introducing *I Don't Like Mondays* by The Boomtown Rats. Jesus Christ, listeners would be weeping into their cornflakes.

She focused on her lap for the rest of the journey, repeating 'this too will pass' to herself as her nerves rattled. And then, with a jerk and a bellow of 'OYSTERMOUTH SQUARE', she had arrived. Making her way along the aisle, she tried to look out to see what awaited her but the glass was steamed up and smeary with water. Down the steps, dread was rising and then came humiliation: at this exact moment, her former colleagues would be going forth assured of their importance in a metropolis and here she was, reversing into provincial insignificance.

The wind and rain slapped her in the face, forcing her to come to. She wasn't, as she expected, facing an air hangar on an industrial estate, which she'd presumed would be Sunshine FM quarters. Instead, she was stood on a blowy prom, lined on one side with little independent cafes and galleries, boutiques, bars and craft shops facing a tiny crescent of sand. To her right was a lighthouse on a rock at sea and her left a small Victorian pier. All very charming, actually, unexpectedly, but where the hell was the radio station? She checked maps on her phone and a red pin sat isolated out on the water. What? Was it on a boat, like some 1960s pirate stations which operated from international waters to dodge licensing laws? She heard a gravelly dour voice, the same misery guts she'd heard on the bus, and looked up at two old-fashioned and rusting trumpet speakers which were mounted either side of the entrance to the pier.

'Next up, a chat with a Mumbles pharmacist who'll be talking piles ...' Then, horror of horrors, a jingle announced she was listening to the breakfast show on Sunshine FM. No, no, it couldn't be ... but it was. A sign pointed up the pier featuring the logo of a faded smiling sunshine in shades above the words 'Ugly, Lovely Town'. That summed up the contradiction of Swansea and Mumbles all right.

Her stomach turned as she began to tread her way on wobbly wooden planks, past an empty cafe, past a lone fisherman, past a seagull pecking on a polystyrene carton of soggy batter. The railings either side of her tapered into the distance, narrowing in a conspiracy of claustrophobia. Two buildings sat at the end – a red-roofed lifeboat station and what looked like a metal cow shed. With the same sun in sunnies grinning like a loony Jack Nicholson. As she approached, the smile seemed to become one of mockery and her radio life flashed before her: growing up with BBC Radio 2, Terry Wogan's dulcet tones tickling Mum as she hovered by the toaster. Her headphones on her walk to school and later uni delivering Radio 1 queens Zoe Ball and Sara Cox. Her ambition then had been poised like a firework, ready to dazzle with its breathtaking display. The reality now was the wet wick and damp matches of soul-destroying disappointment. The weather forced her onwards, there was nowhere to shelter, and as she pushed open the corrugated door, she felt as if she was entering the gallows. A thought crossed her mind of running away right now before she was ensconced in this Godforsaken place. She'd go straight back to London, work in a shop or something, anything. Eat baked beans and get an evening job too. Live at Mum and Dad's and save and save and …

But she had never quit before – even when it had all gone wrong. Besides, running required instinct and decision and Charlie did her best to stamp out that sort of thing. If you stood still, maybe no one would notice you after a while. Even so, for the first time in her life, she considered legging it.

2

The kettle began to shake as it boiled and boiled, unable to turn itself off, and filled the grotty galley kitchen with a billowing cloud, reminding Tina Dooley of the steam room at her old five-star hotel gym.

It was the closest she'd get to a spa in a while, possibly forever, she thought, as she flicked the switch and waved her hand through the mist, clearing the memories. She'd have to send yet another reminder to health and safety to get it fixed.

From the cupboard, she took a Twinings Calming Camomile teabag out of the box, unmarked with her name because everyone else here drank builder's. It was her single luxury – everything else had gone. If only she could've saved one of her bone china cups and saucers . . . Don't you dare go there, not first thing on a Monday, lady! Material goods were merely things – they do not matter. Her daughter, her husband, that's what counted. The Sunshine FM mug was good enough and she was lucky to have this job and a roof over her head.

That didn't stop her fingers from trembling though. A wave of fear and frustration followed – just as she'd got used to her circumstances, something was unsettling her. The man on the bus who'd stared at her on Friday was there again doing the same this morning. It wasn't a leer, not that that was acceptable, but at least she could've understood that. Men did that all the time, ask any woman. And Tina had had her fair share of that, resembling, so people said, Julia Roberts with long wavy caffè latte hair, brown eyes, a disarming smile and legs up to her neck. She would blush if anyone said it out loud but she still made heads turn, even though she considered herself a bit creased round the edges at the age of forty-two. Not that that was old but she was going to be fifty before she knew it.

No, the way the man looked at her was more unnerving because it was as if he knew her. As if he knew she was home alone while Gareth was away. Worse, she'd had the feeling he was going to talk to her on Friday – she'd seen him rise when she did, hesitate and then sit back down again. Today he had stayed put but his eyes which tracked her as the bus pulled away from the pier had burned holes in her trench coat. And he knew her stop, which made her uneasy because she kept work and home entirely separate. An overspill from one into the other would ruin the harmony she had toiled to create – because nobody here at the radio station was aware of her set-up. Being office manager had come to her with no favours or sympathy: it was something she had won for herself after twenty years without a proper job. At work, she could shut the door on her agonising and lonely private life, giving her a rest from despair and paranoia. Because events had changed her ... so was it possible she was being a teensy-weensy bit oversensitive? Possibly, she reluctantly conceded, yes. The man looked harmless enough, didn't he? Smart too, not suited, but presentable in an open-necked white shirt, tidy jeans and a navy-blue quilted jacket, not dodgy at all, in fact. Clean-shaven, barbered greying hair, blue eyes. Six foot, late forties. Oh, listen to yourself, you're not doing an appeal for *Crimestoppers*, she told herself. Maybe he did know her or Gareth – her husband was very well connected. That was probably it. It was silly to worry. She was feeling like this because she was away from her roots, leading a new 'anonymous' life.

Cardiff had been home, lately the posh five-bedroom detached house with glorious landscaped gardens in Lisvane, but also previously in Ely, the rough-round-the-edges part of the city where she had been born and bred which pulsed with community. Being rich had been isolating, actually, and because their fortune had come from 'new money' she'd never felt equal to the others in her circle, who'd quickly dropped her. So Townhill in Swansea, where she now lived, reminded her of Ely. It had a reputation but it was full of heart and decency. She was lucky with her colleagues too, who told her she'd made a real difference in the few months she'd been here. They might've teased her for looking like a Mumbles wife who lunched but that was all the ammunition they had; she ran such a tight ship considering what the station was up against in terms of talent and resources, and it was done with fondness. She had always known how to survive – picking things up quickly was how it had to be in Ely – not necessarily academically, although she hadn't done badly at high school, but amongst people, knowing the chat and working out the rules because you only ever had one shot at an opportunity. That's how she'd got the job with no career behind her – OK, she'd probably been the only one with a brain cell to apply but she'd seen the similarities of running a home with an office: managing diaries, supplies, filing and payroll, it'd be a cinch compared with the demands of a go-getting husband and high-achieving daughter. Tina had always scrubbed up well too, even though she now dressed in charity-shop buys. That was the thing, having lived on the inside, she knew wardrobes were expunged of last season's trends, sometimes still unworn, and dropped at the Cats Protection up the road before the prosecco at their personal-shopping styling sessions had gone flat. Come on, she thought as she returned with her cuppa to her position front of house in reception, she was very fortunate. Respected here, appreciated and—

'Sil-ly bloo-dy wo-man ...'

Oh no, the booming outburst coming her way could only be that sack of old sprouting spuds, Ivor Mone. At least it was off-air this time. The one difficult person here who treated her like a dolly bird at his disposal, he was a dinosaur of a DJ who'd somehow survived extinction despite countless Ofcom investigations upholding complaints about offensive language during his broadcasts. His history was a string of apologies, one suspension and a to-be-arranged course on equality and diversity.

'That producer, she put a jingle on when I was still talking,' he grunted.

Probably to stop him mid-flow.

'Coffee for the talent,' he demanded, somehow keeping hold of the roll-up fag between his lips as he coughed up a ball of phlegm.

'Kitchen's over there, Ivor.'

He grunted, before pushing past a lady entering the

building and going outside for a smoke, as he did every opportunity he had – during songs, news, sport, travel and weather, cutting it so fine he often returned wheezing into the microphone.

Tina dropped her grimace and turned to the dripping-wet visitor, who pulled down the hood of her waterproof to reveal a heart-shaped face, emphasised by a severe braid, although a few springy curls the colour of champagne had broken free around her temples.

'How can I help you?'

The woman tried to match Tina's smile but it didn't reach her big hazel eyes. She had both hands gripped on her shoulder bag, as if she was trying to protect herself.

'Hi … I'm Charlie Bold, the new—'

'Charlie! Hi!' Tina cried, holding out her arms and then bringing her palms together as if she was in prayer, 'The saviour of Sunshine FM! It's great to see you!'

Really great because this station needed some new blood. A transfusion of it, to be precise, to halt the anaemia of flagging figures. The boss, Mervyn Davies, was apparently so alarmed by the decline he was afraid he was heading for the chop. Charlie, with her glowing reference, would inject some metropolitan magic. Although she wasn't looking particularly luminous, it had to be said. More pale and sniffy. Perhaps she was London cool? Or one of those who came alive when she stuck on her cans. Tina had seen that before so she wasn't concerned.

'We're so thrilled you decided to join us!' she added brightly, trying to drown out the depressing sound of REM's *Everybody Hurts*. It was a bone of contention that Ivor got to pick his own playlist when everyone else had to go through the head of music.

Charlie went to say something and Tina heard her dry mouth click.

'Thanks,' she said in a small voice. 'Although I'm not sure about the saviour bit.' Then she gulped.

The very best in the business tended to be perfectionists, Tina thought, as she received Charlie's clammy handshake.

'Get here OK?'

She nodded stiffly.

'Sorry about the weather! The sea air must make a change from the smog though! So ... welcome! Or, as they say in Wales, *croeso*. Let me take your jacket. Have a seat. Can I get you a tea or a coffee? Then I'll give you a tour, show you the studios, the loos, the important stuff! And I'll run through a few things, just the usual.'

'Um ... OK,' she said uncertainly. 'Er ... coffee, please. Milk, no sugar.'

Tina buzzed Lowri and then she clapped her hands. This was proving quite hard, getting a word out of Charlie. Odd because usually these types were full of themselves.

'I'm a bit nervous,' Charlie blurted suddenly in a husky London twang. 'I haven't been the new girl for years.'

'Don't worry! Everyone's really friendly here.' Apart from Mr Mone, the one who barged into you, Tina didn't say. She didn't want to scare her off. Not when she was so spectacularly talented. 'And you're a high flyer, you've nothing to be scared about!'

'High flyer? Is that what they said?' Charlie squeaked. 'They must have been really desperate to get rid of me.'

Tina laughed at the look of panic on her face. So that was her bag! Self-deprecation was a lovely change from cocky and arrogant big-heads.

'Right, so I'm afraid you won't be starting until you've done a health and safety briefing, which will be later today. You're booked in at 11 a.m.'

Was that relief she saw as Charlie exhaled slowly? Tina tittered. This one had character, she could tell.

'You met or should I say bumped into our *Morning Mumbles* breakfast DJ,' she said, nodding to the fog of smoke outside. 'Ivor Mone, been here twenty years. Calls himself a legend. That's one way of putting it! He's our longest-serving member. On from 7 a.m. to ten. After that it's *Mumbles Matters* 'til one, featuring Ed Walker, remember him? Former Radio 2. Had a breakdown. Bounced back. Sort of. More "Alan Partridge, eat your heart out". *Good Afternoon* is with DJ Disgo – bit of Welsh for you there, translates as, you guessed it, disco. His name's Colin, really lovely boy, he's all about cheesy choons. *Home Time* starts at 4 p.m., news and music with Sian Lewis, our total pro, and then at 7 p.m. it's *Evening Mumbles*, which will be—'

Tina was stopped in her tracks by the stench of fag breath.

'Charlie, this is Ivor. Ivor, this is Charlie Bold. Our new face.'

He barely nodded at her. It was his customary greeting – the rumour was anything more enthusiastic might make his ginger shredded-wheat toupé slip.

'Charlie Mould,' he said, scratching his genitalia. 'Pleasure.'

'It's Bold,' Tina said.

'I heard you the first time.' Then he addressed Charlie. 'Don't listen to her. Knows nothing about radio. Any questions, just ask your Uncle Ivor.' He winked gruesomely at Charlie. Don't touch her, Tina thought, we don't want a harassment case on her first day. Tina needed to get shot of him and she glanced across into the control room. Yes! Phew.

'You're wanted,' she said, thumbing Ivor's eyes towards the glass cubicle where his producer was tapping her watch dramatically as if she was playing charades.

'Good luck, Mould,' he sneered, walking off, the elbows of his brown cardigan almost threadbare. 'You'll need it. Nobody has ever made *Evening Mumbles* work. They all die a death. DJ Death, that's what we called the last one.'

'DJ Death?' Charlie said, the most animated she'd been, jerking forward.

'Just a joke,' Tina tried to reassure her but Charlie was white.

'I don't mean the death bit … I meant the DJ bit.'

'You'll make it your own. I spoke to Stig Costello and he was singing your praises.'

'But … but I'm not a DJ,' she said, breathlessly. 'I'm the assistant, aren't I?'

Tina tilted her head and examined her. She was curling up before her and her eyes were pleading. This was not an act of deadpan. This was genuine distress. What exactly had she been told?

'No, the circular said assistant presenter.' Tina put on her glasses and clicked on her computer to find the text.

'It didn't! Did it?'

Charlie crumpled with a whimper as Tina read out the job description. Early evening slot, two hours, co-hosting a show which required experience, creativity and influence to establish a don't-miss programme in a challenging slot. Although, she broke it to her, there was no co-presenter: the plan to spice up the show with a team of two had failed. Charlie had been the only one who'd been put forward. It struck Tina then that Charlie had been telling the truth when she'd said Orbital FM had been desperate to let her go. Dear God, they'd been sold a kipper.

'I had no idea. I've been stitched up. Stig sorted it out, the paperwork, everything ... I'm sorry but I can't do it.' She'd come alive with determination. Tina was confused by this display of confidence which she'd been so lacking before.

'But we've run a week of promos and everyone's expecting you to start tonight!'

'I can't do it ... I just can't ... sorry.' And she was getting up, backing off, grabbing her coat and her bag, moving quickly to the entrance.

'Charlie! We need you!'

Tina wasn't following this at all: she was used to people throwing themselves at her for placements and chances, so much so she sympathised with Simon Cowell when he was faced with desperadoes at the *X Factor* audition stage.

But her declaration didn't fall on deaf ears. Instead, it hurtled into and slid down the slammed door which thudded definitively shut as the slight figure of Charlie Bold disappeared into the rain.

3

Delme Noble cursed his takeaway cappuccino as the sting then the singe cauterised his fingers.

Merri had offered to double-cup it at the counter of her cafe, Cheer on the Pier. But of course, he'd been in a rush and hadn't had a moment to waste on that – he only had himself to blame. As bloody bastard usual. He hurriedly swapped hands and absent-mindedly took a slug, scalding his top lip and tongue. Great. Only he could suffer third-degree burns in a torrent of rain when he was soaked through because he'd lost his badass treated-rubber coat. As for carrying a brolly, that was out of the question: blokes didn't use them unless they were ... well, organised. And he'd needed his other hand to eat his double bacon and egg croissant. Jesus, he was a walking disaster area. Scrub that, he was a squelching disaster area in sodden shoes which weren't even his. They belonged to Rodney. Del had found them deep under his sofa when he was failing to find his charger at home in the smart marina this morning. He couldn't locate his Chelsea boots so he'd put them on instead because they were a tidy bit of brogue, he'd thought, laughing at their top lad behaviour on Friday night. They'd only gone for a pint but came in at 6 a.m. Rodney had kicked them off when he'd crashed here and ended up walking home in his socks. The trouble was these Ted Bakers were a bit too big for him and he'd nearly tripped in his fat-boy run for the bus. He could feel his feet flopping inside like fish as he made his way quickly up the slippery boardwalk to work, which, now he came to think of it, was a health and safety matt— aaargh!

He just about stopped himself from falling on his arse, although had that happened at least his backside would have cushioned the blow. And miraculously, he'd saved his breakfast. It was the spilling of drink that would've caused problems. Whoever had invented the plastic lid was a genius. He'd known who once, when he'd done his training: it was all to do with the McDonald's lawsuit when that woman, Stella what's-'er-face, had sued for millions after being scalded. She got a bad press, she did, actually. Accused of greed when in fact she'd been horribly injured and her action was a result of negligence. Del was all for protecting people. Like his brother, he thought. That's why he'd got into this business.

If it was slidey on this bit, imagine what it'd be like by the entrance to Sunshine FM, where a leaking pipe sprayed like a fountain. He'd have to give facilities a nudge to get that sorted. But for now, he'd get one of his yellow 'caution' cones from the stack outside the emergency exit. He took a massive bite of his pastry, announcing to no one it was 'cowing lush', before tucking it into his suit pocket – priorities, son – then picked up a cone and went round the front to do a risk assessment: predicting the trajectory of someone coming out, seeing the danger zone and bypassing it. He positioned it by the entrance and there! Awesome job, son! Health and safety was often the butt of the joke, its policies seen as overzealous, inflicted by killjoys as evidence of political correctness gone mad. But they forgot the vast majority of rules and regs were there for the well-being of staff. Accidents changed lives. He knew that only too well. Oh yes, he was born to do this, even if not everyone agreed with him. Well, this cone showed he wasn't just on top of it – he was the boss of it!

He gave himself a cheers and took a self-congratulatory sip of coffee, but ouch, the roof of his mouth sizzled. He flinched at his scorching stupidity – and then found himself flinching again when he heard a clatter and a cry of '*oof*' beside him. The cone was spinning round in circles next to a person on the floor, grabbing an ankle. See? He was the soothsayer of hazards. The duke of hazards, if you like! That was a good line, he'd use that in his briefing today for the new DJ.

'Ow!' It was a woman. Probably in heels. Why did women wear them? They were a menace in terms of both balance and physical damage to the spine, knees, tendons and toes. But, oh, she was in trainers. That shut him up.

'Who put that cone there?' she screeched as if she was fresh off the set of *EastEnders*.

'Did you fall into it?' People were very clumsy, in his experience. Especially him, it had to be said.

'I fell *over* it. It was right in the way.' She spoke through gritted teeth. Bloody hell, she was seething. It was only a little tumble.

'No, no. It was there to warn of a wet surface, all risk assessed.'

'What? Somebody thought it was sensible to put a cone by a door?' She shook her head and rubbed her leg, making a bit of a meal out of it really.

'Here, let me help you. I'm a trained first aider.' He reached for her but she batted him away. Talk about touchy.

'I'm not going to do one elephant, two elephants, you know.'

'What are you on about?' she said, trying to put weight on her foot with a sharp intake of breath.

'Chest compressions and kisses of life. Resuscitation. It's actually quite easy to …' He trailed off when she dropped her head. 'Does it hurt?' he said, getting to his haunches, fearing his trousers were going to rip. He really did need to trim down a bit. Be like he used to be.

'Yes. It's twisted. It's really sore.'

'You ought to get up. You'll be soaking. Let me – fuuuck!' She'd got up onto her knees and her head had knocked his coffee over his groin and he was in agony. 'My nuts! I've got roasted peanuts!'

'Let's call it a draw then,' the woman said, putting out her hand for him to pull her to standing. Her voice had softened, its harsh Cockney edge replaced by one of those estuary accents with a pleasant winding drawl.

'I look like I've wet myself,' he said in between gasps of pain as they held each other up. The woman rolled her eyes at him and then winced. 'Right,' he said, keen to move on away from his privates, 'come in with me and I'll do you some rice.'

'Rice? How will rice help? I need a bandage.'

'Rest, ice, compression, elevation,' he said, recovering his professionalism, which let's face it was never far away.

'I can't go back in there,' she said, horrified.

'We have to. That's where the first-aid stuff is.'

'But—'

'No buts,' he said, guiding her towards the door, 'this happened on work premises. It needs to be logged in accordance with company policy.'

She was so gobby this one that he feared she'd protest and loudly. But as soon as they'd got into reception she went quiet and the flush of adrenalin in her cheeks had faded to porcelain. Her eyes looked glassy too. It was the shock, experience had taught him that.

'Morning Tina! *Bore da*!' he called as they passed her desk. 'Make way for the casualty!'

Tina stared open-mouthed at him then her, watching as they hobbled into the corridor, away from the studios into the back offices which overlooked the sea. Except the vista from his pokey room was the lifeboat runway which traumatised him every time it launched. Therefore his blind was shut.

'Take a seat, there you go,' he said, pulling up another chair where she could rest her foot.

'Won't they mind? Having strangers in their office?' She was looking warily to the door.

'No, they won't mind. Because ...' he said, patting his crotch with paper towels before grinning at her, noticing his stomach was in danger of popping his shirt buttons. 'This is my office! I'm the health and safety guy!'

'You?' she cried. 'Unbelievable.'

That was rude – and it wiped the beam off his face. He scrabbled around his suit pockets for his ID lanyard with the intention of waving it at her but he remembered he'd mislaid it. Typical. He was cross at himself now as well as her.

'Oh, I'm sorry. Am I not tending to your health and

41

safety needs even though you weren't looking where you were going?'

'I was. That cone was in a ridiculous place.'

'I'd put that there to avoid—'

'You put it there? That's classic, that is.' She put her head in her hands.

There was no need for that. 'Look, I don't have to help, you know. Fortunately for you, this isn't a job, it's a vocation, a calling. I'm doing this out of the goodness of my heart – it's not as if you work here.'

'I do, actually,' she spat. And then quieter, 'Or I did until I walked out.'

'Sorry?' This one's moods had more swing than Tiger Woods.

'I'm Charlie Bold, the new—'

'*Evening Mumbles* DJ! I'm doing your induction later! It was supposed to be at 11 a.m. but I've been double-booked. Although ... hang on, you won't be doing it if you've left us already?'

She sighed. 'I thought I was coming here to be an assistant to a presenter. Not as assistant presenter, which I've just learnt is now sole presenter. On air, live. That isn't what I do.'

'But that's good, yeah?' he said, 'Most people would die to get their own show.'

'Believe me,' she spat, 'I would rather die than do that.'

How bizarre. She seemed made for radio with her opinionated and 'full of it' personality. With a distinct whiff of London wanker about her. Except now she looked pop-eyed and scared. Small too, although most were small compared to his six foot two stature. It had to be the injury making her like this.

'Tea? A couple of sugars to pep you up?'

She shook her head. 'That rice you mentioned?'

'Right, yes, now where did I put the doctor's bag?' He moved his eyes around trying to recall if it was in a drawer or ... somewhere else. Accidents weren't that common at Sunshine FM. He liked to think it was because of his razor-sharp instincts. More likely, though, it was because there wasn't actually much to decapitate yourself with in a radio station.

'It's up there on the window ledge, between the hard hat and goggles,' she said, with a faint but still-detectable weariness.

'Yes, so it is. Exactly where I left it,' he lied, unzipping the green kit, finding a bandage and chucking it her way. 'So that's rest, compression and elevation. I can get you some ice from the kitchen.'

'No, it's fine. Don't worry.' She took off her trainer, slid down her sock and began to wrap up her ankle, which was looking a bit swollen. He felt a rush of responsibility and before he knew it he was apologising and she was too, 'for ... your ... that', nodding at his nethers. He almost cracked a joke about 'not many women getting intimate with him without knowing his name' but remembered just in time he was the gatekeeper of standards, not a purveyor of unwanted sexual conduct. So he decided to introduce himself instead.

'I'm Delme Noble, by the way.'

When she didn't say anything back, his mouth ran away with him. 'Del Boy to the lads, Del-icious to the ladies.' Oh balls. What had he said? He sounded as crap as those blokes who called themselves the Archbishop of Banterbury. 'I'm not really delicious to the ladies. It's a play on words, that's all. Not a very good one.'

The hint of a forgiving smile crept along her lips. It was quite amazing how it lit up her face – she seemed cherubic with those big ... what colour were her eyes? Brown? Green? And she was really pretty he saw now, and kind-looking and it made him want to confess and unload and reveal himself. To admit he wasn't very good at anything. Just look at the mess on his desk and the industry certificates which hung wonkily on the wall. He wanted to say how he tried his best, he really did, but sometimes he wondered ... but he couldn't finish the sentence in his mind because if he did, then he'd be letting everyone down. Which he was basically doing anyway by being shit at his job.

His mates had laughed when he'd announced he was going into the industry ten years ago. They'd said it was like a vegan going to work in an abattoir, a nun in a brothel. Mam and Dad had asked him if he was really sure because it wouldn't 'fix things'. Even the head of the course had taken him aside and suggested he might not be cut out for it. He'd said it nicely: not that he was easily distracted and chaotic but 'spontaneous', 'fun' and 'creative'. But he refused to listen because he had to do it, to right the wrong. You couldn't give up – you had to stay on the see-saw. Nothing was easy: there was always a struggle if something was important. And nothing had been more important to him in his life. There was a child at stake and Del needed to man up. He was thirty-five years old FFS.

'Anyway,' he said, sitting forward, chin up, smacking his palms on his hefty thighs, 'you don't want to listen to me banging on. Must keep on keeping on! So, I expect you have some things to do, people to meet. Shall we say we'll reconvene after lunch … actually … looking at my diary, I'm in meetings until 4 p.m. so if we do your briefing then?'

'I can't stay here!' Charlie said, full of alarm. 'You can't have a DJ who has a fear, no, a phobia, of public speaking.'

'Ha! Good one.'

She stared at him and bit her lip. Jesus Christ. She wasn't having him on. Those shakes were for real. But this wasn't his problem: he had so much to catch up on.

'You'll have to chat to HR about that. Marilyn is lovely. She could get you on a course or something … Right, so if you can sign in the log book, say you've been bandaged up and it's all sorted …' He pushed it towards her, expectantly. 'We can get on then.'

'I'm serious. I'm not doing this.'

Del rubbed his sideburns with his fingers. This wasn't good. Her eyes looked watery too. He had a few minutes before he had to see whoever's initials he'd scribbled against 9.30 a.m. Switch on the old charm, tell her she'll be all right, then off she'd go. He might get a mention in the weekly dispatches if he convinced her to stay. That was always good for the appraisal. Last year's hadn't been too positive – that collapsing ladder thing had gone against him. Which reminded him, he still hadn't actioned the fire alarm timetable which he'd been tasked to do.

'Remember your job application? All that stuff that made you stand out to the controller? Yeah? We've heard you're top of the range.' That's what they'd been told. Although why she was here in Swansea no one knew. If Del could get away, he would. But he'd spent most of his entire twenties away – this was his chance to rehabilitate the mistakes of his youth.

'I never applied per se. My name was put forward. I was forced out of my job for not being 'bubbly' enough. This was the only place with a transfer.'

Oh dear. It was all starting to make sense. Of course Sunshine FM wasn't going to get the equivalent of new boobs, fillers and Botox. Or, for equal opportunity reasons, a penis extension. But it wasn't his business to deal with her crisis. He needed to get on and the only way he could do that was to encourage her to leave his office. He scratched his stubble in thought, realising the only way he'd achieve that was to spell it out to her.

'Listen, I'm going to let you into a secret … you don't have to think of it as public speaking because …' He paused to do a pretend look around in case anyone would catch him saying this '… no fucker listens to Sunshine FM anyway. Yeah?'

'Really?'

'Well, not anyone under the age of dead. Our demographic audience is in a coffin, our call-ins are either about trimming garden bushes or hospital waiting times. And I'd bet most of the people who do tune in have forgotten to put in their hearing aids.'

She was thinking about it, he could see. But was she desperate enough? He went on.

'And I take it you're not royalty?'

'What do you mean?'

'You're not on the public payroll. Unless you've got job offers coming out of your ears? The BBC on the phone offering you Steve Wright's slot? Capital FM offering you a blank cheque?'

Charlie shut her eyes. 'No,' she whispered.

'Well then, I don't see what alternative you have.'

She swallowed hard and took a big brave deep breath. His gift of the gab had worked and he imagined chalking one up on a scoreboard; this would be a good example of ironing out a wobble when he was next in a corner. All she needed now was encouragement.

'Nerves are good. They prove you're alive! Just live a little, yeah? Go with the flow! Fly by the seat of your pants!' he said, feeling the whoosh of the words. Surely that was an irresistible invitation? His heartbeat was applauding – if only he could live like that.

Charlie let off a vague rumble of agreement. Cracking! That was more like it!

He rubbed his hands together. Nice one. She got up and he turned to his computer, feeling a real sense of achievement. Who said health and safety was dry? He was a suit, yes, but he understood humanity – and it was only twenty-five past nine on a Monday! He was the guru of health and safety! A guiding light in the midst of mayhem! The one who could soothe and inspire. The Buddha of plan B, C and D! Oh yes, how had he ever doubted himself? He could see she was in awe of him, full of wonder and grateful he had top tekkers people skills.

'By the way,' she said from the door, obviously, well, probably, buoyed up by his persuasive powers to live large, 'where's the best place to get a ham sandwich? Nothing fancy, like a deli. I don't like mayo or mustard or anything. Just plain.'

His jaw dropped. Oh my lord. He had underestimated this one. She had as much balls as a castrated puppy. There was no way she'd be back at 4 p.m.

4

'Coming up later on 103.5FM, don't miss our new *Evening Mumbles* DJ Charlie Bold! Before that though, it's time to talk cremation with Bob 'The Undertaker' Burns. He'll be here after this ... *Light My Fire* by The Doors ...'

'What are you doing here, Charlie?' Delme said, looking up red-faced over his right shoulder from the floor where he was lying on his front. With no explanation or embarrassment whatsoever.

'For the 4 p.m. health and safety briefing. As instructed.' Although from this angle she was getting more insight into his actual briefs: the scrunch of jazzy boxer short material was poking out over the top of his trousers.

'Well, I never.' He rolled over, still not shedding any light on why he was panting. This morning his dark brown hair had been shiny and styled in an undercut à la *Peaky Blinders*, shaved closely on the sides with a groomed sweep of length on top. Now it was a whirl of waves and sticking up at all angles as if he'd been rubbing his head with a balloon. Incredibly, he remained quite handsome – yes, she had noticed his azure eyes which

48

creased playfully, the twitch of smile on his dark red lips and his perfectly straight white teeth. 'I didn't think you had the guts!' Oh, but he was coming across less 'Noble' and more of a tactless nob. How supportive of him.

'My pep talk worked then, eh?'

No. She was here because Zoe and Libby – and Jonny too, she knew, once he replied to her text when he saw what a pickle she was in – had ordered her to conquer her fears. Their support had come just when she'd been at peak mess in the ladies where she'd heard a promo for her show piped into the toilets. It had made her wonder if she could get out of it by feigning a fainting fit at the microphone. A tangle of panic, with a fat tongue and a sweaty brow, she'd asked herself yet again 'could she do this?'. Their cheerleading was a resounding 'yes'. A rash of capitals from Zoe shouting 'GO FOR IT!' and 'BELIEVE!' and most convincingly of all from Libby, 'It's a much smaller station and audience – just pretend you're in a room chatting to me.' She'd felt a flash of something powerful, like anger or frustration, that they hadn't told her what she'd wanted to hear. In other words 'Get out of there'. But she'd read and reread their messages and realised she had to do it, not least because she had to eat. For there were emotional reasons too – reasons which went to her very core. She had never actually dealt with what had happened that had led to this: the life-changing character-altering incident involving that bloody conniving woman, Isabella, that had rendered her speechless and ruined her career.

After that, Charlie had apologised to a clearly relieved Tina, who'd overenthused with an indiscreet 'Del didn't put you off then, did he?', revealing what Charlie suspected was the general opinion of him. Then it was all a blur of introductions to the big cheeses and being shown to her desk. Her meeting with the *Evening Mumbles* producer and broadcast assistant would come before the show, they liked to keep things as fresh as possible, they'd have loads lined up. OK, she could just about get her head around that. Take a long lunch, you'll be here until 9 p.m., she was told.

So she'd taken her slightly less ailing ankle to Cheer on the Pier, where it was white, bright and like a beach hut, with big windows to enjoy the view – although today's rain turned it into a bleary windscreen of snaking water trails. One of a handful of customers, she'd picked a comfy blue and grey striped sofa over a picnic table and with a spray of Rescue Remedy, she'd repeated the mantra 'you can do this' as she took in the decor of orange lifebuoys and starfish, spray-painted green anchors and waves beneath nautical rope lanterns. Looking back, she should've seen the signs: the foam of her decaf coffee had a sad face, created by the glum barista whose name of Meredith had been shortened quite unsuitably to Merri. But her ham sandwich was decent and she managed to get some things down on a notebook for the meeting, such as 'Strong opening song to define the show' and 'Phone-in? Monday magic? What's happened to you today to give you a lift?'.

She was sure the team would make allowances for her: she was an old banger, came from Traffic, had had no warning she was hosting and was new to the area. With that, Charlie realised she felt better – and Jonny would back her up when he responded. She knew he'd be in the gym or prepping for tomorrow's show so she wasn't worried. The eerie calm remained now, having passed the last opportunity to back out. Standing here with Delme meant she was in the system. And, glory be, within a few hours, her first day would be over. It was just the talking out loud bit to strangers she had to get through.

'Right, I suppose I better get going then,' he said, not moving, wiggling his feet which were in odd socks. 'I was doing press-ups. It's my new idea – screen-break exercise! Office workouts to get you fit and ripped. Yeah? Like it?'

Delme was beaming at her with delighted eyes as if he'd discovered the meaning of life. She smiled at his preposterous proposition – as if people would do burpees with co-workers without fear of ridicule. He got up – and banged his head on the edge of his desk.

'A few things still to iron out, safety-wise,' he said, rubbing his crown sheepishly, 'but I think head office will love it. O-kaaay … let me find your file … where did I put it?'

Then the phone rang, which led to a series of emails and a lengthy conference call followed by a hunt for the projector remote and a wider search in the building for a replacement. At five, he began a rambling narration of slides detailing her rights as an employee, where to find the first-aid kit ('you've already been introduced, ha ha') and taken her to the evacuation points in case of emergencies. Then, he announced flamboyantly with a wave of his clipboard, it was time for the last-but-not-least module.

'Cutting it a bit fine, aren't we?' said a beardy balding man whose experience was written all over his craggy face as they got to the control room, where a young woman raised her hand in a wave.

'Roy, Charlie. Charlie, Roy. Producer meet DJ. That's Joanie, the assistant. Won't be long, just finishing off.'

Roy shook his head and exhaled deeply. 'Please make it snappy. We haven't had our meeting yet. There's the running order to go through, Joanie's managed to put some stuff together. It's gone six. On the air in fifty-seven minutes.'

Fifty-seven minutes? That was so soon. Too soon.

'Delme!' Charlie cried. Her nerves, which had been simmering during Delme's recital of the top ten accidents in the workplace on their walk to the studio, were on the boil again.

He tapped his nose conspiratorially. 'Distraction! The art of killing the fear!'

'You've just made it a million times worse,' she said, feeling her heart cantering and her stomach churning. Less than an hour, bugger all preparation and – still, Jonny hadn't come back to her. Where was he?

Suddenly she was face to face with the presenter's black leather hot seat, like the one off *Mastermind*, trapping its victim in a spotlight. All it needed was some straps and it'd resemble an electric chair. In front of it was a throbbing yellow microphone adorned with the smiley sunshine logo. A desk of switches and screens. It was as familiar as a bloody flight deck. And she was going to crash land.

Fright had taken hold of her yet on went Delme, explaining 'electrical risks' and 'cable ramps' and 'headphone strangulation' – did he just say headphone strangulation? Maybe she could get out of this by doing that – but she could only focus on the clock hands ticking. It was a pure sound devoid of any echo, thanks to the soundproofed walls, but they boomed in her head.

'I can't do this,' she said, feeling woozy. 'I mean, I know I have to but I don't know if I physically can. Get the words out.'

'Course you can!' he sang. 'It's mind over matter. And you have no problem speaking your mind to me.'

'That's different!'

'How? Radio is just chit-chat.'

Chit-chat. The domain of the easy breezy person who feels confident in their own skin who hasn't ever had a catastrophe on live radio. Even if she was willing to discuss it, which she wasn't, she wouldn't do it now to a stranger. She shook her head violently, backing away from the dashboard.

'I'll get you some water, that'll help.'

He went to the door and pulled hard. And the handle came off in his hand.

'Oh,' he said, staring at the silver lever, then at where it was supposed to be.

He dropped to his knees and started to rattle the metal knob around in the hole to try to get it reattached to the spindle. But it kept slipping off.

'Oh,' he said.

'Oh, what?' she gasped.

'Let me just try again ...' And then, 'Fuck.'

'Fuck? Oh God, can't you fix it?'

'Nope. Don't look so scared! You look like a Welsh lamb who's clocked a jar of mint sauce. I know a man who can. The on-call facilities guy. Get the headphones on and tell Roy.'

Trembling, she stuck them on and felt their weight, like a memory of her failure. 'Roy,' she said, hoarsely, leaning into the microphone, 'we're locked in.'

'Oh, Christ. I asked Del to get that sorted last week. Put him on.'

An animated conversation took place with Delme apologising as Roy turned puce and Joanie betrayed her sweet elfin face topped with a violet pixie-crop by mouthing 'wanker'.

'Can you try to get us out your side of the door? Joanie, can you ring the facilities guy?'

But it became clear as time pressed on and on – and on – despite shoulder shoves and Googling 'how to get out of a door that's lost its handle', they were stuck.

'Maybe we should smash the window?' Delme said, sizing up the glass separating them from Roy and Joanie with a karate-chopping hand.

'TELL HIM NO!' Roy yelled to Charlie. 'That'd cock up the sound! And cost a fortune to replace and it'd put the studio out of action.'

Charlie didn't need to explain – Delme got the gist from the way Roy was shaking his fist.

'Chill, chill,' he said, standing back then shrugging. 'We'll have to sit tight then. The fix-it guy only lives an hour away. Won't be long.'

'An hour? Oh my God.' That'd be halfway through the show. The show she had never presented before in a place she had never been to with spluttering skills.

And then, thank the lord, Charlie felt her phone vibrate. It was a text from Jonny! He'd get her through this. He had to. He always knew what to say.

But oh no ...

You're not going to go do it, are you? Walk away, you won't be a failure in my eyes. You know your limits, that's what I love about you. You can always live between my place, your parents' and Libby's, get some temp work. Sorry for late reply, was getting my 10,000 steps in. XXX

She was stunned on so many different levels. There was a lot to digest: the L word for starters. Was he saying he loved her? He hadn't said it before, although neither had she, but if so, why now? They'd only been apart twenty-four hours and that wasn't unusual so was it the distance? She felt a speck of pleasure that he was missing her so much, then a stab of guilt that she'd hardly thought of him because of the stress. But then again, he could've meant it in that way that people did, casually, as a turn of phrase. Yet hadn't her heart spiked when she'd read it, betraying her own true feelings. Did she love him? She was hovering, that was for sure. Then there was the offer to sort-of live with him ... They'd discussed how that couldn't happen – he saw sleep as the elixir of breakfast show survival and he'd only recently started sleeping over at hers on week nights. Once she'd bought a roll-out mattress so he, or more usually she – because his work came first – could bed down on her floor so he wasn't disturbed.

Next, his advice, which had come too late. She couldn't blame him for that – she'd felt the same earlier. But he'd only just replied – couldn't he have come up with something more supportive knowing she was about to go on the airwaves? Yet hadn't she wished the girls had said the same? Wasn't that her desire underneath the ice-thin surface which was cracking as the seconds went by. She quickly forgave him – he was telling her what he thought she needed to hear. He was her number one fan. It wasn't that he had no faith in her. Not at all. He had wanted to save her from pain – although they didn't discuss what had happened between them on their trial run at a relationship any more; she knew he needlessly carried the responsibility for its collapse and this was his sweet way of making it up to her and showing he was devoted. But there was no more time to analyse it: everyting in this shambles of a tin-pot place was in the balance, it could tip either way ... was her confidence in the black or red? Where did her destiny lie? Back at Orbital, begging for a shift? On the scrap heap scrabbling for a way back in? Or here?

'Charlie, standby. Thirty seconds.'

She was about to find out what she was made of. The handover was coming, she'd heard that Sian Lewis on *Home Time* signing off and the adverts were playing. An adrenalin surge whipped its way around her body. Was this heading the way it had gone when she'd bombed two years ago? She had the same tight throat, galloping pulse and tummy spasms of that night which had ruined everything, when her mouth had opened but nothing but howls had come out.

'What about the running order, Roy?' she rasped.

'No time to go through it. You're going to have to think on your feet.'

Think on her feet? When one of them was still aching? How would she be able to do that? One idea that's all she needed ... one idea then two, three, four would come along, just like buses ... buses ... Suddenly, miraculously, she had an idea. A stupid crackpot idea. But it was all she had.

'Del, get your headphones back on. You've got to help me.'

'I'm going for a curry, sorry.' He was scrolling nonchalantly on his phone.

'How? We're trapped.'

'Twenty seconds,' Roy said.

'DO IT!' she yelled and he jumped at the force of her command and then into the seat beside her. He scooted himself up to the other microphone and got comfy, bouncing up and down matching her flipping insides.

'So what are we going to talk about then?' he said, looking excited. The total madman.

'Crush ... on the bus?' she said, thinking of the old lady who'd met her husband onboard and the guy shyly eyeing up that girl. 'Would that do? Who's your crush on the bus? Tell us who's caught your eye on your way home from work?'

His eyes lit up and he pointed a finger to the ceiling. 'Yes! Because there's always someone you see that you like ...'

'... but you're too scared to talk to.'

'Genius. In the circumstances.'

'Ten seconds. Phones off.'

It all went quiet as the jingle began playing ahead of 7 p.m. There was the news bulletin, the sport, the weather and then a fanfare of trumpets began as a voiceover announced 'Your all-new *Evening Mumbles* on Sunshine FM ...'

Delme looked expectantly at Charlie. Charlie opened

her mouth, half expecting her heart to leap out. Delme nodded at her. Her chin moved up and down but nothing. Charlie took a breath ... she was back in the hot seat aged thirty-one when she'd signed her own career death warrant. Silence. It was happening again. She couldn't speak. She was paralysed and terrified and everything went blank. Roy hissed at her to get a move on: more than a few seconds of dead air and the station's back-up player would automatically kick in. No drama or anything but it was The Worst Thing That Could Happen in this game - unprofessional and unforgiveable.

Delme made some crackling noises into the microphone to pretend there were technical issues. His eyes were wide and he was gesturing with his hands for her to say something.

'Charlie?' Joanie said in her ear.

Tick. Tock. Tick. Tock. Everything had turned slow-mo. The rush of blood was coursing in her ears. And still she was silent. Tick. Tock. Tick. Tock. Her skin was crawling, her chest was compressed as if she was in a bra two sizes too small.

'Good evening, Mumbles!' Delme said, out of nowhere, in a cheerful delivery while giving her a look which said 'If you aren't going to talk, you weirdo, I'm going to have to do it for you'.

Charlie heard Roy take an in-breath.

'Welcome aboard the Mumbles Love Bus with Bold and Noble!'

Joanie flew into action and started typing furiously.

'I'm the driver and she's the conductor. We want to know who's your crush on the bus. That person you see every day who gets your heart racing but you just can't find the courage to talk to …'

It was good. It was very good. Charlie felt something rising – it was admiration for Delme's improvisation. She thought of Isabella's conniving shit-stirring, Stig's betrayal and every single person who had given her the swerve when it had all gone wrong for her. She didn't know Delme at all but this person, this wonderful human being, had stepped up. She had to do it too. Bollocks to the doubters, bollocks to the people who thought she was all walk but no talk. She wanted to show them and Jonny, Zoe and Libby that she could get over this. And what was it Delme had said? No fucker with any of their marbles was listening. She swallowed and went for it, praying something resembling the English language would appear.

'Let … let … us know,' she stammered, thrown by the feat of speaking, 'on the usual number …' What *was* the number? Joanie calmly reeled off the contact details in her ear.

'0345 103 1035,' Charlie repeated, as she felt the warmth of Delme's hand reach for hers to tell her she was doing OK, 'send us a text or get in touch on Twitter @SunshineFM. We want to hear from you. Because to-night … the Mumbles Love Bus is going all the way!' She moved the fader and seamlessly the first bars of music kicked in.

It was *Love Train* by The O'Jays, not exactly right but given the situation it was perfect. She'd done it! She'd managed to talk on live radio! She'd only gone and found her voice.

'Woohoo!' Delme yelled, grooving along with a huge grin on his face as Joanie gave them the thumbs up through the window.

'That wasn't quite what we expected,' Roy said, 'but let's run with it. You just about pulled that off. Bloody hell, you had me there, Charlie. Del, well done, mate. Let's keep it going. Texts and tweets come up on the screen, keep an eye on that.'

'I've got this mate who is obsessed with a girl on the number seven,' Delme said. 'But he's frightened of looking like a stalker. I mean, what's happened when it's OK to swipe right on a photo for some meaningless shag—'

'But you can't risk actually talking to someone in the flesh to get to know them, right?' Charlie said. 'We can do modern dating versus the old-fashioned way.' She could raid the bank of Zoe's disasters, without naming names obviously.

'Good. Just bounce off one another, like it's a chat. Mind your language though,' Roy said as Delme raised his palm for a high five.

'Hit me, Bold,' Delme said.

'If I must, Noble,' Charlie replied, with a weak return of her wrist.

Then she let out a very long and shaky breath. Because there was still an hour and fifty-six minutes to go and she would spend all of that trying to surf the waves of fear rather than sink. But with Delme by her side, she knew, or at least hoped, that she stood a chance of survival.

5

As Destiny's Child closed *Evening Mumbles* with *Get on the Bus*, Tina switched off the radio and pinched her nose.

Poor Del was going to get a rollicking for this stunt, she thought, as she cleared the draining board of a single saucepan, plate, fork and tumbler.

The Mumbles Love Bus was inspired when you considered Charlie was not, as had been previously advertised, a DJ. It had shown too – Tina could practically feel the heat of Charlie's discomfort through the speaker.

But the boss was going to go ballistic when he found out the string of events that led to the health and safety guy turning co-host.

With Sunshine FM a small fish in the parent company's big pond, Mervyn Davies would be eaten alive if he challenged Stig Costello's Orbital FM trickery to avoid paying Charlie any redundancy. On top of that, there'd be complaints coming at him from all angles. From the head of music for the abandonment of the playlist, although all credit to Joanie, their little gem, for improvising with transport-related tracks such as *Drive* by The Cars and The Beatles' *Magical Mystery Tour*. From marketing and the station manager for the tone of the show – yes, you could argue buses were packed with the over-sixties but all that talk about dating and apps was wildly out of the grasp of their elderly demographic. From the production director for the off-the-hoof content. And from facilities who no doubt hadn't been informed the door handle was playing up – yes, Del had even let it slip on air they were locked into the studio because he'd forgotten to report it. It wasn't slick and seamless – it was rough and ready. God knows what the listeners would make of it.

While Tina would declare her portion of the blame for not being thorough enough to find out Charlie was a dud, the person who'd get it in the neck would be Del. Not just for the obvious – moonlighting minus permission – but because he was the easy target, the one who, time after time, had fallen short of what his duties required of him. 'Go easy on him,' she'd told HR whenever he was in the mire, because everything he did, he did out of goodness. But it was hard to defend him after he'd set off the sprinklers by lighting candles on Diana from sales's birthday cake and winded Danny from IT with a heavy-handed Heimlich manoeuvre when he was barely coughing on a piece of turkey at the Christmas do – all the more ridiculous because Del had been wearing a festive 'elf and safety' costume. It wasn't that he was nasty or devious or underhand, because he wasn't, he was lovely. Keen, enthusiastic, spontaneous, the life and soul. It was because he was simply the wrong man for the job. Tina feared for him, she really did. And this would probably be another screw in his coffin.

All in all, she thought, it had been a shocker of a day. A car crash. Or a bus crash to be more precise. There was no one to confide in or chat to – she knew nobody, deliberately, because making friends would mean revealing personal details and she'd had enough judgement to last her a lifetime. Instead she spoke to herself while she put the dishes from her one-pot tuna pasta tea into the cupboards which even though she'd bleached still looked grimy.

It took just five steps to get to the sofa in her flat. Open-plan living was how the landlord had described it. It was nothing of the sort. She'd known open-plan living. She'd owned it. A flowing white space of bespoke craftsmanship, of sleek hi-spec hi-gloss handleless units, polished concrete ten-seater island, floor to ceiling slide-back glass doors, a vast L-shaped sofa and a flat TV embedded in the wall. A huge cooler filled with vintage wines, metal dome pendant lighting and stylised potted bamboo and orchids to bring the outside in. While it hadn't been her first choice, Gareth had a very persuasive tongue and in retrospect she'd loved its clean and fresh feel. He'd been right: it had matched who they were – an 'about town' couple who entertained their many friends with fine dining. One day, he said, when they were older, he'd make sure she got her rambling cottage although if it was up to him it'd be a stately home. Would that ever happen now? she wondered, surveying the damp end-of-terrace shoebox that was her home. No hall, corridors or places to pause, it was a rectangle bookended by a front door which came straight into this room, with her bedroom and the bathroom on the right, and a back door. The odds of ever getting the open wood shelving, ceramic apron sink and vase of blowsy roses on a farmhouse table were heavily stacked against her but because Gareth was a mix of daring and hardworking, if anyone could do it, he could.

At least she had her garden. Although it was as far as you could get from her old one of landscaped lushness, she'd gravelled the paving stones, introduced planters of honeysuckle and lavender and climbers of jasmine and clematis, transforming the grey square of weeds into a private oasis of joy. Upstairs were nice too, as were next door – in fact her street was full of people who stopped to chat and kept an eye out for parcels. OK, you could hear sirens and the swoop of the police helicopter every now and again but that was inner city life and it drowned out the quiet of no friends popping by to confide in. The worst bit was not having Gareth to cuddle up to. They'd been together since they were seventeen – having spent more than half her life with him, she ached for him. She even had done when he'd stayed overnight in Swansea if he was entertaining clients at the company's headquarters. There was never any silence here though – she wouldn't allow it. She couldn't stand to listen to Ivor Mone, so traitorously Radio 2 went on first thing and she kept it on when she was out, not just to deter burglars but to welcome her when she got in, switching over to Sian Lewis until teatime when the telly took over. Tonight she'd listened to Sunshine FM to hear how Charlie had coped. Now she'd grab a couple of hours of channel-hopping company while she flicked through her *How To Grow Veg* book, which was her goal this summer. She had room for a mini greenhouse where she'd try tomatoes, lettuces and cucumbers plus a small area for potatoes and runner beans. Gareth thought she was barmy! His old man had had an allotment which delivered stringy beans and tomatoes vandalised by slugs he was forced to eat as a kid. That was why he insisted on perfectly shaped carrots in fancy cellophane. But Tina needed to nurture something – their two beloved Weimaraner dogs, Ronnie and Reggie, had been rehomed because it would've been cruel to lock them up in here. She was also working now when she hadn't for years. Poor Bobby, her tom cat, had been run over, and it was plain selfish to get another when she lived in such an urban area.

Darcy had a life of her own too: Tina didn't begrudge it, in fact she saw it as her daughter's right – it was proof Tina had done her very best for her. Darcy had exceeded her parents' academic achievements: their twenty-year-old child was at Leeds University, the first of both families to go, studying French. It was silly, really, but she needed something to take care of until Gareth came home. She missed him so much and the time they had together was never enough – but it wouldn't be like this forever. Just until they were back on their feet. Such was life when you were financially ruined. She felt her chin begin to wobble – as much as she tried to keep them at bay, and she managed most of the time, guilt and sadness were always waiting in the wings. The shock, humiliation, self-pity and anger were long gone, she couldn't change anything that had happened. Guilt and sadness, though, were the residue of turmoil; she had to live with them, accept them. Even though she hadn't been at fault, people had been affected. She felt the responsibility because she was Gareth's wife: she believed in unity in the bad times as well as the good. They had too much shared history to pick apart. She also believed Gareth hadn't meant to do it: he had been ill. His downfall hadn't been sudden, like riding a helter-skelter, it had been like a lift stopping and pausing at every floor on its descent. If you were in trouble, sometimes whatever you did to try to reverse it made it worse. He'd said it'd been a relief when he'd reached his lowest ebb: the only way is up now, Tina. She repeated it to herself over and over. Even so, her breathing had become shallow. Thank God then when her phone rang and she saw Darcy's name on the screen. She would never let her child know she was suffering. She took a breath, switched herself to auto-pilot and picked up with a smile.

'Hello, darling! I was just thinking about you! This is a nice surprise.'

'Hi Mum. Got a sec? Just a quickie, I'm on my way out.'

'Course! What is it?'

'I'm really sorry to ask but I need some money.'

Tina's stomach dropped. Keep it together, woman, she told herself. 'OK ... what for and how much?' she said, as if it was a reasonable request from Darcy.

'I don't know yet, I'm pricing it up, but I want to go to France for the summer to get some experience because I'll have my placement there next year and some of the girls are going. We're thinking of Paris and we'll need a deposit for a place and I know things are tighter but I was hoping you'd be able to help because my job at Starbucks won't cover it all. I'll get work out there, you know, but ...'

The innocence of her daughter, as if things were that straightforward, hit her throat. But she couldn't let her down: Darcy's life had to be better than hers had been. That's what she had always vowed, that was her *raison d'être*. 'Wow, that sounds a good opportunity. Of course I'll help.' God knows how but she'd work something out.

'What about Dad? Will he mind? Although I suppose he's raking it in now in Dubai!'

Tina's insides curdled – but she had to stay strong for her daughter. 'Why don't you email him?'

'Yeah, I will,' Darcy said.

'I can speak to him too,' Tina said, relieved she wasn't telling a lie this time. 'I'm seeing him on Wednesday.'

'He's back? You should've said, I'd have come down. I haven't seen your new place yet either.' She was so young, so trusting.

'It's only a flying visit. I'm getting an hour with him. In from Amsterdam first thing, out to Dubai early evening. I've got the day off so I'm going to Heathrow to see him.'

'OK, cool. Thanks!'

'Great. Everything good your end? You having fun and working hard?'

'Yeah, cool. I'm off out now, there's a party so got to go.'

'Take care then, be good. Love you, Darcy.'

'Love you. Bye!'

Then she was gone and this time Tina was powerless to resist the onslaught of emotion which charged into her and held her down, forcing her to steal gulps of air when the sobs robbed her of breath. What kind of mother was she to lie to her baby? To make excuses that stopped her from visiting to see the truth? She didn't care about herself. She only ever wanted to protect them. But what was protection? She'd wanted to tell her everything but Gareth had warned her against it. We spent years raising her to be happy and to have the best money could buy and it would make her question everything, he'd said.

What if she finds out, she'd countered. He had an answer for everything though: she won't. She doesn't live in Cardiff any more, she's got her own life. As long as Tina did her bit, Darcy would never know. But it wasn't as if she was small and you could weave a story to keep her innocence. She was an adult. Gareth had the trump card: if she finds out, she'll direct her anger at you. She'll never believe another word that comes out of your mouth. You'll have covered for me, he'd said, and she'll have no respect for you and you'll never have the same relationship again. And she loved her daughter so much, so, so much, she couldn't bear the thought of losing her. It felt wrong though, it went against everything Tina stood for and had brought Daisy up to be. That was just the burden of knowledge, he'd said, and it would be unfair to tell her to ease that weight on your shoulders. What should she tell her then? Because she had to say something. The rules were thus: they'd downsized because they didn't need the space any more – and Swansea was a stone's throw to the countryside and beaches of the beautiful Gower. A bit of financial bother meant Dad had to work in the United Arab Emirates where it was tax-free. It'd only be for seven months and they'd done two already. Reassure Darcy it was a moment in their lives. His absence wasn't unusual in fact; he'd never been there in the morning for the school run or at night to tuck her in. He was away at head office once a week too – that was the price of earning enough to give them a lovely lifestyle. And what would happen if it messed up Darcy's degree?

Do it to protect her, like the wonderful mother you've

always been. So she had. With all her heart. And most of the time she could carry it off. And she'd still do so because she'd begun the lies now.

But she knew it came at a cost – like now, when she felt so wretched and ashamed, and had God descended and demanded she give up her life to make sure Darcy was safe, she would sacrifice herself there and then.

6

This is what it must feel like to be Zoe Ball! Simon Mayo! Tony Blackburn! Del thought, on a high, as if his veins were fizzing with full-fat Coke.

Two hours of chat, laughter and jokes – his obviously – had whizzed by and there hadn't been a prompt in sight. No guidelines, no rules – apart from language, natch – just pure unadulterated instinct. Winging it, letting it roll, just doing and being and going with it. He felt immense. He was champion of the world!

'What a show!' he said to Charlie as they left Sunshine FM and stepped into the darkness and drizzle. 'I'm buzzing! Buzzing! I haven't felt so ... alive ... in years!'

Adrenalin was bursting from every pore and he had the urge to run – so he did! Dashing up the pier, he held up his arms, shut his eyes and stuck his tongue out, catching the rain drops, feeling his suit jacket flapping behind him as if he had feathers and ... he had to stop because he was out of puff. Jesus, he was so unfit. It was symptomatic of his lazy living which at this moment he saw was a straitjacket of restriction and repression. He held on to the railings, hearing the waves crashing in time with his heartbeat, his breathing making clouds in the air. As he waited for Charlie to catch up, a little voice asked if he might possibly get into trouble for tonight. Would he be regarded as a guerrilla for acting without authorisation? But he'd had no other option – in fact, his brain decided, he'd ensured the health and safety of his colleague and the station. He'd saved it from silence. And the door handle had been fixed by the call-out guy, so that had been a bonus. It had felt so right, so good.

'Drink?' he asked, when she reached him. 'To celebrate? Bold and Noble after hours on the night bus? Honk, honk!'

Her hood was pulled so tightly around her face it was as if he was seeing a baby being born.

'You must be joking,' she said. 'Aren't you drained from that?'

Del saw now her eyelids were heavy with exhaustion and her shoulders were rounded.

'It's been a long day.'

'But you don't have to be in until lunchtime from now on! Not like me! Come on! There's no way I'm ready for bed yet!'

'You're an extrovert, you feed off nerves and excitement. I'm an introvert, nerves and excitement hollow me out. Sorry, I'm shattered. I'm just going to catch the bus and go home. Sort myself out, try to relax after what happened.'

She had this weird way of understanding things, as if she had an insight into how he ticked. It was an area in which he clearly lacked.

'But it went brilliantly! We were amazing! OK, nobody actually rang in to tell us who they fancied but we got away with it!'

'I hate getting away with it. It means you're going to get found out.'

'Bloody hell, you're full of the joys, aren't you?'

She sighed and walked off, heading along the road for the bus stop, her head down, oblivious to the prom which glittered with lights and the steamed-up windows of restaurants and bars, still busy even though it was a Monday in March.

'Wait!' he said, 'I'll come with you. Where's home?'

'The city centre. I thought you were going out?'

'I am! I can get off there and then head to Wind Street.'

'Wine Street? Really?'

'W-I-N-D pronounced as in wine. It's party central, clubs and pubs. Then I can cab it back to mine. I'm in SA1.'

They'd reached the stop. Just in time too, there was a bus coming.

'What's SA1?'

'The Marina. Vibrant waterfront living, loft apartments, smug. For someone who doesn't want to be found out, you haven't done much in the way of research, have you?'

'I didn't want to come here. My hand was forced. I'm going to resign tomorrow. I can't keep this up.'

'What?'

Charlie shrugged then got on board, followed by Del. After a fumble for his pass – it was in his back trouser pocket, which he could've sworn wasn't where he'd put it – he sat down beside her.

'You can't resign,' he said, as she took down her hood which released a bouncy boing of corkscrewed hair.

'What's going to happen tomorrow?' she said.

'Er ... I'll get in with a sore head, probably get a bollocking for something, charm my way out of it, eat

72

my weight in an all-day breakfast at Cheer on the Pier ...'

'No. I mean on *Evening Mumbles*. Because I just about survived tonight. And that was completely and utterly thanks to you,' she said, 'and I'm so grateful. But the only way I'll be able to do it again is if you're there and that's not going to happen.'

He hadn't actually thought about tomorrow. 'Yeah ... I s'pose. But I loved it! I'd do it again, no problem. It's just wanging on about bullshit and I'm good at that.'

She shook her head. 'I noticed. But they'll never let you do it again. It was a one-off. I'm just being sensible. Like you should be. Go home. You'll be back in work within, what, ten hours?'

Sensible. He sighed through his flapping lips like a horse. She was right. He was a suit, not a performer. Reined in and for a good reason. He was where he was through choice, he reminded himself, to try to make the world a safer place. His flat was a mess, he'd had a string of late nights and he could order a curry, watch something on Netflix, fall asleep in his bed for a change. It was nice and warm on the bus and the loll of the motion was soothing. They went quiet and he took out his phone. He had a million messages – someone had heard him on the radio and passed it on.

'Awesome, mucker!' Rodney had written.

'Dee Jay Del on the decks. Total. Lad.' That was Cooky.

'You're as lardy as Steve Wright in the Afternoon, buddy!' Typical Jonesy.

'On fire, baby!' His ex, Fflur, added a million flame emojis and he felt his groin respond and then retreat when he heard Mam's voicemail. Ever since he'd started working for Sunshine FM, she'd deserted Radio 2 in an act of loyalty. She was nice like that, doing it for him. Her lovely soft voice announced 'Delme! It's Mam!' and what followed was an effervescence of tinkly laughter and shock that her boy had been on the radio. 'You were a natural! So funny, everyone thinks so, Dad even switched off the rugby thing he was watching to listen. Crush on the Bus! What a good idea! Although that woman with you was a bit of a wash-out but you were the gentleman, filling in the gaps. That's my boy.'

Boy? He was thirty-five. But still it made him feel loved, like he was small again. She was the best ... she was lovely ... and, oh no, she was ruining it.

'I saw your brother today. He was asking after you. Hoping you'd see him. I know it's hard but Samuel—'

He deleted the message and smacked the phone on his thigh. His elation burst as guilt waved over him. His big brother, his best mate, he missed him so much. Sam had been his hero. An absolute legend. A beast of a boy then, a hulk of a man. Now he was a child again. The head injury had robbed him of his future, his identity, even his appearance, reducing him from an athlete to a limping shapeless gurning blob. Dependent and simple. The language Del used was deliberate – to hurt himself, to punish himself for his failure to handle what Sam had become.

Losing him had been the worst thing that had ever happened to Del. Mam said his pain was proof of his love but it was torture. Seeing what had happened to him when he'd had so much potential. Del had never got close to any blokes again. Dad tried to compensate, offering pints and nights out, but it was wrong and it made him sour in his company. OK, he had a load of friends, masses of them, but that was deliberate so he couldn't make any intense bonds with one person. That was what manhood was, right? A show of steel, of independence. Bromances were just a Hollywood invention to flog films. He spread himself thinly on purpose because there was less chance of being hurt. That's why he'd avoided going to visit Sam in his assisted living flat. He couldn't bear seeing him like he was. The last time, two months ago, when Sam had given him a stickman drawing. It had made Del weep. He'd promised him he'd put it up on his wall but, with shame, he'd folded it and put it in a drawer. It had killed him. He rubbed his face with his free hand and tried to think of something to say to Charlie, to take him away from this terrible sadness. But nothing. He would never sleep tonight. He'd watch that day, that disastrous day of the accident, on replay on the backs of his eyelids. Please, God, make it stop.

His mobile vibrated in his hand. It wasn't God but Rodney and that'd do.

'Where are you, son? It's Rodders. Coming out?'

Del heard shouts and name-calling and banter in the background and it drowned out his own despair. He needed a drink. Not beer but a drink drink.

'Yes, matey, where are you?'

'Wind Street.'

He said a prayer of thanks. Sometimes the boys would do the Mumbles Mile and he couldn't do that. That had been his and Sam's stomping ground, where they wouldn't have to pay a penny all night, getting greeted with cheers and slaps on backs. When his brother had been a household name. Fly-half for Wales, the most revered position. Max Boyce had created the myth of the fly-half factory where a production line turned out number tens. Sam Noble had been one of them, talked about as if one day he'd be the greatest ever.

'Whereabouts?' he said.

'At the bar with the sandpit, know it? Next door to the molecular cocktail thing.'

'Yes, butt. I'll be there now. Just coming into the bus station.'

'Where are you going?' Charlie asked.

'To get Angel Rangled.'

'What does that even mean?'

'To get mangled.' Still she didn't get it. 'Pissed. Angel Rangle, Swansea City legend. It's slang.'

Tired of her now, he stood up, feeling unsteady with the rev and brake of the vehicle, but he didn't bother to hold himself steady. If he fell, he fell. He didn't care. It meant it was going to be one of those nights. He heard Charlie call his name. But he ignored her and willed the door to swish open, poised to escape, and as soon as he felt the rain spit on his face, he jumped out and headed off into the night where he hoped he could get so pissed, he wouldn't remember anything any more.

7

'I've got a crush on the bus to tell you about. It was on the number four this morning. The previous two were cancelled, it was jam-packed. Like being in a bloody scrum.'

～

Here Charlie was again, trembling at the microphone, waiting for the jingle to end and *Evening Mumbles* to start.

So much for slamming her letter of resignation on Tina's desk this afternoon. It'd been whipped out of her hand and thrown in the bin in a manner that suggested Tina wasn't a steel magnolia but a steel daffodil. 'We need you, Charlie,' she'd said, simply and firmly, but with eyes that shone with determination and kindness. Within minutes, Roy, Joanie and Delme had been summoned. The producers arrived quickly. Delme shambled in bleary-eyed, with dried egg from his all-day breakfast on his tie. Tina had then laid it on the line.

'Mervyn Davies isn't happy. But we have no one waiting in the wings. We can't have silence for two hours. We have to make this work. Charlie can't, or won't, do this alone.'

She wanted the ground to swallow her up but there was no extended guilt trip; Tina continued with her astute assessment.

'Del, he wants your guts for garters, but I've told him I will personally take all responsibility for you on *Evening Mumbles* if you want to continue alongside your usual health and safety work – there's no extra pay, I'm afraid, but you said you didn't mind. You can remain co-host until Charlie finds her feet.'

He beamed despite the back-handed compliment.

'Roy, Joanie, you are the best we've got. Can we make this work? Do we have a deal?'

Charlie had seen her colleagues' heads nod. Sickeningly, it was down to her to give the final yes. Their faces had turned to hers and were waiting. Oh God, it had been horrific: she'd felt like she was in freefall, her fingers desperately scrabbling for her comfort zone that was beyond her grasp. She was out of kilter, not acting herself. She hadn't been since last night. She'd offended Gen when she got in, refusing a glass of wine and going straight to her bed. She'd replied to Zoe and Libby's 'How did it go?' texts to say she'd hated it and ignored their supportive replies to stick with it. It was Jonny who had sided with her – thank goodness for him. At least he had something to base his opinion on, unlike them. He'd been so caring to listen right up to the end online even though he should've been asleep and he'd agreed wholeheartedly with Charlie that it had been a stretch for her. She was so lucky to have his honest opinion – friends only told you nice stuff, which proved how nice they were. Their 'Go, girlfriend' cheerleading was also a pressure in itself: she didn't want to let the side down, ever, but why wasn't it all right to admit what they saw as shortcomings but she saw as facts? Why didn't they see that as a strength? Not every girl could or even wanted to run the world. With your other half – and Jonny was her fitting jigsaw piece, she was pretty sure of it – you got the truth. That's not to say resignation didn't scare her: it marked another cliffhanger. That was probably why she had a lingering, tetchy feeling of ... what was it ... anger? Having to put herself through this for others to see what she already knew? Perhaps it was the old disappointment in herself resurfacing, which she'd buried so deeply but had bobbed up bigger than before. Why wasn't she stronger, more re-silient? Why couldn't she grab life by the balls like other people? Why was she putting herself in the firing line when it was obvious she had only just scraped through the show? She had nothing to offer, she concluded, she'd already been found out. In Jonny, she would find all she wanted and needed, not least a safety net. OK, he hadn't mentioned the L word in his text but she didn't need to hear it because his devotion was clear. What was wrong with going somewhere you were wanted and wanted to be? This risk in Swansea had well and truly lived up to jumping without a parachute. It was no good. The fear had reared up and she'd composed her 'thank you for the opportunity but it's not for me' note. But she was so useless she couldn't even resign properly.

'Charlie?' Tina had said, hopefully, laughably, as if she was kingmaker. 'If there's anything we can do to help ... if you wanted to talk about anything ... about your difficulties?'

They'd all looked at her, Delme with a big probably-still-drunk smile, Roy and Joanie, expectantly with raised eyebrows. As if she was part of the team – and she hadn't felt that for a long time. At Orbital, she'd thought she'd been needed, that's what had kept her going in day after day, but she'd discovered to her detriment she'd been tolerated until they could no longer humour her. The guys at Sunshine FM though wanted her to do this: not her specifically, it could've been anyone, but she was here. If she refused, Roy and Joanie would be in the shit. She'd be dumping on them and they hadn't asked to be paired up with her. Her name would be mud – or muddier. They were willing to work with what they had – the DJ with the public-speaking phobia. If they could do that, then she owed it to them. And while it made her squirm to admit it, another reason she relented was because she didn't have the guts to say no. They all had bills to pay. With a heavy heart, she'd agreed, batting away the offer to talk about the reasons for her confidence issues – because how could they fix that in five minutes? – and been bundled off by Roy and Joanie to prepare for the show. Delme was excused because he had his day job to finish and besides, he was good at hitting the ground running.

As they'd taken their seats around the table, Charlie thought they'd have been within their rights to give her a bit of a dressing down. But Roy and Joanie had got down to business and addressed her as if she was a fellow professional and not the inept mutant she was. It was too early to tell if Crush on the Bus spoke to the listeners, Roy had said gruffly, but in his opinion, it had legs – or wheels. It was all they had too. They just needed to get people to call in. Charlie suggested dedicated Facebook, Instagram and Twitter feeds which Joanie got OK'd by the social media manager and then she was off, asking people to get in touch. Happy she was of some use, Charlie slowly reconnected with the industrious part of herself and by the time Delme bounded in, with his second wind thanks to a dripping kebab, she didn't feel so afraid. There was still the self-doubt but she managed to drown it out with work until she found herself back in the cans and ready to go.

Again there were the shakes, sticky palms, cold toes and damp armpits as she was counted in. Again she stuttered and Delme had to take over with the introduction. And again she eventually managed to find her voice and chip in with a welcome. It wasn't any easier but it felt more familiar this time and joy of joys, after the first plea for Crush on the Bus callers, Joanie was putting someone through. Except in her excitement, Joanie had overlooked something: the old codger was complaining about being squashed like a sardine on the number four. Delme was too busy snorting through his nose so Charlie began to chat away happily about traffic with him for a good ten minutes, which she'd thought was a good recovery. Her experience did count for something then! And by the looks of it, the boss thought so too because when she looked up into the control room she saw the tall, wide and badger-haired Mervyn Davies, whom she recognised from the rogues' gallery of Who We Are up in reception. How nice of him to pop in! There was some kind of discussion going on and oh, he was jabbing a sausage finger at Roy who had his head in his hands.

'Charlie,' Joanie's voice said, 'can we have a quick word? In here? Delme, you take over.'

As Charlie left the studio and opened the door to the production suite, she heard the words 'Get her off air!

She's God awful.' Mervyn swivelled round and without even looking at her, marched off with a whiff of body odour.

'Right,' she said, quietly, 'I see.'

'Bloody unprofessional of Davies to do this mid-show,' Roy said.

Joanie dropped her eyes to save Charlie's humiliation which coursed her body – at least the hot flush made a change from the icy grip of terror.

'I tried to argue, Charlie,' Roy shrugged.

'It's OK. Not unexpected.' And a part of Charlie was relieved that her torture was over.

'It's just … he said people didn't want to hear about jams and roadworks at this time of day. They're home, they want to be eased into their evening, entertained. And, he wasn't happy when you couldn't pronounce Cwmrhydyceirw. That's where he was born.'

There was no point arguing back. They had a show to get on with.

'Thanks for taking it on the chin.'

Charlie managed a nod, exhausted now the threat had finally been lifted. Anyway, for all her weaknesses, her jaw was granite – she'd taken more punches than most.

She picked up her bag and coat. 'Tell Delme, from me,' she said, 'it was a pleasure. Sort of.'

8

Tina's eyes were trained only on Gareth when she saw him across the room. The old shiver down her spine was there, just as it had been every time they met, from the day they met. Twenty-five years of shivers, from the first aged seventeen on the dance floor and the moment he turned around to drink her in as she walked down the aisle on their wedding day a year later, to every morning when they woke together and every night when he returned home.

Time had taken them on the most incredible journey – their faces showed it. His green eyes were lined from laughter and pain, his once-jet-black hair now greying. But in their weathered skin, they had survived everything life had thrown at them and she wouldn't have changed a bit of it. Because she had taken her vows and taken them seriously, wanting to provide the safest of nests for their daughter. And seeing him like this, here, convinced Tina she was putting Darcy first.

Gareth held out his hands, tugged her to him with strength to defy his tiredness and she was folded into his chest, her favourite place in the world, forgetting the standard issue orange bib over his designer denim shirt. Before, he'd have worn it casually around the house but now it was saved for 'best' for her visits, to show that beneath his prison number he remained the man she loved. She pressed her forehead where the collar ended, feeling his warmth. He still smelled the same, even more so without aftershave to hide it. Musky and manly, he was her everything. She took his unshaven cheeks in her hands and touched her lips to his but quickly; their displays of affection were private not public property. They had to be. On her first visit to Swansea Prison, when her emotions were unfettered, before she knew better, they had been barked at by a guard, reminded it was strictly minimal contact.

'You look beautiful, Tina,' Gareth said softly, showing her to her seat.

Being under his gaze, she felt a shyness borne from their separation. He'd always loved how she'd dressed and it was even more important to keep that up for him when they snatched these precious times together. She'd hardly believed it when she found the cream tweed LK Bennett skirt suit in the charity shop. Not that she would tell him that she could barely afford the tenner it'd cost because she didn't want him to know how different her life was; he was aware, of course, but there was no need to spell it out and bring him down. He'd been through enough with his illness. The thirty minutes to do her make-up and hair in front of the mirror in the ladies at work was designed to draw him in and block everything out, the noise of the other visitors and the clatter of furniture, to give him a focus away from the peeling walls and wet tissues scrunched in hands. The generous spray of her almost-empty Chanel No 5 scent, which she saved for him, would leave a trace of her on his clothes to mask the stink of cabbage and acrid bleach. The aim was upmarket and elegant, to show him he was above this, that she was coping; a promise of what awaited him when this was over.

'And you're as handsome as ever,' she whispered, not wanting to be overheard for this was as close to intimacy as they could get – there was no opportunity to caress or tease, confide or cry.

'Have you eaten?' he asked, sliding his leg between hers, resting his calf on her knee, before reluctantly pulling away.

'Of course not,' she smiled, 'I thought I'd wait for you.'

'Good, this place, Morgans, it's the best boutique hotel in Swansea, they do a lovely bit of grub.'

It had been their go-to restaurant in the days when they hadn't had to think about bank balances. She played along, happy to see he was in a good mood. Because he wasn't always like this.

'What will you have?' she said, coquettishly, as if they were in the luxurious surroundings of wingback leather chairs and dimmed lighting rather than plastic and flickering fluorescent strips.

'The braised daube of beef, creamed potatoes, sautéed spinach and the red-wine jus.' Oh how he needed it. He'd lost weight: the ordeal was taking its toll.

'Of course! As always! Pan-seared salmon for me.'

'And to drink? Bollinger?'

'Well, I caught the bus here so I'm not driving . . .' The matching Mercs were long gone.

Gareth laughed a little then he dropped his head and she saw the fins of his skinny shoulder blades. He had never been slight before. Ever. He'd had muscles and abs and pecs and a smile and an attitude that sang he was blessed by the gods and the luckiest man on the planet. Coming into this imposing Victorian high-brick-walled jail with its security and searches and sniffer dogs didn't break her – she was tough as old boots on the whole: look how she'd coped with it all. With dignity, even though she'd been screaming inside during the terrifying 6 a.m. door-battering arrest, the court appearances, the 'send him down'. Losing everything they had, moving away from home, reinventing herself so she could be closer to him. No, it was the small things that would break her when she allowed herself to cry later and this would be one of them. For now, it was 'put her brave face on' time.

He resurfaced with an edge, narrowed eyes and a clenched flexing jaw. 'How are you? And how's my princess?'

She knew he meant: had Darcy found out? 'Good. Great.'

His expression relaxed and he winked. She felt a rush of relief that she was doing her bit.

'Well done, love. I know it's hard.'

Hard? It was damn near impossible to keep Darcy in the dark. Unthinkable. But what else could she do?

'How are things with you?'

This was the worst bit: she'd read online how it was important to share troubles but how could she? He had suffered in so many ways. He didn't need to know about the burden of carrying this alone, the loss of her self-esteem, pretending to her colleagues she was dashing off to Heathrow for a champagne and oyster fumble in a hotel at the airport, the man lurking in her nightmares who grabbed her on the bus. Neither the happiness she had at work, of doing a job well – despite personal issues, specifically what to do with Charlie after she was taken off-air last night – and managing on pennies so she could save something each month for their daughter. But she had to give him something or he'd think she was hiding something. Not that he was jealous or suspicious but she could only imagine how his mind would boil and come to false conclusions in the small hours in his single bed.

'Your mother's fine, her op for her knees is in May so I'll take a couple of days off to see her although you know what she's like, she says she'll be up and at 'em. Darcy's busy, full of life. You're best off where you are with this weather, work is a slog and last night I had leftover tuna pasta bake for tea. Trust me, you're not missing anything.'

'Anything to report from Darcy?'

'She needs money.' She managed to suppress her wince as if they were discussing family life over dinner. 'Uni stuff.'

'I'm so proud of you all, you know that, don't you?' he said, his eyes watering, 'You especially. It's not fair on you to be alone with all of this.'

'She's wrapped up in her own thing, love. Good job you were dreadful with mobiles before this or she'd never accept you couldn't get yours to work in Dubai.'

'Any emails?' he asked.

'Not really. Penis extentions and men who want to meet me in Russia, you know. One from Darcy. About the money.'

'Have you answered it?'

Oh, how ashamed she'd felt pretending to be him,

talking of the heat and the high-rises and the sandstorms and the traffic.

'Told her she can have as much as she needs?'

'How? No!' Because she was supporting Darcy with bits and pieces, trying to pay for her own rent and bills plus put aside anything spare but it was double figures rather than hundreds or thousands.

He swallowed hard and looked around before he dropped his voice to a whisper.

'Don't get excited or angry and raise your voice OK, but I'll get some sent to you.'

She fought the shock as well as she could, keeping her shaking hands on her lap and directing her stare at his chest.

'What? What money?' she gasped.

'Emergency money.' He checked around him again and bit his thumbnail.

'Where from? Gareth … you're not … oh God, please don't jeopardise any of this.' He'd pleaded guilty to get a shorter sentence. He wasn't actually guilty.

'It won't. I had to hide it, you know why. Otherwise it would've been seized like everything else. It's for Darcy.'

The apple of his eye.

'You don't have to do anything apart from—'

'I don't want to know.' She felt sick and stunned; he'd kept this from her, they didn't have secrets. This was unfamiliar territory.

'Listen,' he said harshly, hissing. Bewildered, she looked up at him. There was a split second when she saw flint in his eyes, a sliver of violence which she didn't recognise. But it was gone so quickly she saw it was the anger of an innocent man.

'Look, we're almost there. Five months and I'm out. I've kept my nose clean. All you have to do is take what's offered when it comes to you. There's someone I know who can handle it, who's been keeping an eye on things for me.'

Was this the man who had been shadowing her? 'Do I know them?'

'No. Just a contact. Why?' His eyes narrowed.

She shook her head. Asking questions would only implicate her.

He seemed satisfied. 'I made arrangements. For you. For us. For Darcy. You don't have to do anything but take in a package.'

If all she had to do was that ... but no. 'I can't.'

Her chest was heaving with the thought of doing what could only be illegal. She couldn't. She wouldn't. Lying was one thing but this ...

A table was thrown onto its side, a scuffle and jangling chains and she was the only one who leapt in her seat.

'It's clean. From before.'

She trusted him. She'd vowed all along to trust him. An inmate was handcuffed and against the wall.

'I'm going to my meetings.'

He was recovering from an illness. A woman with tattoos and roots and facial sores was crying.

'It's for our princess,' he said, pleading with his eyes, 'for our number one daughter. Little Darce. Daddy's baby. Please, Tina ...'

She twisted her wedding ring in thought. He wasn't like these criminals. He was her loving husband and an adoring father. Her happiness depended on their happiness. And she'd sooner die than let them down.

9

Before anyone had said a word, Delme knew he was done for.

Their awkward faces put him right off his All The Meat takeaway pizza. He'd been looking forward to his pre-show snack since lunch, too. The slice in his hand wilted like a disappointed willy as a snail of grease from his first piece trickled down his chin. He chucked the box on the table in surrender.

'The game's up then,' he said. For why else would Marilyn from HR be here?

'Nice touch, Maz. To do it in front of everyone,' he said as Roy and Joanie rose to leave the control room.

'I've been trying to get hold of you since ... the matter arose.' Marilyn, fair dos, did look sheepish. More so than usual with that white perm and cream fleece.

'I popped out, I was hungry. I thought I'd need a feed before *Evening Mumbles*. The voluntary work I do for no pay to make sure there isn't two hours of silence. The work I'm doing alone because the actual DJ employed to do it was dragged off mid-show last night and I had to carry on and pretend she'd suddenly come over all queer.' His sarcasm was as thick as the crust on his abandoned fourteen-incher. Delme immediately apologised – the only person here responsible for what was about to happen was himself.

'No need to go anywhere,' he sighed at the escapees, 'it'll save me having to explain.'

They retreated from the door just as Charlie walked in, pale as anything. When she saw Delme, she stopped dead, mortified. Hang on, she'd been ordered off the airwaves yesterday. She wasn't supposed to be here … unless … she'd been asked to come back?

'You know already, then, Charlie.' He pinched the bridge of his nose in anguish.

'I'm afraid head office got wind of the door handle incident,' Marilyn said. 'They view it as a fire risk. A breach of health and safety. I'm sorry to inform you you're being suspended.'

'Of course,' he exhaled, undoing his tie and top button in capitulation. No one bothered to protest that it was a disproportionate sentence – everyone knew this was the straw that had broken the camel's back. He'd had so many incidents, so many chances…

'Gutted for you,' Joanie said, reaching to him, her eyes as sad as a bird with a broken wing.

Roy shook his hand and gave him a commiseratory smack on the back.

'Security escorting me from the building then, Maz?' He looked around dramatically with hunched shoulders and thought about raising his wrists to be cuffed.

'I don't think that's necessary,' she winced.

Bless her, he felt a shit for taking it out on her. She'd stuck her neck out for him so many times she could've given Marie Antoinette a run for her money.

'I'm so sorry, this is all my fault. If I hadn't dragged you on the radio you'd still have your job.' Charlie spoke quietly, neck bent, looking up at him from beneath her eyelashes, wringing her hands with the guilt. But it had nothing to do with her, not really.

'It was a long time coming. I'm sorry you're having to do the show by yourself.'

At this reminder of the elephant in the room, Charlie froze and her eyes went wide; her body said she was less battle-ready, more rabbit in the headlights.

'Can he stay?' she blurted loudly to make sure she was heard, as if this was her final request. 'Just for a bit. Until I've got myself settled? Because I have zero confidence. Dumped yesterday for being rubbish and now reinstated out of sheer necessity. Please? If he wants to that is? If he doesn't mind? If I can see him then it might help.'

It couldn't be easy for her. Frogmarched from the studio last night, hovering around today, waiting for the push, once they'd found a legal way of doing it and somehow finding herself back at the helm again. Everyone waited for Marilyn's verdict.

'I'm leaving now,' she said, steadily. 'Don't let me down, Del.'

Delme hugged her for what would be her last act of kindness. Because he'd come to a decision. 'I won't touch a thing, I promise. Nothing to worry about, you know me and trouble ...'

'That's what I'm worried about,' she said, patting his shoulder. 'I'll ring tomorrow. Do my best to sort this out for you.'

Good luck, he thought, because that would be that. He

wouldn't be coming back even if he was cleared because it was obvious he'd used up his nine lives.

'Bastards, looking for a reason to get rid of you,' Joanie said as soon as the door shut.

But the funny thing was, Delme got it.

'I'm just not meant to be doing health and safety, am I?' he said, with his palms in the air. He was being released, that's what it was. It was like a weight off his shoulders to be honest. What he'd do he had no idea but there was a tingle on his skin at the prospect of freedom.

'You're going to contest it though?' Joanie said.

'Nah. No point. Guilty as charged. I'll be on full pay until they sack me off. I'll start looking for a new job tomorrow.'

He turned to Charlie. 'They got the top guns in to replace me, then, I see.'

'Don't! No one else would do the show. It's jinxed and everyone knows it,' Charlie said desperately.

Poor thing. As the football chant went, she was shit and she knew she was. Or more accurately, when they'd scraped the barrel, she'd been the last one in there. Why hadn't she told them where to stick it? He didn't dare say it because he didn't want to make this worse than it already was for her. Anyway, she wasn't that bad but he couldn't say that either. Note to self, he thought, don't apply for any motivational speaking positions. What she'd done showed balls. That was the way to do it.

He fisted her arm softly. 'You'll make it work, I know you will. You've got more guts than ... well, me,' he said, looking down at his bulging waistline.

'And no fucker's listening, right?' she said feebly. It

wasn't a statement, it was a question loaded with insecurity as if she was seeking moral support. Delme's bum clenched at her self-doubt. So many people had a sense of entitlement, usually men to be honest, with no bricks and mortar of experience – just a pair of testicles roaring them on. Yet here was she, so feisty and clever, but wracked with a crippling lack of faith in her own ability. Where was her immunity?

'No fucker's listening,' he repeated firmly. 'Break a leg.'

'If only. Twisted ankles are my thing.'

Charlie tried to smile but it was a brittle one – she hadn't made a joke, he realised, she was saying she couldn't even break a leg properly, as if she was incapable of doing anything right. It was too late to offer any more encouragement because she'd disappeared.

'Dearie fucking me,' he mumbled as she reappeared through the glass like an exhibit in a zoo. Not an animal furious at being caged but a creature who wanted to curl up and hide. He almost couldn't watch. If he didn't, though, she'd pick up on it. He willed her on as she shuffled around, crossing his fingers in his pockets. But she looked numb and detached, barely glancing at the script.

'OK?' Joanie said over the 7 p.m. jingle.

Charlie shrugged from the slump of the chair. 'I might just let rip a string of expletives,' she said. 'Then it wouldn't be my problem any more.'

Roy and Joanie swapped nervous looks.

'This is going to be a disaster, why did I agree to it?'

Charlie wasn't talking to them – she was talking to herself and it was getting dangerously close to show time.

'Charlie, look at me,' Joanie suddenly said, leaning forward over her desk with an intensity borne of desperation. 'Look at me!'

She did as she was told through dead eyes – the news was going to sport, there wasn't long left. Delme itched to save her and considered what would happen if he jumped in. But it wouldn't be him who would be affected – everyone else, Roy, Joanie and Maz, would get into trouble and he'd promised.

'Listen,' Joanie said, 'I've got an idea. I wouldn't normally do this but needs must.'

Charlie almost looked interested.

'I know someone with a crush on the bus.'

That did the trick!

'Who?' Charlie was suddenly animated.

'Me,' she sighed. 'If I do it, it might kick it all off.'

'You'd do that? To save my skin?' This was one step beyond. Just like Madness.

'You got any other ideas?'

'No.'

Time was running out, the sport was coming to an end.

'Just say we have our first confessional and I'll do the rest.'

Joanie got up, grabbed her phone and ran out of the control room to ring in as the *Evening Mumbles* intro began.

'Hieveryoneit's*EveningMumbles* …' Charlie gabbled, her hands flapping.

'Slowly,' Roy commanded.

Delme felt sick.

'It's Wednesday … March the sixteenth … we've got a

person on the line ... Crush on the Bus person ...' Now monotone and talking at a funeral director's walking pace, she had as much bounce as a dead kangaroo. She was appalling. Come on, Charlie! Come on!

Quick as a flash, Roy put on *Live to Tell* by Madonna as background music. 'Go, Charlie.'

'Hello,' Charlie said, uncertainly.

'Hi,' Joanie echoed, playing it cool, waiting for Charlie to find her mojo. You could've heard a pin drop as she searched for it.

'So, tell us about your crush ...' Charlie was shielding her eyes from Roy and Delme, holding her forehead with her hands, staring down at her microphone.

'My name's ...' Joanie paused for inspiration, 'Violet ...'

Nice one, as in her hair, Delme understood.

'Hi Violet,' Charlie said, a smidgeon more warm than a robot. Delme prayed she was defrosting. 'Who's the lucky bloke? What's he like?'

'Well ... he's ... tall,' Joanie said, shyly, 'but not, you know, huge. Quite ... lean, yes, lean, that's what he is. Really gorgeous looking, shoulder-length hair, dark brown, wavyish with the most beautiful chestnut eyes.'

'Have you ever spoken?' Charlie was keeping it together.

'Never.'

'Made eye contact? You know, any lingering looks?' This was a bit better.

'We've smiled a few times. It makes my heart beat so fast and sometimes I can't bear to look ... Do you know what I mean?'

'Like he's not real? He's too perfect?'

Delme felt his chest loosen. And Roy sat back too.

'Yes, exactly that. Because you'd never put us together, he's sort of romantic-looking, in a Poldark kind of way! Dresses like he's a New Romantic or something!' Her voice grew stronger as she talked with passion. 'But I admire it, that look, it's hard to pull off and I know it's weird but he totally carries it off.'

'Why do you say you'd never put you together?' It was almost as if Charlie had blocked everyone out and was behaving as if she was having a girly chat.

'Because ... ha, well, there are a few issues ... but I don't think I'm in the running. He'd never go for someone like me. He's too beautiful.'

'Don't put yourself down. You sound lovely to me! Not to mention courageous ...'

This was better, much better.

'I suppose, but I think I'd like to do the admiring from afar, better not to be disappointed.'

'What bus does this dandy highwayman go on then? So we can all have a butcher's!'

'From town to Mumbles, 2, 2A, 2B, 2C, 3 and 3A. Every day, sometimes there and back!'

'A double dose!'

'Oh, yes! When that happens, I have to try to get a seat or my legs threaten to give way!' Joanie laughed.

'Maybe he'll be listening, maybe he'll know it's you? If you're the Poldark of public transport, then please get in touch – maybe we can do a bit of matchmaking, fix up a date.'

My God, she even managed a giggle. Charlie had done it! The emergency services could stand down!

'Thanks, it feels nice to let it out, you know.'

In that moment, Delme sensed a connection between

the two women – like Charlie had appreciated and built on Joanie's rescue. Roy was giving his anchor the thumbs up as the first ringing notes of Tears for Fears's *Shout* began.

Still, Charlie stared at the microphone, coming to terms with what she'd managed to do. Joanie reappeared and took her seat again, mumbling 'I'm never doing that again'. But then she gave a cry.

'You won't believe this, team, but the switchboard has just come alive.'

'Really?' Charlie said, looking up, finally facing her squad with a pair of flushed cheeks.

'Yep. A bit like you! Now let's do this!' Joanie said with determination as the three of them began to chatter about what came next. It was strange for Delme to see them from the outside of their bubble – but he was OK with it, he'd just been visiting after all. And he was happy for Charlie: she wasn't the alchemist of radio gold – not silver or bronze either. But at least she'd found her mettle and she'd have this to salvage when she was replaced. Should he say goodbye, he wondered. He was going to go for a pint to think about things and then have another five pints to not think about things. Maybe see Fflur, she'd been messaging him a lot lately, pissed texts, slightly off her head with hilarity and emojis and kisses. What harm would it do to see her? Lots, probably. But he was in the shit already. He went to wave but the crew were deep in talk. And nobody noticed when he slipped away.

'Saturday on Sunshine FM ... still to come, sounds from the sixties, and our resident fitness expert Maureen Roberts, who'll be telling you how to keep fit from your armchair ...'

～

For the first time, Charlie actually felt like she was seeing Mumbles. All week she had barely noticed her surroundings because she'd been so focused on surviving. It was probably a good job too – had she spotted the Welsh version of Mwmbwls, she'd have swallowed her tongue trying to pronounce it.

Now she had made it to Saturday morning, staggered to have pulled off a not-too-terrible show, she could finally stop to breathe in the salt and seaweed. With the spring sun shining and the air still, it was like a sparkling jewel today, as if it was showing its best side for Jonny's benefit. The sky was so vast and blue it could be somewhere on the Mediterranean riviera. Shoppers and promenaders mooched lazily in T-shirts and brunchers sat outside cafes in shades, while dogs snoozed on warm pavements with one eye open for titbits of toast. For the seaside, it was as far from 'kiss me quick' as you could get. There was a quaint charm in the run of brightly coloured boutiques and bakeries, galleries and gift shops along the two main streets, Mumbles Road, which ran parallel to the shore, and Newton Road, which led upwards inland where the twelfth-century Oystermouth Castle sat regally, overlooking its domain. Yet there was also a cosmopolitan feel to the place, its gentrification in bloom with tuk-tuk churros vans, parents cycling with kids in trailers and bistros using blocks of wood and jam jars to serve food and drink.

It begged the question: why wasn't Sunshine FM targeting these people? It was such a lost opportunity. Their listeners were dying because they were dying.

'Where do you fancy eating then?' she sighed happily, rolling away the knots from the week in her shoulders.

'You choose!' Jonny said, squeezing her hand. 'Anywhere you like. What about here?'

He nodded at a pricey-looking place which boasted its own kitchen garden and a menu board of three courses for twenty-five pounds. 'Gluten-free options, micro herbs, non-alcoholic spirits. How ...'

'Expensive?' she laughed.

'I was going to say unlikely! Although, it isn't as bad as I thought it'd be here. You know, considering it's Wales, Charlotte,' he said with a naughty glint in his eye. She loved it when he called her by her full name: it was like he was telling her off which gave her the thrills.

'Shh! You'll get us thrown out!'

'Would that be so terrible?' he said wolfishly. He swung her round and into his arms, which made her excited. Just as excited as last night when they'd devoured each other the minute they were in her bedroom. And this morning when they'd done it twice. TWICE!

'You back home with me?' He buried his nose in her neck and Charlie was weak with lust.

'Stop!' she cried, 'I need to eat.' To keep her strength up!

'Yeah ... good point. We need to keep our strength up.'

They were so in sync it was ridiculous, Charlie thought, kissing him hungrily.

'Food,' she instructed when she came up for breath. 'How about here?' she said, pointing at a little Italian. 'I like the sound of their all-day breakfast pizza. Wild mushrooms, crispy prosciutto and cherry tomatoes. Like a posh bacon roll.'

'Hmm, they've got red-and-white trattoria tablecloths. Never a good sign.'

'You sound like a snob!' she teased.

'I am not!' He looked horrified. 'I'm just saying that it's a lazy rustic hackneyed cliché. If we're going for a bacon roll, then why not just get a bacon roll?'

'Right then, if you're not a snob and you want a bacon roll, how about Cheer on the Pier, my new haunt for my lunchtime ham sandwich?'

'Perfect!'

Yes, she wanted to say, you are. For agreeing to come to Swansea when she'd found out the last train for London on a Friday went before she'd finished work. For not being put out when she'd suggested she meet him not at the station but in Mumbles because the Sunshine FM crew had invited her to their traditional Friday night drinks – she'd wanted to get her round in to say thank you for helping her through her first week. For not belittling their celebrations of more Crush on the Bus callers or telling them he thought Charlie should leave because she'd been treated so badly. It wasn't that he necessarily would've done but she was super-sensitive being the new girl. He hadn't hogged her either, letting her chat away to Joanie and Delme, who'd come out of habit.

She'd got to know Sian too, the *Home Time* presenter, who was so on the ball and experienced, Charlie was in awe. In her late forties, she'd jacked in her big anchor job in London for a better quality of life; her appearance, of outdoorsy wear and scruffy blonde hair, belied her precise radio voice. Her three kids were only young but they could already surf and Sian had been able to buy a huge place with the sale of her house in Islington. Plus Charlie had met DJ Disgo, the cool as a cucumber twenty-eight-year-old muso who dreamed of doing his own club night. Roy and Ivor had sat apart from what they'd called 'the youngsters' but they seemed happy enough. Jonny had taken it all in his stride until they'd got in at hers and his desire – and hers – had gone nought to 60 mph. He made her feel cherished and dangerously close to loved although she wasn't going to bring that up! She'd never told anyone she'd loved them before because she'd never been in love before – infatuated yes but not this ... this entwined soulmate feeling. She would wait until he said it first: for this was a marathon not a dash to the line. He felt it too, she knew, by the way he kept asking if she was OK, really OK, not just saying it OK? But she didn't want to dwell on all of that doubt and humiliation. She wanted familiarity and routine again – just doing what they would've done in London of a weekend. Although it was hard when Merri addressed them in a Welsh accent so drippingly ripe she should've worn a bib.

'What the hell are you doing in here on your day off?' Merri said at the counter, where Sunshine FM was talking chair yoga.

Charlie laughed. Merri's default was cynicism, as if she was world-weary. But what was she, early thirties? Her triple-pierced ears, savage square-cut blood-red bob and a T-shirt which declared 'I'll stop wearing black when they invent a darker colour' said edgy young woman. Yet she had the air of an old exhausted lady. It amused Charlie because it reminded her of London. So she'd come in every day at 12.30 p.m. for her lunch and a carton of homemade lasagne to warm up in the office microwave. (Which reminded her, she had to cook a batch of meals tomorrow once she'd done a proper shop, something that had been eating away at her all week.) Merri's emoji coffee foams told you what she was feeling each day. On Monday there'd been the sad face, Tuesday had been rage, Wednesday rolled eyes, Thursday death and Friday sleepy. What would it be today?

'I'm showing my boyfriend, Jonny, the sights.'

'My condolences,' Merri said, with a smirk on her scarlet lips.

Jonny sniggered. 'Two bacon rolls then?' he said to Charlie, who nodded.

'Plus coffee, for three pounds each?' he asked, amused, before adding too loudly, 'What a mug. You'd pay at least a fiver for the roll alone in London. What a bargain.'

'It's on me,' Charlie said, knowing the train cost a bomb. When it came to her making the journey, she knew he'd pay her way. She led him to a squishy sofa where they took a minute to sigh at the emerald sea before their lattes arrived.

Charlie leaned in and saw a broken heart on hers – poor Merri – and some hands on Jonny's. He failed to notice and took a slug before she had could point it out.

'Thanks,' Charlie called to Merri, who shouted back, 'Don't mention it. Please, don't mention it. Don't mention anything in fact. I'm not in the mood.'

'At last, someone who isn't a simpleton!' he said, picking the side with a cushion. 'Because that Del's a fool, isn't he?'

'That's a bit harsh,' Charlie said, prickling at his criticism. But then she'd thought the same on first impressions. 'He was the one who helped me break the cycle.'

'By the looks of him, he probably breaks everything he sits on.' Jonny made a pufferfish face to illustrate Delme's size. Charlie was taken aback – Delme wasn't fat, he was what you'd call cuddly and actually, you didn't notice it at all such was his large personality. Why would Jonny say such a thing? It was mean and uncharitable, he should be thanking this man for making her face her demons, unless . . .

She arched her eyebrows at him over her cup.

'All right, I admit it, I'm jealous,' Jonny said. Charlie knew she shouldn't be pleased at this sign of insecurity – it was a negative unhealthy emotion. But he wasn't the possessive type and he only meant it in a flattering way, as proof of his attachment to her.

'He had you to himself all week. Lucky sod.'

'You don't think a health and safety guy would steal my heart, do you? Not when I'm with a breakfast DJ!' she said, licking the froth from her top lip.

'Nah, course not,' he winked. 'But I miss you, you know that don't you? Not just here …' He patted his chest and then gave a quick point at his groin as he said 'or here …' which made her giggle. 'But here.' He tapped his head as his eyes bored into hers, which made everything around her disappear and her insides loop-the-loop. 'You're my muse. The one I imagine I'm talking to, trying to please when I'm on air and it's killing me …'

Stick me in the freezer, she thought, or I'll melt.

'… knowing you're going through this when it's all too much for you.'

'I'm coping,' she said earnestly. 'I've surprised myself a bit. Although I've had to ban myself from listening to you in the mornings.'

'You're not listening? Charming!' Jonny fake-harrumphed.

'I get too upset otherwise.'

'Sweet,' he said, wrinkling his nose. 'How long do you give it here then?'

'It depends. The boss has apparently agreed to keep me on until they find someone to replace me.'

'You must feel so shit about that. So out of control.'

'Yeah, I do.' He knew her so well. 'But I have to go along with it, I can't let the others down and there's the money.'

'You can always stay at mine, remember?'

She felt all goosebumpy that he was reminding her of his text. She drew breath to ask tentatively how that'd work, you know, if she did come back. But the bacon was here. And she felt a strange relief on Jonny's behalf that it wasn't a limp and greasy offering but a fanfare of succulent rashers bulging from between warm and white floury doorsteps.

They took their first bites and chorused appreciative noises which reminded her of the sounds that had come from within her as they'd made love this morning. She flushed with heat – and then embarrassment – when she saw her landlady hovering with a wave. Had she heard them doing it? That was one very tempting thing about making the move home, she thought, having privacy, not having to cover up outside of the bedroom. Jonny had so much body confidence, and rightly so, he was lean and toned, and she loved to watch his muscles working as he moved. She was more shy when it came to parading around – she was slight, yes, but cellulite-pocked and had a wobbly tummy and even though he told her she was beautiful, she didn't believe it of herself.

Charlie beckoned Gen over – she had to introduce Jonny to her seeing as they were under the same roof. Gen floated over and Charlie saw she wasn't in her usual casual yoga pants and loose T-shirt but radiating chic with red lipstick and straight silver hair falling down past her shoulders onto a simple grey smock on which rested a statement necklace of plastic thimbles and thread. She looked so wealthy yet she lived in a modest home, it was quite a contradiction. A younger woman was with her.

'I thought it was you!' Gen said, 'Sorry to barge in. This is Claudia, my daughter. I meant to introduce you this week so you could meet someone your own age but we were like ships in the night, weren't we?'

Charlie suddenly realised how she must've come across since Sunday – rude, self-indulgent and self-obsessed. With shame, she realised she hadn't even sat down for a chat with her, not once. She hadn't even asked how she'd come to live in Wales when she was obviously from Scotland. And here she was offering her smiley daughter – who was just as stunning with raven locks, almond-shaped eyes and apples for cheeks – as a friend when she needed one. Immediately, she invited them to join them at their table.

'No, no, we won't. We've just had coffee. I just wanted to say hi.'

'Lovely to meet you, Charlie,' Claudia said warmly, with a Welsh burr. 'We'll catch up again.' And they left, unaware of how their presence – and their legs up to their elbows – caused jaws to drop.

'Wow! They're so glamorous!'

'Not as gorgeous as you,' Jonny said, leaning in to kiss her forehead.

'Cheese.' Merri was rolling her eyes as she collected their empties.

'I'm sorry?' Jonny said, irritably, which made Charlie tense up. This was her local now, she didn't want pubes put in her sandwiches.

'I said cheese,' Merri replied. 'Next time try some of the local cheese.'

Charlie and Jonny widened their eyes at each other. It was a bit off that she'd stuck her oar in.

'Meet you outside,' Charlie said to him as she picked up her bag and followed Merri.

'Everything OK?'

'Trust me, they're all the same,' Merri said.

'Who are?' Charlie asked, confused.

'Men,' Merri said, wiping down a table, 'They're all prize plums. I'm praying for you.'

*

Well, what did you say to that? She clearly had issues and to interrupt them like that showed she didn't just have a chip on her shoulder but a battered cod too. Charlie let it go – it was too busy to find out more. Besides, Merri didn't look the type to want to bare all on the shopfloor. On Charlie's way out it hit her that that was what had been on Jonny's coffee foam. A pair of praying hands. And next to Charlie's broken heart it could only mean one thing. Merri had been treated badly by someone special. Seeing a loved-up couple had been painful. Charlie remembered how that felt when she lost Jonny the first time. Merri's outburst had been a venting at them, not because of them. The poor thing.

Once Charlie was out of Merri's eyeline, she practically threw herself at Jonny; she was so very fortunate to have found a decent, lovely, sexy, handsome, compassionate man – she would do everything it took to keep him.

II

Del woke up to find every part of him was aching – and suddenly remembered why: his ex was in his bed.

Shit. He stretched out on the sofa. Well, he tried to but his arms and legs hit the ends. No wonder he was in pain: he'd been scrunched up on the two-seater in his clothes from last night with just a coat over himself. Her heels and handbag were abandoned on the rug. Fflur had asked him to go with her into his room, for old time's sake, but he wasn't like that. He'd been weak enough to answer her booty call last night when he'd been supposed to be having a drink with the boys. Pissed and already at sea because he'd lost his work focus, he'd latched on to her. But when it came to the crunch, he couldn't go through with it, he couldn't have lost himself in her curves and soft creamy skin. For her, it'd be a casual shag but for him, it'd undo the untying of his heart from hers. Ultimately, he knew she'd take him off in a wild direction when what he needed was to be sure of foot.

He'd loved her so much but they wanted different things. Like kids. She was younger than him by seven years: she wanted to have fun. As a nurse, she saw suffering and death all the time – Del was the perfect antidote to that with his effervescent spirit, his not taking anything seriously and his spontaneity. The way he'd suggest going to Dublin, Amsterdam or Brussels for the night, which they did; how he was up for gay bars and roller discos, sometimes in the same night; how he could whip up a meal from a near-empty fridge. It wasn't, though, as if he'd wanted children, like, tomorrow, just at some point. But Fflur had laughed at him: he was the least responsible person she'd ever met! That was true on some levels, he'd admitted, but he felt as if she couldn't ever see him being anything beyond a clown. He was sick of that act, he'd been doing it all his life: he'd been the family comedian, the class joker at school and college and then the holiday rep with a rep when he did it for one summer and ended up doing it season after season around the Mediterranean until his wake-up call. He was thirty-five, for God's sake, and time was ticking. He wanted to know where their relationship was going but she was all about the chill. His mates thought he was mad for ending it – they were mostly being 'herded' into marriage or fatherhood. Del had been best man, what, five, six times? No one had ever asked him to be godfather though. Kids were what he thought he wanted, she'd said, what he *should* want: he was lying to himself – his job was part of the problem. He was fighting who he was. He felt the conflict in him now as he sat up and rubbed his eyes. He saw his big brother Sam on his eyelids – that was another off-topic subject. Fflur had never really wanted to know much about him and what happened. No point dwelling, it wasn't your fault ... all that. She didn't even show much interest in the one kid he already had in his life – his niece, Rhian, whom he was seeing today.

Del got up and headed for the shower, tiptoeing past his door in case she came at him with her lovely messy red bed hair and asked to join him. And he didn't dare go into his room for clothes either. So he dressed in what was on the floor – yesterday's tracky bums, T-shirt and hoody. It was Sunday, after all, and where he was going he'd end up sandy and sticky anyway. Not risking a coffee, he wrote a note for Fflur saying he had something on. Then he slipped out into bright sunshine and after a quick espresso and egg muffin at a marina cafe, he got a cab to Langland Bay, a Blue Flag beach on the glorious Gower Peninsula, where Rhian lived with her mam and step-dad.

Becky and Sam had split up when Rhian was three – Del was amazed she'd stuck with him for that long because how could you have a relationship with Sam the way he was? It was the hardest decision; Del's family couldn't have loved her more, and she'd been doggedly determined to make it work. But as time passed, it became clear it was useless. Now Becky was with Spencer, who was a part of the family now. Of course Rhian saw her dad but Spencer was there doing the day-to-day caring and protecting – as far as a twelve-year-old would let him. Del made sure he was in her life too. To keep a promise he'd made at his brother's side when Sam had his accident. That also meant he could appease the accusations that he'd turned his back on Sam: how could anyone say that when he doted on Rhian?

And here she was, waiting by the row of sparkling white and green-trimmed Edwardian beach huts, one of which he leased.

'Duncle!' she called, waving, using the name she'd

christened him when she was small and couldn't string Uncle Del together.

'All right, nipper,' he said, feeling his steps bounce at the sight of her. He could see Sam in Rhian: whereas Del was dark, taking after Mam, Sam was like Dad with sandy hair. Rhian had the same sunny looks, an upturned triangle for a nose, freckles and a round face. They were a tall family and she was no exception, sprouting up seemingly every time they met. 'Where's Mam and Spencer?'

'I'm twelve. I'm allowed to walk down here by myself,' she eye-rolled. But the way she swung her legs on the wall showed she was still a child.

'I know! I'm just asking.' He gave her a quick hug, which he was still permitted to do, but kisses and piggy-backs were long gone.

'They're at home. They said to go up with me after for lunch. Can I do your nails and make-up after? Or face-paint you? Go on!'

'All right,' he said, grudgingly, but secretly loving the attention. 'No photos though or it'll ruin my image.' He unlocked the hut and Rhian set out two deckchairs, flopping down and squinting at him wonkily.

'Are we going in today?' she said, which was always the first question she asked. She was a water baby through and through, just like her dad.

'It'll be freezing in there!' He chattered his teeth for effect and tried to distract her with a bag of marshmallows. 'I'll do us hot chocolate on the stove, yeah? How about we play rugby first?' He reached for a ball and flipped it in his hands.

'After,' she pouted, crossing her arms. 'Why don't you ever want me to go in?'

'I do!' he said, knowing she was right. He feared the water: the way it could swallow someone then spit them out near to death. 'It's just it's only March, you'll get pneumonia.'

'I won't! I only want to paddle. I can put my wettie on.'

She stood up, sensing his inability to refuse her. He'd rented this hut specifically for her, for them, to spend time together. Just because he had a thing about the sea he shouldn't pass it on to her.

'Go on then,' he said, throwing her his old hooded changing smock – which he hadn't used for years – and her wetsuit.

'Why don't you come in?' she said, muffled from beneath the towelling mass.

Why not indeed? he mused as he watched a seagull gobble a chip as thick as its neck. He and Sam had been brought up by the beach: learning to bodyboard was as natural as learning to walk round here. They'd spent whole summers catching waves on this beautiful sweeping shoreline – in between wrestling one another and chucking a ball around. Sam always said the time he'd spent playing on the sand with Del had made him faster and more explosive on the pitch. But Del hadn't been in the sea for years, not properly, not deeper than his height, not cutting through the water with his hands, ploughing through currents and having the ocean all to himself.

'Because I don't want to frighten anyone,' he said, grabbing a wad of his tummy. 'Your uncle is a fatso. Too many pies.'

'Get fit then!' she said, leaping into star jumps, 'Then we can go in together!'

She made it sound so simple – why wasn't it that straightforward? Why couldn't he get himself sorted? It was time, looking for work, socialising. It was an excuse, he thought, getting up as she commanded, 'Come on, let's go!'

Rhian took off down the steps to the fine, soft sand, where a breeze lifted her hair, and he marvelled at how free she was, despite everything. He skipped down, feeling overwhelmed and grateful that somebody thought him trustworthy and mature enough to look out for her. But he and Becky had always got on, she was like the sister he'd never had. They didn't talk about really deep things, neither of them wanted to go back there, and she didn't nag him to see Sam like Mam and Dad. Becky knew Del was trying to deal with things his own way. Just when he was able to handle the change in Sam, his brother would floor him with something so heart-breaking, it would set him back again. He hadn't found the strength to build himself up, not since January when they'd last met. But Becky understood that by being with Rhian, Del was with Sam.

After a while, he realised his cheeks were aching as his niece cartwheeled ankle-deep in the sea, ran in up to her knees squealing at the cold and back out, her black silhouette gleaming from the water. This was pure joy: seizing the moment, living in the now. It was fresh and vital, not at all like he had been, when he'd seized the day, the night and the dawn. When work rolled into play then work again without sleep in Malia, Kavos, Magaluf, Zante, Ayia Napa and Playa de las Americas. Those days had been crazy with a capital K … big beats, clubs, women, booze, fights … Oh, hello, there was one going on along from him, loud voices carried on the wind, a man and a woman who, he thought, looked like Charlie and that bloke of hers. He screwed up his eyes and yes, it was them! He wasn't surprised – her boyfriend had been a bit shifty, a bit off with him, in that classic 'back off, she's mine' way that some blokes behaved. He hadn't said it out loud – his body language had though. Jonny, that was his name, had pulled himself up to his full five foot squirt, coming up to Del's kneecaps, and postured about the small-town vibe which reminded him of his native Lincolnshire home. Del had noticed too that he was all smiles and nice when Charlie was with him but as soon as she was out of earshot, he had made a few jokes about the lack of craft beers and olives as if he was in bloody Shoreditch. The point of Friday night drinks was to be inclusive – Roy and Ivor would never have gone somewhere fancy. Then there was the London shit and his 'Big I Am' job, his millions of listeners, his Twitter following. But his way of talking was fake, like he was performing. Del had wanted to say 'All right, butt, I'm not interested in you or your bird' but that would've been half the truth because he liked Charlie loads. Once he'd got past her funny ways, which he guessed was what London did to people, he'd found her to be a laugh, self-deprecating and she was brave with it.

They were a weird couple: he was uptight whereas she was … what? Sort of guarded and aloof and terrified of taking her foot off the gas but then she'd had the balls to actually do it and she'd done OK; she'd become softer, more open, someone you could talk to. He still didn't know why she was so hesitant because when she got going she had this magic of listening, like she'd done with Joanie, of drawing people in and them telling her things. Which this Jonny was doing right now, judging by the way he was flapping his arms at her. What a dick. Del pulled up his hood, not because he didn't want to get involved but because if she saw him, she'd be embarrassed. She'd told him after a glass of wine they were so compatible and never rowed, her eyes lit up like neon love hearts, and actually that may have been right because the way she looked now she was dumbstruck. Like she was in front of a microphone that first time on Monday. Maybe this was their first argument?

He turned his eyes back to Rhian ... and searched for her ... and searched again. But she wasn't where she'd been. Immediately his heart was thumping and he was scanning the sea for her but there were just surfers coming in at him and he moved forward, desperate, not caring that his trainers were wet, and his socks were too, his tracksuit bottoms heavy and his thighs freezing as he waded in, trying to catch a glimpse of a flash of blonde or black. Where the fuck was she? His mouth was dry and he heard his voice sounding strangled as he shouted for her. It was like when Sam had gone, when the waves had turned red and he'd dived in and gone down, seeing his body lolling in slow motion, swaying like seaweed in between the rocks, his muscles loose, his head back and oh God ... a billowing cloud of claret coming from his head ... when Delme had frozen in shock and someone else had come to his rescue ...

'Duncle! Look what I've found!'

He swung around – and thank God. It was Rhian to his right, just a short stretch away, crouched down, melting into the rock pools. He felt the blood rush to his head and he caught his breath, so relieved she was safe. How had he let himself be distracted? He was so stupid. His eyes smarted as he blinked hard to hold back the tears and he raced over.

'It's a starfish! It's huge!' she said, peering at the rusty creature with fascination.

The words 'I thought I'd lost you' came rushing up his throat but he couldn't say that – he couldn't taint her with the exact same phrase he'd said to his brother over and over at his bedside in the hospital in Palma. Sam had been twenty-five and on his stag do, unaware his fiancée was already pregnant with Rhi, flying over with ten mates to meet Del in Magaluf where he was working. They'd been egging each other on, tombstoning into the sea. The rest had made it and Sam was last to go. But he'd been unlucky, that was how the doctors had put it, and he'd suffered severe head injuries when he crashed onto a rock.

How naive Del had been thinking he'd get his big brother back: after a medically-induced coma, a transfer back to Wales and months of rehab to get him walking, he finally realised he'd never get Sam back. Now, twelve years later, he was thirty-seven and in an assisted-living head-injury centre half an hour from Del. It could so easily have been him and he wished it had because he'd never had potential like Sam. Seeing him reduced to nappies and drawing with crayons, stuck there, while Del's life went on, while Rhian grew out of nappies and crayons, surpassing her own father, had changed him. He'd thrown away his spontaneity and buckled down, trying to flatten his anger and grief. But the change hadn't altered Sam's fate and Del's desperation was still finding cracks in his body, seeping out, fuelled by the light and love and laughter and all the things his brother was denied. Like Rhian. God, he needed to talk to somebody about this. But everyone else had moved on. He didn't want to drag them back there or trouble them.

'Why are you soaking wet?' Rhian said, giggling, suddenly aware of his dripping clothes.

'I thought I'd try out the water,' he said, gulping back emotion. 'I didn't want you to get the glory of going in.'

Then he turned his back to her, pretending to dust off the sand on the ankles of his trousers. And as he looked up, he saw Charlie's eyes on him, her brow furrowed as if she'd seen him lose the plot. She was quite still and he wondered if she would come over. But then Jonny was upon her, he'd gone from shouting to looking as if he was apologising, and he had his arms around her and was trying to lead her away. And after a hesitation that pushed and pulled between her and Del like a magnet, she was gone.

12

Tina had wrestled with what to do all week but she was decided. She'd have one of Merri's coffees, which always seemed to propel her into action, then go for it. She pushed the door of Cheer on the Pier with purpose and ordered herself a double-shot cappuccino.

'I'll bring it over,' Merri said, nodding to the corner of the cafe. 'Sunshine FM is having an outside broadcast by the looks of it.'

Tina saw Del, Charlie and another woman at a table. She'd rather not join them – she only had half an hour of lunch left and she needed that time to steel herself. But there was nowhere else to sit. Any chance she had of changing her order to a takeout went though when Charlie saw her and waved. She seemed much happier than ten days ago when she'd arrived a quivering wreck. But Del ... oh dear, he looked terrible: withdrawn and pale, his face lined with worry. Charlie read her mind and pulled a quick grimace to warn her as she grabbed a chair.

'Tina, this is Claudia, my landlady's daughter. She works in Mumbles so she's joined us.'

'Hi,' she said, turning round to reveal such beauty, Tina almost gasped. She was like one of the Corrs sisters but lovelier.

'And I'm Del,' Del said, sticking out his hand, 'un-employable.'

'Don't say that! You'll be cleared, I'm sure of it. It's just a warning, that's all.'

'I'm not going back, what's the point?' he said.

'You'll be snapped up then.' It was just a question of finding his vocation, he was made to do something fantastic. 'As long as you don't go to any interviews in those joggers.' Although he looked far more himself, far more at ease than when he was in a shirt and tie, which had seemed to constrain him. He was naturally handsome, big too, robust-looking, and so not made for a suit. 'If I can help, you know I will,' Tina said with heart. She was very fond of him personally and he had brought so much to the team.

'Thanks. But don't start giving me any "this happened for a reason" shit. Charlie's done that to death.'

But maybe she was right? He sure as hell wasn't made for rules and regulations no matter how hard he tried. Perhaps he had a point about quitting while he was ahead. He gave a dramatic sigh which travelled the length of his frame. 'I'm so annoyed … I was OK with it,' he said, launching himself at his beef and laverbread burger, 'but now I've looked for a job, there's bloody nothing.'

'Don't give up!' Claudia said, with feeling, but unaware of Del's back story. Incredibly, he didn't go gooey-eyed at her – it seemed he was immune to her charms.

'It's shit without you,' Charlie said, 'I'm barely managing. Roy says Mervyn's happier with me than he was but I need you back. Otherwise …' She mimed a slash across her neck.

Tina felt the heavy weight of inside knowledge on

her chest. Mervyn wasn't happy, at all, but the search for an emergency DJ had been fruitless. It had to be a permanent appointment: there couldn't be another temporary jockey thrown in there because listeners needed a connection to stay faithful. The latest figures were due any day, plus Mervyn was making noises about a focus group to find out just how bad Charlie was going down. If only Del was allowed to keep doing the show. He'd made it work: in just two shows they'd created their own little double act, bouncing off each other, and they'd had a chemistry that was the elixir of the wireless. Where Charlie faltered, Del had brought her on, where Del got overexcited, Charlie had calmed him down. But security had all been briefed: he wasn't to set foot on the premises. Now there'd be no chance to see if they'd retain the older fans and attract the young.

'I wish I could help, Charlie, but ...' His sentence evaporated and Tina saw Charlie gulp.

'It's OK, I shouldn't be so selfish, thinking of myself.'

'What you need,' Del said, 'is an actual crush on the bus romance – or a date at least.' That was him all over – so giving in spite of his own downfall. It was probably his weakness too.

'I wish. That would be amazing. It is picking up though,' Charlie said optimistically. 'Every night this week we've had callers ringing in. And I've got tweets and messages, look ...' Charlie took out her phone and scrolled quickly, holding it up to show the Crush on the Bus Facebook page, before reading some out.

'Tall, dark and handsome on the number forty-one. You let me have your seat. Fancy a drink? Small, blonde stranger.'

'Lovely lady with the dog who cocked his leg on my briefcase on the fourteen. I'd love to take you for an ice cream – bring the dog and I'll bring biscuits. Secret Admirer.'

'To the man I spilled my water on this morning on the ten, I meant to ask you out but I bottled it. Brunette in pink mac.'

'See?' Del beamed at her. 'What are you worrying about then?'

But Tina sensed it would all be in vain. She looked at her lap because she didn't want her eyes to show her doubt. A pair of biker boots appeared: it was Merri with a tray of coffees.

Charlie peered at the drinks and muttered, 'That's uncanny – I thought you did them about you, not others.' She gawped and looked very worried as if she'd realised something.

They all looked at her, puzzled.

'Merri does foam emojis. Mine's the scream face. It's like she can mind-read.'

They each inspected theirs and … wow. Tina couldn't believe it.

'Yours is a ring, Tina, which is because you're loved up,' Charlie said, hitting the target in one sense but missing it by miles in another.

'Mine's an aubergine because I'm a dick,' Del said, which made everyone laugh.

'And mine's a crying face,' Claudia said. 'Which is spot on. I've been dumped. Yet again.'

'You?' Charlie said, incredulous, speaking for Tina and Del too.

All eyes turned on Claudia, who twiddled a strand of

her shiny black hair self-consciously before deciding to let it out. 'I have no luck with men whatsoever. It takes me ages to like someone, even longer to say anything. They think I'm cold and difficult, you know, but it's because, I dunno ... maybe I am?'

'Maybe it's them?' Charlie suggested with wisdom. Tina had ten years on this lot, give or take a few, and she felt the relief of her own security.

Claudia shrugged. 'I'm beginning to think it's my fault that I've never been in love. Like there's something wrong with me. Who'd have thought it ...' she said, then explained, 'I'm a bespoke high-end underwear designer ...'

'Got any catalogues?' Del asked, getting shushed by the women for Claudia to continue.

'I've a boutique, Lux Lingerie, tucked away off the main road, ridiculous isn't it? I create all sorts, bridal lingerie, honeymoon stuff, for people who are in love. Yet I know nothing about it. Maybe I should try wearing my own pants rather than M&S ... my Lux brand are hand-wash only and I can't be doing with that!'

'You'll find someone,' Charlie said, touching her arm, instantly connecting with Claudia's sorrow, 'I truly believe that. Look at Tina, eh!'

'I am lucky,' Tina said, confessing easily in Charlie's warmth, feeling blessed to have Gareth and Darcy despite the agony it caused her at times. 'Have you found yours, then?'

Charlie nodded furiously. But then she stopped. 'It's so weird, right, Jonny is the best, my perfect fit ... but we had an argument at the weekend and we never argue.'

'Oh dear. What happened?' Tina said. 'It is OK to fall

123

out you know, though.' It was worth pointing out that relationships had to be worked at, savoured, appreciated and evaluated.

'I know, but he's cross with me for staying here. He thinks I'm a mug. Not because of the show or anything, or you guys, but because I'm a dead woman walking. I know he's only saying it because he thinks I'm worth more. But I said I couldn't just leave after a week. How bad would that look? I have to try to get something positive from this nightmare, don't I? It'd feel like I was giving up ... on myself. Wouldn't it?'

'Well, yeah, obvs,' Del said, pulling his head back into his shoulders before he touched his neck, counted his chins and grimaced.

Charlie examined him and stared unblinking as if she wasn't expecting him to agree with her.

'He's not doing me down though,' she said, in the way women tried to justify men's behaviour. 'We're fine now. He sent me flowers on Monday, a beautiful bouquet and some chocolates. Organic handmade ones. His favourite flavour so I'm saving them until Saturday when I go to see him.'

Del didn't look impressed but Charlie was oblivious, swooning over her gifts.

'It's probably just the change, you being here, you'll get used to it,' Claudia said.

'Yes, I agree.' Tina knew how change could challenge the happiest of situations.

'Well, I reckon if you're with someone it should be easy. You love them for the way they are, you go with their flow. Or am I being male about this?'

Tina saw Charlie's forehead frown – it was always

the way when someone was good at advice, they struggled with their own situation. But then it was difficult for some to see the wood for the trees when their own emotions were involved. If something wasn't working. She'd never had that. As far as Tina was concerned, love was something you couldn't force – if you felt something for someone, that was it, you were done for. That was how she was with Gareth. God knows, many women would've walked away but Tina was in love with him. It was that simple. With that, she got up, made her excuses and left, to solve her dilemma. Darcy needed money. Tina had a way of giving it to her.

She found the dusty shop in a sorry alleyway that was littered with wrappers and cans. Gareth didn't need to know, he wouldn't notice anyway, but if he did she could say she was getting her wedding ring cleaned. It was far from dirty but Gareth's offer had been though – she wouldn't be able to touch his emergency fund without worrying. She believed it was from before, when he was a respected financial director. But this was Darcy, she couldn't be dragged into anything. Tina still had the original cheap golden band he'd slipped on her finger, she could wear that in the meantime. This upgraded one, bought when they'd been flush from his earnings, was on a different level.

As the door of the pawnbroker tinkled, a man with small circular specs and a polishing apron looked up from behind his glass counter, which was full of silver.

She inhaled for courage and prepared to wrench off the eighteen-carat white gold ring decorated with brilliant diamonds which had cost five thousand pounds back in the day. It didn't resist though as she'd expected – instead it slipped free and there was only a faint mark where it had sat for years. It was a sign that she was doing the right thing, she told herself. She laid it before him and his eyebrows momentarily peaked. He examined her, assessing her groomed appearance, and she knew he was thinking 'What's a woman like you doing in here?' She wasn't like his usual customers, she guessed, who came in for payday loans. Then she heard a jangle as he reached for what looked like a bunch of keys but turned out to be magnifying tools to inspect the quality of her pledge.

'How much?' she asked as he put a mini UV torch to the diamonds.

But even before he drew breath, knowing she would take whatever he offered, she was saying goodbye, as well as a prayer that she would be able to find the cash to buy it back before Gareth was free.

13

'Tonight between seven and nine, don't miss our brand new Sports Social Club looking ahead to a weekend of rugby and football. Next on Sunshine FM, DJ Disgo but first … Rihanna and *Farewell*…'

◦◦◦

'Tonight's show's cancelled? Just like that?' Charlie cried, throwing up her hands before common sense coughed politely in the corner of the conference room.

'I'm sorry, Tina,' she said, falling back into the chair. Tina didn't deserve the hairdryer treatment: the decision hadn't been hers. All credit to her, she looked as wounded as Charlie felt. 'It's just very late notice. What about Joanie and Roy because they shouldn't have to be involved …'

Tina squirmed out of awkwardness.

'Oh. They're working on the show, aren't they?' Charlie dropped her head in embarrassment. It was just her who'd been dropped.

'They aren't happy about it if that's any consolation,' Tina said.

It did help, actually, it meant she was right to feel part

of the team. But then two plus two equalled four, she realised.

'So what does this mean? Is that it? Because my replacement hasn't been found. Unless that's happened and I'm the last to know?'

'No, no, you're still the presenter. Tonight is an experiment. Mervyn's playing with the schedule. He's panicking.'

'So am I,' Charlie said, feeling the stuffy air catch in her throat. 'This is the beginning of the end, isn't it?' She knew she was just keeping the seat warm but so far it was barely above freezing. As ever, she'd been in denial, thinking it'd take longer than this. One step closer to getting the elbow brought back all the humiliation she'd felt in the past but this was worse because there was no offer of another position as there'd been at Orbital. She'd be out on her ear before she knew it without anything to show for her efforts. At her next interview, if she ever got one again, she could hardly say she'd lasted a fortnight but had learned a great deal about herself. They wouldn't give a monkey's.

'I'm going to be straight with you, Charlie. It could be the beginning of the end, yes. Mervyn is looking to blame someone for the figures. You saw them in the group email?'

She had – they were nothing short of appalling.

'It's not your fault, how could it be when you've only just got here? But he's in a corner with head office breathing down his neck. If listeners keep dropping off then advertisers will go elsewhere and profits will fall even further. The sports show is a way to appeal to the core audience. He has to be seen to be doing something.

The focus group didn't help either. Del had been a hit, but that option's gone, they love Crush on the Bus, that's good, but—'

'Not enough, I know. I thought I was onto something, even though I knew it wouldn't last. But I'd hoped ...' Charlie felt tears rising and she sniffed and swallowed to hold them back. It wasn't news that personality wasn't her thing. But overcoming an inner battle to speak live clearly wasn't enough. Why should it be? There were millions of people out there who could do what she struggled to do. What did she expect? A round of applause for doing her job? And yet, she'd gone further than that. She really believed it: her stutter and dry mouth was less frightening to her now. Through sheer bloodymindedness and desperation and doing it for Roy and Joanie, she had improved a smidgeon. Last night, for example, she'd spoken to a lovely woman whose husband had proposed to her on the number sixteen to Pontarddulais and she hadn't mumbled once. Then there were the confessionals coming in from lonely hearts who were tweeting and calling in slowly but surely – she listened to their tales of unrequited love and fantasies from afar and gave them hope that they'd find their someone, she could tell by the lightness of their goodbyes.

'Some said they liked your touch,' Tina added by way of sympathy. 'How you let people talk. For example,' she reached for a sheet of paper and read aloud a comment, 'one person said, "At first I thought the gaps she left were a bit weird, like she was lost for words, but then I realised she was giving callers the opportunity to breathe and then fill the gap with more information." Someone else said "She's nice, the girl next door, makes a change from big-head DJs." And another liked your, and I quote, "understated bit alongside Delme Noble's enthusiasm, they were like a double act".'

'That horse has bolted though.' Charlie rubbed her face and blew her cheeks. 'This is a nightmare. When I wanted to leave, I couldn't. Now when I want to stay, I'm being told I probably can't.'

She'd stepped out of her comfort zone and look what had happened: she'd been found out. Just as she had predicted.

'Well, yes. But ...'

The contradictory tone in Tina's voice made Charlie look up.

'You want to stay, do you?' Tina was double-checking.

'Yes!' Charlie said, then 'No.' Because she was torn between her head and heart – or her bank balance and her homesickness. She was making the best of things here but perhaps Jonny had been right during their set-to on the beach when she'd seen Delme halfway into the sea fully dressed. He'd since told her it was to save his niece's goggles but the way he'd looked at Charlie from the shore, when she'd stared at him, he seemed to have been communicating some kind of distress signal. Or maybe he had been reflecting her own? Delme backing her up in the cafe had stuck with her too. It was easy for him to say she should stick with it here – he was all for the gung-ho and bravado. But he didn't know her back to front like Jonny, who would be empathising with her based on what he instinctively felt was best for her. The note that accompanied the bouquet and chocolates had said he was only thinking of her and she had nothing to prove to anyone. And she ached for him, every time she thought of him, and she was afraid that one foot here and one in London would mean they'd grow apart and she couldn't lose him.

'You could still turn it around,' Tina suggested.

'How? You've heard what they think of me. As bouncy as a piece of concrete.' She was edging back towards Jonny, she could feel it.

'Charlie, you need to ask yourself this: what are your strengths? There may be something you can think of, something you could introduce to make the show more you. Keep Crush on the Bus, that's working. But you need something more … Look, I know you're off to London, go now, catch an early train, have a good think and we'll chat on Monday.'

If I come back, Charlie thought.

An hour later, she was on the train to Paddington, feeling as if she'd made the great escape. She was going home a day early! Jonny had even cancelled Pilates to make the most of the extra night. She'd catch up with Zoe and Libby too, and get the chance to see Mum and Dad – she was so excited she squeezed herself, dreaming of all the things she'd get up to. And yet, in the back of her mind, Tina's words were waning away. She tried to forget about them but it was like a sore throat, impossible to ignore. Sick of the whole drama, she gave in, producing her notebook and pen to make a list of ideas, knowing that if she put something down on paper then she would've dealt with it and wouldn't need to think about it again until Monday. What could Charlie do to make *Evening Mumbles* her own?

She'd come up with Crush on the Bus, surely she could

think of something else. But what? List-making used to be easy. Now ... there was nothing. It started to get her down and she thought about heading to the buffet for some train booze. The problem with that though was it might make her maudlin, she was in such a see-saw mood, it could go either full-scale hilarity or misery. No, she needed to get this homecoming off to a stable start. She wouldn't put on a brave face, she wouldn't moan either – she just wanted to forget about everything she'd been through this past fortnight. Good job then the next forty-eight hours were packed with plans. Jonny tonight, Libby for lunch, Zoe for early-evening drinks, dinner with Jonny then a Sunday roast with her parents. And what if she decided she wasn't going back to Swansea? The possibility made her heart stampede with the agonising thrill of staying in London. Would she ever dare to do that? Could she cope with the guilt of letting down Roy and Joanie, the risk of a terrible reference and the fear of what next? Was she capable of turning her back on her new friends and her landlady, abandoning her trinkets and books, knowing she'd never go back to claim them? Or was it a question of being delighted the bad dream was over and relief that her friends hadn't visited her in Swansea, pretending to her she was living her best life? She'd be doing Gen a favour too: she would turn Charlie's room into a workshop when she moved out because Claudia had lots of sewing jobs for her with the wedding season coming up ... But she wasn't like that. Not like Delme and his spontaneous ways, which weren't exactly making him happy. Just make the most of this, now, she told herself, as she put away her pad and settled back to stare out the window, seeing herself superimposed on a racing landscape of fields and sheep, then, the closer they got to London, on buildings and high rises.

The stress ebbed away and she began to look forward to seeing her girls. They could have a proper chat because she'd missed that so much: the simple pleasure of a face to face rather than missed calls and voicemails because her working hours were so antisocial. That wouldn't matter though, they'd dive back in as they always did if one of them had been away on holiday.

It was all-standing by the time she reached Reading and her anticipation grew at the prospect of being back in the bustle of the best city in the world – a proper city with zones and districts, boasting grandeur and land-marks at every turn, wide open green spaces and busy streets, squares and alleys, culture and food from every corner of the world ... although obviously she'd be going to her old haunts because she'd had enough of breaking out.

She picked up her phone and declared she was nearly there to Libby, Zoe and Jonny and sat back waiting for them to cheer her on. She was coming home! And then her elation took a nosedive as Libby and Zoe both asked to change the arrangements. Stuff had come up; Libby could do drinks tonight because she had a wedding fair to go to with James tomorrow and Zoe wondered if Sunday was possible as she had a fifth date with a bloke she really liked tomorrow night. It meant a reshuffle and Jonny had already altered his night for her, plus she didn't want to mess her mum and dad around. Crushed, she felt sidelined and let down, as if they had forgotten what she was like: how she needed order and predictability. Had they already moved on? Was she now an inconvenience? Perhaps they didn't need her shoulder to cry on any more. Messages went back and forth and they settled on coffee tomorrow morning, the three of them, but the compromise cut Charlie deeply: she would be squeezed in as a matter of convenience. On top of everything else, of this torturous trial, its relentless uncertainty and soul-destroying degradation, the miscarriage of hope which left her empty and bankrupt, it hurt so much that when the train screeched into platform three and she was swept up in the mass exodus and thrown out into the concourse and into Jonny's arms, she wept tears of self-pity into his neck.

'It's OK,' he said, gently, kissing her tears and stroking her plait, 'you're with me now. It's all too much, isn't it?'

She couldn't deny it this time as the emotion of the last two weeks poured free.

'Yes,' she said, looking up at him, 'all this change, it's been so hard.'

'I know. It's OK to admit it didn't work out. You tried and that's the main thing. I'll look after you Charlotte, I'll never let you down. I ...' he said, pausing to look deep into her eyes, 'I love you.'

'Do you?' she said, swelling in her chest.

'Yes!' he said. 'And I don't expect you to say the same, I don't need to hear it. Don't say it just because I have.'

He knew her so well but she was ready. She opened her mouth to tell him she felt the same but he put a finger on her lips.

'Come on,' he said, taking her bag and folding his hand into hers, 'let's go home. I've made a spaghetti bolognese and I've even changed the sheets! We can watch some telly and cuddle up. Maybe think about asking for shifts at Orbital? I could pull a few strings, you know, now that you're back?'

And she nodded and smiled, letting him take the lead to the underground, because it was what she wanted and needed to hear when she'd taken a chance and it hadn't paid off; when her heart and head had united and were waving like a white flag.

14

Del examined his paunch in the mirror, pulled it in and then when the effort made his muscles twitch and his breath shudder, he released it with a huge puff.

The clocks had gone forwards and he had an extra hour of daylight at his disposal. Usually he loved this time of year because it promised so much: more time to go out and about and the prospect of new adventures.

But he wished it was winter so he could pull the blinds and slob out on the sofa, eating Doritos and drinking bottles of beer. Correct that, he thought, taking in the Doritos packets and bottles of beer that were on the floor by the sofa: he wished he could eat and drink more of them. Because he was in a state of lethargy that would've made sloths look energetic. He was sluggish, actually he was slug-like, and he looked around as if he was seeking trails of slime from his greasy diet.

What was wrong with him? Ten days of what he should've considered as freedom and an opportunity to turn his life around had come to nothing. Instead of leaping on it as a positive force as he would've done in the past, Delme had found himself succumbing to a negative state of mind. If this carried on, if he didn't start properly looking for a new job or finding something worthwhile to fill his days, he'd be the size of not a house but this block of apartments. He knew the answer: it was staring him in the stomach. He had to focus. Get up as if he was going into the office. Tart up his CV. Register at agencies and sign up for alerts online. Get himself into shape mentally – and physically. If he got moving, his mind would sharpen and think of all those endorphins ... But his spine started to slump.

Come on, Del Boy, where's your oomph? he thought, trying to work himself up into action. The temptation to flop back down in front of the telly and ring for pizza and call Fflur to hang out was so strong but something urged him on.

Fear of being left behind when his mates were in the race and he was farting around at the starting line? Shame that he'd brought this on himself? Facing up to his head-in-the-sand denial over his brother? Or was it just his natural state coming to the fore? To keep moving to the beat of his impulses? Thinking made him jittery and rest-less. Staying inside suddenly became a very unattractive prospect – his feet started to itch: he had to out-run the voice in his head.

Into his bedroom he went, chucking clothes out of his cupboards to find shorts, a long-sleeve T-shirt and old trainers and going out, racing down the stairs, into the early evening and onto the coastal path which ran for hundreds of miles around the whole of Wales. Here, in front of the marina, he could see the entire curve of Swansea Bay. To his far left were the smoking industrial towers of Port Talbot steelworks and to his right, in the distance, Mumbles. From the shape of the twin rocks off Bracelet Bay which, legend had it, French sailors had compared to a pair of boobs, '*les mamelles*', that had given the town its name. Beyond, to the lighthouse which stood as the last defence against the sea.

The late afternoon sky was wide and blue, fringed with orange at the horizon, suggesting a classic of a sunset. He let himself stand for a minute with hands on hips to take it in, vowing not to forget how awesome a view it was. If he could remember this feeling of calm it inspired in him, that he was just a tiny part of this enormous planet, and of his fortune to have this on his doorstep then he could ... do what? Perhaps channel what he was into something good for once? Because he was realising now that he was never meant to be a bloody health and safety guy with his loose grip on policies and appendages. It hadn't been the answer to his broken heart: it had just made everything worse. He'd been fighting himself, going against who he was. Had he put people at risk?

The thought sickened him. What if someone had been badly hurt as a result of his ineptitude? He needed to come with a health warning, he did. How had he thought that was the answer to his brother's fate? His decision to ditch holiday repping had been right, he knew that instinctively. He'd seen so many others burn out from the demands of twenty-four-hour partying. But he'd knee-jerked too hard by strapping himself in.

He turned to the pathway and saw it stretching on and on and it was like he was seeing his own journey ahead. It was a huge task he had on his hands yet if he could take it one step at a time then he might be able to become a better version of himself. He dreaded the pain ahead but with a sniff of the salty air he knew nothing would be as painful as what he'd been through with Sam.

Before he knew it, he began to jog west towards Mumbles. Immediately, his calves were asking what the hell he was doing and his stomach jiggled as if it was having a laugh at himself. But he went on, not caring that he was overtaken by proper runners and Lycra-lacquered cyclists. Slowly, slowly, he told himself as he found his groove. The temptation was to streak ahead and feel alive: but he knew that he'd tried that before. Moderation had always been a foreign concept – it represented boredom and predictability. But neither total restraint nor total excess had worked for him. There had to be another way. He tuned into the even tempo of his feet hitting concrete, resisting his brain crying at him to feel more and go harder, listening instead to his chest and thighs which were in harmony. His breathing was heavier, the small of his back was damp from the effort of this first go at exercise in years but he knew if he pushed it, he'd give up. And he wanted to keep going for a while, even if he became so tired he had to walk. This was about going forward, not giving up. Of course, his mind pleaded with him after a while to stop and turn around but he bargained with himself: just to the next tree, just to the next tree. By the time he got close to Blackpill Lido, he reasoned – ha, reasoned! when was the last time he'd done that? – he could turn back on himself.

Twenty minutes of walk-running was a long time to start with – he was panting and his legs were hurting. If he pursued pride, he'd pull a muscle and bugger his chances of doing this again tomorrow. It wasn't about playing it safe – playing it safe wasn't him, he'd never be capable of that. It was about recognising he'd done well today and done enough to make sure he could do it again the day after. He felt good – very good – and a sense of satisfaction that his muscles were moaning. Get used to it, lads, he thought, as his heartbeat started to drop – and as the sun was doing the same, he noticed. He spied a bench further up the promenade and decided he'd sit down on it when he got there to watch. Someone else had the same idea, he saw, but it didn't put him off: talking to strangers didn't phase him but … ah, it was a woman. He'd make sure he'd sit on the edge so he didn't look like some heavy breather. When he got closer he realised she looked familiar. The end of her long blonde plait was between her fingers and she was deep in thought, nibbling her hair like it was one of her beloved ham sandwiches.

'Charlie,' he called, giving her the chance to invent an excuse that she was just leaving. Instead she came to and did an unnecessary budging up and shifting her big bag to show he was welcome.

'Hi, Delme,' she said, making him smile because unlike everyone but his mother she always insisted on using his full name. But then after his excruciating 'Del Boy' introduction on the day they met, he didn't blame her.

'What's occurring, mush?' He plonked down next to her and apologised for his sweaty sheen. 'Been for a run. Well, more of a plod.'

'Well done, you!' she beamed.

'May as well, seeing as I'll have a lot of time on my hands.'

'It's a very constructive thing to do when things are uncertain, so they say. It can give you space or you can use the time to sort things out. I'd say it's probably a bit of both. How's it with you?'

She had some weird sixth sense, this one. He twisted his body round to face her and admitted it. 'Bit of both. Scared, worried, but trying to work it all out.'

'I felt the same when I was transferred here. Like my identity had gone. I was Charlie Traffic but then it meant nothing here. That flailing feeling hasn't really gone away.'

'That's the weird thing – I've never really felt connected to my job in the way you did in London.'

'I hope you don't mind me saying this ...' she said, pushing a stray coil of hair behind her ear.

'Go on, I can take it!' he laughed. 'But I'm a waster?'

'No!' She almost jumped out of her seat. 'Not at all! You're so colourful and vibrant and approachable ... but—'

'Here comes the but.'

'Listen! What I'm saying is you probably weren't a natural for health and safety. You're more than that. So much more! Like, the new guy is such a jobsworth, so grey and ... perfect for it. But you ... on the radio, you came alive, as if that was what you were meant to be doing. You're such a people person. You can't contain that – but you kind of know you have to be responsible at the same time, if that makes sense? There'll be something out there for you that lets you be both.'

'Wow, yeah ...' Had she just stepped inside his head, poked around and plucked out his innermost thoughts? How else could she have summed him up so easily and so simply when she barely knew him? He was kind of gobsmacked at her assessment and it took him a second to come to. 'Although I'm getting on a bit for fresh starts and finding myself.'

'You? I thought you were late twenties!'

'Young face. Immature, really. Anyway,' he said, embarrassed he hadn't even asked why she had a long face, 'why are we talking about me on the scrapheap?'

'Yeah, well I might be joining you at the Job Centre tomorrow.'

Shit. So soon? 'How come?'

'The show was pulled on Friday night, Mervyn's shaking things up because the station is on the decline, so Tina said.'

'No way,' he said. He hadn't heard the gossip because he'd gone on a bender with Rodders on Friday.

'I felt like walking there and then. But she said I might be able to save myself if I came up with something extra by tomorrow. Build on my "girl next door" appeal.' She shook her head at the label, which she'd highlighted with air quote fingers. 'I hoped I'd be able to think of the something extra when I was in London this weekend but nothing.' She stared out to sea and shrugged but her tapping fingers gave her anxiety away.

'Is that your bag packed then?'

'No, I came here from the station. I didn't want to go back to the house straight away. I fancied some fresh air after getting the old London black bogies. I may as well not unpack because frankly I expect to be back on the train this time tomorrow.'

'That's crap.'

'Yep,' she said.

'At least you've got London.' Because he only had here.

'That's the trouble. London was bloody awful,' she sniffed. 'I was really upset when I got there and Jonny told me he loved me for the first time and it was all lovely but then he got it into his head that I had left Swansea for good. But I was all over the place. He went mad at me this morning when I said I felt I should give it one last go. I dunno, we used to think exactly the same way ... I hardly saw my mates either and I had to pretend to my parents I was fine so they wouldn't worry.' She put her hands to her head and groaned. 'It's all building up and—'

'Tell me, what?'

'I'm really confused. I just feel ... not myself. Like, I knew who I was until this. But now, I don't know what I want, only what I don't want.'

'Which is?'

'To fail again.'

He felt as if he was getting closer to knowing more about her. And gingerly, he tested the water. 'Is this to do with why you were frightened to talk into the microphone?' He was sure it was connected. What had happened to make her lose her self-worth so terribly?

She paused, fiddling with her hair again. Then she sighed. 'Yeah. It's all connected.'

His heart went out to her – as much as he felt like he was wading through peanut butter, he knew he would somehow keep going. But she looked stuck. He had to help her – and he knew just how.

'If this was a friend talking, what would you tell them to do?' He expected her to realise what he was up to and give him a look of disgust for laying such an obvious trap. Instead she leapt in, her cheeks glowing from the orangey sky.

'Everyone is afraid of failing,' she said, emphatically. 'Everyone has failed in some form or another, it's just

143

people don't talk about it. Living in fear isn't living at all, really, is it? It stops you from going forward. Failure is human – it's what you do about it afterwards, how you learn from it, that's important. It's a life lesson, it can teach you so much, give you motivation and actually you'll find out how strong you are. Look at how far you've come instead, listen to your gut, not what other people say you're capable or incapable of. If you're uneasy about something it's a sign that something isn't right. But it doesn't mean it's wrong – it just means you're making progress. Set yourself small goals instead of one big one and go for it!'

It had tripped off her tongue so easily, surely she had to see it.

'There you go then!' he said, slapping his palms together.

'There you go what?' she said, the glowing eyes she'd had during her speech extinguished.

'That's your answer.'

'What is?'

'Are you being deliberately *twp*?'

'What does that even mean?'

'It's Swansea Welsh for stupid! What you do best, Charlie, is listen and think and give good advice. Yeah? And you could do with taking your own advice, by the way.'

'Mmm ... oh!' Her eyebrows shot up.

'Yeah! Get me?'

'Do you mean ...?' She sat forwards and he could see the cogs whirring. ' ... I could be an agony aunt?'

'Bingo, Bold!'

She exploded out of her seat and stood before him

with her arms wide. The backdrop to her silhouette was pink and purple and it looked religious – she was only missing three wise men. Except she was directing her worship his way.

'You genius!'

He could cope with being one of those dudes on camels, he thought, delighted to have given her some inspiration.

'That could work alongside Crush on the Bus. A phone-in! That's it! That's the best thing I can do. It's about all I can do. What can I call it?'

Her eyes danced, darting from his left one to his right in concentration. He couldn't help but feed off her energy.

'Mumbles Grumbles!' he said.

She laughed and then frowned. 'Too ... people ringing in to complain about pot holes.'

She had a point. 'To Boldly Go!'

'I'm not in *Star Trek*! How about Love Matters? Or ... not love is in the air but Love is on the Air ... no ... too long and would anyone get it? Dear Charlie?'

'Call Me? Call Me Maybe?'

'How about sunshine something ... Ain't No Sunshine ...'

Then she clicked her fingers ... 'Bring Me Sunshine?'

'As in Morecambe and Wise?' He attempted a sitting down version of Eric and Ernie's skipping dance.

'Yes, but it's more than that isn't it? It's a classic, about looking on the bright side, fun, laughter and love. What do you think?'

She was nervously clenching her teeth as she waited for his opinion.

'I think it's … brilliant! The station will love it, there's a name-check in there, it's positive, it says you're there for people.'

'Do you, Delme? Do you think it's good enough?' she asked, pleading almost.

'Yes, Charlie. I think you are good enough.' He said it on the level so she'd see he meant it. Then he realised his slip – he'd praised her rather than the idea. And she knew it because there was a flicker of embarrassment about her, the way she dropped her eyelashes and touched her nose. There was a 'thing' then between them, an awkwardness, and she began to fuss with her arms. Then he did the same, feeling goosebumps, wanting to pat them down in case she thought he thought things about the thing. Then, what if she had goosebumps too?

'Right,' she said, getting up and faffing some more, 'I'm going to go to mine and make a list for Bring Me Sunshine.'

'Right,' he echoed, feeling a jolt of surprise because he'd gone shy and he never went shy. They made a dog's dinner of saying goodbye and good lucks all round and he was glad of the descending darkness to hide behind.

As he walked off, he felt his tummy popping. He'd never really had a girl friend before. Ahem. A friend who was a girl, he meant, who he wasn't involved with. He was one of the lads. But there was a fascination about her, some kind of gravitation towards her. He didn't fancy Charlie, he didn't think. She'd just got under his skin. It was the way they could talk, how they shared stuff, and he wanted to share more: tell her about Sam and for her to reveal why she had the losing-her-voice funny turn. It was bizarre because she was pretty much everything he wasn't. In which case, this lightheaded feeling he had had to mean something else. Perhaps it was the after-effects of his jog. Or hunger. There we go, he thought, that was it because he hadn't eaten for at least two hours. Yes, it was definitely hunger, he told himself. Definitely.

15

Tina imagined she was putting them to bed as she carefully covered seeds with compost.

Sleep tight, see you soon, she thought, placing a dozen little pots in rows in the plastic hothouse she'd bought yesterday. And then she shook her head at herself: was she that lonely she was talking to cucumbers and tomatoes?

The answer was yes. She had no shortage of human contact: the warmth of people around here meant she could have a chat whenever she wanted. It was the knitted bond of everyday friendship she missed, to pour her heart out to, to receive reassurance that this harrowing time of her life would pass. The circle she'd been in had shut her out and the mates of old in Cardiff would send the occasional message, checking she was OK, but they had their own problems and often worse ones. But then had she become close to anyone, she wouldn't be able to bring up Gareth's stretch because she couldn't risk Darcy finding out. God knows how she hadn't been tipped off with all of the social media out there. The local newspaper, thank God, hadn't covered the case, whether it was by error or having no one there to report it. And luckily, Darcy was geographically and emotionally distant from Cardiff – she'd had a disjointed childhood, moving from a state primary to a private secondary, losing ties with her early past and many of her teenage friends had been boarders from different parts of the country. Without these two factors, never would she have dreamed of keeping things from her.

Tina's main concern was if she got used to sharing her pain, it might mean she became lax about it and the words would slip out at the wrong time. Yet how she wished she could confess to her situation. Particularly after Gareth's weekly letter that had been waiting for her when she'd got in from work. It was the strangest thing getting mail from him. In all the years they'd been together, they'd never had cause to write to one another because they'd never been apart. From the sight of his oddly beautiful upright handwriting on the prison issue lined A5 paper to the regulation second-class stamp on the envelope, it affected her deeply. He'd never been one to sit down and talk about his feelings; he'd shown his moods through action, whether that was stomping around out of stress or bringing her breakfast in bed: his letters then were as if she was getting to know him all over again. But there was no reading and rereading them with fluttering eyelashes in a romantic mist. She would take them in, then put them away because they were so very painful. His first few had been stark through shock because he hadn't been held on remand during the court case. It had been a list of facts: the blur of entering the first night unit, a strip search, getting his number and his clothing, being held with five other blokes in a cell, one who was withdrawing from drugs and the other put on suicide watch, handed pamphlets about prison policies, meeting an 'insider' who explained the system, being assessed by a nurse, needing a shower but not getting one. He was transferred to a double cell, sharing with a guy who was in for drug trafficking. No privacy curtain around the toilet. The noise from nutters kicking off, clanking doors, shouting. Finding work in the laundry for pennies a week. Locked up for longer than they should've been. The overcrowding. Terrible food, stews and curries and gristly meat.

Then he'd opened up, revealing how he had learned to cope – as one of the older ones there he'd found his role as a 'daddy figure'. He looked forward to kit change, when they'd get clean bedding and shaving gel, which he tried to eke out so he could be nice for Tina's visits. He was keeping his head down, helping others with literacy problems to write their letters, reading books, going to the chapel for quiet. Gareth was putting on a brave face.

But as time went on, she noticed he'd become more expressive. He'd always been private but now he spoke openly, not caring if his letters were picked to be read by prison staff.

This one was full of how much he loved her, how much he missed holding her hand, speaking to Darcy, the walks he wanted to take with her and the cuddles he wanted to share when he was back home. He spoke too of darkness and boredom, isolation and fear and it was all so very overwhelming for Tina.

His terminology changed too, talking of screws and ghosting, bird and nonces, which made her flinch. Gareth was institutionalised, he would be changed by this. Yet she had to contain this agony within.

She took a big breath, zipped up the greenhouse to keep in the heat from the last bit of evening sunshine and got to her knees to work on a patch of weeds. Little by little, she went through her Monday: the subdued atmosphere without Del's 'good morning!', Ivor Mone's perverted delight in his absence and Charlie, almost confident but certainly determined, who pulled Tina aside to see what she thought of her agony aunt idea. This girl was the definition of feel the fear and do it anyway, she'd thought, and Bring Me Sunshine could provide the depth that only Charlie could bring. To support her, Tina had promised she'd tune in tonight.

Soon, her mind was still and she heard only birdsong, distant cars and the rustling of leaves in the breeze while her naked fingers minus the sheath of gloves pulled at straggly plants in between a beautiful gathering of bluebells, getting dirty to feel clean. This was therapy for her soul, absorbing her in a meditation connecting her to the earth: fascinated by a disturbed worm burrowing for cover or a snail nibbling on a leaf.

She heard footsteps coming from the alleyway beside her garden and she listened in as she always did: people on their phones saying they were almost home or on their way out, quick steps and slow steps, skipping kids and the thud of trainers. Sometimes the whirr of a bicycle or the pant of a dog on its walk. There were arguments too, laughter and kissing − all signs of life which made her feel less alone. But then the feet that had been approaching did not fade away − they stopped right by her wall. Maybe it was a shoelace being tied or a rearrangement of shopping bags between hands. She craned her neck to hear, kneeling back, hearing just her breathing now. Any minute now the person would continue on their way ... except they didn't. She got up and went noiselessly to the bushy mess of clematis affording her a screen. It'd be nothing, she prayed, peeking through – then her heart leapt as she saw him. That man again. The one she'd seen on the bus. She covered her mouth with her hand and swallowed a scream, wondering what the hell he was doing there. Was he local? Was it a coincidence? It couldn't be because he was looking at the far end of her boundary.

Anger erupted inside of her and she wanted to shout go away, leave her alone. But it froze in her throat because she was by herself and had no back up. Would he be able to scale the wall? Was that what he was planning? Because actually he looked almost fearful himself in a strange way and he wasn't up close: his back was against the other wall and he was staring at his feet and then rubbing his forehead.

Then he was gone and the air inside of her flew out and she flew back inside, locking the door in a flurry of bolts and keys. Should she ring the police? But she couldn't bear an officer coming in here – it would remind her of the arrest and questioning.

Instead, she pulled down the kitchen blind, flicked on the radio and began to chop an onion, taking her frustration out in heavy, clumsy slices, which pricked her eyes and gave her a justification to cry. Weeping, she banged the frying pan down on the hob and she slammed cupboards and the fridge door until she ran out of steam, sitting down on the floor, feeling spent and weak, yearning to feel arms around her. To take the weight off her heart and her shoulders, to soothe her, to give her a safe space where she could unload without judgement or blame. But where the hell would she find that?

16

'Bring Me Sunshine on *Evening Mumbles* ... call in with your worries and woes. And let Charlie Bold bring you sunshine ...'

~

Here we go, Charlie thought, as Joanie put through the very first caller on Bring Me Sunshine.

This was the last throw of the dice, what it all depended on – her job, her livelihood, her confidence. Not much then, yeah? she heard in her mind, in a voice very much like Delme's. If it tanked, she was out on her ear. So she had to make it work. Failure was not to be feared, she'd learned from the past – she'd said it out loud to Delme yesterday, hadn't she? Not that she'd realised it applied to her then and there but later in bed when she'd gone over their chat, which had left her buzzing. It had been an epiphany: it wasn't that she couldn't run back to London, it was that she wouldn't. Not until she'd cracked it. Jonny would come round: he'd see how much she needed to make peace with herself. He hadn't as yet – he'd sent a frosty goodnight before he went to bed and she hadn't replied because she didn't want to ruin his early night. A gift, a fancy calming candle made from essential oils and probably unicorn musk knowing Jonny's charm, had arrived this morning. Gen had presented it to her when Charlie was making coffee and toast – she'd called him straight away to say thank you. He'd gushed at how fantastic a weekend it had been but there was neither an apology for his mood on Sunday nor a backing down that she was right to stick to her guns.

'Trouble in paradise?' Gen had said, picking up on Charlie's tense jaw when she'd joined her in the sitting room.

'It'll blow over.'

Gen examined her then returned to her cross stitch, humming a tune. After a few moments, she'd held up her almost-complete piece of work, a quote of something or other in a romantic cursive font bordered by a floral delight of red roses, pink tulips and yellow sunflowers.

'What do you think? It's for one of my Etsy customers.'

'Lovely!' Charlie had said, all smiles, which slid off her face when she'd read the words: 'If I was meant to be controlled, I'd have come with a remote.'

'They start off nicely then slowly they try to isolate you, make you doubt yourself and then they trap you. All the while declaring their love.' Charlie felt she was being pierced by Gen's blue eyes.

'Oh, no, Jonny's not like that,' Charlie said, horrified. It was very odd, Gen had met him too. And he'd only been lovely to her.

'I didn't say he was.' Gen blinked slowly at her. 'This is for a customer. And I understand why she ordered it. Claudia's father, I was drawn in by his charisma. But underneath he was insecure. The only way he could feel powerful was to make my world all about him. I had to leave in the night with Claudia when she was a wee one with just the shoes on our feet.'

'From Scotland?' Charlie asked, feeling terrible she hadn't given Gen the time of day since her arrival. It was like she'd dismissed her as a middle-aged woman with nothing of interest to say. How could she have misread and misjudged her? Gen just wanted to build a relationship with Charlie.

'Edinburgh, aye. I worked at the DVLA there, the Driver and Vehicle Licensing Agency, got a transfer to the headquarters here in Swansea behind his back. This may not be much,' she gestured around, 'but it's mine.'

'And it's gorgeous,' she said, admiring the mix of vintage and modern furniture which was stylish yet cosy, 'I've been meaning to tell you.'

'Thank you, I got by with extra sewing jobs while Claudia was small.'

'Like mother, like daughter.'

They ended up having a second coffee together, filling each other in on the main headlines of their lives, until Charlie realised the time and had to get ready for work but promising they'd do more together. But Gen's story stuck with her all day; for some reason it made her question things with Jonny. Yet when you set aside the argument, they'd done their blissful London mooching and smooching. They'd talked shop and the burn of hearing how fab the new traffic presenters were hurt less when he asked for a brainstorm with her and she'd suggested service station outside broadcasts and a car share karaoke competition.

Hang on though, he had started to message her much more, asking who she was with and what she was up to, but then that was the distance. Perhaps he was feeling vulnerable? Because he'd said he loved her and while she'd felt ready on Friday, it seemed to get stuck in her throat when she'd tested the words out to herself on the loo or in the shower at Jonny's. Zoe and Libby hadn't been so cautious – they'd whooped about him saying it first. Libby even suggested it was payback but for what? Because Charlie had explained it had all been a misunderstanding when they broke up back in the day. It made her feel uneasy but she didn't get a chance to explore the idea because neither of them asked how she felt: they brushed over it and then Zoe went on about this guy she had the hots for and Libby banged on about wedding dresses and venues. The hurt of being lower down their priorities was still there but Charlie understood they had entered new phases of their lives, just as she had.

Giving all of them the benefit of the doubt was a no-brainer – these people were her nearest and dearest – but she had to forget them now. This was when she needed to invest in herself. Easier said than done.

The new segment had been heavily trailed as soon as Roy and Joanie had produced the blurb, going out from 2 p.m. Charlie had battered the Facebook and Twitter feeds with plugs. Tonight's *Evening Mumbles* was dedicated to helping the lovelorn. Basically, they'd thrown the kitchen sink at it. And, hallelujah, barely three minutes in, someone was on the line. Charlie's reaction was to quake – cacking it was the polite way of putting it – and she saw the glass shake in her grip when she took a swig of water to swallow her nerves. But as soon as she moved her face towards the microphone, placed her elbows on the desk and held her headphones with both hands, she felt it: she was where she was meant to be.

'Hi there,' she said softly into the ether as Joanie instinctively knew to dim the lights. This wasn't radio as far as Charlie was concerned but a one-to-one.

'Hi, Charlie.' The woman's voice was understandably hesitant. Charlie needed to make her feel safe.

'Hi, lovely, how's it going?'

'Well, you know …' Her wobbly exhalation crackled down the line. Charlie knew exactly how she was feeling, she'd been there herself.

'I know. Would you like to tell me your name? You don't have to, of course. Or make one up. Whatever you're comfortable with.'

'It's … Gail. From Townhill.' She'd stumbled over the letter G but it was impossible to tell if she really was who she said she was. She was quietly spoken but her South Walian accent was like syrup, thick and sweet, familiar sounding now that Charlie had opened herself up to the city.

'So, Gail, what's up? How can I help?'

Gail breathed a heavy sigh; in it, Charlie could hear her emotional load, from the strain of sorrow to the weariness of defeat.

'No one would think it because I look happy on the outside … but I'm lonely, crushingly lonely. I go to work and that's great, that's my lifeline, but when I leave … I go home to nothing, nobody. I just feel so ashamed.'

The poor thing, Charlie really felt for her. 'You know the funny thing about loneliness … you're not alone. But people don't talk about it, that makes you so brave for coming on here. It's like some kind of dirty secret in this day and age when we're supposed to be living our so-called best lives. And there's a pressure to be out there, mixing and making the most of things. Have you tried to speak to anyone about it? Friends, family, a partner?'

'We're separated at the moment, it's very hard on us both. We're still in touch, we love each other very much but we can't be together for various reasons. I accept that, just about, but it's the effects of it. My family don't know we're living apart, it'd cause too much anguish, and I know he'll come home to me, eventually. I know he will. But it just feels like my life's on hold. As for my friends, well, they have problems of their own. People tend to back off when you're effectively single. Money's tight as well … it all feels so hopeless, like I'm trapped.'

There was not a sound in the studio – Charlie knew Joanie and Roy were waiting with bated breath to see how she dealt with it. But somehow she understood this woman's plight and knew what to say.

'Gail, let me tell you,' she said, with passion, 'you're halfway there by acknowledging it. And thinking your life is on hold means you understand you need to press play. The issue here, to me, isn't the people in your life: it's how you feel about yourself, as if you aren't worthy of taking part in it.'

Charlie heard Joanie whisper 'yes' but it wasn't to her but to herself. The silence from the producers told Charlie they were letting her take charge. And they realised any interruption would break the spell.

'They say you can feel lonely in the middle of a crowded room. I have done, so many times in my life. But I think the way to stop loneliness is to start looking at yourself, to see there's a gap inside of you, but with compassion. Accept how you feel and connect with it: see your worth, find out what brings you joy. Do those things and you will feel loved and part of the community again. Does that make sense?'

'Do you mean as in do things to fill my time?'

'You can do but you can't fill every second. But if you find out about yourself then engage with it, then those seconds and minutes and hours when you're doing nothing won't be so uncomfortable.'

'I see!' Gail's voice curled up at the edges in a smile. 'I think I get it ...'

A flame inside of her that Charlie had been unaware of jumped taller and shone brighter.

'Acknowledge your feelings, accept them without judgement, tell yourself it's OK to feel the way you do, then make new connections through your own interests, but take it slowly and don't compare yourself to others, therein madness lies, right, because you are you, not anyone else.'

'You're right,' Gail said, as if she was having an awakening.

Charlie realised her eyes had been squeezed shut and her fists clenched as if she had been willing Gail on. She released them and felt a wave of affirmation flow through her body, tingling her scalp and tickling her fingers and toes.

'So ... perhaps if I do some things I enjoy I might feel better?'

'You've got it!' Charlie said, 'It could be anything. A walk, a date night by yourself, say a cinema trip or a meal or a night in with a bath and a book. Cook something you like that you haven't had in ages. There are meet-ups you can go to, volunteering opportunities—'

'I do like meeting new people,' Gail said. 'Maybe I could try a class or a club?'

'Exactly. You might find through all of this that the people who've been around you are the ones who make you feel lonely.'

'Wow, yes, you could be onto something. Thank you so much, Charlie.'

'My pleasure,' she said, bursting. 'And tell you what, we'll send you a special Bring Me Sunshine mug. Can we do that, team?' She hadn't known that was coming – it just popped out. But it was the stuff of her childhood which she'd heard on the radio all her life.

'Sure thing,' Joanie said into her ear.

'The boss, she says yes!'

'Thank you! You really have brought me some sunshine.'

The bars of Stevie Wonder's *You are the Sunshine of My Life* struck up and Charlie sat back in her seat, puffed out of her cheeks and felt ... not exhausted but exhilarated. Vital and real, as if she'd done some good, not just for this Gail but herself. Assured and bold – Bold! – that's how she felt, and able, and all without a script. Delme would be proud of her spontaneity!

She looked up to Roy and Joanie for the first time since Bring Me Sunshine had started and they were both pumping the air with their fists.

'That. Was. Brilliant,' Joanie said. 'The lines are lit!'

'Terrific radio, Charlie,' Roy added. 'Now we're cooking!'

'Ready for the next one?' Joanie asked.

'Absolutely,' Charlie said, as she felt the ghosts of her past loosening their grip on her heart.

17

He might be banned from the building but Del wasn't going to miss out on tonight's Sunshine FM Friday night drinks.

Charlie had had such a mega week he wanted to see her. He'd listened every night – staying in was the new going out, right, according to his new regime – and she'd ruled the airwaves with her soft but stirring slot. He wasn't going to go mad, he just wanted to be amongst people and soak up their excitement having been confined to his flat in his pants and on his laptop since Monday.

Setting up stall at 6 p.m., he'd bagged a table in the old git pub and waited for his former colleagues to arrive. First was Ivor, who'd muttered darkly about changes afoot and 'bloody women' as he supped his real ale. Blazer and jeans man Ed Walker wandered in, pausing at the door with a well-rehearsed smile as if he was posing for photos, and bought himself and his ego a double gin and tonic. Colin Disgo got a quick round in, although he was on the Diet Cokes, then Sian popped in for one glass of white wine because she was en route to hosting a businesswomen in Wales event.

Trouble was he'd built the night up and no one was really interested in how he'd filled his workless week.

Colin and Sian were in and out, Tina couldn't make it because of a fancy charity dinner she was attending, Ed was full of the past before video killed the radio star and Ivor's interaction was limited to an accusation that Del was 'a poof' for ordering a half. 'Don't want to end up an old soak like you, butt,' he'd said. There was no point outlining his quest for moderation to him: Ivor was an old-school neanderthal who thought any deviation from his way of doing things cast doubt on a person's sexuality. It was only when Charlie, Joanie and Roy burst in awash with airwave adrenalin at five past nine that he realised he hadn't been craving company per se. Just theirs.

'Delme!' Charlie cried, flushed and bright-eyed. 'How are you?'

'All the better for seeing you lot,' he said, getting up to go to the bar with her. 'I've been stuck in the nineteen seventies over there with Smashey and Nicey.'

She let out a large laugh. It was the first time, he realised, he'd seen her looking at ease with herself. What was it about her that seemed different? Hmm. He examined her then it hit him. Her hair. Rather than her standard severe plait, Charlie had it in a ponytail and there were loose tendrils of gorgeous blonde curls around her face, which was fresh and relaxed. It was like a mask of tension had come off, yet he hadn't realised she had been wearing one before now.

'What you been up to?' she asked, which touched him because she'd put him first above her feelings. Which was why she'd smashed it with Bring Me Sunshine. Waiting for her to go live on Monday had given him a touch of liquid bowels but from the off, she'd smashed it, connecting with callers, winning their trust, teasing out their problems, on anything from unrequited love and cheating partners to widows wanting to find someone special and healing family rifts, and rewarding them with solid advice. Her confidence had rolled over into Crush on the Bus too, where she'd been able to tap into her sense of fun.

'Never mind me, mush! You're hawt!' He performed a microphone drop and gave her a 'booom'.

She waved his compliment away. 'Hardly!'

But he could see by the way her blue eyes sparkled that she was being modest for his sake.

'Honestly, it's like you've overcome all the nerves,' he said. 'You've saved the day and yourself.'

'Yeah … thanks, Delme,' she said, shyly, 'I do feel like I've crossed some kind of bridge. I look forward to the show now, can you believe that? It's so weird – the agony aunt bit has shown me I can cope with the unknown in a way. I couldn't have done it without those two though,' she said, nodding at her team. 'Or you.'

Joanie presented pints for Roy and Del, white wine for Charlie and then held up her bottle of lager in a toast to *Evening Mumbles*.

'How's life then?' Charlie asked, taking a big swig. Radio was obviously thirsty work.

'Not bad. Quite good to be honest. I'm running every day, watching what I eat, reading up on mindfulness … and shit.' The swearage was to counteract the inevitable embarrassment that would make its way up his neck and onto his cheeks. But none came – it was a change to have an impressed female friend rather than a sarcy male one.

'Nice one!' she said, impressed.

'Thanks. Yeah … I thought I'd be drowning my

sorrows in the pub, stuffing myself in all-you-can-eat buffets, having Netflix marathons and spending my way out of it. But ... it's like I've been given a chance to sort of reset myself. Oh, check me out, I've turned into a Buddhist wholegrain and pulses wanker.' He bowed his head and put his hands in prayer.

'No! It's good! But it's funny, isn't it, like, you're finding routine and I'm trying out spontaneity? Hey, by the way, have you contacted IOSH to see if they can help?'

He was touched. And flattered that she'd looked into his suspension. The Institution of Occupational Health and Safety was the professional body which supported workers in the industry. But he shook his head. 'I kind of want to see what happens, really. Need to sort my head out first. And how can I defend myself when I was the sloppiest health and safety person ever?'

He pulled up the sleeves of his shirt and Charlie gasped. 'What?' he asked, alarmed, looking around him for evidence of something gasp-worthy.

'Your tattoos!' she squeaked, with bulging eyes, which even after half a glass were looking a bit glassy.

'Oh, yeah.' He was so used to the sleeve of ink which ran from his shoulder to his forearm on his left side that he forgot it was quite a statement. 'From my youth.' From before his brother's accident. Unlike everything else in his life, he'd spent ages working out what he'd wanted, finding the right artist, producing sketches and it had taken months to build up the flow of deep blue waves and white crests, which was inspired by that print called *The Great Wave Off Kanagawa* by the Japanese dude Hokusai. In his head, when he had had it done, it was a nod to his love of the sea and its strength, and a symbol of his love for his brother. After the accident though, he'd considered having it removed and there were nights when he'd woken with blood on his sheets and under his fingernails having scratched at it during nightmares. Over time, he'd learned to blank it out, almost not seeing it when he saw himself in the mirror. What it represented now, he wasn't sure. He'd swing between thinking it was a sign of life's rough times and then of beauty ... it changed according to his mood. And in the end he hadn't had it lasered off because Sam always asked to see it. Or he had when Del had regularly visited.

'Wasn't it painful?'

'Bloody nightmare!'

'I was going to get one once,' Charlie said, 'when I first got to London. But I bottled it. Good job really.'

'Why?'

'Because, get this, it was going to say *carpe diem* on the inside of my wrist. Seize the day. Me! As if.'

'Dangerous, that. I did too much seizing the day, that was my trouble.'

Charlie remembered something and pulled out her phone as another wine appeared under her nose.

'My friend, Libby, who I used to live with, she found this note under my bed. She's turned my room into the spare. Anyway, look ...'

There was a snapshot of a piece of paper on which the words 'By the Time I'm 30' were written and underlined. Numbered one to four, she'd put down 'live abroad', 'be a breakfast DJ', 'have my own place' and 'planning barefoot beach wedding'.

'We each did a list when we'd just got to London. I was twenty-three. Look at the naivety of it!'

'You're in Wales, that's abroad!'

'That's what Libby said. The rest of them though. Nope.' She shook her head energetically.

Oh, hello, went his curiosity as if it was a meerkat on its back paws, popping up on patrol. Was she saying she wasn't anywhere near marrying that Jonny twat? Had she rumbled his Mr Lover Lover act? He stopped himself, shocked at how he'd leapt to such a conclusion – and wondering why he had. Oh no, it wasn't because he was seeing her differently, was it? He had to test himself. Her mouth was moving and her lips were making him feel funny, they were in high definition, in fact the whole of her sparkled and the rest of the room was grey. How did your brain go from liking someone as a person to finding them attractive when you got to know them? Stop. Right. There. She's a friend, don't sully it with horrible bloke stuff. You're only feeling this bond because she's in the same boat as you – not sorted.

'Same here, apart from the property bit,' he said, handing back her phone and gulping his pint, looking to see who was left here. Ivor and Ed had gone and Roy was draining his drink as was Joanie, and they were getting their coats, saying goodbye and mentioning early starts and being knackered. Charlie had edged herself onto a stool and showed no signs of wanting to go. Then she pointed up with her finger and her eyes flashed.

'I'm going to do a new list! You can do one too! Things we want to happen by the time we're ... actually, let's not put a limit on it because it'll only make me cry when I look back and they haven't happened. Perhaps we should call them life goals instead? Or ... how to seize the day? Yes! That's it!'

'What is it about you and lists?' That was better – lists were not sexy at all.

'They make me feel as if I've achieved something. Or not!' she said, laughing.

'You have! You came here not knowing anyone and made it work. That's something cool.'

She considered it and a smile crept onto her lips. 'Maybe ... yes!'

The night went on and he found her increasingly lovely and open; it was as if she was blossoming like a flower. A pissed one. Because before long, she was swaying and rolling her eyes when she mentioned her boyfriend. He found out Jonny was on a stag do this weekend so she was staying here; she wouldn't see him next weekend either because her friend was visiting; and she thought it'd be good for them because things had become a bit strained between them. Which pleased him, as awful as he knew it was to admit it. Drawn to her, he began to prod a bit, to find out why exactly she'd had a public-speaking phobia. What had caused it? But she groaned and waved his question away with an 'It's complicated' and she swivelled the spotlight back onto him, asking if he had a girlfriend.

'That's complicated too,' he said, thinking of Fflur's hold on him, which was fading but not as quickly as he'd like. Then who the kid was when she saw him on the beach? Why had he gone in the sea up to his thighs? And he started talking about his brother and the accident. But when she asked 'Where is he now?' he couldn't go into it. It'd make him morose and he'd get drunker. It was late and he didn't want to end up making love to a kebab with his mouth.

'Right, I think I'm ready to go,' he said, to persuade himself. 'Want to share a cab?'

'Go?' she cried. 'I'm not going home yet! Come on, let's go to a club or a bar! We can work on our lists! *Carpe diem*!'

It was so tempting to keep this night alive. But he'd vowed to stay true to his new mindset. What was seizing the day? Before, he'd have seen it as living life to the max, living in the moment. And he'd have been the one shouting for the party to carry on. Yet he'd thought about this and he'd wondered if seizing the day was more about being able to prepare for tomorrow. Like, making the best use of the day so you were well enough to do it again and again and again over weeks and months and years ... The mess he was in was down to too little self-control.

'No, I've had enough.'

'Boring!' she sang as they left the pub and he searched up and down the street for a taxi.

'Behave! You need to go to bed.'

'This,' she declared, throwing her arms wide, 'is the new me. Brave and ... out with the old and in with the bold! I want to get the bus!' she said. 'I want a crush on the bus!'

'The buses have stopped. It's too late.'

He searched for the cab company on his phone and he heard her squeal.

'Look!' she said, 'That's so sweet!'

A convoy of bicycles were making their way up the prom, their handlebars and helmets lit up with fairy lights. It was a magical sight – like a mirage, almost, of twinkliness. If you forgot the bikes you could almost imagine they were wisps somersaulting along in the darkness.

'Oh yes, that's the Night Ride. Cool, isn't it?'

'I want to do that! I want to do that!'

'Not in your state,' he shot back.

'Do you mind?' she said, swinging round and clutching at his shirt with two big handfuls. He put his arm out to steady her because she was on the verge of falling over.

'Hey, guess what …' She'd forgotten her defiance just like that and she was pulling him in to tell him something with a whisper. 'I think Tina phoned in to the show.'

'What? Why?' She had a charmed life. Charlie was off her rocker!

'My first ever caller, said she was called Gail, from Townhill, Welsh accent. Said she was lonely.'

'Really?' he said with doubt. Tina was forever dashing off somewhere to see friends. And Townhill? 'Why would she say she was in Townhill? It's hardly *Real Housewives* territory. The only reason she'd go up there would be for the view!'

'I know but this Gail said her and her bloke were separated, like Tina is, but she didn't go into it, probably because it'd blow her cover. I didn't realise it at first but when I thought about it … I'm convinced it was her. I'm going to help her.'

It was hard to take Charlie seriously, such was her slur. But he couldn't be arsed to get into this.

'That's nice, if you think she needs help then go for it. Bloody cab company is engaged.' He put his phone away and wondered how he was going to get her home.

'Do you remember,' she said, still holding onto him, 'when we first met and you made me trip and I twisted my ankle?'

'How could I forget that?' he groaned.

'I thought you were a total bloody idiot!'

'How nice.'

'But now ...' She tilted her head and gazed up at him, her hair lit up behind by the moon making her look like an angel. Who'd had too much of the communion wine. 'I think you're brilliant. In fact ...'

A strand of her hair was caught in the breeze and it tickled his chin. That was why he shivered. Honest to God.

'I think I fancy you!' She giggled, then covered her mouth and did wide eyes in fake shock at herself. If she hadn't filled her tank with lady petrol, he might've entertained it.

'You don't, you're twatted, that's all.' What was it with pissed birds? He was an option if they were wearing beer goggles. But not to be taken seriously when they weren't. It was so depressingly familiar.

'I am but I still do. Just a bit, a teensy weensy bit.' She made a minuscule gap between her thumb and forefinger, shutting one eye to focus on it, to show how little she felt. 'You're just so nice and you're always so positive.'

'Yeah well, that's a pointless philosophy degree for you.'

'I mean it!' she insisted.

'Yeah? If you do, tell me when you're sober. Then I'll believe it.' He said it brusquely but she was wearing him down.

'Phisopholy?' she struggled to say. 'You did that? Wow, you are deep.'

He couldn't help but laugh. 'It was the easiest course to get on through clearing because my A-Levels were crap.'

His heart was getting gooey, like it was a baked circle of Cenarth cheese. Thank God for the cab ... He waved it down and instructed her, 'No throwing up, all right?' Then he poured her in, let her fall asleep on his shoulder, woke her when they got closer to town, got her address out of her, took her to her front door and used her key to let her in. He took her number and gave her his in case she needed anything, then he got back in the taxi with a sigh as his phone began to ring. Fflur was booty-calling.

'Where to?' the driver said. 'Need a stiff one? Wind Street's open, mate.'

He thought about it. It was progress, he realised, because he'd never have thought about it this time last week. He'd have just done it. He put his phone away.

'No, ta,' he said. 'The marina. It's home time.'

'Right you are.'

'But if we pass a kebab place ...'

He was cleaning up his act – he'd resisted so much tonight and he could get a grilled chicken one. After all, moderation was about dabbling in the bad as well as the good, yeah?

18

Charlie's advice on Bring Me Sunshine had been a lifeline.

Tina had inhaled every word she'd said about loneliness and she'd known if she was going to get through the next three months, she had to do something with her time to find a way to cope.

And so that was why she was in a semicircle of women sat on conference chairs in a little church hall in Townhill. All shapes and sizes from all walks of life, they could've been a book club or knitters, the WI or community campaigners. What they were though were wives, partners and families of prisoners, whom Tina had found online promising 'no judgement'. They met once a week on a Thursday night to share their stories and offer support over home-baked cakes and cups and saucers of tea. She'd rung the contact number, spoken to Jayne, the lady in charge whose soon-to-be ex-husband was serving five years for domestic violence, and had known there and then by the welcome in her voice that she would go along. Bring a bake, she'd been told, and last night she had had a go at a Victoria sponge which had turned out well for her first go since Darcy was small. She'd relied on M&S for entertaining back when they'd been flush.

Socialising with other people was a strain because she feared she'd let something slip: she hated herself as she did it, but she had to make up excuses to get out of work drinks on Fridays. Here though, the nerves she'd felt as she'd pushed open the creaky old door soon disappeared because she was among people going through the same thing as her. There were nine of them: the oldest, sixty-five-year-old Linda, whose son was inside for drug dealing; the youngest, twenty-two-year-old Lily, who brought bonny babe-in-arms Bella, born after the dad had been sent down for armed robbery. To look at them on the outside, you'd never know they were like her. But as soon as they came together, they felt the safety and Tina recognised her own haunted eyes in theirs.

Each introduced themselves with explanations of who they were, what their loved one – or unloved one in Jayne's case – had done and how they were managing.

Now being Tina's turn, she released her story with relief.

'My husband, he's serving, we hope, seven months for fraud. He didn't mean to do it ...'

She saw a couple of women drop their eyes and Tina realised they'd heard it all before. 'What I mean is ... he did it, he was guilty, he knows he did wrong, but he developed a problem and he couldn't get out of it ...'

A few nodded in empathy and it gave her the strength to continue.

'He was a gambler,' she said, looking down now at her writhing fingers in her lap.

A hand reached out from beside her and settled her twitching arms. She felt a stillness that had evaded her for months; this was her moment to get it all out there.

'He'd always been into the horses, a couple of pounds here and there on big races, but then he worked his way up; we came from nothing, you see. He was an accountant, a very good one, but as he earned more and more, a huge salary it was by the time he got caught, he'd place bigger bets, chasing the wins, trying to make up for the losses. He hid it so well. Or perhaps I didn't pay enough attention?'

There was a collective shake of heads, of forgiveness.

'I'll never forget the day when he was arrested ... the police came at dawn, it was terrifying. I was shivering in my nightie, feeling so exposed, asking why they had to take him away now, why couldn't he have a shower? But he acted as if he'd been expecting it. He went without a row, admitting it straight away. I had no idea. It was as if I'd been introduced to a stranger. I'd been spending all that time, unaware. He'd said he hadn't told me because he didn't want me to suffer but when I think of what I was buying ... fresh cut flowers every week, the choicest cuts of premium meat and vintage wines and handbags and ...' She still felt the blow of her naivety.

'He was charged, appeared in court, bailed and eventually, after a long investigation, jailed, not in Cardiff, but in Swansea, here because there was no room near us. I had to up sticks overnight. All the assets were taken, the house went, he owed so much. Three hundred thousand pounds, he stole. He'd siphoned off money from the business, a big motor company which specialised in luxury cars with dealerships across Wales. They caught him when we were away in St Lucia, they found out because finance agreements hadn't been settled. The boss checked the account and my husband had paid sums into his bank and various companies which he'd set up. They say these crimes are victimless but the company was almost ruined, people were laid off, families were affected. All because of his gambling. His addiction. It took over his life. He goes to the meetings in the prison, to stay clean. But I can sense he's different to how he was when he went in. I'm so frightened he'll start betting again and we won't make it when he comes out. Worst of all, my daughter doesn't know ...' Her voice cracked at the betrayal. ' ... and I wish I'd told her but he begged me not to. She's having a whale of a time – we don't want her to pay for what he did.'

Tina wiped away her tears but she felt cleaner than she had in months. 'So that's me. Who I am.'

The room was quiet for a while as the women took it all in before Jayne thanked her for her honesty and reminded everyone that what went on inside these four walls stayed in these four walls. That was their only rule. Then it was refreshments time and chat broke out over forkfuls of lemon drizzle and Tina's sponge, which she noticed went down well judging by the appreciative murmurs. Conversations covered everything from legalese and what did such-and-such a term mean to the shame they felt by association and the pain of having to do all the mucky jobs with their men away. Every word she heard was familiar – it was like being hugged.

'Tina, this is Abbie – she's a newbie too,' Jayne said, introducing a well-dressed woman in her late thirties who'd just come through the door. She'd been running late, but she wasn't going to miss the cake. 'You might have a bit in common,' Jayne winked. 'Her fella's one of those "respectable" criminals too.'

'Hi,' Abbie said, with a big smile. 'Tough, isn't it, being one of those spoiled bitches, eh?'

That was exactly it – that was how spouses of white-collar crimes were regarded, as if they were complicit. 'How could you have not known?' She'd been asked that by one of her rich friends as if she should've been asking Gareth every night, 'How was your day, darling? Did you steal anything?'.

Tina nodded in recognition as her heart bloomed. For here was somebody who would understand exactly what she was going through. And maybe, just maybe, she could make a friend.

19

'Bring Me Fun! Bring Me Sunshine! Bring Me Love!
Tune in for more advice from Charlie Bold on Monday
night, Sunshine FM's very own agony aunt!'

~~

'Oh! Imagine getting your wedding photos done
here!' Libby gasped, taking in the towering stone
walls of Oystermouth Castle and its hilltop sweeping sea
view. 'It'd be perfect! So romantic!'

'Yeah,' Charlie agreed. It was pretty spectacular from
where they were standing on the thirty-foot-high glass
platform overlooking Swansea Bay, which was sparkling
in the spring sunshine. Below wasn't bad either, with the
medieval building's maze of deep vaults, secret staircases
and banqueting halls. 'You'd have trouble getting James
here though.'

'Yep. He gets a nose bleed if we leave London,' Libby
admitted, 'but a girl can dream.'

It was Saturday afternoon and Charlie was in heaven
showing her friend the sights of Mumbles. The worry
she'd had of distance between them dissolved as soon as
they met at the station this morning. For fear of Libby getting the wrong feel of the place, Charlie had immediately

explained the concept of what Dylan Thomas had called his 'ugly, lovely town'. Don't judge it by the concrete, wait until you see Mumbles, she'd said with passion. And did she know Swansea had recently been judged as Britain's most beautiful city by researchers who'd looked at quality of life and proximity to the coast and all sorts of things?

It had come out in a gush, because she wanted Libby to enjoy herself. There was also the potential snob factor that Londonistas carried with them, sometimes not even being aware of it, which made them wrinkle their noses at provincial-by-comparison places. But Libby was enthusiastic about the fresh air and the space – and she worked out what Charlie hadn't yet managed to do. 'You really like it here, don't you?' she'd said, simply.

Yes, she did. Very much. It had come to feel familiar and dare she say it, like home. Especially now she was getting closer to Gen, who'd put down her cross stitch hoop to say hello when they stopped by to drop off Libby's bags.

'And I'd heard Wales was stuck in the past,' Libby had said with impressed eyebrows at Gen's latest masterpiece, which read: 'A woman's place is in the revolution'.

'Hardly,' Gen winked, 'one of the world's first female industrialists was from Swansea. In the early nineteen hundreds, Amy Dillwyn rescued her father's loss-making factory and turned it into profit, saving three hundred jobs. Plus she took on the plight of striking seamstresses who worked at the Ben Evans store, the Harrods of Swansea, and campaigned for the vote for women. She was a pioneer! Didn't need a man to save her!'

Gen was like a fortune teller – the sentiment turned

out to be the theme of the weekend. Charlie and Libby left on a high, chattering away on the bus into Mumbles and over lunch and ice creams on the pier, where Charlie had shyly pointed out Sunshine FM. How could it match BBC Broadcasting House? Libby, though, had shrugged. 'Who cares what it's like? You're the happiest I've seen you in ages.' And right on time, a trailer for Monday's Bring Me Sunshine rang through the pier speaker. 'It's you,' Libby cried. 'See! You've done it!'

She loved Libby for not making her feel small and understanding she had made a breakthrough. It was the same up here, in the castle. Libby could've laughed and cracked a gag about it not exactly being the Tower of London as Jonny had. She began to wonder what he was doing on one of his oldest friend's stag do. He hadn't wanted to go, he'd wanted to see her. But it wasn't going to be a stripper-vindaloo sort of thing. They were wine tasting in Budapest. Charlie had felt she should be flattered but actually, had it been Libby's hen, nothing would've stopped her from going. Just then, an idea came to her as they made their way out of the castle to the prom.

'Hey! Have you sorted your wedding-honeymoon undies yet?'

'No!' Libby grimaced. 'There's so much on my to-do list. I should put you in charge!'

'That reminds me, I've got a new list to tell you about. You'll be so proud of me – it's called How to Seize the Day!'

'What! Amazing! You're a changed woman!'

'I know! I came up with it last week. It's about the only thing I can remember from the night out, mind.'

Apart from telling Delme she'd fancied him. What the hell had she done that for? He was just a friend and she'd been drunk and it was only because he was male that she'd translated her feelings into a crush. It was utterly mortifying and so she'd decided to treat it as something that had never happened, burying it deep and sticking a ten tonne weight on top of it. Anyway, he'd been very gentlemanly about it, texting her the next morning to see how her head was without reference to her stupid behaviour. She wasn't going to drink ever again after that – well, not until later with Libby at a lovely restaurant she'd heard about in the city. Charlie swiftly shut the door on her embarrassment.

'Oh, there's somewhere I want to show you ... it's just up here. Gen's daughter designs underwear, you might see something you like? I've never been in though so I'm not sure if it'll be what you're looking for.'

'Wow,' Libby said, clapping eyes on the shopfront which was as far from edible pants as you could get.

First, there was the sign for Lux Lingerie which was written in a flowing golden cursive font. Then there was the dressed window of divine brassieres and stockings which were draped over a Victorian silver velvet deep-buttoned chair, lit up by a standard lamp and reflected in a freestanding gothic mirror. Behind that was a plum-coloured curtain which was open a crack at the top as if it was offering a glimpse within. Together, the effect promised a tasteful emporium of femininity with a hint of seduction. Charlie and Libby exchanged looks of wonder and went in, where their mouths opened even wider in astonishment. A gallery of hand-drawn undergarments through the ages ran across the three walls, from knickerbockers to camiknickers and from net petticoats to pointed bras. Spotlights fell on collections of lace and silk, which were artfully strewn across vintage furniture including hat stands and dressers, chaise longues and occasional tables in a kind of elegant striptease. And there at the back sat Claudia, her head visible over a sewing machine, nodding in time to the music of a 1940s swing band.

'Charlie!' she said, 'Hi!'

'This is Libby, she's getting marr—'

'I want all of this,' Libby said, gasping. 'But is it me? I don't do ruffles or meringues.'

Claudia tilted her face and in two seconds flat she'd sized her up.

'I'm thinking you need something classically seductive. OK, so you've got the most amazing skin. It's like porcelain and your hair, it's titian. Your best colours will be green, pink or blue.'

'Really?' Libby said, unconvinced. Charlie knew Libby's radiators were only ever lined with wholesome no-frills cotton undies in black or white.

Claudia got up, rifled through drawers of tissue-wrapped lingerie, taking out bras and knickers and basques and long gloves in the most gorgeous shades of emerald, navy and blushing pink. She pulled open the changing drapes, guided Libby to the huge mirror inside and held them up against her face. Instantly, her features lifted and popped like a goddess.

'She's amazing,' Libby whispered to Charlie as Claudia found her tape measure.

'I just look into a woman's soul, that's all,' Claudia said, humbly, before getting to work.

*

An hour later, once Libby had placed her order, they took the weight off their feet for a preprandial cocktail.

'What a day!' Libby said, beaming. 'But it's been all about me so far.'

'I'm just glad we could do all of this together.'

'So ... how's everything going with Jonny then?' Libby's eyes were shining in a kind of expectant way.

'Ok-aaay,' Charlie replied, not wanting to strike any more matches of hesitation because what if the whole damn thing caught fire?

'Any news?'

'No.' What was she on about?

'OK,' Libby said, suggesting she'd been fishing and now she'd change tack. 'You think you'll stay here for a while then or ...?'

'Spit it out, woman,' Charlie said, stirring the ice and mint leaves in her mojito with her straw.

'You know!' Libby was pulling a big grin.

'I don't,' she hissed.

'I thought he was going to say it last week. Oh, come on, don't be coy!' Libby leant over the table, wide-eyed, willing her to divulge whatever it was she was supposed to be hiding.

'Say what? What was he going to say to me?'

Libby's face dropped. 'Oh, shit. My big mouth. He actually hasn't, has he?'

'No. But you have to tell me now.' That was the rule when women accidentally let something slip. Everyone knew that.

'Bugger,' Libby sighed. 'Right, don't say I've said anything but the reason Zoe and I said we couldn't make it when we were supposed to when you were in London last week ...' Charlie felt a gush of relief that there was a reason for them messing up the schedule – it meant her radar was working. 'He'd contacted us and said he was going to surprise you on the Saturday.'

'But he didn't.'

'No, we realised that when we saw you.'

'I wondered why you two kind of talked at me rather than to me.'

'Yeah, we were thrown by it. I thought he'd have said it by now.'

'No. So? Libby! Tell me!'

'OK, OK. Look, he's going to ask you if you want to officially move in with him. Take it to the next level.'

Charlie near choked on her drink.

'What do you reckon then?' Libby said once the coughing and eye-watering had stopped. 'Isn't that what you want?' It was code for that which women their age weren't supposed to admit to for fear of letting the side down: mortgage, marriage and kids.

'What do I reckon?' Charlie spluttered. 'What do I reckon?'

Libby gestured with her hands to get her to explain.

But there was so much in Charlie's head after this revelation she could only wonder where the hell she should start.

20

Delme reached the crest of the coastal path with his chest pounding.

It wasn't because he was feeling the effects of his four-mile run from Mumbles because his fitness had improved fast and furiously in the two weeks since he'd cleaned up his act. The scales showed he'd lost almost twelve pounds in that time, taking him down to thirteen and a half stone, achieved by exercise and cooking stuff from scratch. Apart from the odd kebab, obviously.

No, his heart was thumping because his legs had brought him to within sight of his brother's place which sat below in the hug of Caswell Bay, the next beach along from Langland. He'd stopped there at his beach hut, thinking that was it, putting down his water bottle, but he'd ended up carrying on. He was gasping for a drink, too, even though it was a chilly grey day. Shit. Why had he come here? Because he'd never intended to venture this far when he'd first arrived on the bus at the pier. Somehow though his thighs wouldn't give in, too deep into a meditative rhythm as he went up and down the sandy and scrubby pathway, following the contours of the cliff, jumping dips and avoiding rabbit holes.

He turned his back on Sam, trying to collect himself,

sticking his hands on his hips and looking out across the choppy steel of the Bristol Channel to north Devon. But that did no good because he saw the flash of orange of the Mumbles lifeboat, the heads of the crew like dots, on a shout, riding the horses of the waves and slamming back down at the mercy of the swell. They were bloody heroes, going out there – he'd thought that at his desk every time he'd heard the inflatable thundering down the slipway and crashing into the water, which had always made his stomach drop and his head pound with flashbacks of his brother's accident. What courage it took to become a volunteer for the RNLI – when the weather closed in and vessels got into trouble, they headed out, risking their lives to save them. He dipped his head and waited for the vision of bloody water to fade. It didn't work so he swung round and dared himself to focus on the block of flats where Sam would be now. Come on, man, you wimp, he raged inside, go and see your brother. Go! His legs obeyed and he found himself racing on tiptoes as he came closer to the beach, the wide open sand, more open than Langland, empty today except for a few surfers.

The air hung around him in a heavy moist fug, as if he was wearing a balaclava, as if he was being held hostage. Go on, keep going, so he did, feeling his tendons protest and his knees jar as the ground became softer. He wanted to hurt himself, he realised, grimacing as spiteful spits of rain mixed with grains of sand whipped by the wind lashed his cheeks. Up past the beach shops and along from the car park, he gritted his teeth and pushed harder, towards the woods, up past Mumbles Lifeguard Club, seeing the building rear up at him. He stopped dead and stared up at the second-floor window, afraid but unable to turn away in case his brother was there. A window licker, that's what some would call Sam: those bastards who didn't know how far he'd come from being laid out in a coma. Not knowing the physio he'd been through. To reach a recovery which doctors had called miraculous. To have set himself a new bar of potential, the therapists had said. Delme sucked back the shame that once he'd regarded those claims as pitiful. Not straight away because he was drawn into the audience praising-be that Sam was alive and vertical, not even a few months in when he was in a wheelchair and learning to walk again but years after, when he realised his progress had tapered off and was near flatlining. The victories, however small, kept coming but to Delme they were diminished because he would never become Sam as he was again. So he would bite his tongue, thrash out his anger on life, make up for his brother's stasis, live life for the both of them when the confines of the office had near asphyxiated him. Because how could it be that a man who'd been a mountain of muscle and strength, who'd inspired so many and been cheered by the thousands, known to millions, how could it be that the dribbling fleshy mass he was now had anything like potential?

He leaned against the protective gate and all he could taste was self-contempt. On his lips, on the skin around his mouth and now, without realising it, on his fingertips as he wiped away tears. Twelve fucking years since it had happened and Delme still wasn't over it. He was fucking pathetic. Why couldn't he accept it? His brother was happy, always smiling. His parents beamed with pride when they spoke to Delme about Sam's latest interest or outing or achievement. Even Rhian, Sam's daughter, took it all in her stride. Why was Delme the only one whose scar wouldn't heal?

He felt sobs coming, his throat throbbing, but approaching footsteps made him hold them in, swallow them down, blink hard and return to standing. He wiped his eyes and pinched his nose and pretended he was just resting for a minute by the sign for Eden House: Acquired Brain Injury Supported Living.

'Do you know someone in there?' a woman in her sixties said to him. She had her arm through a man's, he was as old as her, both wrapped in coats and hats and smiles. 'We've just come out, we have, seen our son who's just out of rehab. He only moved in last week. But isn't it wonderful in there, Bill?'

'Superb, it is,' Bill said. 'They've got everything they need. Their own en suite rooms with kitchen and a sofa and telly. But communal areas too. Plus the biggest grounds.'

'The staff are fabulous. Our boy, well I say boy, but he's twenty-eight now, he's doing things I never thought he'd be capable of. And the loveliest thing, he's made a mate and you'll never believe this but when he was a teenager, he idolised this rugby player called Sam Noble, you might have heard of him?'

'Wonderful player, absolutely wonderful,' Bill said, exhaling with passion as if he was the dragon on the Welsh flag.

'Yes, well, they're friends! On the same floor. Our son, Tim, he didn't really remember at first but we took a DVD in and watched it together with Sam, about Welsh rugby, and Tim got it, he was so excited! That Sam, he was thrilled too.'

'I reckon they could put a touch-rugby team together in there, there's enough of them!'

The lady laughed and then leaned in conspiratorially to Delme.

'It's lunchtime in there. If you're quick, you might get a bite to eat! Tim's making beans on toast. With the staff, of course, he'd burn himself if he was left to it. But even so, it's independence, isn't it? I never thought he'd be capable. But the possibilities, well, they've just opened up for him. It's not the potential he had once, granted. But it's just a different kind of potential and the effort is just the same.' How could it be so easy for her to see that? 'Right then, come on, Bill. Off we go.'

Delme hovered, undecided, his head a jumble of thoughts which he had to unravel. Potential. The way Tim's mam had put it, potential wasn't about being the best of everyone. It was about realising your maximum performance given your situation. Development wasn't a one-size-fits-all. Sam had as much potential now as he'd had when he was a rugby star: the parameters had changed, that was all. In fact, perhaps he had achieved more since his accident because his limits had been much tighter. Maybe then he had more potential because so much was against him? In which case, the question Delme had to ask was: was he himself reaching his? It was an undisputed no. But if someone showed him pity, he'd be insulted by the belief he was somehow inferior. The medical people didn't pity Sam. They helped. They saw his life as viable as anyone else's. Understanding this was like standing in a wind tunnel: it rushed through him, reaching his every cell. He finally saw that he needed to help himself too, beyond the wholewheat pasta and exercise.

Sam would be so chuffed to see him. But … but, but. He didn't feel ready. He had to sort this out. Become good again. Because the next time he saw his brother it would be for forever, a regular thing, always there, never letting him down. He just needed to do some things first.

So he ran back over the beach, up the cliff, down to Langland, necked his water, then on and on until the pier was in his sight. Sunshine FM had called him in later – Tina had let it slip he was going to be told he would be reinstated if he agreed to sit a refresher course. The investigation had apparently concluded that his list of misdemeanours hadn't threatened anyone's life and head office would be wide open to be taken to an industrial tribunal if they got rid of him for a few minor incidents. He'd wondered if he should go with it for security reasons – he could just brush up his knowledge and keep his head down.

He knew now though he would tell them thanks but no thanks. He had to face his fears once and for all.

21

'Tonight, Charlie Bold boldly goes where Sunshine FM has never gone before ... live on the bus for a Crush on the Bus special!'

~

An outside broadcast, she'd said. It'll be fun, she'd said, exciting, a crowd-puller even.

How about doing an edition of *Evening Mumbles* on the number four? It's one of the busiest routes, taking in the city centre, the university and two hospitals – they'd be taking the show to the listeners, picking up new ones, young and old. Just imagine if they could get people to admit to a crush on the bus?

But oh dear, Charlie was ruing the moment she'd suggested it, to massive approval from Roy and Joanie. Because the temporary-now-permanent health and safety guy Brian had been an absolute pain in the arse all week with reams of paperwork, form-filling and risk evaluations. If only Delme was still around – he'd have at least made it jolly. But he'd gone, even though he'd been told that the nearly completed investigation was heading towards a warning and reinstatement. How she missed him – odd really, seeing as she had spent little time with him. But when you met someone you got on with, you just knew: like when she'd first got to know Libby and Zoe, it was obvious they'd connected. Charlie hadn't seen Delme in ten days, which had given her enough time to 'forget' about her silly crush confession. All it had been was an appreciation for what he'd done for her, he'd been her crutch that was all.

This afternoon had been one long sound quality and equipment-testing check after another and she'd retreated with her script and a bottle of water as a pretend microphone. It had given her too much time to think. Over stewed polystyrene cups of tea, she had tried to concentrate on tonight's show. But inside the echoing bus station terminal her mind kept straying: her heart and her head weren't at war, they were at sea.

Once she'd got over the initial shock of Libby's revelation that Jonny was going to ask her to live with him full-time, Charlie had felt uneasy. Not because she didn't want to live with him – it was a massive deal, a show of commitment and a natural next level of a relationship that so many desired and had to drop hints to reach.

What troubled her was that he hadn't mentioned it that weekend when it'd been an obvious time to pop the question. Perhaps he thought it'd be too much on top of her work problems. That was the nice way of looking at it. Her fear was he'd decided against it. Maybe he was having second thoughts, questioning if she was for him. In the four days since the beans had been spilled, she'd become wracked with insecurity. Now she was the one waiting for him to reply to her texts, poring over how many kisses he left, and preoccupied with 'what ifs' when he didn't pick up her calls. He sounded normal when they did talk but when it came to face to face this weekend on his visit, would she see something in his eyes?

In the meantime, the thought of sharing a home, their home, became a marvellously tempting mirage. All right, she'd seen a change in him but that was from the testing transition of living in two different cities when they'd had it so easy before. Being under one roof would take that pressure away and things were bound to return, no, improve, on what had been. She could just imagine waking up to his sexy bed hair each morning, going to sleep in his arms every night. They'd get up early on Saturdays to find the finest ham at farmers' markets! Take lazy Sunday baths! Even cleaning together to meet Jonny's meticulous standards would be fun! It was so thrilling. And safe. Apart from the job bit but she'd thought about it and Jonny was so well connected now, he had a good chance of finding her something.

Yet this return to London, putting down roots and building a solid foundation for the future could just be a daydream. And her anxiety now sneered at her gut-inspired list of How to Seize the Day.

She'd composed it on Sunday once Libby had gone, still firing on girl power. Hammy inspirational quotes did not feature – Charlie had wanted it to be a bespoke personal set of goals that would motivate, not pressurise her. Curled up on her bed, she had devised a daily, easily achievable, sometimes silly, checklist in the notes section of her phone which she felt would make her feel more alive. For example, and in no particular order, in a scattergun of bullet points rather than neat and numbered, she would …

- Try new sandwiches at lunch – nothing too adventurous, just a change from ham.
- Talk to strangers – NB. Not weirdos – just friendly faces.
- Be curious – don't let yourself get too comfy at work and in life.
- Find out about where you live.
- Tell people you love that you love them. (Not when drunk.)
- Wherever you are, be there in your heart and mind as much as you can.
- Be yourself. (Whoever that is. Believe you'll find out who you are.)

The sense of achievement and excitement had ebbed though as she sensed Jonny's withdrawal, whether it was real or in her head. If it came to the crunch, if he did ask, would she choose this life here, this bizarre winding B-road which could be built on sand for all she knew, over the trusty tarmac of the M4 direct to London of mortgage, marriage and kids? Of course not. Mervyn had gone quiet lately, which was a good sign, but who was to say he'd stay that way? This wasn't a long-term situation. So she'd stuck to ham all week.

'The bus is ready to board,' Joanie called, just as Charlie was coming to the conclusion that she'd bitten off more than she could chew tonight – how could she give advice when her head was scrambled eggs? How was she going to cut through it?

It turned out all she needed was to see the Sunshine FM stickers on the windows of the bus, the mobile studio on the back row and the microphone being pressed on her to rove the aisles. Except the clarity wasn't a good thing; it was more of a hideous dawning that she was about to be exposed. On the pier, she could hide her nerves. But here in public, people would be looking at her, waiting for her to stumble, maybe even filming, ready to post a howler on YouTube. How hadn't she foreseen it?

The engine started and the rumble of the floor went up her legs to meet the shake of her hands and Roy was counting her in as passengers embarked with 'What's all this then?' on their faces. It was horrible. Damn you adrenalin, damn you, she thought. Jonny always said it was like flicking a switch when he went on the radio, as if he became someone else like an actor. But that had never worked for Charlie; she couldn't be anyone but herself. She caught a woman's eyes shining at her from behind a pair of tortoiseshell specs sitting halfway down and decided to talk to her.

'Welcome to our first ever Crush on the Bus on the bus,' Charlie said, flatlining. The woman nodded slightly and raised her eyebrows in an encouraging fashion. This person wanted her to succeed, Charlie realised, and it gave her a boost to be on the receiving end of a stranger's kindness. 'We're on board the number four and we want to know – could this be the love bus? Will the wheels of motion inspire some emotion tonight? I'm Charlie Bold and this ... is *Evening Mumbles!*'

It's Just a Little Crush by Jennifer Paige began and Charlie breathed out heavily, falling to her seat as the bus took a corner; she'd been bouncier but she'd made it to the music break, that was something. Joanie gave the passengers a quick brief and asked for volunteers. A round of 'ooh' went up and a heckler shouted 'Not bloody likely!' but then the woman Charlie had addressed raised her hand, shyly announcing that she was a regular listener. Not of Sunshine FM in general but of *Evening Mumbles*. She loved hearing people's stories and Charlie's advice and she'd come here tonight specifically to get some from her – she'd even come up with her own crush codename! Wow. The hairs on Charlie's arms stood up. Was that a stirring of her ego? She only ever associated egos with arseholes. Whatever she was, she wasn't one of them. And how could one person inspire this minuscule but distinct effervescence in her veins which, now she was aware of it, seemed to bubble up over her fear? Would she look beyond herself and see she had made a difference to someone who had no vested interest in her? All she'd been worried about had been getting paid and getting through it but here was another reason to do her best. Suddenly, her chest was rising and her shoulders were relaxing and maybe this hadn't been such a shitty idea after all … With an intake of breath and a grit of her teeth, tentatively, she went with it, because this was her best option.

'Ladies and gentlemen, we have our first confession!' she sang, back on air to cheers. OK, Joanie was geeing them along with applauding hands over her head in true warm-up style but it replaced the thud of Charlie's heart in her ears. She sat down next to the woman and promised herself she'd do her justice.

'With me here is a very brave lady,' she said, blocking everyone else out, including the craned necks of the pair sat in front of them. 'Would you like to introduce yourself?'

'Hi, Charlie, I'm .... Specs Appeal. Specs because of my glasses and appeal as in an appeal for help.'

'I like it! It's deep! Interesting and honest,' Charlie said, intrigued.

'Do you think so?' She flicked her long brunette hair away from her face as if she was flowering before her.

'I do, yes. So what brought you here tonight?'

'Well, I've got a crush on the bus but ...' She hesitated, looking afraid. Charlie took her hand and gave it a squeeze. '... I'm ... a widow. I lost my husband Paul three years ago. Cancer. It was very painful ...'

The bus stopped at traffic lights and a ripple of sympathy from the passengers could be heard.

'My friends and the kids, they say it's time I got back on the dating scene but I'm scared.'

What a woman she was: her voice was cracking from the memory and she was in the grip of fear and yet she was confronting it.

'That's natural,' Charlie said to her, 'What of?'

'That I'll forget him.' Her chin wobbled and Charlie felt hers quiver too. 'He was wonderful. Kind, funny, really funny, he was.' She was staring into space now, her eyes glistening with love. Charlie was given a great big dollop of perspective by what this lady had been through. 'A great dad and so full of life. If I met someone else, wouldn't it be like I'm cheating on him?'

Oh, it was awful – she hadn't just been through the torture of losing him, she was piling the pressure on herself too. Charlie desperately wanted to lighten her load, to show her there was another way.

'It sounds like you're seeking permission but I can't give you that. Only you can give it to yourself.'

Charlie saw a movement out of the corner of her eye – it was the driver nodding in agreement as he watched them intently from his rear-view mirror.

'You're entitled to be happy. Would he want that?'

'Yes. He wouldn't want me living in the past.' This was good – Specs Appeal seemed to understand what she had to do. But could she do it? The bus began to crawl forward as red turned to orange.

'Do you feel happy in the other areas of your life?' Charlie was probing to see if Paul was a bruise at the surface of her skin, which would mean it would all be too soon. There was total silence – everyone sensed this was a crossroads.

'Yes, actually. I'm me again, a new me, I can't change what happened. But there's a gap ... where he was.'

'Do you feel you want to fill the gap? Because that might suggest you're not ready. But if you can see it instead as a heart-shaped memory box that—'

'Yes! It can be like a photo album!' An 'Ah!' went up at Specs Appeal's smile and the engine purred with happiness as it picked up speed.

'Exactly, to open whenever you want to look at it.'

'Then it won't feel like a hole. Because otherwise I'm good, I'm busy, lots of friends, lovely family, I began volunteering at the hospice where he'd been ... after Paul went.'

'Wow. What a tribute to him. That's such a positive.'

'Yes and now I work there full-time on reception.'

Charlie was full of admiration for her. And she was waiting to see if Specs Appeal would take the next step. 'So, are you here because you want to move on?'

Her eyes lit up. 'Yes ... I do, so much. I see now that

I don't have to leave Paul behind, do I? I can carry him with me always, even when I meet someone new.'

Charlie didn't have long before the next stop so she went for it. 'Someone like ...?'

'This lovely guy who gets the 8.23 a.m. He's got lovely curly blond hair, big build, you know, cuddly, he wears glasses too. He looks a thinker, about the same age as me, mid-forties. I think he could be a librarian or an academic, he always has a big rucksack with him, he's always got a book on the go, in fact that's what I call him, Mr Bookworm! And he's very polite, he's given up his seat for me before.'

'What a gent!'

'I think so! But I haven't spoken to him beyond "thank you". And I'd like to. Because life is about living, isn't it?'

The bus was slowing down and Charlie saw a line of people on the pavement beneath a bus shelter. It was time to wrap it up and go to some music.

'Life *is* for living. You know, I think we can all relate to that.' Me, especially, Charlie thought, realising she hadn't only helped, she'd been helped too. 'So Mr Bookworm, if you're listening and you feel the way Specs Appeal does, then please get in touch!'

Specs Appeal stood up to go as the doors swished open and she left, waving, to a huge round of applause. The energy on board was incredible! And it lasted for the rest of the show. Almost two hours later, as the bus made its return to the bus station, Joanie passed her a piece of paper. Charlie squealed when she read it. This was even better than her seamless combination of Bring Me Sunshine and Crush on the Bus.

'Oh my word, guys, listen to this,' she said. 'Mr

Bookworm has only rung in! And he's got a message for Specs Appeal ... coffee at the library cafe? Let us know how it turns out!'

The bus roared when Charlie finished and she couldn't help but punch the air. It could be their first real romance! Just imagine if they got on! What if they fell in love? She'd have to get herself a dress for the wedding, she thought, laughing at herself as she helped pack up.

Afterwards, as she stepped off the bus, her heart leapt when she noticed it wasn't dark: it was twilight and the long nights were over. And the sun was burning brightly in Charlie's soul. By talking to a stranger and being in the moment, she'd ticked off two things on the list she'd supposedly screwed up and chucked in her mental bin. More than that though, this bizarre winding B-road in Swansea had turned out to be a journey of self-discovery. It might only have been one person trusting her but it was one more person than she'd had in a long time. It gave her a sense of meaning and definition – a purpose and fulfilment in finding her niche. It could be fleeting but now she'd experienced it, she wasn't sure she'd be willing to turn her back on the possibility of feeling it again. So where the hell did that leave Jonny?

22

The bone-shattering bang of the door behind her, Tina felt like she'd been thrown up from the prison's belly out onto the street.

Gareth had asked her to do something dreadful, not to mention illegal, and she was a mess of guilt and outrage, compassion and despair. She'd put her foot down over the money he'd wanted to give her, refusing point blank to accept anything in case anyone got wind of it and his claim it was clean was tested. To jeopardise the time he had left inside was insane. He'd cried when she'd told him she'd pawned her ring – she had to confess to that, she didn't lie to him. His own wife, he'd said, having to sell her soul because of what he'd done. It had set him off and Tina had wished she'd never told him. Yet they were partners and equals and while she always vowed to keep her visits bright, sometimes her worries tumbled out. Even so, from now on she knew she wouldn't open up again to him – it wasn't worth it, particularly when he was suffering. She would only confide in the girls at the prisoners' wives support group.

Gareth had been in a terrible state this afternoon: gaunt, pasty and pained by what could only be depression. His denim shirt had been replaced by a greying white T-shirt as if to say he had given up. He was having trouble sleeping not just because his cellmate snored but by panic which would rise up in the dark. Waking after a fitful night, he was hit by the realisation he wasn't in his own bed with her but on a hard, narrow excuse for a mattress, scratched sore by the blanket and his nose full of the stench of piss. The food was shit, the company even worse; he could see why people topped themselves.

He missed her, and being unable to talk to Darcy – he'd do anything to hear his daughter's voice. But she'd find out the lie if he rang her: it'd begin with a prison officer asking if she'd accept a call from the nick? Someone in here had a mobile but he was charging favours and money Gareth didn't have to use it. If only he had his own … He'd looked up at Tina with bloodshot baggy eyes, the twinkle gone, the green murky. There was a bent screw, he'd said, brings stuff in, nothing dodgy, just to help us get through this nightmare … Oh God, no, she'd whispered. But he had implored her with his eyes – he just wanted to talk to his wife and his daughter.

He had left it hanging, not demanding she do it outright but the suggestion was enough to make her blood run cold. When the visit had ended and they'd hugged goodbye, his lips had tasted of tears and desperation. It frightened her because he was showing he was prepared to take a risk. A gamble. And did that mean he was again in the jaws of addiction? She told him to seek help but his shoulders had drooped, defeated.

She absolutely wouldn't do it for him. It was too much to ask. And yet … if she couldn't speak to Darcy, if she was in his shoes … That was the problem, she couldn't bear to see him like this, so far from who he'd been. No, no, no.

She took a big breath, looked up to the blue sky wispy with clouds and reminded herself she had things to do. But not before she wondered how it would look through bars. This half-day off work had to be put to some use, she thought, putting on her sunglasses, walking to the bus stop, travelling home to Townhill, calling at the chemist to buy some hair dye to get rid of her wiry greys, which she'd noticed were multiplying. She was incredulous that once she would have thought nothing of spending at least a hundred pounds for a cut, colour and blow-dry with maybe a pedicure thrown in plus acrylics for more money while she drank a chilled glass of wine. If they ever had wealth again, she would never go back to that mindless cash-splashing. And then she felt the alarm of having wondered if Gareth would steal again. What a dreadful wife she was.

The climb up to Townhill didn't distance her from her disloyalty and she couldn't bear to look out onto the city's very best view of Swansea Bay in this sunshine. If he couldn't see this then neither could she. Instead she focused on the lines of weather-beaten beige houses stacked row upon row on the hill where trees barely broke the skyline. She sought out abandoned sofas in front gardens and smashed glass on the cracked pavement. She crossed the road to avoid the PCSO on patrol handing back a mug of tea to an elderly lady at the door. She ignored the laughter of old friends stopping to talk on their way to the shops, the happy kids on bikes and the sign for the community centre which had something for everyone. Denying herself the close-knit atmosphere of a place with so much togetherness, willing to see the bad because she didn't deserve the good.

But it seemed luck wasn't on her side today because she heard her name being called from the other side of the street. It was Abbie, who was waving at her from the entrance of a hairdressers.

'Fancy a trim?' she shouted. 'I've had a cancellation. I'll do it for nothing, it's on me.'

Tina felt her face break out into a huge smile. 'Oh wow, really?' she said when she got up to Classy Cutz. 'Won't the boss mind?'

'No, I won't!' Abbie laughed, showing her into a gorgeous little place which was decked out in a romantic Regency style.

'This is yours?' Tina said, taking in the soft pink walls and darker dusky alcoves, symmetrical on both sides of the salon, winged leather chairs and a small glass chandelier. It was lovely and had the intimate air of a boudoir.

'All mine. It's my baby,' she said, pointing at a seat and taking Tina's bag and coat. She wrapped her in a gown and the two women looked at one another in the elegant rose gold mirror. Abbie's skin glowed beneath her honeyed highlighted bob and her figure was amazing even though it was in the traditional hairdressing uniform of black T-shirt tunic and leggings. Tina looked drab now that her three-quarter-length wide-sleeved teal ribbed knit dress was under cover. The black of the cape made her look drawn.

'What do you fancy?' Abbie asked.

'Some of what you've got!'

Abbie swept her fingers through Tina's hair suggesting this and that. She agreed with it all, whatever it was she was saying, because she had relaxed in an instant, enjoying the touch of another person, the physical contact reminding her how she missed the rapport of female friendship.

'Easy! Coffee, tea, something stronger?'

'Only if you are!'

'Tell you what, I'll pour you a prosecco if you agree to pour me one once I've finished doing your hair. I can't be drunk in charge of scissors, can I?'

'Deal!'

'OK, sit tight, I'll just go and make up some colour and get you a glass.' She disappeared into a back room and Tina sighed with utter contentment. It was so nice being looked after. Normally she wouldn't have accepted such an offer but she'd been caught at a low ebb. There was also the sense that they had established some kind of connection when they'd met, almost comradeship. From that first introduction which lasted only fifteen minutes or so, Tina had liked her and it seemed mutual – they were two women who'd known the good life and it had been taken from them. Both were standing by their men and trying to be upbeat. They hadn't seen each other since then, Abbie hadn't come to the meeting last night, so this was a chance to find out more about one another.

When Abbie reappeared with a mixing bowl and brush, Tina realised the radio was tuned in to Sunshine FM. It all seemed to fit, it was easy and the conversation flowed from the go. They only lived round the corner from one another, they were both home alone and they watched far too much telly. Abbie though knew to leave her with a magazine when the foils were on and she was under the heater, to say nothing when she was washing her hair and doing the most wonderful head massage, only to pick it all back up again when she feathered her wavy hair to chin-length, did the blow-dry then styled a sweepy fringe and added some product to smooth it into shape. The colours lifted her complexion, made her eyes shine amber and took years off her.

'I love it Abbie, thank you so much. You must let me repay you somehow. How about dinner at mine one night? If you can make it.'

Abbie put her hands on her heart and accepted with grace.

'That'd be lovely. There's not much to do of a night time, is there?' She produced another glass and Tina did the honours while Abbie sat down beside her, both turning to give themselves a cheers.

'Do you have any kids or family around?' Tina asked. 'Lots of women in our position say that helps.'

Abbie shook her head and a sadness fell upon her. 'No. No kids. As for my family, they've disowned me.'

'Good job you've got this place then,' Tina said, wanting to pep her up.

'Definitely, I don't know what I'd do without it. Work keeps you going.'

'Same here. Although no one there knows.'

'How did you manage that? I couldn't have kept it quiet round here if I'd wanted to. People love to gossip. And I expect my ex helped spread the muck.'

'How do you mean?'

Abbie puffed her cheeks. 'It's a long story.'

'I've got time. You don't need to go into detail if you don't want to.'

'Bitter ex, he didn't want kids, I did, so I left him. Met

someone else who turned out to be a criminal. Serves me right, in his eyes. And I suppose I've done things I'm not proud of.'

'Haven't we all?'

'It's not as if I wanted to be involved with a convict. The thing is, I know if I was in other circumstances, I'd get rid of him. But I'm like tainted goods now. I'm thirty-eight and this might be my last chance to have a baby. I never even fell pregnant with my ex but with Eddy, I have been. Once. I feel like I'm getting closer. As if it could happen and I can't deny myself the opportunity.'

Tina's heart went out to her. To stick with somebody because you wanted to have a family wasn't advisable but it happened. She wasn't one to judge because she'd fallen pregnant within a few months of deciding to try for Darcy. She'd never known the devastating loss of miscarriage nor the temperature-taking and cycle-plotting to conceive. But she had known the yearning for a baby, when her body had craved to carry and birth and hold the greatest gift of life. It had come on suddenly after her and Gareth had been married for a few years and she'd never known wanting like it. She had been lucky. And could she honestly say she wouldn't do the same thing if she was Abbie?

'Sometimes there are things we do that don't make sense, that we know are wrong or questionable at the very least but we only do it because of love, whether that's for a man or a child.' Tina knew this only too well.

Abbie gave her a grateful smile. 'You're a diamond, Tina. Not many people are so understanding.'

'You know what?' Tina said. 'Let's just not talk about our woes again. Stick to the happy bits.'

'You're on. About that dinner,' she said, bashfully, 'I know it's short notice but I don't suppose you're free tonight are you?'

'I'll have to check my very busy schedule ...' Tina said, deadpan, before rolling her eyes at herself. 'You're on. How does veggie lasagne sound?' Because she had the stuff at home and she could get a salad on the way back.

'Bloody lush!' Abbie laughed. 'I'll bring the wine. I don't know about you but I'm in the mood to let my hair down a bit. It is Friday night! Can't have too much as I'm working tomorrow. Just enough to slump into the sofa.'

Tina knew just what she meant. It had been a long time since she'd had the pleasure of putting the world to rights with a friend. Even if it was Friday the thirteenth.

'Suits me,' she said.

Abbie held up her glass. 'To friends. New ones.'

'Oh yes, I'll drink to that,' Tina said, feeling the warmth not just from the prosecco but from finding this sparkling gem of a woman in the darkest chapter of her life. There would never be enough money in the world to buy this kind of happiness.

23

'It's the *Sunday Morning Love-In* on Sunshine FM. Diane has asked for Marvin Gaye's *Let's Get It On* for her husband Steve on this their fortieth wedding anniversary. Good on you, Di! And Steve, pal, it looks like you've pulled …'

~

They'd actually had a brilliant weekend so far, Charlie thought, as she lay beneath Jonny's arm that was heavy with sleep.

Watching his naked chest rise and fall and his long eyelashes flutter with dreams, she saw that he was every inch the man she'd originally fallen for. But better! As if he'd accepted where she was and who she'd become.

He'd been really happy to see her, meeting her after work on Friday with a surprise reservation at a posh restaurant which he'd paid for, no arguments. Over dinner, he was attentive but not suffocating, he listened to her talk about Libby's visit and the praise she'd had for taking the show on the road and he told her funny stories about the stag do.

Yesterday he'd taken her to the Dylan Thomas Centre to catch the exhibition she'd mentioned, then it was a lazy lunch, back to bed for the afternoon and out to the cinema for an arty film they both wanted to see. They had laughed and talked, flirted and snogged, just like they always had. Neither of them had mentioned Charlie's return to London because it would be like breaking the spell – they'd had enough ups and downs lately. They were living in the moment and Charlie was glad of it. She hadn't really spent much time thinking about him asking her to live with him anyway – the show took up most of her brain space: she had been in a purple patch ever since the outside broadcast with callers and crushes galore. Plus, she'd only had ham sandwiches twice for lunch this week – she'd branched out into chicken, avocado and mayo at Cheers on the Pier. Jonny had been so impressed!

And because he'd been supportive, she felt certain that when the subject of moving in together came up, she'd be able to express what she'd come to feel: that if this happiness continued then they could build up to it. That was the mature way of doing things – her fear that he'd gone off the idea had just been a knee-jerk reaction of her insecurity. The return of their perfect equilibrium, the one they'd had for almost a year now, made her relax. She had something else that mattered to her as well as him, her job, and she felt more complete. What was the rush anyway? She could stick it out here for the meantime and it'd take a while to get her half of the savings to put down a deposit on a flat.

The radio switched itself on, her 9 a.m. wake-up call kicking in, and Marvin Gaye was being introduced on Sunshine FM's request show *Sunday Morning Love-In*. Let's Get It On, oh yes, she thought, let's. She gave the bed a mischievous little wiggle to wake him up. And he responded with a slow stretch of his neck as he came to.

'Morning,' she said, feeling very sexy indeed, mirroring his longing against her thigh.

'Hi,' he said, blinking a few times, before Jonny ran his warm hand lightly along the curve of her body. 'Fancy seeing you here.'

Desire fountained inside of her and she moved closer so they were skin on skin.

'Where else would I be?' she said, with a smoulder, waiting for him to tease her some more, sliding her fingers past his stomach.

'Hmm,' he said, moving in to kiss her shoulder, which he knew she adored. 'I dunno ...' She surrendered immediately and shut her eyes, tilted her chin and gave in to lust. 'How about ... Exeter?'

Strange. But she let it go and giggled, expecting there to be some punchline. 'Mmmm,' she said, 'go on ...'

'I'm serious,' he said, now motionless.

Her eyes flew open and she saw he was.

'Exeter? Why would I be in Exeter?' she said uneasily.

'With me.' He began to stroke her hair, which as usual had boinged up even bigger overnight, fanning the pillow.

'With you?' she asked suspiciously, not having seen this coming at all.

'There's a job going, an afternoon show. I'm sick of the early mornings. And I was thinking that maybe you and me, we could get a place. You know, together.' He gave her a big smile and raised his eyebrows as if he'd just offered her a chocolate cock. But she'd lost her appetite now and was mystified.

'What about London?' Because that was where he was meant to be asking her to go. Where she'd expected him to say.

'I'm done with London. Like you are.' He said it confidently as if he knew her back to front.

Like she was? Was she done with London? She didn't think so, she had assumed she'd go back at some point. 'Why do you think I am?'

'Because you've fit in so well here. Little city life suits you. It just made me think I should do it too. And then this job came up and then when I accepted it at the interview—'

This was too much to take in – this fitting in of hers which hadn't been natural at all, the condescension of little city life, this job, what interview? 'You've accepted? I didn't even know you had applied let alone gone there.'

'It happened quickly and it's hard to talk when I'm in work and you're in work and … I thought you'd be pleased.'

This was all so loaded with assumptions, it made her jerk up the bed and pull the duvet up over her. 'But London is where I'm from! Where I'd be going back to once I got things sorted like getting a new job.'

'Oh … right.' He sat up and crossed his arms, his face looking on the turn like a bottle of week-old milk.

'You need to explain.' Communicate. Which was what couples did.

'You've made it work here, you can make it work there.' He shrugged. There was an edge to him, as if she was being difficult and she'd spoiled his surprise. Had it even registered that she hadn't just fitted in like a jigsaw piece – it had taken everything to get where she was now.

Another move wouldn't be a click of the fingers – why didn't he understand that? 'It's gorgeous, you'd love it. A total change from London. I didn't even know I was sick of it before I went there. You should see it, it's a small city, a cathedral city. Outdoorsy. A quayside. Walks and water and even Michelin restaurants. So it's obviously going places.'

She didn't care if it had wheels, a drinks trolley and an airport marshal waving orange paddles at it.

'Perfect for … children growing up. Safe. Perfect for us if we wanted to …'

My God, he had already painted the nursery and had her in maternity dungarees. He seemed to realise what he'd said. 'Not that that's happening yet. But … I need you.'

Was she supposed to be flattered?

'But I've got a job here. And a few friends.' She picked up her phone. 'Look, Delme sent me a text to say they'd all missed me at Friday night drinks. I'm part of something here, can't you see?' She'd been so touched by it because she hadn't seen him for two weeks now.

A vein in Jonny's neck stood to attention. 'Delme! That idiot.'

She felt a defensive wave of fury. But she kept a lid on it because it would only complicate matters. He'd accuse her of standing up for him because she had feelings for him and she'd parked all of that – Delme was just a mate and that night out when she'd shamed herself had faded from memory. She thought of him now as someone who had been there for a reason – to help her when she'd needed it. Nothing more. It would be entirely irrational to make something more out of it.

'He's my friend, like Joanie and Claudia are. We look out for each other.'

'I'll look after you!' he said.

'I don't want looking after, Jonny!'

He gave an exasperated harrumph. 'What is it you want then, Charlotte?'

'A bit of consistency actually. Things are only just settling down for me.'

'I'm offering you settling down!'

'I don't mean that. I mean that I've pushed myself and I'm in a new place and—'

'So you want excitement? Make your mind up!'

'Listen, you've had time to think about all of this. You've just sprung it on me. And it's not as if I want either excitement or routine – it's not as cut and dried as that. What I want is not to be in a rut like I was but that doesn't mean I want to live some kind of wild and crazy life. I just want to keep what I have for now.'

'You're not making sense.' Jonny was cross with her. And she was angry now too. Because she felt duped, as if his show of manners and consideration this weekend had been exactly that. A performance. As if he had been feathering her fall. And all those assumptions he'd made: the restaurant he'd picked when she knew this place better than him and could've asked her to choose; the wine he'd tasted; the starters he'd ordered; the Dylan Thomas books he'd bought as if he was suddenly Mr Number One Fan.

For God's sake, this would never have happened if he'd asked her to move in with him in London. Not Exeter. Where she'd never been, knew nobody, had no job, no contacts, no nothing. Only him. Just then *Every Breath*

You Take by The Police came on the radio – how was that romantic? It was about a possessive lover …

'You have to be in control of everything!' she blurted out, instantly regretting going for his jugular.

'Oh, I see!' he said, nodding furiously. 'That's what you think of me, is it?'

'Jonny,' she said, reining in her emotion, trying to soften herself. 'I'm sorry. That came out wrong.'

He turned his back on her and got his legs out of bed, resting his head on his hands. 'I don't understand this. I'm asking if you'd like to have a future with me, that's all this is.'

It was true and so many women – including herself – wished for commitment and a happy ever after. Christ, she knew that from all the calls to Bring Me Sunshine. But something about it sat uncomfortably in her throat like a chunk of ham sandwich she hadn't chewed properly.

'I know,' she said reaching to his back, expecting him to throw her off, 'I just need to finish what I've started here first.'

But Jonny turned round and his eyes were willing her to believe him. 'I was wrong to say you wouldn't be able to cope when you got here … that you should've cut your losses and come home. You've inspired me, Charlotte. You've made me see that sometimes it works out, taking a risk. And I've realised what I really want and that's you. Forever.'

Finally, he was being honest. 'Oh, Jonny. That's so lovely. And I want to be with you too but not until it feels my job is done. Exeter sounds great and you should go and we can talk again about me maybe moving down. Is that OK?'

He nodded slowly, still looking hurt but in a way that suggested he'd get over it.

'Come here,' he said, pulling her towards him and nuzzling into her neck.

'I just want to help people, that's what I'm good at.'

'I know,' he murmured into her ear, rocking her back and forth in his arms. 'But you've got to think about helping yourself too. Promise me you will. I love you.'

'I promise,' she said, shutting her eyes as they swayed as one. They'd closed the chasm between them and reached a new level of understanding. And she knew if they could just keep this balance that telling him she loved him could be just around the corner.

24

Across the heaving cafe, Del could see a cappuccino coming his way and he braced himself for one of Merri's insulting foam works of art. What would it be today? A single middle finger flipping him the bird? A scowly face? Or a turd? All of the above were fair comment really because life hadn't been sweet to him of late.

A month of job hunting had thrown up precisely nothing and he was beginning to worry. His savings were obviously non-existent, such the dickhead he'd been, and he hadn't bothered to sign on, thinking he'd be back in work before he'd filled in the paperwork.

Mam had been great, getting the shopping in for him, and Dad had got him a few shifts on a building site through one of his mates. How had he been so reckless, he sometimes wondered – and had overheard Dad say the same to Mam after Sunday lunch. Why has he done this to himself? And signing up for *that* course with the last few quid to his name? He was chasing the past, that's what it looked like, Dad had said.

Mam had whispered over the dishes not to worry, she had faith in Delme – he does his own thing, always has done, love, and health and safety wasn't him at all, really, was it. Bless her. She understood, kind of, why he'd left Sunshine FM: it was so he wouldn't be reckless again. It had been a leap he'd had to make. He had a calling – that was what his course was about – he just had to find out what it was he could do in the meantime for cash.

And it was hard going trying to be creative on applications when you had a CV of health and safety, holiday repping and a degree in philosophy. This was the problem: he looked as if he didn't know if he was Arthur or Martha, like he was in a career maze rather than on a Roman road. He stuck to his one rule though: he wouldn't go backwards - despite what his father thought. What did that leave him with though? An online personality test had revealed he was a 'spontaneous idealist', suitable for roles like cartoonist, teacher or public relations but he couldn't draw, he didn't want to be in the classroom and he had no clue about marketing and sales. There were plenty of big companies around here but sending covering letters to Swansea City Football Club, a TV company, Amazon and the university had been fruitless. Of course it had been. Then he'd turned to an agency but he didn't have a car to get to the places he needed to go. He knew he looked choosy – but he wasn't. The worst thing for him to do would be to go into another unsuitable desk job.

Luckily, Rodney had paid back a loan Del had forgotten about as soon as he'd heard he was unemployed so he was living off that. He'd slashed back his expenditure – and his waistline – so no booze or junk food, instead surviving on pasta and rice and lots of beans. This coffee that was en route to him in Cheer on the Pier was a once-in-a-while treat. He'd go stir crazy if he didn't come out from behind his screen at home. And he always saw someone he knew from the station. Never Charlie though. He'd heard from the guys that over the past few weeks she'd thrown herself into her job as if her life depended on it. She was either tied to her desk or out and about, meeting interesting people for the show. He'd listen to her some nights and had heard how she'd come on. He'd like to see her, definitely, because she'd been all over the place the last time he saw her. That was the night she'd got ratted and told him she fancied him. The strange thing was, ever since, he'd wondered if he might have the hots for her too. Not in that lame 'because she said it first' way but he'd noticed how pretty she was and how easily they got on before she'd said anything. It had been a shock for her to say it and that was why he hadn't really registered it until later. Although, maybe he felt this thing for her because they'd been through something quite mad and intense in a brief time. That sort of thing stirred up emotions, didn't it, like when you had a holiday romance ... Not that they'd been involved like that. Anyway, this was all beside the point, she was with someone, he was getting over Fflur and he had enough on his plate being out of work, his course and sorting himself out in the head so he could see his bro.

'There you go, Del,' Merri said, slinging his coffee down. He peered to inspect it only to feel short-changed.

'Where's my emoji?' he asked as she threw used cups, cutlery, plates and serviettes from surrounding tables onto her tray.

'No effing time. Too busy. The new girl who started on Monday never came back. I haven't had a chance to scratch my arse since Tuesday and any hope of training someone up to cover me for half term so I can be with my daughter is as slim as a streak of piss. And you want an emoji.'

She gave him a look of utter disdain. Which was a bit rich seeing as he was a regular, not like these fair-weather customers who only came out in the sunshine. The season was in full swing: early May was having one of those swoony heatwaves which people had learned could be their summer. Then again, she had a point – this place was rammed with day-trippers, walkers and shoppers and she was struggling to keep up. It was only 10.30 a.m. but already it was boiling in here.

'Any chance of getting some air in here?' he said as he took a swig. 'Great coffee.'

'Go for it,' Merri said, her cheeks as red as her hair, her nose beaded with sweat.

'Can I? Do you mind?' he said, getting up and pointing to the doors and windows. 'Oh and I think the dog bowl needs topping up.'

She consented with a distracted nod, her face taking in the growing queue at the counter. He wouldn't bother her any more, he decided, he'd just do it. So he took another gulp then went round the cafe throwing up the old sashes, pulling back the French doors to the tables outside where he put up umbrellas, wedged open the entrance and refilled the plastic ice cream container which doubled as a cup for canines. He stopped for his drink and felt a lovely cooling breeze on his temples and on the back of his neck and received a wink from Merri, who immediately looked fresher. While he was here, he thought, he might as well help so he picked up a tray which had been left on a chair and did three journeys to collect dirties. Then he saw the stack of unwashed crockery by the sink at the far end of the kitchen and what else did he have to do? He might as well help out.

Ten minutes later, after gazing out the window at the lighthouse which stood brilliantly white against the blue sky and sea while he worked, he'd caught up with the mess and was rinsing his own mug with satisfaction when Merri gave him a 'pssst' from the six-ringed cooker and grill. She was single-handedly whipping up the goods for orders of crêpes, breakfast bruschetta, avocado and bacon on toast and Welsh rarebit.

'What do you fancy? Cheese and ham croissant, eggs benedict, sausages?' she said over her shoulder as she expertly attended to each pan without panic, adding mustard and seasoning here and tomatoes and pancetta there.

'Oh, well, I would but ...' He patted his stomach for effect but in reality he should've been patting his wallet because he couldn't afford it.

'It's on me, you idiot. You're fading away.'

'I'd hardly call losing two stone "fading away".' He was proud of his trimmer waistline but prouder still of his fitness which he'd worked on so much he was ready to face his demons, well, physically at least.

'Don't argue. This is to say cheers for helping.' Merri gave him a rare smile, which in her world equalled a flic-flak across the tables.

'No! I'll just have the coffee on the house, it's fine.'

'You bloody well won't. I'll do you eggs benedict. Making some now.'

It did smell delicious. 'Go on, then,' he said. 'I'll eat it in here.'

'I know you will, butt,' she shot back with glinting eyes. 'Because staff eat in the kitchen.'

'I'm sorry. Did you say staff?'

'You got anything better to do?'

He opened his mouth but she got in there first. 'No, didn't think so. I need a hand. You're free. Would you be able to help? Minimum wage, I'm afraid, but loads of tips. Plus all food and drinks on the house.'

'Um ...' It was a tempting thought but a bit sudden. Although he did like sudden. And then she actually stopped what she was doing, turned round to face him completely and said the word 'please' in such a way he saw a shard of vulnerability through her hard coating. He could fit his hours round the course, he'd be earning again. He might even get to see Charlie ... and the rest of the Sunshine FM gang. 'Maybe ... yeah ...'

Merri gulped. 'Serious?' Her defences had come right down – she was soft as shite underneath that sharp fringe and funereal black clothes. 'I can't fail here,' she said quietly. 'My ex doesn't pay maintenance, my daughter only has me and my mam, we live with her. Lil's only six but she needs a good role model in me. I've never had another job. Worked here since school, took it over when the boss retired, he still owns it but one day I'd like to buy it. So ...'

He had to look away from her because he was filling up so he picked up an apron that was hanging on the back of the door. 'Yeah, of course. Just for a bit.'

'Thank you,' she said, solemnly as he fumbled with the ties. You just never knew people, what they were hiding. He cleared his throat then rubbed his hands and stuck on a grin.

'What do you want me to do, chef?'

Then just like that, she was tough as boots again. 'Clear the tables, take orders, I'll show you the till then I can wash up and cook.'

'All right, sorted,' he said, just as a thought popped into his head. 'How about I put on some activities for the kids during half term? Whenever that is?'

'Couple of weeks.'

'Then your daughter will be able to come along for a bit? If that suits you? I've got a niece who's into art and she could do face painting?'

It was the first time he'd seen Merri smile in a long time.

'From now on, you are going to get the very best emojis on your foam,' Merri said, plating up and sliding Del's brunch across the stainless-steel surface to him.

'No more aubergines?' he said, stopping it with his fingers like he was in a western.

'No more aubergines,' she vowed. 'Now get on with that sharpish.'

Oh yes, chef, he thought, as he dived into a pile of the sunniest hollandaise sauce and eggs on the most gorgeous buttery triangles of Merri's seeded bread. Once he'd finished it, all too quickly, he got to work and immediately fell into the groove. It was physical with all the walking about, mental with the chit-chat and emotional because he suddenly felt much better about himself for doing something. This life wasn't so bad, after all, was it?

'Hey! Delme!'

His heart went mad – he knew that voice. He whipped round to see her grinning. 'Charlie!'

Del would hug anyone, he was a hugger, but for some reason he felt shy and self-conscious – if he cwtched her would he look overenthusiastic, would she read it as something else ... did he feel something else? But she was coming for him and he had his arms wide like she was a long-lost person of importance from his past and their bodies met – she was lovely and slotted right into him – and they both chorused 'ah!'.

They unclinched and laughed, both aware their greeting was entirely ridiculous for two people who had known each other mere minutes in the history of the world.

'Are you working here?' she asked with surprise, taking in the tea towel over his shoulder.

It crossed his mind to say he wasn't. He just liked wearing a pinny. But this was a moment of unadulterated happiness. Which was madness. Instead he said 'Yeah!' with a gummy smile like he was a simpleton.

'Wow!' Thankfully, she was behaving the same way.

'Only until I get something else.' He did the cash finger-rub to look a bit more with it. 'Needs must.'

'Oh, I know the feeling. I'm on lunchboxes from home and instant coffee. Being careful. But today I thought "What the hell, I need a proper coffee".'

'You are a proper crazy woman!' he said.

They both guffawed like idiots. It was nice, really. Really nice.

'I haven't seen you in ages!' he added. 'What's it been? A month?'

'A month!' she said.

'Time flies …' When you're having, what, fun? A personal crisis? 'How are you? You look great.' Lovely, in fact, he thought, with her hair down and wavy. And she had cute dimples, he'd never noticed before.

'You too! You're all … you know …' She waved at his body and her cheeks pinked up which made him do the same. It was hot in here, mind.

'Yeah, I'm on a health kick. Running and eating

sensibly. But you, well, check you out, doing really well on the show. Good on you!'

It was like a love-in. But not that, he corrected himself. A like-in. That was what it was, yes.

'Oh, thanks,' Charlie said modestly. 'It took a while to settle in though.'

'But look at you!' It was all he could say because he felt tongue-tied. And in trouble, if he was going to be honest because he felt recharged by her company and they were only doing polite conversation. Yet unless he was completely mistaken, she looked just as chuffed to see him. How would it be if they ...

'Excuse me, can I order another coffee from you or do I have to queue up?' Not now, he wanted to hiss, as Charlie took a step back while he dealt with the customer. Wait, he wanted to say, don't go!

'Yep, coming up. I'll sort it.'

Charlie mouthed 'See you soon' and he was distracted by a request for tap water from someone else. By the time he'd pointed out the jug of iced water on the side where people could help themselves, Charlie was being served by Merri at the counter. He was gutted. He stared at her, and stared and stared, until his ankles were rammed by a buggy containing a crying kid.

'He dropped his biscuit on the floor,' the little boy's mam said. 'A tragedy, obviously. He had had most of it though.'

'Oh, mate,' he said to the devastated toddler. 'So near yet so far, eh? I know how you feel.'

25

The conference room was electric with whispers and theories when Mervyn Davies's personal assistant swept in.

That shut them up, such was Marissa Lloyd-Jones's steely presence. Over half-moon specs, she glared at the gaggle of faces from production, technical, sales, marketing, promotions, music and programming, waiting for the clock to strike 3 p.m. On the dot, she began to read from a prepared statement, which would be simultaneously released to the shareholders and trade publications. The upshot was that after five years here, station manager Mervyn Davies was leaving to work in head office for the group which owned bags of radio stations, including Sunshine FM. It was some role in procurement where he'd be looking at asset management, whatever that was. That was all Tina needed to know. In other words, he'd been kicked out. Murmurs dominoed through the staff: they got it too. It was no surprise – while Mervyn had grown the station back in the day, it had become stagnant; Charlie had seen it from the moment she arrived. It wasn't moving with the times.

'Mervyn Davies would like to take this opportunity to thank you all for your dedication,' Marissa said, almost suffocating under her own glee – and hairspray, by the look of her stiff feathered silver helmet – at having been the one to break the news. But she had more up the sleeve of her pant suit.

'Taking over the position will be ...' She paused for effect, dragging it out, when yes, everyone was asking who would be replacing him. ' ... Sian Lewis, our presenter of *Home Time*, on an interim basis. She will be talking to you all next week. She's in the studio now preparing for her show.'

'What about our jobs?' someone called, asking the burning question.

'Everything is under review. Any further concerns? No? Good. Just to make you all aware, I shall be taking early retirement – it's obviously time for new blood here, that's the way things will be going.' Then she marched off, no doubt to go and sharpen her talons.

As soon as the door closed, noise erupted. Everyone was united in fear at the threat to their livelihoods. But the re-action was divided when it came to the new head honcho. Sian Lewis! sang those who were pleased it was an insider or a woman or simply a respected broadcaster who gave Sunshine FM its only bit of gravitas. Sian Lewis? groaned the mostly older men, led by Ivor Mone, of course, who cited tokenism and 'bloody equal opportunities'.

'Here we go,' he said to Tina, 'the lefty liberals are going to turn us into Radio 2.'

'Wouldn't that be dreadful,' Tina laughed as his face went from claret to purple, 'to be that successful with a wider range of listeners.'

'We're local, for the locals, reflecting the locals, that's what we are,' he panted. 'Oyster fishermen at heart.'

Charlie appeared and raised her eyebrows at Ivor. 'Back in the nineteenth century, yes, before the sea was over-fished, the oyster beds were polluted by industry and what remained was finished off by a disease which swept through Europe's oysters in the nineteen twenties. There is a small farm off Mumbles today but nowhere near the size of what it once was when hundreds were employed by the industry. Now, oysters are just one part of what Mumbles is about.'

Tina couldn't help but smirk at Charlie's show of knowledge.

'What do you know about it?' Ivor said, flapping his cardigan. 'You've only just got here.'

'And I see it how it is,' she said, keeping her calm while his was already halfway up the M4. 'It's a beautiful bustling place, alive and kicking. Tradition is great but that doesn't mean it has to exclude the new. Anyway, tourists have been coming here since the nineteenth century, when the Mumbles train started carrying not just coal but passengers. Then they came for the pier, the bandstand concerts, skating rings, coconut shies. The Edwardians loved the amusements! People still come for a day out. Look what's here! Lovely beaches and restaurants, homes and schools. Young families, professionals, foodies, retirees. It's got something for everyone.' Charlie was bouncing – just like her hair, which Tina hadn't seen her wear as loose before: it was half-up half-down so that it hugged her shoulders like an explosion of Verve Cliquot curls. 'What if we can harness this energy we've got and broadcast it and get listeners from Swansea and even further afield?'

'So says the DJ with stage fright.'

Tina gasped at his low blow because that just wasn't the case any more. But Charlie didn't bite and her flush was from passion, not humiliation.

'You want to turn this place into London!' Ivor seethed. 'Make it one of those places where people wear funny beards and eat foreign food.'

'And people get the top jobs on merit, not because of their gender,' Charlie said, which Tina wanted to applaud. Ivor sensed he was on the losing side.

'Typical women, sticking together,' he said, throwing them dirty looks as he stalked off with his cronies.

'Unlike men like you,' Charlie said to his back, finally revealing her irritation.

'Don't worry about him. He's just worried he's going to get the elbow.'

'I have no idea how he's held onto breakfast for so long.'

'Friends with Mervyn, at a guess. Hey, you've done your homework, you're the font of all Mumbles knowledge! You put him in his place.'

'I've been reading up on it, getting my bearings, that's all,' Charlie said.

But that wasn't 'all': this was down to her blossoming confidence, her connection with listeners and her desire to invest in Mumbles rather than just seeing it as a temporary stop as she had in March. And thank God because the station was going to be under Sian's scrutiny – anyone who didn't cut the mustard would be gone. Only the best would remain.

Talking of whom, Charlie said: 'So Sian then? She seems qualified to take on the job. Not that I know her at all really.'

'She does keep her cards close to her chest. But she's a steady pair of hands, very experienced and worldly.'

The crowd was thinning out so Tina and Charlie headed back to the kitchen for an afternoon reviver.

'How are you then, Tina?' Charlie asked as they waited for the kettle to boil.

'Good, thanks.' Tina felt brighter than she had for ages. It was down to Abbie, who was becoming part of her daily life with messages, quick drinks after work and coffees on Sundays. Darcy was revising for her exams and planning her Paris trip. And Gareth hadn't mentioned the phone again in her visits. There were three months to go until he was free – if she could keep a lid on it, then the family would be reunited in August for his annual birthday bash. The question of Darcy seeing where she and Gareth would be living wouldn't come up because she'd make damned sure they met up at his mother's – Pat was in on it too and boy, would she do anything for her son. Including the offer she'd made the other weekend when Tina had gone to visit her after her knee op: she'd sell her house in Cardiff, which was worth a mint now because of rising prices, and they could use the money to buy a home as long as there was an annexe for her. It wasn't ideal but beggars couldn't be choosers. If they could get it sorted by Christmas, when Darcy would return, then she wouldn't ever have seen Tina and Gareth in the one-bed flat. The worry was Pat would insist on staying in Cardiff but Tina needed to be here for work – she was certain Gareth would back her up. Who knew how long it'd take for him to find a job? As the breadwinner, she'd have some influence and she'd started looking up ramshackle countryside cottages which needed doing up. That was as close as she would get to her dream but it was a chance and she'd take it if she could.

'So what do you get up to outside of this place?' Charlie said.

'Oh, this and that, you know.' Tina smiled and fiddled around for her tea bags in the top cupboard because she didn't do personal details.

'What are you up to tonight then?' Charlie had relaxed back on the kitchen worktop and Tina could see she was comfy.

'Just the usual.' Keep it vague, keep it dull.

'Knowing you, dinner somewhere nice, eh?'

Tina hid herself behind the cabinet door and bit her lip. Letting people think she was a lady about town was different to lying. With such a direct question in such an intimate setting, she couldn't do it.

'Not tonight, no. Just me on my tod. I'll do some gardening then have some supper and watch telly.' She shut the door and gave a bright smile to show she was very happy with that.

But Charlie nodded with a sad face. 'It must be hard being married but living apart.'

'I'm used to it now,' Tina said, all jolly.

'Yeah, it does take a while to become normal. I had that at first with my boyfriend, being long-distance. It's like you approach the time together with too much expectation or you pick up where you might have left off last time but they might be somewhere else in their head. You read stuff into things that you might not do if you saw each other more.'

This was excruciating. Tina knew exactly how she felt.

Prison visits were all about pressure. If Charlie carried on like this, Tina would crack like an egg. She busied herself opening and shutting the drawer, looking for a clean spoon, anything to avoid eye contact.

'Hey, don't know if you fancy it but there's a thing at Cheer on the Pier on Bank Holiday Monday. Delme's putting it on as a community thing, the loony!' Tina clocked Charlie's face light up. 'He's after volunteers. Would you like to come with me?'

So relieved her life was out of the spotlight, Tina agreed straight away.

'Brilliant!' Charlie was very enthusiastic. 'Because it's nice to get out, isn't it? I get lonely sometimes, I don't know lots of people yet and ...' Her voice faded out and she gave Tina a funny kind of look, expectant almost.

Oh my. Tina realised what she was getting at. That she thought Tina was lonely too. Oh, Tina yearned to say how Charlie had helped already thanks to her advice on the radio. But if she admitted that she listened to it most nights then Charlie might guess her whole demeanour was a fraud. Thankfully, the kettle was rocking and Tina couldn't make her cup quick enough, not wasting time to find a spoon to take out her teabag and scorching her fingers instead. She needed to distract Charlie, to move the conversation elsewhere.

'Good old Del!' was all she could come up with.

Remarkably, it did the trick. Here was Charlie, as emotionally astute as you could get and on the cusp of registering Tina's act didn't quite add up, but her entire face changed. It relaxed into a big soft-focus smile.

'Oh, yeah, Delme's just brilliant, isn't he? Like how could he just jump from here to the cafe whilst getting fit and doing it all so effortlessly when if that had been me I'd be crying under the duvet?'

'He's just one of those naturals at life,' Tina said. 'Cheers people up.'

'I know! Even Merri! She's not doing depressing foam emojis any more! I can't help going in to see him, he makes me laugh. I'm meant to be cutting back on Cheer on the Pier coffees too, I'm supposed to be saving,' Charlie said, losing her sparkle.

'How come?'

'Well, my boyfriend wants me to move in with him at some point so I thought I'd better get some cash together for a deposit.' She didn't look delighted about it.

'Where? Here? Or London?'

'He's got a job in Exeter. Starts soon.'

'Are you leaving us then?'

'God, no. Not for ages. To be honest, I'm too busy to even think about it seriously really. And I love it here. That's why,' she said with naughty eyes, 'I keep having sneaky posh coffees. And Delme's got me trying new things for lunch! He refuses to do me ham when I ask. The other day I had a turkey and pesto panini and it was yummy. I don't know what's got into me!'

But Tina had an inkling why. It wasn't what had got into her but who had got under her skin. Delme Noble. Tina said nothing though and made her excuses to go back to the office. As much as she loved being part of Sunshine FM, she couldn't afford to be drawn into people's lives because they'd expect the same intimacy from her.

26

'It's all the fun of the fair on Mumbles Pier today so come on down for a celebrity-packed afternoon featuring none other than our presenters! This is Bonnie Tyler and *Holding Out for a Hero* ...'

~

Charlie was bent-double with laughter, unable to breathe it was so comical.

Delme was inside a cerise inflatable ball with just his head, arms and legs poking out. He was grappling with his mate, Rodders, who was in identical get-up, before a crowd of cheering kids in an arena he'd set up on the Cheer on the Pier decking. It was like sumo wrestling but less loincloth and more plastic. The size difference made it all the more hilarious: you'd have expected Delme's height to have given him the advantage. But the opposition being squat and wide meant he just had to deliver a nudge and Delme would windmill as he fought to keep his balance. She was supposed to be umpiring but when Delme was bounced onto his back like an overturned woodlouse with flailing limbs, she had no puff inside her to blow the whistle. Instead she could only wave her hands weakly to declare the winner.

'You're going to have to lube me up to get me out of this,' Rodders said as he pulled Delme to his feet.

'You're sweating like a Tory MP under investigation so it shouldn't be too hard,' Delme answered in a flash, nodding at his bald head shining in the sunshine.

'You should know about investigations.'

'Hilarious. I was cleared. Wanted my freedom. Didn't want to be a slave to the man.'

'And look at you now. Sticking it to them! In a giant blow-up ball.'

The pair snorted through their noses and shook hands to show it was all part of their banter. Charlie could see the affection they had for one another and she felt a pang for Libby and Zoe. Friendships of old with nicknames and in-jokes were so precious – just look at Delme and Rodney, real name Michael, but so called after *Only Fools and Horses* because they'd seen themselves as a double act ever since their schooldays.

'You're like brothers you two,' she said. Rodney quickly looked at Delme, his eyes full of alarm. What had she said? But Delme hadn't heard her, missing her comment because he'd been taking the costume off over his head and she saw Rodney stand down. Blokes were funny in their pairs, never really talking about intimate stuff, preferring to communicate through piss-taking.

Delme beamed as he pushed back his floppy fringe and pulled down his T-shirt which had crept up his stomach. Charlie found herself admiring it – not just because he'd worked so hard to lose a few inches but because she saw a sinew of hip bone, the dip of his belly button and a line of dark hair going … below. Dear God, woman, how inappropriate when there were children around. And to think of him in that way at all. Especially when she was spoken for, she thought a little bit too belatedly.

Over the last few weeks, things with Jonny had calmed down and they'd found a rhythm in their weekend relationship. They didn't talk much in the week due to their schedules. Jonny was preoccupied with working his notice and sorting his move to Exeter while Charlie was immersed in Sunshine FM: having survived Mervyn, she was determined not to get the chop again under Sian's watch. But when they got together, they fell into their secure routine of reading the papers over brunch, afternoon naps and meals out. It was a harmony of sorts because when it was like that, Charlie didn't have to think about Exeter – she was content as things were and there was little room in her headspace for anything else. If Jonny brought it up, she'd remind him her thoughts hadn't changed. He'd swallow it down, most of the time, but should she mention she found London increasingly busy and smelly, he'd see it as her coming round to his way. But it was the sea air she'd craved.

Their first anniversary had been spent camping in the Gower, the area of outstanding natural beauty up the road from Mumbles, where they sunbathed on the glorious beach of Rhossili Bay and beat the tide by walking the mile-long rocky promontory called Worm's Head. But Jonny, it turned out, had a thing about sand and moaned when his sleeping bag turned into the Sahara.

They had a much better celebration in London on the following Saturday night at their usual restaurant at their usual table, sharing their favourite parma ham and mozzarella bruschetta before they'd dared each other to have something different. But Jonny hadn't liked his fish stew so she'd given him half of her chilli pasta, which had been pleasantly kicky. No presents were exchanged – they were saving after all, well he was, she didn't like to tell him it was as much as she could afford to come and see him and go halves on everything – but they had had a bottle of champagne. It was perfectly them, he'd said, nothing too showy, still waters ran deep. The only flashpoint was when he'd tried to pick her brain for his Exeter show but she had exhausted her own supply of ideas for *Evening Mumbles*. She had a brilliant one which she was working on, something big that needed so much planning it was taking up most of her thinking. He'd gone into a sulk and only came out of it when she'd said she was going to go cake-testing with Libby followed by drinks with Zoe. He had a surprise for her instead, afternoon tea on the Thames, he'd had it in the bag for ages, so she'd had to cancel her friends, and then she'd gone home. That was the trouble, the thing she regretted most – losing that day-to-day contact with the girls. Seeing Delme and Rodney playing their game of verbal ping-pong gave her a twinge of sadness.

'Staying around for the kids' dance-off?' Delme asked her. 'I hope DJ Disgo's done a decent playlist. *Agadoo* and *Gangnam Style* rather than his niche off-air favourites like deep trance and goth rave.'

'Definitely!' she laughed, feeling the familiar exuberance inside of her when she was with him. It was fondness, she thought, he inspired it in everyone. 'You've done such a fab job putting this on. I mean look at it!'

She swept her arms wide and took it all in. Happy children, happy parents, lots of them and all buying ice creams and drinks, sandwiches and chips from Cheer on the Pier.

The weekend presenters were covering the late spring bank holiday. Nobody else could've persuaded the DJs on their day off to come in and do their bit. Colin Disgo had put on *Oops Upside Your Head* and was sat on the floor with children of all ages, from toddlers to teens, showing them the routine; Ed Walker's grimacing head was poking through a hole which superimposed him in an old-fashioned striped bathing costume while being wet-sponged; even Ivor Mone was involved with hook-the-duck, after his offer to do Punch and Judy was deemed to be a cover for his misogyny.

'It won't be like this all week. It'll be less interactive on my part from tomorrow, I'll be back inside. Merri's mam is only helping out in the cafe today.'

'But look at what you've done! It's like a Sunshine FM carnival!'

'It helps that Sian Lewis is here though.' He tapped his nose confidentially. 'Everyone's shit scared they're going to lose their jobs.'

Sian had delivered her first speech to the troops last week, reassuring everyone in one breath that things would carry on as normal but in the other warning of a shake-up. It wouldn't happen for a few months. She would be reviewing the programming schedule and handing recommendations over to her successor, whoever that would be. What she was looking for was ideas, new voices, ways to increase the listeners. To get out into the community. There needed to be tie-ins and promos, content for young and old. It was a challenge but she was sure the team had it in them.

'But genius of you to invite her and her kids. And telling everyone she was coming.' It meant he was inundated with offers of help to show they'd taken her comments on board. Charlie had leapt on it herself by handing out Sunshine FM stickers and pens beneath the speaker which broadcast the station.

'I know right.' Delme huffed on his fingernails and shined them on his top.

Just then Joanie ran up excitedly. 'My crush on the bus is here!'

'Oh my God! No way!' Charlie said, looking around for clues. She was about to ask who it was but Joanie had dashed back to a long line of people waiting for her glitter tattoos. She was sharing a stall with Delme's niece Rhian, who was doing face painting.

'Oi, Del Boy,' Rodney said, returning with a teetering triple-scoop chocolate-wafer cone. 'There's a bird over there who keeps giving you the eye. She's lush. Lucky twat.'

Delme didn't even look to check her out. 'Leave it, Rodney. I'm on a spiritual journey at the moment. Women are off the menu.'

Charlie felt herself relax at that when she hadn't even realised she'd tensed up. Rhian, holding hands with Merri's daughter Lily, came up to him and he ruffled her hair.

'I've only got eyes for Rhian. All right nipper, how's it going? Having fun?'

'Yes, Duncle!' the girl said, all freckles and long blonde hair. 'Joanie says my face painting is brilliant!'

'My mam says you can have tea for free here with me!' Lily said, cute as a button. She had a butterfly's wings on either cheek and in character, she flew off, taking Rhian with her.

'Is her dad here? Your brother?' Charlie asked.

Rodney dropped his ice cream and it splatted all over the floor. Delme shifted uncomfortably on his flip-flops and Charlie saw Rodney exchange a look with Delme. There it was again. A change in the atmosphere.

'It's just I haven't got any ... brothers or sisters ...' Charlie said, trying to explain herself but knowing without reason she was digging an even deeper hole. 'If I did I'd be on about them all the time.'

Delme's face kind of collapsed as if he'd been winded with a punch in the guts. Everything seemed to stand still then as she looked into his eyes trying to work out what was going on. But he had pulled down the garage doors, closing her off, staring out to sea, looking lost.

'Oh look, that bird's coming over. Go on, Del Boy.' Rodney suddenly pushed him so Delme almost knocked into Claudia.

'What a stunner,' Rodney murmured.

Of course it would be Claudia, Charlie realised. She was one of those women you could only wonder at when you saw her cheekbones, tumbling black hair and damson pink lips – and Charlie accepted it without a fight. She hadn't remembered Delme going doe-eyed when they'd met in the cafe all those weeks ago but then he took everything in his stride. The way he'd been completely non-plussed when Charlie had cringingly said she fancied him, well, it must happen to him all the time.

'Yep,' Charlie agreed, 'and she designs underwear. Luxury lingerie.'

Rodney made a noise which suggested he found this

even more exciting and she felt a lurch of sickness in her stomach. She could only watch as Delme made Claudia laugh. They looked great together, there was no denying it. Both tall and lean, they could be starring in an advert for Gap. The bubbles of happiness she had been feeling today went flat and when Claudia waved her way, mouthing see you soon, Charlie reprimanded herself for being so mean-spirited. Even though she was thirty-four, Claudia had never been in love, she'd been ditched once they'd got their way, when they found out she wasn't some sex siren in silk undies but a seamstress in cotton M&S pants. She deserved a good man and Delme was that. What had got into Charlie? Why did she even care? She had Jonny, for crying out loud, who was practically begging her to walk down the aisle. So she managed a smile as Delme returned to Rodney's side.

'You jammy bastard,' Rodney said.

'What?' Delme at least had the decency to look embarrassed.

Rodney shook his head and leaned to Charlie. 'This one here, he only dumped his last girlfriend Fflur the Flirt because she wasn't interested in commitment. That's a man's bloody dream that is! Then he pulls Mrs Knickers!'

'Oh, too much, mate. Too much,' Delme said, recoiling, 'and cheers for the potted guide to my love life. For the record, had Fflur said she was ready to settle down, I'd have bitten her arm off.'

'Married with seven kids by now? Under the thumb?' Rodney teased.

'You're the one getting married!' Del's voice had gone squeaky. 'Rod's missus, Sal, is lovely,' he said to Charlie. 'Far too good for him.'

'He's right.' Rodney shrugged. Then he was back on the scent. 'Not forgetting that one the other week who threw herself at you when she was pissed.'

Charlie thought she might throw up.

'That was Fflur,' Delme said urgently, colouring up, making it totally obvious he'd told Rodney about the night he had to escort Charlie home.

'No, it wasn't!' Rodney crowed, folding his arms with satisfaction. 'The other one after Fflur had called you up and stayed over. I remember!'

Oh lord, he *was* fighting them off with a shitty stick. And he supposedly wanted commitment, this guy whose concentration bounced around like a space hopper. It sounded like he was a player. Not that that was any of her business – it was just disappointing when she thought he was better than that.

Charlie couldn't look at Delme. But she couldn't look away or at the floor because she was part of this conversation so she focused on not dying of shame. More than that, she was having to pretend she didn't know what they were talking about because she'd said to Delme she'd had no memory of anything that night bar coming up with her How to Seize the Day list.

Which was exactly why she was in this awful situation. It was like a smack on the forehead. She felt herself zooming backwards away from Delme and Rodney, seeing her frantic figure standing beside them, watching herself come to the cold realisation that she had lost her head.

For this wasn't the real Charlie, telling a man she barely knew that she had the hots for him. It was as if she'd been on a wave and it had crashed down and lost all of its power. She'd been kidding herself and now she was burned out from this little fantasy that she'd created that she could be someone she wasn't. She didn't really know these people. She didn't fit in.

The new sandwiches and the talking to strangers, being curious about where she was living and taking charge at work; coping with her fear and taking part in the moment – they were all a pitiful denial of who she was. Be yourself, ha, what had she been thinking? Seizing the day was alien to her, she had to face it. And laughably, the one thing she hadn't done, telling people she loved them, spoke volumes. What was it that was stopping her from giving her heart one hundred per cent to Jonny? He was her one proper chance of having it all – why was she on this self-destruct mission?

Accepting her uncrazy safe self would be the only way she would get through this. She needed to be brutally honest with herself; strip herself back to bones. But at least then she could start to be true to herself. She had to forget seizing the day. Do her job as best as she could. Live as she'd intended when she'd been on that train coming here for the first time. Resist the rushes of elation to avoid the dips of despair ...

With that, Charlie returned to her body and then backed off, muttering that she had to go and she'd catch them later, allowing herself one look at Delme, whose concerned eyes followed her retreat until she could bear it no more and turned her back on him.

27

Delme shut his eyes as he knelt in prayer, collecting himself before he faced his demons.

His fingernails were full of sand, there was salt on his lips and a boom of his pulse in his ears. This was what it had all come down to – this was his chance to redeem himself.

Never had he taken anything so seriously in his life. Steady, measured and focused, he'd done the hours in the classroom. No longer the clown as he'd been at school, he fought and beat the urge to crack a joke. Not wanting to forget a thing, he'd been meticulous right down to not just having one pen but an emergency stash. The info was all up there in his head – beach theory, life support and first aid, he knew which flag meant what, how to monitor sea conditions and CPR resuscitation. He'd proved himself fit enough with timed swims in the pool, treading water, surface dives deep into the water, lifting and two hundred metre beach runs in well under forty seconds. Now he was taking on the toughest test of all, putting it into practice in a practical assessment in board rescue. He was 'saving' Andrea today but little did she know he'd be trying to save himself in the process too. He was the oldest by a mile, studying for the National

Vocational Beach Lifeguard Qualification – the rest were students paying for forty hours of tuition so they could earn through the summer. As expected, they got a lot of mileage out of *Baywatch* references. For Delme, however, this was far more serious. It meant he would be able to live with himself and for himself. To right the wrong of seeing his brother flail in the water and being frozen and unable to do anything about it. To get himself a job. To give his spontaneous side an outlet. To seize the day by giving his best, not doing his worst so he could do it all again tomorrow. For Sam, for his big bro.

He'd lived and breathed this course: it had taken up so much of his body and brain. It had been physically and mentally intense, the most draining thing he'd done, even topping the binges of holiday repping when he'd turn up still drunk after no sleep. But the wholesome food he was eating and lack of alcohol had given him a clear mind; the shifts at Cheer on the Pier and his runs and swims in between meant he only briefly felt his thighs aching, his toes smarting and his biceps throbbing before he fell into deep, restful sleep. Yep, Rodney was right when he'd said he'd turned into one of those clean-living wankers. But it was only polite when you were snogging a plastic doll during a kiss of life that you didn't stink of last night's beer and kebab.

Yet he still wondered about Charlie, which for some reason was quite often. Rodney hadn't mentioned her specifically by name when his big mouth struck the day they'd wrestled on the pier; thankfully Delme hadn't said whose indiscretion it was, but Rodney may as well have.

Charlie had blushed so hard and he knew that she hadn't forgotten that night. She'd tried to, though, that much was clear. He understood why: she'd see it as an embarrassing case not of beer goggles but of beer-talking bollocks. She didn't fancy him – it'd been a momentary rush of tongue moving before brain. But he'd found it endearing. Unlike his ex Fflur's soulless shag tactics. They were oceans apart, those two. He hadn't seen Charlie since then, in two and a half weeks, and he'd found he missed her popping by for a chat. Quite often he'd catch himself flicking his eyes to the door when a blonde walked by.

Claudia had though and they'd arranged a drink soon. How had that happened? He'd been bamboozled into it by Rodney, on the back foot after Charlie brought up brothers and sisters, struggling to think clearly, blurting out if Claudia fancied going out sometime. She was gorgeous and friendly but he didn't have a thing for her like that and he doubted she did for him. Still, he was in it now and it was no biggie.

Delme had a swig of water: he was warming up in more ways than one, simulating the paddle out to sea on his rescue board while the sun beat down on his wet suit. June had very kindly delivered some decent weather. It was warm today on Caswell Bay Beach but with an onshore wind which had turned the sea choppy, just like that day in Majorca … he had to put that out of his mind or he'd be done in. Adrenalin had to be his friend, not his enemy. He couldn't fuck this up.

The instructor signalled it was his turn so Andrea led the way, running into the sea, diving down and emerging further out and swimming deeper to be the unconscious casualty. He waded in and felt the force and cold of the water which collided with his calves and thighs, threatening his balance, and he had to work hard to steady the board as he alighted. Hunching down on his knees, he propelled himself forwards, *come on, come on, come on*, cutting through the sea, making sure he was shoreside until he reached Andrea's bobbing body where she lay on her back, her chin tilted up with her mouth and nose just above water. He slid his legs off the board while twisting himself so he could lay across it widthways, getting a face of the freezing swell, placed an arm under her nearest one, using his palm and fingers to support her jaw, the other hand reaching under her to cradle her. He checked for breathing and pretended to give five rescue breaths, mouth to nose, before rolling the board back while pulling her over it until her armpits rested on the side. The buoyancy helped but she was playing the role well so he had a job to shift the deadweight of her legs round so she was lying on her front on the board. Then he went behind her and paddled for his life back to the sand. It took only a few minutes but he'd felt every second acutely as if it was for real. But it wasn't over: he shouted 'Call 999' and went through the motions of CPR, rolled her into the recovery position and covered her up to keep her warm. He felt the hand of the instructor on his back and the scene around him came back into focus and he became aware of his own body again. Still on all fours, he felt the sting in his eyes, the water pooling off him, his panting as his pulse started to drop.

Andrea jumped up to applaud Delme, clasped her hands together and simpered, 'You saved me! My hero!'

The others on the course laughed until the instructor raised his finger, making Delme drop his head in fear. Had he been too slow? Got the position of Andrea wrong on the board? Forgotten something? Perfectionism wasn't a part of who he was – he'd been slapdash all his life. Yet this job demanded getting it absolutely right because lives were at stake. He squeezed his eyes shut and waited for the verdict.

'Textbook, guys. You've just seen a textbook rescue. Good job, Delme.'

'Awesome, Hoff!' someone said.

'Hoff!' Andrea cried, 'Yes! He's the David Hasselhoff of Mumbles!'

Applause and chanting broke out and Delme got up, stunned and blinking, finally letting himself grin like a loon. He'd done it. He had begun the process of forgiving himself for being unable to help when Sam needed him: it was as if a weight was lifting from his heart and leaving a space he could fill with happiness. And he was one step closer to being strong enough to see his brother.

28

Tina's phone buzzed with a text from Abbie – she couldn't make it, she was really sorry to let her down at the last minute but something had come up.

Sighing with disappointment, she politely messaged back that she hoped everything was OK, before self-consciousness tumbled in. She must look a fool with flashing red, blue, yellow and green finger lights on her knuckles. She switched each of them off and leaned back against the railings at the entrance of the pier, glad to be fading into the dusk. But then insecurity snaked inside of her as she wondered if she'd put too much into her new friendship. Abbie's excuse was vague, suggesting she didn't owe Tina a specific reason for blowing her out. Maybe she simply didn't fancy it but then why couldn't she have just said she was tired? Perhaps though it was a holding back as if they'd made friends too quickly, not really knowing each other. Yet sharing her company was easy and straightforward, it had been from the instant they'd met. But Tina now asked herself if she had given off needy signs; she didn't think she had, but you never knew how you came across.

Although come to think of it, Abbie had come up with this crackpot idea to join the Midsummer Night Ride, not Tina. She'd agreed to come because it sounded fun: it'd fill an evening and it would be a healthier option than a glass of plonk in front of the telly.

It was a puzzle but, hey, she wouldn't try to analyse it any more because how could you ever get inside someone else's head? She turned to look out to the horizon, drinking in the sight of still, petrol sea which met the purple sky. Still warm even though it was just after 9 p.m., she felt the softest of breezes on her forearms. Five minutes here then she'd head home.

'Tina!'

Charlie appeared at her side looking worn out and wan. She took in great big lungfuls of the balmy air as if to revive herself. 'It's so nice out here, still so light, especially when you've been in a studio for the last two hours. What you up to?'

'Well, I was going to take part in this thing called the Night Ride—'

'What?' she gasped, leaning in, momentarily animated. 'The cyclists who ride the prom with fairy lights in their spokes and on their handlebars?'

'Yes and tonight it's a special one because it's the longest day. The summer solstice.'

'Aren't you doing it?' Charlie looked doleful again.

'I was going to.' She switched on her finger lights and waggled them about which seemed to cheer her up a bit. 'But then my friend cancelled and I felt a bit ... you know ... like a saddo.'

'Oh, OK.' Charlie didn't move a muscle though or announce she was off home. Standing there with a downcast face, it was obvious she wanted to have a go – or that she didn't want to be alone. Tina felt weak in the face of her sadness: here Charlie was helping everyone she could on air and there was no one to help her. She knew she shouldn't, that she'd regret it if she got closer to her, but she couldn't help herself.

'Unless you fancy it?' Tina said.

'Really?' Charlie said, her eyes shining in the twilight. When was the last time someone had been kind to her?

'If you want. I don't mind either way but if you want some company?'

'I'd love to!' she cried, making Tina glad she'd offered. 'What about a bike though? Where's yours? And a helmet? And lights?'

'It's a tenner including all the hire of the gear and there's refreshments too. But if we're going to do it, we need to get there sharpish, the bikes leave at half past.'

'Let's go then!'

So they dashed up the prom, craning their necks looking for a crowd lit up like a fairground. Now they'd decided to do it, Tina realised she did want to have a go, not least because of Charlie's infectious enthusiasm. 'I haven't ridden a bike in years! This is going to be brilliant! Oh, is that it?'

It couldn't be anything else! A load of people in all sorts of neon regalia including glow bracelets, hi-vis jackets and flashing glasses were gathered around a pop-up tent decked out in fairy lights. Some were already on their bikes with strings of LED lights woven through their spokes, leaving trails in the air as they wheeled around.

Tina and Charlie swapped looks of glee as they joined the queue. Once they'd signed up, bought some glow necklaces and rings and were kitted out, they heard a whistle – and they were off! It was like a party on the move, a multi-coloured conga of cycles making its way down the promenade.

'Woohoo!' Charlie sang as they picked up speed and moved en masse like a magical murmuration. And as darkness fell, Tina soon forgot her sore saddle, feeling the joy too, laughing along as passers-by stood and watched, waving with beaming smiles.

'This is amazing!' Charlie said across the handlebars as the sky finally let go of the day.

'It's crazy!' Tina sang. 'Ridiculous! But so much fun! Although I do feel bit underdressed compared to all these fairy wings and tutus!'

'Who are the Night Riders, I wonder?'

'A bunch of cyclists who want to ride at night, I guess! No interest in being the next Bradley Wiggins by the looks of them – there's not much Lycra in sight.'

'How funny! I love it!' Charlie giggled, her cheeks dancing from the illuminations.

After a while, the route double-backed on itself and as they turned around, they both took a pause. 'Oh I needed this, Tina! Just to do something ... I dunno, pure, for the joy of doing it for no other reason or agenda, without worrying. Just to be.'

Tina understood that: it was a kind of mindfulness. 'It's like being absorbed in the actual moment, isn't it?' she said as flocks of riders swooped at and away from them, laughing as some performed wheelies and others cycled hands-free jiving with their arms.

'That's exactly what it is!' Charlie said as if she'd been struck by inspiration. 'Because I've been so bogged down in ... stuff, lately.'

Tina waited, unsure whether to encourage her to

continue. If she became her confidante, then she would be drawn into a friendship and she'd vowed she'd keep work people at a safe emotional distance. Charlie took the choice away from her.

'I've been wondering what I'm doing here, where I should go,' she said, sinking down on her seat, her eyelashes low. 'I thought I'd conquered something when I came here, that I'd found a new and improved me but ... Oh, listen to me, I don't want to burden you.'

'Please, it's fine.' Because Tina realised she was indebted to Charlie. 'You really have come out of your shell, Charlie. You should be proud of yourself.'

'Maybe at work, yes. But when it comes to my private life ... it's kind of backfired. I saw my boyfriend Jonny at the weekend. I went to London and I thought I'd be glad to be myself again with him but it all just felt flat. Uncomfortable. Like I'd outgrown it or changed shape. I felt like I couldn't breathe in London. Here, it feels like home. But how can it when I could lose my job in the review? I've improved at work but have I improved enough? And what if it's "last in first out"? I don't know ... Maybe I should just cut my losses and go with Jonny?' She took a huge sigh. 'Something's just not right and I don't know what. And I'm supposed to be an agony aunt!'

'It sounds to me like uncertainty ...'

'About Jonny?' Charlie hurtled in as if that was at the forefront of her mind. Her eyes dropped and she bit her lip. It was obviously about him – perhaps she just hadn't accepted it. On cue, Charlie began an argument with herself. 'But we're Jonny and Charlie, we're peas in a pod, meant to be.'

253

'But do you love him?' Tina asked, getting to the crux of it.

'I don't know,' Charlie said in a small voice. 'I really care about him, we've got our own jokes and routines and I thought I was getting to the point of telling him I loved him. I'm beginning to think it's cold feet – that I'm frightened of making a commitment to him because it involves another life change. And yet I want nothing more than to be sorted, to have a family of my own one day. It's making me tetchy – I'm finding fault with him when he's no different to how he was. Maybe if we lived together it'd all fit into place?'

Tina was overcome with sympathy. Charlie was clearly at a point in her life where she felt she needed to take control. Moving from home was disorientating – Tina got that, so to have to do it all again would be overwhelming. She wondered if Charlie was putting too much pressure on herself and it cancelled out whatever her gut feeling was. There was also the possibility that Jonny wasn't the right person for her. Tina wouldn't say it though, it wasn't up to her to force the issue.

'There's no rush, you know, you're still young.'

'Did you feel any doubts? With your husband?'

Charlie's question fired up an intensity in Tina's heart. She couldn't keep it in.

'Honestly?' She owed her this. 'No. I just knew. I'm not saying every relationship is like that or should be like that, it's just how it was and is for me. Everyone's different. That's not to say we haven't had our rough times …' Tina stopped herself elaborating '… but when they've hit, there's a kind of solidarity that we tackle them together. Because ultimately while things can be

254

difficult, it's always felt easy to be with him.'

'Easy ... comfy, hmm.' Charlie turned the words around in her mouth then looked to the sea which had become the sky. A few neon stragglers coming towards them were ringing their bells and Tina put a foot back on the pedals and grabbed the handlebars. 'I should talk to him about it,' Charlie said.

'You should.'

'Thanks so much Tina, for listening,' Charlie said, with grateful eyes.

Something maternal rose up in Tina and it poured out before she could stop herself. 'Well, thank you so much for your advice. On the radio. I listen in a lot. What you said about loneliness to your first ever caller. You said about not dwelling on it, using your time to do what you enjoy and I've done that and I feel so much better.'

Charlie's eyes widened. 'Do you know, I had wondered if it was you that called in to the show. I had this feeling and—'

'Me? No! It was that lady ... what was her name?'

'Gail. No, I know it wasn't you! I did for a bit but then realised we had a mug sent to her to an address in Townhill.'

'Exactly!' Tina snorted. 'What would I be doing in Townhill?' she said, feeling bad about this show of snobbery. 'Although it's a good place to think up there.'

'Funnily enough, there was a man outside Sunshine FM the other day, asking for a Tina from Townhill.'

Tina's laughter caught in her throat.

'I told him I didn't know of anyone obviously,' Charlie said. 'But he didn't look a nutter or anything. Tall, grey hair, smartish.'

Panic gripped Tina. Him again. He must've seen her coming to work. He could've blown her cover. Who the hell was he? He was getting closer and she was scared. She couldn't engage with it or Charlie would sense something was up. Tina knew you had to fake it to make it so she gave a breezy 'How weird!' before she pushed off hard and pedalled fast until she was out of breath, overtaking the slow coaches, putting as much distance as she could between her and the fear.

The cover of night, the chaos at the finish of handing over bikes and helmets, and thirst, helped her contain herself. Charlie's chit-chat, which flowed freely now she'd got stuff off her chest, filled the journey on the bus to the city centre and it was only after a hug and they'd gone their separate ways that Tina could rub her face and exhale, acknowledge her concern about that man and reason with herself that if it wasn't a coincidence then it might be to do with Gareth. Perhaps, she thought as she got on the number twelve to Townhill, he was the contact Gareth had on the outside. And she could always tell him if he did approach her that she was absolutely not interested in getting involved with anything that could jeopardise her husband's freedom. Gareth would sort it out, he could tell him to back off.

Calmer and closer to home, Tina took out her phone to see if Abbie had replied but she decided before she'd even looked that it was fine if she hadn't. What would be would be, she thought, instantly lifted as she saw she had a voicemail from Darcy. She would've liked to talk to her tonight, but it was too late to call back and she was weary from the ride. She'd just listen then ring her back tomorrow.

'*Hi, Mum,*' Darcy said, her innocent voice full of youth and hope, minus the worries of the world. My God, Tina had been right to protect her. '*Just wondering if you wanted to meet up? I haven't seen you for ages, not since January. My fault, obvs, too much going on here. Anyway my last exam is coming up but after that I'll be around.*'

Tina had never been one to hassle her daughter to visit or turn up out of duty – she loved the fact Darcy had her freedom. And without it, Tina would never have been able to maintain Darcy's unblemished adoration of her father. So when Darcy was available, Tina would jump at it. So yes, she could take a few days off work, get on a MegaBus and go to see her in Leeds. She didn't want her coming here, not to see her home rivalling Darcy's student digs with its damp walls and condensation.

'*Hey, can you believe Dad's entered the twenty-first century!*'

The excitement drained from Tina just as she reached her stop. She stumbled out into the estate.

'*He's just messaged me from Dubai with his new mobile! Said he thought he should move with the times! He signed it off with lol, though, which he probably thinks means lots of love. Anyway, got to go, revision calls. Love you, bye!*'

A phone? Where the hell had he got that from? Who had brought it in for him? And why was he risking his good behaviour? Her blood was icy – then it began to boil as she raged at his stupidity, marching hard towards her door. Of course he wanted to contact his daughter, it was only natural, but by doing so he was jeopardising everything. His release, Darcy's future and everything Tina had worked so bloody hard to hide. If Abbie hadn't cancelled tonight she would've turned to her to let off some steam. But then they had agreed to steer clear of their misery. She needed to work this out for herself. Suddenly it hit her. Gareth had done this because she was failing to keep him happy. For if he was to put himself and the kids and their family in such peril then it showed he was desperate and prepared to take a gamble. There was only one way to deal with it, she realised as she put her key in the lock: she had to make sure he felt more loved than ever before.

29

'It's Monday, it's miserable, so let's hear your top moans on *Mumbles Matters* with me, Ed Walker. Here's Annie Lennox with *Here Comes the Rain Again ...*'

⌇

Charlie's head rested on Jonny's shoulder as the train rocked back and forth on its way to London. She breathed in his scent, woody from the posh B&B toiletries after their shower together, and sighed with happiness.

He looked down at her tenderly and kissed her with a smile. It felt like she was in an old-fashioned film – he'd upgraded them and there was still an air of glamour in the hush and leather seats of first class.

'Almost there,' he said. When he caught her disappointment he tried to reassure her, 'I told you, not to worry. Everything will work out.'

To the heart-breaking screech of the brakes signalling their separation, he picked up her bag, took her by the hand to the door and they embraced passionately like movie stars, making the most of their last moments together. Jonny murmured 'I love you' in her ear and she felt it rising inside of her, on the tip of her tongue and she was about to say it when the wind was taken out of her by another passenger's elbow poking her in the ribs and a suitcase bashing her ankles. What a missed opportunity! The emotion was stuck in her throat and she was being bustled off at Bristol for her connection to Swansea, leaving him to carry on to Paddington. Don't get upset about it, she thought, because it was a positive that she was ready to say it. Floating in a bubble of joy, she found her platform, boarded the train and took a seat, certain she had solved her inner battle.

It had been the loveliest weekend in a long time. Exeter had been wonderful with its sunny and vibrant riverside setting, foodie restaurants and grand Roman history. The icing on the cake though had been talking to Jonny about her worries. So much so, when she was helping him to look for a flat to rent on Saturday afternoon, she'd begun to imagine what it would be like being here. With him.

She'd cried her eyes out as soon as she'd arrived, unable to bottle it up any longer. In a quiet corner of a cafe, she had poured out her uncertainty about her job, where she was going in life and yes, even him. But Jonny hadn't been upset or angry, just soothing and sweet. He'd expected it because she was unsettled and naturally that meant she would question everything. His calm was hypnotising, potent too, because she saw he was right. Swansea had always been a stepping stone for her, it was never meant to be forever, and if she did lose her job, then incredibly, he had one lined up for her here. His soon-to-be boss was enthusiastic about him building his own production team – she was guaranteed a position and wouldn't it be fantastic to marry his talent and her ideas? Charlie was so flattered he thought that much of her professionally and it wasn't just a safety net but a tempting and very real prospect. It was a win-win, he'd said. Like the good old days when they'd worked together! If she got the axe, if Sunshine FM thought so little of her, then she could come straight to Exeter. If she didn't, then she should see it as a goal achieved and she could stay there and save for a while until … the words had hung in the air and remarkably she had grabbed them and clutched them tight because what had she been thinking, that there was something more, something better out there for her than him? Was she prepared to throw it all away for a fleeting and, frankly, unhinged, crisis? The drunken Delme declaration thing had been a silly symptom of her wobble, that was all.

As they'd walked the streets of Exeter yesterday, Jonny had been so supportive about the all-consuming idea she had for Sunshine FM, agreeing it fit Sian Lewis's expectations of fun, community, strengthening the brand and attracting younger listeners while retaining its base. He could see it working in Exeter too, with a bit of tweaking …

The city was pretty amazing – like a London village minus the dirty bits and so much more polished than Swansea. It was a middle-ground kind of place. Pretty much perfect for her – Charlie Bold hadn't been made to live near the edge let alone on it. And as Jonny had pointed out, London was no longer an option with Isabella back there. If Charlie ever set eyes on her again … The woman who had come between them was returning to Orbital as a senior producer – the cheek of her, brazenly revisiting the scene of her shame. Charlie could've sworn Jonny told her she'd been kicked out for what she'd done. But like he said, it had been an emotional time, and perhaps that's what she'd wanted to hear. Luckily, Jonny would be gone by July when she was due to start.

Back in rainy Swansea, Charlie dumped her stuff and then went to work, full of resolve. She needed to nail it – whether it kept her her job or not, this was about pride and pluck.

At her desk she sat down and took out the ham sandwich, orange juice and Walkers ready salted crisps she'd bought on the train earlier. It was seven minutes past one and she wasn't alarmed by the echo of her days at Orbital FM – Charlie saw it as a sign that she had done her flipping out and the scales had tipped back into equilibrium. She was in control. Routine was not the enemy; neither was going with the flow. With order in her backbone, she could be the person she needed to be on her radio show: it was a satisfying conclusion, smoothing off the sharp corners, feeling whole and content. Munching away, she realised she'd never felt she'd known herself better.

Joanie walked in, shaking her floppy fringe which was so wet the violet had turned purple.

'Bloody hell, you look like a dog with two dicks. Good weekend?' she said, throwing herself onto her seat with an oomph.

'Brill,' Charlie said, unable to hide her smug grin. 'You?'

'Quiet. Boring. Opposite of yours by the looks of it.'

'Well, I've got some excitement lined up for you.'

'Yeah? A hot date, non-stop sex and undying love? I doubt it knowing my luck.'

'Oh, mate,' Charlie said, sidetracked by Joanie's miserable face. 'What about your crush on the bus?'

'That's not happening. I did think we'd made a connection, you know, eyes meeting across a crowded pier but turns out I was wrong.'

'How do you know?'

'I just do. God, I'm one of those who'll be single forever, I know it.' Joanie swigged from her takeaway coffee and kept swigging, indicating the personal chat was over. 'Oh, good news by the way … Specs Appeal and Mr Bookworm are going on their third date tomorrow.'

'What? That's amazing!'

'Yep, she emailed.'

'Let's get her on tonight!'

'Already asked but she wants to wait until they're a proper item, which is fair enough. But she wanted us to know.'

'Ah! That's nice.'

'Shame though because we need something fresh, something good, something to show we're rising to the challenge of Sian's review. Unlike Ed Walker …' Joanie rolled her eyes and they both winced as he asked listeners to give him their top Monday moans.

'That's what I was talking about earlier! When I said I had something exciting for you!' Charlie cried. 'So, Sian wants us to connect with the listeners, get acquainted with them, grow the audience, reach out to the under-sixties.'

'Yes.' Joanie sat up.

'She liked the carnival Delme put on, didn't she?'

'Yes.' She took the biro from her mouth.

'So how about we do it on a grander scale. Sunshine FM's party on the pier. Call it …' She clicked her fingers for inspiration.

'The Party on the Pier?' Joanie suggested.

'Ha, yes! We could hold it on … say, August bank holiday weekend, we could do a special broadcast on the night, invite Specs Appeal and Mr Bookworm as our guests of honour, if,' she said, crossing two sets of fingers, 'they're still an item. We could have local bands, get sponsorship, maybe a parade …'

'It'd need a hell of a lot to stage.' Joanie looked sceptical all of a sudden. 'It'd be expensive for starters. A health and safety nightmare.'

'Yes, but I reckon advertising will want to get on board. People need to be seen by Sian to be doing something upbeat.'

Joanie thought about it. 'You're right. It's worth a try. Perhaps we could get Del to help?'

'No,' Charlie said quickly and firmly. There was no need for him to take part. 'He doesn't work for us any more.' And Charlie needed to steer clear of him because he was a distraction. A diversion that had sent her down the wrong road. She'd got lost because of him and she didn't want another U-turn. From now on she was going forwards. And both Roy and Sian agreed too when they took the idea to them for the nod later. It was ambitious but that's what the station needed, the boss said. Chuffed to bits, Charlie and Joanie bounced out of Sian's office.

'Who'd have thought we'd be where we are—' Joanie said to Charlie, on the way to the studio.

'After the start I had here, eh? I know.'

'It's amazing what confidence can do.'

This was the moment when Charlie could've told Joanie all about what had happened to her that night in front of the microphone when her big break broke

264

her. Their friendship was deep enough now for Charlie to go into detail but for the first time in a long time, she felt no need to pick at the scar. It all seemed so long ago. She'd tortured herself enough. It was done and dealt with. Life had turned a corner: her head was brimming with suggestions for the party, she was loved up and her heart was filled with excitement for what was to come – starting with tonight's show. And when her first caller rang in to Bring Me Sunshine, it was as if the universe was listening in.

'How do I know if he's The One, Charlie?' asked Dawn from Uplands.

Charlie raised her eyebrows at Joanie through the dividing window at the sixty-four million-dollar question. Where did you start with such a biggie?

'Tell me about him, how you met, give us some background.'

'We used to work together, we were friends first but there was always a spark between us. So we started dating and that was two years ago! We're recently engaged, which is brilliant – he's so amazing in every way. But ever since we decided to get married we've been arguing a lot. And now he seems distant. I can't work out what's changed. I thought he and I were destined to be but now I'm frightened we might not be.'

'Oh, don't be frightened! I'm sure there's an explanation. What sort of things are you arguing about?'

'Marriage things, really. You know, the venue, the menu ... I suppose it could be the stress?'

'Yes, it may be, but it should be a joyful time too. Is it that you want different things?'

'No, we want the same. I know it's unusual but he's

into the planning as much I am. I think it's me, getting on his nerves.'

'In what way?'

'I want whatever he wants. He gets annoyed when I say I want him to choose.'

Ah, so now Charlie was getting somewhere. 'So tell me, do you believe in The One? Love at first sight? Soul-mates?'

'Oh yes, absolutely.'

'And do you do everything together?'

'Everything.'

'So if he gets cross or frustrated with you, do you have anywhere to go?'

'Well ... our bedroom, if that counts?'

'Not out with friends or to the gym or for a walk or family or ...'

'No! Why would I? I need to fix things if we fall out. He's my world!'

'How's your self-esteem?' she asked gently.

'What? Erm, OK. I s'pose. I mean ... not great. I need to lose a few stone for the wedding, although he says I'm perfect the way I am ... And I'm not the most interesting person you'd come across. Basically, I'm so lucky to have him.'

Bingo. Charlie got it.

'Dawn, you know what, I believe in The One, most of the time, like I believe in the power of love and hope. But I also think you can analyse too much what things mean – look too far for deeper meanings, catastrophise when we encounter discord. I'm hearing lots of stuff about him but not enough about you and who you are. I truly think we need to have a relationship with ourselves and friends and interests as well as relationships with lovers, otherwise that becomes your be-all and end-all. We aren't who we are because of our partners. Self-confidence is more important than having someone else's love and ours shouldn't depend on that. Do you see what I mean?'

Charlie heard the penny rolling and drop.

'I do ... yes. I suppose I do read a lot into how he is with me and it affects my mood and makes me needy. Like I worry about us but my friends, they say we're the best couple they know. And that makes me frightened that I'll lose it and I'm not good enough to have it.'

'There's no such thing as perfect. If you think something is, it puts an enormous amount of pressure on it. Maybe instead, you need to look outside for a bit? Broaden your horizons? Do something for you as well as him? Maybe he'd find that exciting? What special skills or interests do you have?'

'Well ... I speak a bit of Italian. He does like it when I order our food in Pizza Express with the proper accent.'

'Well, why not go to a class?'

'I could, I s'pose ... he says I should choose the honeymoon but I wanted to do it together. But I could get my Italian back up to scratch and we could go to Rome ...'

'There you go! The Eternal City!'

'For the eternal couple! *Grazie mille*! And *ciao*!'

Charlie couldn't help but laugh. Dawn was a hopelessly devoted romantic; it ran right through her like a stick of rock. And to be honest, there were worse things to be in life.

30

'So what do you reckon?' Delme said, pulling out a brown faux-leather chair for Claudia across the chequered beige and white-tiled floor.

She sat down and took it all in: from the formica tables and hat stands to the bulbous glass salt and pepper pots and vintage rounded sterling-silver sugar bowls.

'It's nineteen fifties diner heaven!' she gushed, amid the clatter of customers who packed the place out. 'I love it! There's so much character.'

'Me too! I can't believe you've never been here.' The family-run Kardomah Cafe was legendary in Swansea. 'The decor is the original stuff from when it opened in nineteen fifty-seven. And check out the staff in lace pinafores.'

'It's like stepping back in time!' she said, her incredible cat-like eyes wide.

'Get this, Dylan Thomas used to come to the cafe with his bohemian mates when it was in Castle Street, before it got bombed in the Second World War.'

'By the Luftwaffe in the Three Nights Blitz. Swansea was razed to the ground.'

'And apparently Alec and Laura—'

'From *Brief Encounter*! One of the all-time great films!'

'Yes! One of the places they met on set was a Kardomah Cafe.'

'Oh, I love that era. You should come and see my shop, I've loads of forties-style designs.'

'Yeah, I'm not sure a bloke can get away with popping into your place on the grounds of "historical interest".'

Claudia laughed and swept her black hair over her shoulder. 'What's the food like here then?'

'Cheap, hot and lots of it! Loads of classics, roasts and burgers, omelettes and jacket potatoes. Knickerbocker glories too if you're partial.'

It was a bit of a busman's holiday coming into a cafe on his day off but it'd been hard enough to find a time they could both make. So after extensive negotiations, Delme and Claudia had agreed to an early lunch on the first Tuesday in July.

'I'm going to have the liver and bacon, I think,' Delme said, rubbing his hands at the prospect as the waitress appeared.

'If you're going retro,' Claudia smiled, 'I'll have the gammon and pineapple. And a pot of tea for two?'

'Nice one. Builder's or Earl Grey?'

'Builder's. Every. Time.'

'Now you're talking.'

Claudia was pretty much the perfect woman. Brilliant company, Delme thought, and they bounced off one another easily. They had loads in common, it turned out. In the time it took for their food to come, he'd found out she'd travelled widely too and they shared a love of *Game of Thrones*. They'd both been to uni in Leicester, that's where she did a lingerie design degree, but home had called, like it had for him. Rugby had been part of her story too: the wives of players had been her first customers and he picked up on how important family was to her – she laid her success at her mother's feet, for teaching her how to sew and more crucially, how being from a skint single-parent family shouldn't hold her back. Claudia was beautiful, there was no denying it. Funny, interesting, creative and deep.

The trouble was there was no chemistry between them whatsoever. As far as the old fireworks went, it was like a very damp November the fifth. No whizz, no pop and definitely no banging. Could he snog her, he wondered, trying hard to imagine it? She gave him a wink of appreciation over her plate which made him guffaw. The answer was one hundred per cent no: it'd be like copping off with a sister. His sleeping downstairs bits were in agreement. And by her unselfconscious behaviour, it was apparent she felt the same. She wasn't watching herself at all, not that she should, and he wasn't either. It was just that when people had romantic aspirations they acted differently, perhaps flirting or acting demure, or polite in a bloke's case. But there was none of that going on at all.

So how did he feel about it? On one hand, he'd love to have fancied her – he'd see it as moving forward from this strange Charlie fixation he was having. Even better if Claudia felt the same and they fell head over heels, bra and corset in love. It'd be easy then, she was local after all, and they could tie the knot, him in his wetsuit, her in her swishy clothes. It'd even get Fflur off his back, who was still sniffing around. But on the other, that was life. He'd just have to hope he'd meet someone at some point so he could have the whole wife and kids thing. And there was relief too, knowing he didn't have to prove himself worthy to Claudia: he could just be Del. The idiot who had dropped peas and gravy on his groin. Delme felt a bubble coming up and he tried to swallow it back down but then when it refused to die, he forgot where he was and let out a small burp. Claudia looked up, quick as a flash. Delme froze and wondered if he'd got it all wrong. He started flapping apologies about manners and how sorry he was, feeling himself begin to sweat at his piggery. But then she let one rip herself. And they honked with laughter.

'I think we both know where we stand,' she said, raising her eyebrows. 'Because, well, I'm pretty sure, you know, that you feel the same ... and I don't mean to hurt your feelings ...'

Del's heart swelled. 'But can we be just friends, yes? Yes! Hell, yes!' he cried before he'd felt he'd gone a little over the top, verging on insulting. 'Not that you're not attractive or anything but ...'

She shrugged. 'Same goes for you. I'm having a great time. But not "like that". You can't force it, can you? It's either there or it isn't. Right?'

'Right.'

'Come on then,' she said, conspiratorially, 'what's your relationship history now that we know we're not judging?'

'Complicated.'

'Ditto.'

'Women want me when they're drunk but not when they're sober because they either think that's all I'm good for or that's all I'm capable of. You?'

'The ones I end up with are dicks but the ones I want

271

are so out of my league they're practically playing for a side on the planet Venus. Still, there's plenty more fish in the sea, right?'

Hmm. Actually, fish stocks were dwindling. He decided not to pee on her bonfire.

'You said when we first met in Cheer on the Pier you'd never been in love.'

'Correct. I get close to someone but it always lacks that extra bit of oomph to tip me over. Something always seems to be missing. What about you?'

'Yeah, I've been in what you'd call love probably once or twice but there's no one I've had a proper connection with. Not with someone I've gone out with, I mean. If it's possible to be able to think you've met someone who you could love if you were given the chance? Which makes me sound like a stalker.'

'No, I get you. Definitely. Completely.' She stared off into space, which made him feel not quite so lunatic for having the hots for a woman who had disappeared off the face of the earth.

'Isn't it weird,' Claudia said, coming back to him with a shiver, 'we can have all the same interests and things and not have any spark.'

'Yeah, I thought that.'

'But then they do say opposites attract.'

'Is that true though? Because I've thought about it,' a lot of late since his course had finished and he was waiting to hear if he'd passed while wiping tables, 'and I can't see how you could navigate stuff if you approach things differently, act differently, think differently.'

But then Fflur had been his supposed equal – that's what everyone had said: the original wild child had met his match. And it had been awesome at first and he'd loved her madly but then it had hurt him when she didn't want to settle down. Oh well. He sighed, he couldn't sit here all day, mooning over matters of the heart, he should get the bill, really. Claudia had said she had to be in the shop by 1 p.m. He checked his watch. She saw him do it and nodded that it was time to go. Once they'd paid, they stepped outside and Del felt his stomach sagging.

'Somehow I've got to do a run later but I think I need to calf first,' he said, rubbing his liver and bacon baby.

'I could do with a nap myself. But I have to go and measure up a bride-to-be for a babydoll negligee.'

'Want to swap?' he joked. 'Not really. I couldn't, not in my condition.'

She touched his arm and smiled. 'Right, well, that was lush. I really enjoyed myself.'

'Yeah! Me too!' he said, putting his hand on hers. It *had* been lush. Really nice to chat, not what he'd expected, but better.

'Cool! Yay! Go us!' she said.

It was the most natural end to a non-date and they gave each other a hug, pleased to have made friends. Then they kissed one another extravagantly on either sides of their cheeks. Delme was mid-laugh when he saw her. And time turned elastic.

Charlie was next to him, on the bus at the traffic lights, looking right at him, and he felt his eyes drawing her in and his heart leaping and his hand rising to wave but as the seconds dragged, her smile had turned downwards. Quickly now, she was turning away. Then he saw her plait – she was wearing her lovely mad hair in a plait, did that mean she was back in her unhappy shell? – and another face. It was Joanie and she was gawping too. Why was Charlie so down on him? Oh, shit . . . He knew what it looked like. A goodbye of kisses and hugs with a stunning woman. Had Charlie read something into the entirely platonic goodbye?

'That's my bus!' Claudia shouted, flushing, pointing at the very one Charlie and Joanie were aboard, and she darted up the road to the next stop.

Oh, no. His legs itched to run behind, to jump on and tell Charlie he wasn't involved with Claudia. But not even his peak fitness could out-pace the thoughts Charlie was bound to be having. She was one of the most articulate, fascinating, emotionally intriguing people he'd ever met and right now, she'd think he was a player, a bullshitter, someone who slagged off his ex and sneered at pissed girls. It was so fucking unfair, he thought, feeling his fists clench. But then reality took over and his hands went limp. Because all he wanted was something straightforward and simple: no drama.

He had to do something. The bus was about to leave, so he shouted to Claudia, 'Tell Charlie there's nothing going on between us!'

But his words were drowned out by the rev of the bus as it pulled off and into the traffic.

31

Tina covered her face with her hands and let out a strangled cry.

Alone on a broken bench at the top of Townhill, this was the only place she dared to let it all out.

Home was sacred, where she tried to lock the door on her woes. Where she would tidy up and listen to the radio, water her vegetables, watch telly and read as if she was content. It didn't always work but she had to at least attempt to find peace within her four walls.

Up here though she could release her tension and fear and visualise the warm evening wind carrying them far away. Tears helped, too, as did the shoulder shudders, as if she was opening the pores of her soul in a detox of her mind. For today's visit to Swansea Prison had left her befuddled with conflicting emotions.

There was concern, there was always concern, for how Gareth was coping inside: the apprehension that she'd find him at rock bottom. The joy at seeing him smile like his old self thanks to her campaign of letters and cards, sent since she'd found out he had a mobile, to remind him he only had weeks left in a cell. The terrible lurch when he'd confessed he had organised the phone drop via the prison officer and a former inmate who'd used some of that stash of money Gareth had, that was clean, he'd insisted, and it had all happened without Tina's hands getting dirty. Even so, guilt lapped at her skin like flames: she had failed him when it came to the mobile even though he'd apologised for even asking her. That's why he never messaged her with it – he didn't want to implicate her. He loved her that much. But what did that say when he had no qualms about contacting Darcy? That, he said, was weakness, their daughter knew nothing of his crime. If he was found out, they wouldn't be involved. She had known there and then if she had been in his position, she would've been tempted to do exactly the same. And his body language and chat showed how much of a boost it had given him. Yet knowing he was breaking the law again, this time with her knowledge, crippled her. It was wrong. No matter how many times Gareth said the screws sometimes turned a blind eye to things because they understood the hell of prisoners being apart from their loved ones. She wished she knew nothing about it because it was like sitting on a time bomb: every time her phone rang or there was a knock on the door she feared it'd be the solicitor informing her he'd been caught. All privileges taken away from him, an extended sentence, more despair. He had pleaded with her to reclaim her wedding ring – use the money, he could get someone to post it through her letterbox. But no, she had been adamant. She had to do the right thing on behalf of them both, for Darcy.

A wave of sorrow washed over her again and she raised her head, this time defiant, determined that she could endure it. She was so high up here she could imagine the curve in the horizon which was aglow with the last strip of light. The stars were starting to twinkle in the inky sky. She was just one person on an earth of billions, she told herself, her problems were tiny compared to the suffering of those living with starvation, poverty and war. This was how she had to think to get to the finishing line, when she would wait for Gareth to emerge blinking into the sunlight when he was a free man. She could see him now, back in the clothes with which he'd gone into the prison, his winter cashmere coat over his arm for it would be too warm for it in August. She had it all planned. She would take up tailored shorts and deck shoes, a polo shirt and sunglasses. They would go to Morgans, their favourite place, where he could change in the gents before he had champagne and the finest meal of his life. It'd cost her but she didn't care. He would have paid his debt to society, he'd have every right to his second chance. She would take him home, bathe him with oils and wash his hair, massage his back and let him sleep for a while until she could wait no longer and caress him awake to make love. That day would be the start of the rest of their lives.

A smile almost touched her lips as she tasted him in the twilight. They would never be apart again.

A movement to her left, another person taking a seat at the far end of the bench, brought her to. Tomorrow, think of tomorrow. Another day closer to being reunited with him. She would go to work, see Abbie at the prisoners' wives group then go for a drink with her. They'd arranged it this week, promising to see one another, definitely. The morning after the Night Ride, Abbie had messaged to explain her absence: she'd had to see her mother who'd had a fall. Tina had berated herself for her paranoia but had learned from it, taking it slower with her now although

Abbie seemed just as keen to be friends, texting silly things such as celebrity haircuts and prison jokes.

Tina had been the one to cancel the next time they'd meant to meet, as she'd been invited to Sian Lewis's for supper. It had been a lovely evening, giving her an insight into who the new boss really was. Sian had wanted to pick Tina's brains about the talent but barely a moment was spent discussing that: they'd gone on a tour of her idyllic courtyard semi in Limeslade, which was a mile from Mumbles, and then set foot in the garden, where Tina discovered that Sian was just as green-fingered as she was. Over wine, they'd got lost in compost and courgettes until her husband had called them in for salmon and new potatoes, leaving them to it because he was putting their children to bed. *That would be me and Gareth*, she had thought then and thought now, under the same roof very soon ...

'Excuse me,' a voice said across the darkness. It was a man and he sounded safe and sane if it was possible to sense that in two words. But his presence hadn't disturbed her either, she realised, and he had obviously not wanted to alarm her because he'd sat as far away as he could without falling off the wooden seat. She wasn't frightened – this was a residential area at the height of summer. It was a humid night so back doors and front yards were open and people were walking their dogs; if she needed help she just had to shout.

She turned to see who was talking to her and could make out the silhouette of someone sort of familiar. A street light shone behind him so she had to put her hand up to her eyes to see better. When she realised who it was, adrenalin coursed her body, her hairs shooting up, her pulse hammering as she jumped up and backed off to the edge of the pavement. It was the man from the bus, the one who had been trying to look into her garden.

'What do you want?' she cried, hearing her own panic, looking around, working out her escape route, registering the elderly couple across the road who she could call to if she needed to. Her hands were on her heaving chest in an automatic act of self-defence and her legs were primed to run. 'Who the hell are you?'

The man instantly held up his palms and moved his body into the bench. 'I'm sorry, I mean no harm. I'm not here to hurt you.' He sounded genuine but there was no way she'd fall for that.

'Why are you following me?' she shot back, her muscles turning to jelly, making her tremble. 'You've got to stop.'

He stayed seated and kept his hands aloft, thinking she would see it as a sign of safety, but she wasn't going to accept that.

'What kind of a man appears out of nowhere in the night when a woman's on her own?' she spat, although she felt braver now that he hadn't approached her. 'What kind of a man follows a woman? Follows her on the bus? To her place of work?'

'Please ... I need to talk to you,' he said, pleading. 'I'm so sorry to scare you.'

'What is it? Because if you do anything I'm calling the police.' She got out her phone without breaking eye contact and held it high so he could see she would do it.

'I didn't know how to tell you. I've been trying to do it but—' He sounded strained and weary but still she couldn't trust him.

'Now!' she shouted.

'My wife, she's having an affair with your husband.' He dropped his hands as if he was collapsing and then his head bent down. 'I'm so sorry.'

'What?' Her lungs were sucking for air and her vision was bobbing up and down in shock. The bastard was playing mind games, trying to distract her from the threat of whatever he really wanted. Her feet began to dance as she prepared to run ... but then he had a defeated air about him. He always had, too, the times she'd seen him shadowing her. And he was rubbing his forehead and then looking at her again. She stopped dead when the moon lit up a tear rolling down his cheek.

'It's been going on for a couple of years. I didn't know whether to say anything but I wanted you to know the truth about him.'

No. No, no, no. It was impossible. Gareth would never do that to her. He had made a huge mistake, yes, but women weren't his weakness. Money was.

'You've got it wrong,' she said, firmly. 'He's not like that.'

He shook his head. As if he knew her husband better! How dare he!

'You're lying! You don't even know who I am.'

He swallowed hard and with apology in his eyes, he said, 'You're Tina Edwards. Your husband is Gareth Edwards. He's in Swansea Prison for fraud.'

'No,' she gasped, stepping away from him, stepping away from his despicable fabrication. 'You're the fraud. You are. Not my Gareth. Why would you say such a wicked, wicked thing? And how did you find me?'

'I went to the court case. I was in the public gallery. I had to see what he had that I hadn't.'

'You're obsessed!'

'If you ever want to talk, here's my number,' he said, producing a card, gingerly rising, holding it out to her, making her take it. Up close, she saw his blue eyes, the silver of his hair, the same upright gait. He didn't look like a pervert or a weirdo or someone out to get her. And if he was, why would he give her his details? He withdrew quickly out of her personal space. Only then did she glance down at the white cardboard rectangle which was shaking between her fingers. It was too dark to read who he was. She didn't want to know either: to see him as a real person would give credit to his outrageous claim. Gareth was her one true love and she was his: there was simply no way he'd go behind her back like that. And when did he ever have the chance? It didn't add up. She refused to believe it. He was a troublemaker. No, he was troubled. She had enough happening in her head to take his problems on board. Tina straightened her spine and lifted her chin, ready to tell him he could take his issues elsewhere. But by the time she'd taken a breath, she saw only the droop of his shoulders as he disappeared into the darkness.

32

'Thermometers at the ready, gang! Have you got a case of Saturday Night Fever? You're not alone, you're in great company ... here come the Bee Gees ...'

～

Charlie switched off her radio and flopped onto her bed. She did not need to be reminded that she was staying in by herself at the peak of the weekend.

Then she caught herself: don't blame it on Sunshine FM, don't blame it on the moonlight, don't even blame it on the boogie. Charlie Bold, it's your fault. For she'd turned down Claudia's invitation to go on a straight-from-work pub crawl on the Mumbles Mile. Joanie had gone, having hit it off with Claudia when they'd been introduced on the bus the day Charlie had seen The Big Clinch. Tina had gone off sick Thursday and Friday so she wouldn't be there. But Merri and DJ Disgo would. Plus Delme. That's why she hadn't. She really didn't want to see him and her together. 'Just brunch,' Claudia had called it when she'd sat herself down in front of her and Joanie on the number 2A but there'd been a twinkle in her eye. She'd sang his praises and Joanie had joined in as if they were the Delme Noble Fan Club ...

Charlie took a deep breath and stared up to her bedroom ceiling. How mean-spirited she was being. How twisted. She'd turned into a green-eyed monster overnight – it was pathetic. She had to get a grip. She was in love. With Jonny, obviously. Not Delme. She had her own happy ever after – why was she pissed off he would be getting his with her lovely friend?

See? This was what he did to her. He made her confused. Think of Jonny, she ordered herself, think of his kind and caring nature, how they'd overcome not one obstacle but two and found themselves an even deeper bond. If only she could see him … But he was visiting his parents in Lincoln; it'd be the last time before he moved to Exeter. He'd asked her to go but it was a long way for a night and his mother was a bit of a manipulative nightmare, always taking him out of whatever room he was in with Charlie to have him to herself. How his dad had put up with it all these years, she didn't know. Well, Doreen was going to have to get used to Charlie being on the scene. Ha! Just think, if Doreen could see her now, sat in her faithful tartan fleece pyjamas, she'd make unsubtle hints about women letting themselves go. But what was the point in getting dressed? She hadn't had a shower either – today had been so lazy, she'd spent most of it up here watching *Friends*, restarting the whole thing on Netflix. Gen had popped her head in but Charlie didn't want to talk, especially not about Claudia.

Her eyes wandered the room. She hadn't put much effort into making it her own – didn't that say everything about how she felt about being here? There were a few framed photos she'd set out, of Mum and Dad on camels in Tunisia, Libby and Charlie at Glastonbury,

Zoe and Charlie at a Christmas do, another of the three of them very drunk on a girls' holiday in Turkey and one of Charlie meeting the DJ Sara Cox at uni. From happy, carefree times when nothing was at stake. Some candles, including the one from Jonny, which was a bit overpowering if she was being honest. Notebooks of lists, nail varnishes, pots of moisturiser. And the cross stitch Gen had given her which had 'Nevertheless She Persisted' sewn in yellow in a cool 1970s bubble font. She picked it up and admired the intricate handwork which had gone into it and smiled. Yes, she had persisted in spite of it all ...

Bang, bang, bang. She ignored the door. Gen would get it – everyone Charlie knew here was out on the town. But the knocking came again. Gen had gone out, obviously. Dear God, Charlie was the only person in the entire world staying in on a Saturday night in her pyjamas and, as she got up and caught a waft of her armpits, stinking. She traipsed out onto the hallway and her eyes hurt from the sudden brightness. She'd been in a fug for hours, her curtains closed, thinking it was perpetual night and yet late-evening July sunshine was streaming through the windows. Down the stairs, she reached the door, pulling its handle, and felt it open with force as Delme toppled in. What the hell was he doing here?

'Charlie! Wahey!' He was pissed. Really pissed. He was a big, smiling buffoon whose face had relaxed so much one of his eyes was wandering lazily until it found her and focused and then twinkled. Him. Why did it have to be him? Why did he have to see her at her worst? She felt herself stiffen and then flush.

'Claudia's not here,' she said, trying to keep him from

coming in any further, protecting herself behind the door.

'I've just been with Claude.' Claude. He'd already shortened her name to a term of endearment. 'Why ...' he said, a finger pointing supposedly at her but aiming drunkenly over her shoulder, 'weren't you there? What are you doing staying ... woah, your hair!'

Charlie put a hand to her head and realised it was loose and free, corkscrewing out and up, past the breast pocket of her pyjama top, as wide as her shoulders and tumbling anarchically down her back.

'It's ... cor! I didn't know you had so much! It's ... it's ...'

'Big.' Quickly, she took the band from her wrist and began to gather it into a ponytail.

'No!' he cried, 'it's amazing! Let it all hang out, man.'

She ignored him – men who admired it were always the ones who'd let her down – and he swept past her, shoulder-barging the wall as he went into the lounge.

He collapsed into Gen's modern swivelling white arm-chair with a huge 'pffft' and stuck his flip-flopped feet on her low circular 1960s wooden coffee table. He made the room look tiny, filling it with elbows and knees, and she was terrified he would trash the lounge with one movement.

'Have you just come from the pub?' she said, hovering, trying to make it clear he couldn't stay. His presence was threatening the antique stand-up lamp with its shade of delicate teardrop crystals, the hanging plant pots, plates and paintings on the wall and trinkets on the shelves.

'Yep.' He threw his arms wide and she tensed as his fingertips wafted dangerously close to a vintage vase.

'"Screw you, I'm hilarious!"' he said, hooting, '"Fuck this shit!" Ha ha! "Piss off, I'm reading!"' He was quoting Gen's gallery of filthy cross stitch. Delme was finding it very funny indeed.

'How much have you had?' It was only seven thirty. Two hours of drinking less the time it took to get here.

'That's the really weird thing. Not much at all. A few pints.' He shook his head in sheer wonder. 'I've lost my drinking superpowers, I reckon. No tolerance any more.'

'Anyway, why are you here? Why aren't you with … the others? Claudia?' She could ask him so directly – he was that far gone he wouldn't get the undertone.

'To see you!' He pushed back the brown curtains which he'd grown. They'd also joined the Curly Hair Liberation Front. He gave her a dribbly grin – and she defrosted just like that. She was so fond of him, she couldn't deny it. He was such a sweetheart and so contagiously lively. Even when he had a wet patch on his T-shirt. Almost immediately, though, his mouth crumpled and he started to sob.

'What's wrong?' Charlie got to her knees beside him, her chest hurting at his agony. 'Has something happened with Claudia? Isn't it working out?' She hated herself momentarily for asking him when he was so vulnerable. But she had to know.

He paused his misery. 'What? No! We're not together! No spark. We're just mates.' Then he pressed play again.

Relief flooded through Charlie. As well as a bit of guilt. She didn't dwell on it – he was so upset she was really worried now.

'I just needed to see you.' Oh, how her soul soared hearing that. 'To talk.'

'Come on,' she murmured, rubbing his hand. He kind of caved into her then, leaning his forehead into the crook of her neck. His breath and eyelashes were hot and wet against her bare skin in an act so intimate it gave her a fluttery tummy. There was so much there: wanting to make his hurt stop, to soothe him, and an unmistakable emotion at his touch that wasn't as one-dimensional as desire. 'Let it all out.'

When he'd finished crying and had a coffee in his hand, he seemed more sober and began to explain, staring into space as if she wasn't there beside him on the sofa, where she'd moved him to safety.

'We were on the Mumbles Mile. I thought I'd be OK. I used to go, there were twenty pubs in the old days, now just a handful … It'd be different, I thought, but it all came back to me when there was a stag do. I heard one of them calling it the Rumble in the Mumbles and it was all wrong, that's not what we called it …'

We? Who was he referring to? But she didn't want to interrupt his flow.

'… and I felt panicky so I went to the bogs and on the way there was a photo of him in his Wales kit …'

His voice wavered and she was mystified who he was talking about.

'… and it got to me, really bad, and I didn't know what to do so I had a couple of chasers at the other end of the bar where the others didn't see me and I was happy then for a bit, that's when I wanted to see you. So I left, got a cab, not even thinking about if it was a good idea … which I now know wasn't … story of my life. I try to rein it all in and this time I thought I'd done it, stepped away from the edge but it's like it comes from nowhere and I act on it. Like an impulse.'

Which is exactly how he made her feel. There was a storm inside of her – the conflict was back, the scales were out of balance and she was fighting, fighting so hard to steady herself.

'I know, Delme, I know that feeling.'

'You?' he said, turning to her, 'When were you ever mad and crazy?'

He said it with disbelief and Charlie sensed a sliver of mockery. From nowhere she felt very defensive.

'Well, had you ever asked me anything about me, about why I turned up here, why I really turned up here, then you'd know.'

His bloodshot eyes went wide. 'I did, I have …'

'Yeah, well.' But now was not the time to go through her shit. 'Anyway, tell me, who is "we"? Who was in the Wales kit?'

Delme's chin dimpled and like a reflex she put out her palm and held it against his soft face. 'This is what it's all about. My brother. Sam. Me and him, best buddies, my hero, really. He had an accident, I couldn't save him …'

Then he told her everything: his rugby-star brother, their happy-go-lucky lives, his former reckless existence as a holiday rep, the terrible injuries Sam sustained, how he hadn't seen him in months because he couldn't accept what he'd become. Leaving health and safety to be true to himself, how being a lifeguard would be the perfect way to channel his spontaneous side and bring him resolution. That was part of it but he knew now he had to see Sam to move forward. That was what he had to do.

Oh, he was so good, she thought, with not a nasty bone in his body. 'I'll help you,' she said, rubbing his back, 'I'll come with you if you like, when you're ready?'

'Would you?' he asked, completely exposing his vulnerability. 'What if I lose it?'

'What if you don't?' she said, softly, feeling the energy between them blooming and the gap closing, feeling so drawn to him. 'He still has promise and possibilities, you know. Everyone does. To love, to give joy. To be your big brother. Just because he's not how he was ... Look at what he can do, not at what he can't. And what you can do for him. He has as much right to be involved in life as you do. Cutting him out does neither him nor you any good.'

'I've always wondered what colour your eyes were,' he said, out of nowhere, sliding his arm along the back of the chair.

She could hardly breathe. There was a strange look to him – a look which shouldn't be between friends. She had to check he meant it. 'Did you listen to anything I just said?'

'Yes. You're right.' He'd seemed to come to and said it quickly. Then he went backwards again. 'They're like autumn leaves, with bits of hot chocolate thrown in.'

He gave her a little embarrassed smile and it was adorable. And sexy. Intense. Dry-mouth and breathy intense. Being this close to him felt like they were in a magnetic field. He was taking in her lips and blinking slowly, sensually, and it was the most overwhelming sensation she had ever had. She couldn't help it, her fingertips met his, setting off shooting stars in her body, and—

'I fancy you too,' he said quietly, carrying on the

conversation she'd started all those months ago. If a naked flame came anywhere near her, she'd combust. It was madness and yet it felt absolutely completely as if it was meant to be ...

Her phone went in her pocket. She saw her trembling fingers pull it from her pyjama bottoms as heat filled her cheeks. It was Jonny. She'd forgotten all about him. Her desire became guilt and then confusion.

'Hi!' she said, gasping, her heart pounding. 'You OK?'

'I wish you'd come with me ... why did you abandon me?' he said in a jokey voice. 'I just wanted to tell you ... I love you.' She realised she'd accidentally put him on speakerphone and her stomach rolled.

Delme jutted out his jaw and groaned before clamping a hand over his mouth. Had Jonny heard?

'Have you got someone with you? I thought you said you were staying in by yourself.' He sounded suspicious and spiky, which was fair enough. If she denied Delme was there, that would look like she had something to hide. Which, frankly, she did, seeing as it had been as if he'd never existed two seconds ago. But Delme would think she was a liar. Admitting he was beside her though meant Jonny might be upset. Her head was mashed potato. Just tell him the physical truth.

'Delme, he's about to go.'

'What the hell is that twat doing there? Is that why you didn't come with me this weekend?'

The whip of his tongue lashed her, the force of his anger floored her. Delme was open-mouthed with outrage, his palms to the ceiling, mouthing 'twat' at her.

'Are you trying to get me back for me bringing up Isabella last week? God, you're pathetic.'

That wasn't it at all! She was hurt he'd think she'd do that.

'Jonny! Calm down.' She turned her back on Delme, unable to look him in the eye. Because she'd been about to say 'we're just friends' but she knew now they were anything but. She stabbed at the phone to turn off the speaker but by the time she had, Jonny had ended the call. She tried to ring him back, once, twice, three times, but it went to voicemail each time.

Charlie was in shock: at Jonny's rage, at herself for an almost infidelity and for Delme's confession. Bewildered too by the feelings she had, now so clearly, for Delme – when she was Jonny's girlfriend. Guilt for what could have happened and indeed what had happened when she had considered herself ready to tell Jonny she loved him, not to mention taking advantage of Delme when he was drunk and emotional. Shame too for considering herself being 'caught' which was bad enough because it suggested intent but knowing too she would've kept going. She hadn't been unfaithful with her body but she had in her mind. She was a terrible, terrible person. Jonny had been entitled to lose his temper. Just as he had done back when it had all gone wrong the first time around. Suddenly her phone buzzed. He'd be apologising, she just knew it. But it was only a text from Zoe. 'You'll never guess what I just heard …' She threw her phone onto the sofa.

'Is he normally like that to you?' Delme asked incredulously.

'No!' she said, horrified, turning round to see disgust on his face. Then her cloak of denial shrank off her shoulders. 'Once before … Oh God, this is all my fault.'

'Charlie, it really isn't. It's mine, I shouldn't have

come. I'm sorry.' Delme came at her with his arms stretched towards her and there it was again, that pull. 'Talk to me, tell me.'

The door slammed.

'Hiya!' Gen was home. 'I'm back from Stitch and Bitch.' Her cross stitch club. 'You OK?' she shouted from the hall. 'I'm putting the kettle on. Fancy tea? Or a wee dram?'

Charlie looked at Delme, wondering. The seconds ticked by as she asked herself what to do. He should go. She was in a state. If Gen saw him here there'd be questions which Charlie had no idea how to answer. She needed to process this tangled storm of emotion first. But should she do it alone or with Delme? Wouldn't that complicate things even more? She called out to Gen in the kitchen.

'I'm going to turn in,' Charlie said, nodding at Delme to go up the stairs. Because she had to start somewhere and while there was so much else going on, her gut told her that somewhere started with him.

33

Charlie shut her door and backed herself against it.

The fingers Del had touched were hidden beneath crossed arms, the eyes he'd seen, of autumn leaves and hot chocolate, were searching the room, looking everywhere but at him. She was still beautiful though. Cute as hell in her pyjamas with her hair like sunburst.

Please talk to me, he willed her from the edge of the bed, where he was perched uncomfortably. Maybe he should get up? Being sat there, she might see it as too intimate, too informal. He hadn't meant that, it had just been a place to wait. But if he stood, she might run. Instead, he shifted so his elbows were on his knees to make himself smaller. So she'd know he was going to coerce her into some confession. He was just as astonished by the chain of events as her. Coming here out of the blue, crying about Sam, telling her he fancied her, hearing Jonny speak to her as if she was dirt. But he didn't regret any of it. Although it wasn't the smartest move to groan so Jonny realised Charlie had company. He could blame the booze for that, or frustration. It was neither. It was a protest. Because Jonny was such a weasel, making out he had been abandoned, joke or no joke. If he hadn't done it though, he'd never have heard him lose it. OK, had he seen him and Charlie just before that, he'd probably have a case for being upset. But he hadn't and the vicious way he'd gone for Charlie was over the top. For the red mist to come on so quickly, to fire off insults and accusations that fast, had to mean this guy had issues. If it was rare that he acted like that, Charlie would've fought back. But she'd kind of tried to contain it as if she knew where it would end up. And then when she thought it was all her fault ... it was textbook controlling boyfriend behaviour. Was that why, he suddenly thought, Charlie had been so down on herself when she got here? It made sense. And she'd have told Del if they hadn't been interrupted. He certainly would've told her what he thought. The words had come to him like that downstairs: why are you with that idiot when you could be with me?

But up here, the air had changed. It had crackled with their electricity before. Now it was rumbling away as if thunder was coming. Just break the tension, he told himself.

'Charlie ...' he said, not even knowing what he was going to say. But it did the trick and broke the storm because she stepped forward and threw out her arms.

'Whenever I'm with you, things happen,' she cried. His eyes widened at the force of her tone – Gen would hear if she wasn't careful. She realised it too, stopping to compose herself. 'You make me do stupid things,' she said, her eyebrows raised to compensate for the quieter way she was talking. 'I was doing fine until I met you. You have no idea what chaos you've caused.'

'Me? I have no idea?' Having to keep it down meant he was waggling his eyebrows at her too. 'If it wasn't for you, for your bravery and your guts, I wouldn't have quit

294

my job or signed up to be a lifeguard or tried to sort things out with my brother or turned up here.'

She crossed her arms again, all stroppy. He sighed. 'Look, you know what I'm trying to say ... You ... me ...'

Charlie stared up at the ceiling. He didn't know what had come over him – actually he did. It was because he adored her. He wanted her and he couldn't bear this.

'It's right,' he said, reaching to her as she puffed out and dropped her shoulders.

Her eyes were on him again and they were kind. Oh God, had he got it wrong? Was this 'being let down gently'? The fist in a silk glove? He looked down and took a heaving breath of disappointment and anger at himself for thinking she'd been serious when she'd told him she fancied him and then backed off and then got carried away downstairs and ... the bed gave as she sat beside him ... here it came.

'But ... you're in a mess, I'm in a mess, this is all ... too much. It isn't that it isn't right between us, it's just that it's wrong because I'm with Jonny.'

There it was. It was as simple as that. That he'd read the attraction between them right was no compensation. It was a case of never the twain shall meet. Unless Jonny, his hopeful heart suggested, got the boot.

'And even if I wasn't with Johnny, then we're not finished with ourselves, are we – you and me?'

She was spot-on: they had come so far on their journeys that they couldn't afford the distraction. He fell backwards onto the bed with a bounce. This was so unfair. He'd met his soulmate, no, his soulmush, and they couldn't be together. She lay back to join him and reached for his hand. Del clutched it to his heart. Safer now, the line had been drawn, they shifted their heads to face one another.

'So let me clarify,' he said, staring at her as if he was staring into her soul. 'It isn't that it isn't wrong whatsoever, just not right at the moment?'

Charlie giggled and their vibrations made their way to him across the duvet and he caught them too. Somehow, it wasn't too crushing. The physical longing of earlier was there but it wasn't the whole picture. It was in there but alongside something deeper, right down to his bones. For the first time in his life, he felt he could be patient. And cautious. Wow, it was a revelation. And she was responsible for that. He didn't want to reduce this to anything so basic, but he could eat her.

'Could I kiss your nose?' he asked instead. It was a small nose, a dainty one, unlike his, which had a nobble on the bone from when Sam had hit him with a cricket bat.

'All right,' she said, rolling her eyes but smiling, making his tummy flip. Gently, gently, he didn't want to accidentally chin her, he dropped a peck on the tip and then withdrew, closing his eyes.

'I prefer that to being kissed on my forehead.'

'Yeah, that's super creepy, sort of paternal. Weird.'

'Jonny does that to me a lot.' Her voice had gone whispery but flat.

His eyes clapped open. 'Yeah, well, he would.' Del couldn't keep the sneer out of his voice. 'Sorry. I shouldn't have said that.'

Feeling a dick-for-brains, he shifted up the bed, to distance himself from it, fluffed up a pillow and settled down.

'Make yourself at home,' she said in a withering tone, sitting up. 'Shall I get you some slippers?'

'A dippy egg for me in the morning, please. Soft-boiled, five minutes, plus soldiers.'

She took a cushion and threw it at him. He scanned her room, taking in the bare walls and shelves save for a few fascinating female things such as creams and jars, pictures and notepads.

'I haven't done much to it, have I?'

'It's the opposite of mine. It's a tip, my place.'

'A reflection of who we are, maybe?'

'Well, yes ... and no. Because actually I don't think we are as straightforward as that.' He was fishing, trying to get her to open up. Specifically about Jonny.

'Possibly. Who we think we are might not be what we are?'

'I see myself as this loser but I've changed a bit. Same as you, I reckon. Not the loser bit. What I mean is, you came here thinking you were one thing but then it turns out you're not. Like you're better than you thought you were.'

'Jonny. You want to know about Jonny, don't you?'

He was that transparent. 'Well, more about you really.'

She shuffled up and sat cross-legged opposite him before picking at her pyjamas. Maybe it was painful for her? He had to go easy.

'Red sauce or brown sauce?'

'Your mind!' she tutted, looking up. 'It just leaps about like a frog!'

'Red or brown?' he said, frowning. 'Come on, answer.'

'Well, it's not as simple as that. Red with bacon and chips but brown with sausages and cheese on toast. You?'

297

'Mayo.' He poked his tongue out and Charlie laughed.

'That's us in a nutshell, isn't it? I'm all "These are the rules, this is what I like" and you're off at a tangent.'

'I don't think that's true, sorry.'

'I tried to live a little and look what happened.'

'What? You're doing brill!'

'Only because I realised it didn't suit me.'

'But you're not the same you, are you, the same as the person who turned up here terrified?'

'I suppose not.'

'And I was doing the extreme polar opposites thing, boring by day, overdoing it by night. And I've stopped doing that. I feel better.'

'Women can't help but throw themselves at you, can they though?' She gave him a hard stare. She was testing him.

'Hang on a minute! I wanted Fflur to commit to me! I didn't take advantage of you either! I'm not a booty call!'

'Aren't you?'

'No! I've been there, done that.'

'So maybe you're not as spontaneous as you think you are?'

'And maybe you're not as rigid as you think you are?'

'Maybe then we're more in the middle than we thought?'

'Maybe we could try to meet in the middle? If we ever got the chance?'

She gave him a sad smile and if she'd plucked his heart strings then they'd hear the tune of Myfanwy, the ultimate in unrequited love.

'You and me, we're so different though.'

'Being the same is a bit of a deceit really, I think. At

first Fflur, my ex, we were so right for each other. You know, mad for it and into exactly the same stuff. Partying, mainly. But then I fell for her, big time, and asked her about marriage and kids and she wasn't interested. It's all surface, that stuff. It's about values and what matters to you. If they bring sunshine into your heart. Lightness to your feet. But a whole heavy bit of grounding too. And you love them for being who they are, no matter what they are.' It hadn't meant to come out as a speech but he had to get across his version of love – so she could see if it matched hers. So she could see if she had that with Jonny. Because this was what it was all about, he was sure of it.

Charlie had a big swallow then made a kind of little whimper. She started waving her hand around her eyes and covered her mouth. He said nothing. He'd obviously said too much. Sitting forward, he said, 'I think it's about time I—'

'Jonny's only ever properly lost it with me once before tonight.' Charlie spoke over him as if she'd told herself it was now or never. 'And that was two years ago, when we split up the first time we got together. This is our second go.'

He slowly sat back and she stopped talking to her hands and started talking to him.

'So, there I was at Orbital, one of the promising stars of the future,' she gave a wry smile. 'Not to be arrogant, but every appraisal I'd had said I was one to watch, I had a great future ahead of me, all that crap. Then Jonny joined as a trainee, we hit it off straight away, he was different then too, I guess. Full of energy and drive and we worked together in production on the late night show.

We did some amazing stuff, well, amazing for the time and amazing considering it was a cheesy radio station for white van man. I was the ideas person, Jonny was the fixer and we'd arrange interviews with celebs on the M25. It was called Stars in their Cars, so it could be footballers or soap stars or whatever. There was the Service Station World Cup where drivers who'd never met each other came together to play football under the same flag, the Orbital Olympics – same thing, different horse, all kinds of silly fun stuff.' Charlie was reliving it all, chattering now, on a roll.

'Anyway, Jonny and I had this bounce, we got together almost straight away, we adored each other. I never thought it wasn't right – everything had gone my way all the time. God, I was so naive. Everything dropped into my lap. My parents had just me, they gave me everything, whatever I wanted or needed. I had so much love. I was so, so lucky. I sailed through school and uni, top marks, a first-class degree, really popular, loads of friends. I was the first one to go into higher education in my family and they treated me like a god. It's so embarrassing to say all of that. Because really I was just horribly sheltered.'

He shook his head. She couldn't help it if she'd excelled at everything – some people found life easy. Besides, he sensed the crash was coming.

'So I was offered a go at presenting the show when the DJ was on holiday. Late night, so if something went wrong it wasn't a big deal. I thought nothing of it, knowing I could do it because I'd never been not able to do anything. That list, the one I told you about, I was crossing them off, the man, tick, the career, tick. I went into the studio, I had the barest of scripts because I was good at thinking on my feet. I was going to be this fearless female – the first woman to DJ for the station. I was going to change the world. I had all the spiel – all tits and wit. And then …' She sank down into herself. 'Just before I went on air, I'd popped to the loo. I was in a cubicle when I heard a voice I knew, Isabella, my producer—'

'The one Jonny mentioned earlier?'

'Yes. She was on the phone, saying something about Jonny, saying he'd finished with me as she'd said he had to if anything was going to happen. They'd had a drunken snog the night before. That morning though, we'd told each other we loved one another for the first time. In bed.'

Delme groaned.

'I just sat there, listening to it, feeling so sick and in a stupor, but then I came to. I had to get back to the studio, I was cutting it fine as it was. When she saw me, I can see her now, Isabella's face kind of collapsed, she was one of those women with statement eyebrows and it was like they were saying sorry but not to me, sorry she'd been caught. I ran back to the studio, so did she, she was trying to explain but I wouldn't listen, I didn't have time. But when it came to the show, I couldn't speak. I broke down. It was dreadful. Silence apart from me crying. If only I'd been silent - the backup player would've picked it up and no one would've heard me sobbing. I was ushered out and put in a cab and then the next thing, on the drive home, I heard Jonny doing the show. The senior producer had called him in and he did the rest of the week, passed with flying colours. So at least he did well out of it.'

'It sounds like he did! He set you up!'

'No, no, he didn't. My DJ days were over because of her. Isabella had practically forced herself on Jonny. She'd done all the chasing.'

'And he could've said no?'

'He tried to. But she was an important person, in with the big boss.'

'Exactly, maybe he did it to get himself a break?'

'It was borderline sexual harassment, Delme.'

'OK, that's possible. But did you ever ask her her side?'

'How could I? She never came back. That says it all, doesn't it?'

'I dunno, Charlie. If it was me, I'd have had a word.'

'But it would've killed Jonny if I'd gone to her. He was furious enough that I'd thought he was capable of cheating on me. If I'd asked for her word too then that would've been it. And we'd never have got back together. That's why he went mad tonight, because trust is so important to him.'

Anger boiled inside of him. How couldn't she see she'd been manipulated?

'And do you wonder why? Because you're the beauty and the brains! He needs you! He's a fraud! He's gas-lighting you!'

'Gas-lighting? I was the fraud, Delme! I couldn't hold it together, no matter what. That's what you're supposed to be able to do on air.'

'You were justified!'

'I was better off on traffic.'

Her denial was quite something.

'What about now?'

'All right, I've improved. But we'll see what happens with the review. In the meantime, there's the Party on the Pier to organise.' She was burying her head in her hands, which may as well have been sand.

'Then what?'

'I don't know!' Charlie eyeballed him, her voice trembling and shrill before she recovered herself. 'Depends. Jonny's got me a job lined up in Exeter ...'

Rage seared through him. He wanted to shout and scream. But he'd be as bad as Jonny. He let it go, with a conscious long blink and a few breaths. He had to wait for her to wake up to him. He had to ask her just one thing.

'If it doesn't work out with him, would there ever be a me and you?'

Charlie took a shaky breath. 'I don't know. I'd like to say yes but ... who knows?'

There it was again. The confirmation that he wasn't seen as commitment material.

'Give me until after the Party on the Pier to work it all out. Could you do that?'

He worked out how many days that was. Fifty. He would wait for five hundred.

'Possibly,' he said, playing it down for himself. Charlie wouldn't come round to him romantically. Not a chance. Too much was going on in her head and there wasn't room for him. He didn't like it but he understood. He'd just say this one last thing in the hope she'd set herself free. 'As long as you stop doubting yourself.'

She gave him a weird look and then reached for him. They hugged and swayed for ages. It was beautiful. More intimate than anything that'd happened to him between the sheets for a long time. For ever. And it was enough – it had to be. Yet who was he kidding? It felt more like a long goodbye.

Some time later, he woke with her asleep in his arms. Reluctantly, he unwrapped himself from her; it would be too awkward to be here in the morning. He tried to free his hoodie for the walk home but she was tangled up on it. He'd have to leave it. He got up ever so slowly, tiptoed out of the room and down the stairs and let himself out. There was a sliver of light on the velvet blue horizon. Birds were chirping and the air was still. A new dawn was breaking. He'd said his piece. Now he had to get on with his life. The trouble was, he felt himself sliding backwards. And just like that, he knew he shouldn't, he knew it could be the start of the undoing of all his hard work, but he'd stop for a mega brekkie from the twenty-four-hour greasy spoon before he went home.

34

Tina honestly couldn't remember ever having taken a day off sick in her life.

She must've done when she was a child – chicken pox or flu, she'd have had one of those. But it would've been a couple of days maximum because her parents had drummed it into her: anything other than imminent death and you got on with it. While love had grown on trees, money had always been very tight when she was growing up. They were a typical working-class family in Cardiff, doing blue-collar jobs to eat and live. She'd subscribed to it wholeheartedly – not really achieving much academically because she couldn't wait to land a secretarial job at sixteen to earn money, self-respect and freedom.

So to have called in for the third day in a row to excuse herself from Sunshine FM killed her. It went against everything she stood for.

On Thursday she *had* been physically ill, she could justify that, just about. Tina hadn't slept overnight after that man's allegations about Gareth and by the early hours, her insides had revolted at the injustice of her husband being unable to defend himself. She had to do it instead, over and over, all day, because he was not that kind of person. On Friday, she'd intended to go in – the show must go on, she'd been through worse, all of that in her head as she got into the shower. But again, her body let her down and she'd sat on the floor shaking until the water had run cold. Her weekend had been spent recuperating with tins of soup, poring over his letters and their conversations for clues of infidelity. But there was nothing, absolutely nothing, to give her reason to suspect him. He had been a devoted husband – everything he did had been for her and Darcy. In the good times, when he'd worked sixteen-hour days and missed school concerts, been late for his own birthday meals and spent Saturdays and Sundays catching up and getting ahead. In the bad too, texting Darcy despite the risk of being caught, and even in his gambling which he'd done to try to chase his losses so his family didn't want for anything. He doted on them all. And she was his queen.

After four days alone – four days of cross-examining him in her mind, four days of not crying because if she did she'd be giving credence to the lies, four days of staring at the wall and scrubbing the same plate in the sink or weeding the same bit of garden for God knows how long – the tremors had subsided and she had recovered her composure.

Today, she could've gone into work for her scheduled half-day, she was healthy enough again, but she was going to visit Gareth. She needed to look him in the eye, tell him how he'd been slandered, make sure he understood she backed him one hundred per cent. He had to know. She'd wrestled with that, wondering if she should tell him. He would be angry but better he knew now and it was dealt with than when he came home and learned for himself if that fool of a man turned up again. Never mind the cheek of saying he was unfaithful – pestering his wife would make him see red.

Stand By Your Man by Tammy Wynette had been playing on Sunshine FM as she'd applied another layer of red lipstick just before she'd left to catch the bus to the prison.

Too right, she had thought. He wasn't perfect, of course not, although he *had* admitted he'd stolen the money straight away; the company was in the process of getting every penny back and no one had died. But he was damn well perfect for her. And so she'd taken all morning getting ready. She'd used some of the posh products Abbie had given her to make her hair shine and she'd taken extra care over her make-up with foundation, bronzer, highlighter and all. Gareth needed to see her in war paint, to know she was on his side. She had toyed with wearing the outfit she'd worn on the day he was jailed. It was a sober white shirt, navy-blue pant suit with courts from M&S which didn't scream money or attitude but hushed a sombre humility. Dutiful wife, the barrister had called it. But today needed something different: a bit of attitude, a reminder that she was his and she was all he needed. And she did feel a million dollars in this fiver from the charity shop high-necked sleeveless emerald midi-dress. The colour showed off her tanned arms, the silky sheen bounced off her cheekbones, the cut hung off her hips and kissed her calves and it was given room to breathe with a pair of silver sandals. Tina revelled in the glances she was receiving, as she stood out on the pavements of Townhill and on the bus amongst the sweating grey suits. Nothing was going to bring her down, she decided, not even the endless roadworks and the stop-start of the wheezing engine. Her visit was at 1.45 p.m., she was supposed to be there forty-five minutes beforehand and the cut-off time was 1.30 p.m. The minutes were ticking by, rather too quickly, and she found herself hurrying people up as they took an age to get their prams onto the step or fussed with bags for their passes or coins. Oystermouth Road was never-ending and she jumped up when she saw the signs for City Hall, which was just opposite. She had three minutes. Thank goodness she was in flats because she was going to have to run for it – and run for it she did when her feet touched the ground. Usually she was daunted by the high grey walls and fearful black door, which was straight from the sitcom *Porridge*. This time she took them on, daring them, just daring them, to slam the door in her face.

'In the nick of time, so to speak,' a prison officer said as he shut the prison gates behind her. 'You're the last one we'll be letting in.'

'Thank God,' she said, 'and thank you.'

Bringing the outside in with her, with fistfuls of sunshine and blue sky, she'd made it just as the clock flicked to 13.30. She'd never been so late. Her normal routine of being searched and expecting herself to fail even though she had nothing contraband on her fell by the wayside – she was too busy catching her breath to worry and she was waved through into a heaving waiting area. There was no chance for her to sit down and read and re-read the dog-eared posters of rules and regulations on the pocked white walls – she didn't need to anyway, she knew them off by heart. The usual suspects, the ones she would take a moment to wonder about from her seat, were ahead of her: the crying babies of women left to fend for themselves, the clamped silence of first-time visitors and the old timers who had by now finished sweet-sucking, their crosswords put away. A bell sounded and the crowd swelled up and towards the door and she felt the flutter of butterflies that she would see Gareth. They became the wings of eagles as the mass of people moved forwards, the backs of their heads no longer down from looking at their feet but erect and darting, trying to catch sight of their loved ones. Blonde heads and bald heads, young heads and grey heads bobbed about and the queue began to thin as Tina reached the door. Here she was, coming for her man, the love of her life, catching a glimpse of him across the room.

Gareth was looking up expectantly, looking for her amongst the crush which was filtering slowly to tables and chairs, and she waved, feeling as youthful as the day they'd met. Beneath his orange bib was an expensive grey shirt she remembered he'd worn on a date night way back when…it made his eyes even greener. How lovely he had saved it for today! Surprises were generally unwelcome ones of late, but this was like a beacon of hope. He stood out from everyone else, his stature was proud this time and he had a huge smile on his face and she could feel the twinkle of his eyes meeting hers … or at least they had until someone in front of her, a woman, blocked her view. Impatient now, Tina tried to overtake but someone had dropped a jacket and they'd bent down and she was elderly this lady, so Tina remembered her manners, who she was, and reached for it to help, placing it on the back of her chair. They shared a look that said kindness meant so much in this sort of place, that whatever had happened and however their men were treated, we, the partners, were still capable of kindness. It would be easy to be cross at their reunion being held up but Tina refused to let it get to her. So she lifted her head up and found him again and walked towards him feeling shy, dropping her eyes coyly, and then lifting them up again ready to embrace him. Her heart was exploding like a volcano! And then the ash began to fall, making her cold, so, so cold.

He hadn't been smiling at her. There was someone else with him. The dark-haired woman who'd been ahead of her, who he was now kissing – not in a friendly way but on the lips as lovers. Tina felt her legs lock in disbelief. Then his jaw dropped when he saw her and he pulled the woman to him. There was something about her body shape but her hair was different ... it couldn't be her ... and there was no chance to check as Tina lurched left then right, her knees buckling, her vision distorted by panic. She was covering her mouth with her hand, a scream was coming from inside of her, and then arms were on her and she was being taken away, seeing pairs of popping eyes on her as she knocked over a chair in her distress, having to be held up by the guards and then in a sequence of shots she was in the holding area, back through security, reclaiming her bag, pushing people off her, refusing help, throwing herself out of the prison where she was fighting for breath, fighting the truth.

Her handbag. She'd been using it the night that man had told her. His card would still be in there. Fumbling and shaking, her fingers found it and she stared, unable to make sense of him. Andrew Thomas, it said, mechanic, with a number. She took out her phone and jabbed the numbers, hearing it ring and then answered.

'Your wife ...' she said, needing an explanation.

'Who is this?' said the man and she could see him frowning, confused.

'Tina Edwards. From the other day. It's true,' she said tightly as the words got stuck in her throat.

'Yes ... I'm sorry. Abigail has—'

The phone fell from Tina's hand. Abigail. The woman she knew as Abbie, whose shape had looked so familiar, who had changed her hair as hairdressers often did. Her friend had betrayed her. With her husband. For how long? Her ignorance, her naivety, they stretched out before her, the emptiness filling her with a shock of nausea. There was so much she didn't know. Another question came to her too ... if she was known as Abigail, could that mean she'd had another identity as Gail? Could it be ... no, surely not. Yet something inside of her wondered if it was possible in this very small world. Thinking hard, trying to get past the howl that was growing inside of her, to work out if it was true, her legs started to propel her across the road, across four lanes of traffic, where she heard beeps and brakes, and on and on until she hit the grass and the prom until she slowly puddled onto the sand. The sunshine was too much now – she wanted only darkness when her Gareth was having an affair.

35

'Tonight on *Evening Mumbles*, it's a special edition of Bring Me Sunshine devoted to ... well, here's a clue, I'll let M People kick us off with *Moving On Up ...*'

~~~

Charlie's heart was going like the clappers when she knocked on his door.

'Surprise!' she sang when he opened up.

'Charlie! What are you doing here?' Jonny threw his hands to his head and then at her in excitement. 'Wow! Why didn't you call?'

'I had to see you,' she said passionately into his collar bone which shone with sweat. Over his shoulder, she saw his trendy one-bed bachelor pad in Ealing was even more minimalist than usual. Boxes marked 'Cookbooks', 'Fitness gear' and 'Tech' were stacked in neat piles around the grey walls of the masculine sitting room. Dust from his energetic packing danced in the heavy London sunshine which flooded through the seventh-floor windows, making it as hot in there as the complex's basement sauna room.

'Ah! I've missed you so much too!' he said, panting slightly, his body warm and sticky as he kissed her forehead then her lips.

She felt him start as if he'd worked out why she'd turned up out of nowhere on a Thursday at 11.23 a.m.

'Have you left? Are you coming with me to Exeter?' he asked, squeezing her tight.

'Not quite!' she teased, wanting to make this feeling last as long as she could.

'Oh,' he said, disappointed. 'Wish me luck for tomorrow then?'

His final show at Orbital FM. She laughed a 'no', buzzing all over, enjoying this perfect moment.

'Tell me then, to what do I owe this spontaneous pleasure?'

It was far from spontaneous, actually. Charlie had it all planned.

'Is it a red hot 999 call? Call the emergency sex services!' He stepped back, delighted with himself. She gave him an enigmatic smile.

'Or have you come to help me pack?'

'Spot-on,' she beamed. 'I'm here to send you packing.'

He guffawed and then when he realised she wasn't, he stopped and she saw his jaw twitch as he tried to work out what she was up to.

'It's just a flying visit,' she said, still smiling broadly. 'I'm working later.'

'You've come from Swansea this morning and you're going back there? In the same day?' His eyes had narrowed and his tongue was licking his lips.

'Yes. It's only Wales. Not darkest Peru.' She was toying with him and she felt a surge of power. This is what it feels like to be him, she thought. It was an incredibly heady sensation but too much of it would give her a headache.

Jonny shifted his weight onto one side and studied her

uneasily. 'Why would you do that on a random weekday?'

Why, indeed. But she wasn't going to put him out of his misery just yet.

'Look,' he said, warily, 'if this is about Saturday night, then I've said I was sorry. I do trust you. Did you get the flowers? And the note?'

The extravagant bouquet with an apology written out by the florist.

'Yes, I did. Thank you.' She paused and held his gaze. 'But I preferred getting these ...' She took out a bundle of papers and handed them to him.

Jonny took them with his fingertips as if they were explosives.

'What are they?' he said, evenly, but with lizard eyes scanning the details, flicking from the sheets to her and to the sheets again, back and forth, back and forth, ticking like a timer. Gradually, once he'd worked out what they were, his mouth fell open. 'Where did you get them from?' His voice was low and threatening.

Charlie wasn't scared because she was about to drop the bomb. 'Isabella.'

Jonny missed a beat. But his recovery was quite remarkable, she'd give him that.

'She is so devious!' he growled, 'Oh, Charlie, you poor thing. See? This is what she's like!'

'A liar, manipulative, a bully, untrustworthy, deceitful—' she said, listing them off on her fingers.

'Yes, yes.' He nodded quickly.

'And worst of all, a weak, insecure fraud who feeds off everyone else.' She was almost there.

'Exactly.' A bead of sweat rolled off his cheek as if he was a Teflon frying pan. 'That's what she is.'

'Not her, Jonny. I'm not talking about her.' She was quite still as she waited to pounce.

'No?' Jonny's voice went up a notch.

'No.' Here goes ... 'I'm talking about you, Jonny. You!'

'Me? Charlie! You don't believe all of this, do you?' he said, beginning to shout, waving the papers at her.

'How do you know what they are,' she pointed out calmly, 'if you haven't even read them properly?'

He opened his mouth and then shut it, knowing he was cornered. How would he react?

'You're so stupid. Have you come up with this on your own, eh? In your deranged mind?' he spat, stabbing his temple with his forefinger.

He'd reacted by attacking her. As she had expected. It was textbook gas-lighting. Full marks to Delme Noble. She'd woken up on Sunday thinking of what he'd said, to not doubt herself. To acknowledge the muddle in her head, which she did as she made a cup of tea, to recognise the see-saw of feelings she'd had for Jonny and how she was never quite sure how he was going to be with her.

In the sitting room, she sat in silence and considered this: he loved her, so he said, but he would lose his temper at her, undermine her and make her question her own version of events. He hadn't been a cheerleader for how far she'd come and he didn't accept her for who she was. And then she'd picked up her phone and read Zoe's text: 'You'll never guess what I've heard on the office grapevine ... Jonny was told either jump or be pushed out of Orbital – what's going on?'.

Immediately, she'd worked out who would know. She Googled Isabella, found her on Facebook and without a single doubt, messaged her, apologising for contacting her out of the blue, she wasn't after a row but she had some questions about Jonny.

Three dark grey dots in a speech bubble came at her ...

Are you still with him?

Just about. I think he's been lying to me.

What's your email address? It's easier if I explain that way. It's quite complicated.

Within an hour, Charlie had the whole story.

'Dear Charlie,' Isabella had written, 'this will make painful reading for you and I'm sorry for that. But I hope it gives you what you need to walk away from him.

'It's a source of shame what I'm about to tell you but please bear in mind what I did was out of some misguided idea that I was trying to limit the fallout from my own mistakes.

'So, I'd just come out of an affair with the old station boss, something I truly wish I had never embarked on. I fell pregnant with his baby at the same time as his wife, with whom he'd claimed he had a loveless, sexless marriage. The trauma of that plus the termination sent me on a self-destructive spiral. I'd gone to an industry do one night, Jonny was there, and we got drunk. I should've known better. I poured out my troubles to him, we talked for hours and then we kissed. I came to, realising my mistake. He didn't take it well: he decided to use it as traction. He wanted me to put a word in with the producer to give him a shot on the show — he thought he was better than you. I refused. Then he told me he'd tell the boss's wife about me and the pregnancy. I had lost a baby, I didn't want her to lose hers either out of shock or a snap decision. I had to do it.

The night of your first show, I waited for you to come into the toilets – I knew you'd go out of nerves and necessity. Jonny was on the end of the line and I just had to repeat out loud what he said to me. I couldn't have done it off my own back, Jonny knew I was horrified about what I was doing. As soon as I saw your face, I regretted what I'd done. Jonny meanwhile was already on his way to the studio to take over. I was so sickened by myself and him, I asked my boss for a transfer and he agreed – he was happy to see the back of me. I just got on with my new job, hiding away, licking my wounds, hoping to forget it. But Jonny's popularity soared and I couldn't escape his face on billboards and on buses. I decided to get him back one day.

I never contacted you after what happened because I was very ashamed of myself. To be honest, I hoped you would see through him quickly, finding out for yourself what he was like. As time went by, my anger turned into defiance. I was headhunted to return to Orbital FM as a senior producer. I didn't see why I shouldn't do it – but I wouldn't go back if Jonny was there. So I contacted him and threatened to expose him if he didn't leave. If he felt he had done nothing wrong, he would've stuck to his ground. The fact he agreed, after a load of abuse obviously, tells you everything you need to know. I haven't told anyone about this but you know how people work things out for themselves. My sudden disappearance, Jonny's rise, his departure, my return ...'

At the bottom, she had attached grabs of his blackmailing emails and mobile phone messages as proof.

Charlie had been disgusted and appalled by the whole thing – but she hadn't felt shocked about his behaviour. She had been able to imagine him doing it. She'd felt sorry for Isabella, even though she'd been in on the set-up, because she had acted under duress. Mostly though, it was relief that her indecision was over. And that gave her clarity. Ever since, she had never felt so clear of mind. So sure of her self-worth. So solid and strong that if she stood in the sea in the largest waves, she wouldn't lose her footing. Not in a storm, not right here face to face with Jonny.

'You're a gas-lighter, Jonny. You created a lie. You undermined me. You swung between charm and anger, all to control me because the truth is ...' she cried, hearing her voice soar. 'The truth is *you're* the fraud. The insecure imposter. The one who wanted to isolate me so I'd never find out what you did. So yes, I am stupid – I fell for it all. But not any more.'

'Delme. It's him, isn't it, who's put you up to this?'

'There you go again! Trying to twist the facts!'

He threw more desperate punches: she was still a useless DJ at that joke of a station.

'So useless you had to ruin my career to steal my ideas to make a success of yourself? Because that's what you did, didn't you?'

She was giving up her only chance of a relationship: she wasn't getting any younger, was she?

'As if I can't survive by myself! You're the parasite!'

She'd burned her bridges now!

'I'm the mistress of my own fortune, you mean.'

Her days were numbered.

She drew breath to deliver the killer blow. Not just to him but at her old self.

'You encouraged me to leave London so I wouldn't ever find out. You told me to stay away from the microphone because it was too much for me. You asked me to come back to London, not because you wanted me there but because it told me how little you rated me. You denied telling me Isabella had been kicked out of Orbital to make me question my own mind. You made out you were saving me when the whole time you were leeching off me. Whenever I looked as if I would wake up, you'd back off to make me insecure. Taking care of me was about controlling me. The "I love you's" were meant to smother me. Your standards were about making me try to please you. You were only happy when I was sad. And I convinced myself I was falling in love with you!' She scoffed at herself in disbelief, rising higher and higher, reaching a crescendo, marching to the door. 'Enjoy your last show tomorrow, if you can face it. You're on your own now!'

And as she walked boldly away, with her head high as if she could challenge the sun to a staring competition, she realised her comfort zone had been a cage all along. She had someone new in her life now to trust – her gut, which was telling her there was no time to waste. Taking action would be her mantra from now on, no matter how big or small.

Starting now, as she headed to Ealing Broadway Station to begin the trek home, with a text to Tina to see how she was getting on with this virus of hers. Then she'd use the train journey to message Libby and Zoe – they'd want the gory details. Come tomorrow, she'd tackle Party on the Pier, because what was she waiting for?

As she took to the stairs at the underground, her plan of attack flew at her like the people flooding towards her: she needed to confirm the marquee delivery and erection, chase up sponsors, contact the Night Riders and the bus bosses to take part in a parade, ask the RNLI if their volunteers wanted to shake collection tins, seek out some live musicians, run her catering ideas past Merri and work out how to get a road closure sorted ... Ha! Gen's story of Amy Dillwyn rang in her ears – she didn't need a man to save her. Like her, Charlie could do it for herself.

The city slowly gave way to suburbia, fields, then Wales and once she was back behind the microphone at a minute to 7 p.m., London seemed far away. That was when her adrenalin ran out and the shock subsided, replaced by the reality of what she'd been through. Despite the hurt, her newly found performer's professionalism got her through the start of *Evening Mumbles* and when it was time to introduce Bring Me Sunshine, she was able to draw on her deep well of emotion from the events of the day without losing herself to tears.

'Tonight,' she told the listeners, 'we're talking breakups. Whether you've known it's been coming or you've been dumped out of the blue, whether you're raw with grief from losing who you think is the love of your life – or even if you know you've had a lucky escape – or it's later down the line when you're still haunted by bitterness and hurt ... I'm here to hear you out. Ring us on the usual number and we'll Bring You Sunshine ...'

By now they were so close in the studio, Joanie could see Charlie was dealing with something.

'You OK to do this?' Joanie asked her in the ad break.

'Is it that obvious?' Charlie said.

Joanie nodded across the studio.

'I might as well do it, eh?' Charlie said, 'Might help me after finding out what Jonny was really like.'

'Oh, Charlie!' Joanie cried.

Charlie gripped her throbbing throat for a second and managed to swallow back her upset.

'I've never been able to hide my real self away, have I? What you see is what you get with me.'

'That's why you're so good.' It was lovely to hear.

'People can tell you're genuine,' Roy added, which was high praise from him.

'Thanks, you two,' she said, touched.

'No problem, lovely,' Joanie said as the red light went back on to show she was about to go live again. 'There's a queue of callers already. First one coming up …'

Charlie took a big breath to calm herself.

'Broken hearts, there's a lot of them about,' Charlie said, feeling the room around her dim and her whole self centre in her chest where she put her hands as if she was trying to hold herself together. 'There's no pain like it, is there? That sudden realisation you're on your own, that the one who would protect you from the hurt is causing it and my goodness, it seems you'll never recover. Everyone says "Time's a healer" but what about when the clock seems to slow down so that every waking second feels like an hour? What about when you can't think of anything else but your loss? When your body aches for that person? When you feel so alone and stupid … Let's see what we can do to make that feel better. On the line, we have a listener from Crymlyn Bog ... what's up, caller?'

'Hi Charlie,' came a shaky voice, 'I'm Katie, I broke up with my boyfriend, my ex I should say, two weeks ago and I just can't get over it.'

Charlie squeezed her eyes shut. 'Oh, bless you. What happened?'

'He cheated on me. It wasn't the first time. We'd been through the whole thing once already last year when he'd got drunk on a night out with his friends and ended up snogging someone and it was horrible. But I loved him, we'd had nine brilliant months, it was just a moment of madness, and I wanted to work through it – he'd said he was frightened about settling down and he'd seen it as a last hurrah, you know, before settling down. And it was fine for six months but then I found out he'd been messaging this girl and they'd been at it behind my back. And I couldn't trust him then, I knew it straight away. He kind of accepted it, he didn't bother fighting for me and I know I'm better off without him and all that but ... I'm just so hurt that I wasn't enough.'

'Katie, that is such an upsetting thing to go through. To be so let down when you'd thought you'd worked it out. I really feel for you. But it shows you wanted different things, that you had different priorities. Hearing that itself isn't going to take your misery away but knowing now that he doesn't match up to your standards or deserve your love will save you so much more pain in the future. You've got to think how lucky you are that you've found out what he's like sooner rather than later. OK, you have lots of shared history, I'm guessing mutual friends, your families are involved ...'

'Yes, we were talking about moving in together.'

'And that's going to make it worse for you. He was your best friend, your lover, your everything. You must have felt as if the air had gone from your chest, that you'd been winded, you were dying ...'

'Yes. I really did.'

'But do you know something, you didn't die, did you? You kept breathing, you automatically took another breath and another and then another. You've survived. You instinctively knew you'd be better off without him – you ended it after all. That's amazing isn't it?'

'Wow ... I hadn't looked at it like that!' Katie said in revelation. It was the same for Charlie – she hadn't known she was going to find a positive way of looking at it, it had just risen up inside her.

'Your gut knew immediately. It's OK to be hurting, it's natural, it shows you're capable of love. Accept it and then let it go.'

'Right ... but how?'

'Do the things you love, whether that's watching box sets and shovelling down Maltesers, mooching round the shops and treating yourself, having coffee and cake or having a nice bath, reading a book or going dancing. But don't go berserk, you don't want to overdo it with food or booze or money or one-night stands because then you'll feel terrible about that too. See your friends, talk it out with them or write it down if you feel like you've been going on about it for too long. Go outside too, look up at the sky, watch the sea, walk or run or hop, visualise yourself moving on. It might feel like you're going through the motions but one day you'll realise you have some distance. Good things are going to happen to you, Katie. I promise.'

Charlie heard the smile in her own voice. It was like she had given herself therapy.

'Coming up, we've got the ex who won't let go, a jilted bride and the woman who's missing her ex's dog ... but first, here's *I Can See Clearly Now The Rain Has Gone* by Johnny Nash.'

36

For the first time in a week, Abigail was at work.

Shaking with anger, Tina watched her inside the salon through a hole in the smashed bus stop shelter, where she could observe her undetected.

At last the bitch was in her sights. Every day, twice, three times a day, Tina had left her place and walked the half a mile through Townhill to confront her. But the coward had put up the closed sign. Abigail hadn't answered her texts or calls or voicemails. This no-show had had the effect of turning up the gas on Tina's emotions – in seven days, she had gone from frozen shock to boiling fury. Tina couldn't even go to her house and bang on the door like a crazed banshee demanding answers because she didn't know where Abbie lived. Of course she didn't. Abigail must've known Tina was Gareth's wife, must've worked it out mid-friendship: it explained the distance she'd put between them when she'd cancelled the Night Ride. It was only one arrangement that had been aborted. But it had made Tina back off for a bit and had tamed Tina's need for her confidence. Abigail was clearly as devious as Gareth.

So to see her snipping away and chatting to her clients as if she had no cares in the world gave Tina a visible target for her fury in the aftermath of seeing Abigail's claws in her husband. She had a good mind to go over there and tell her she was a home-wrecker, to shame her in front of her customers. Oh, the temptation ate away at her – her fists clenched at the prospect of a showdown. She exhaled deeply. If she stormed in, she would never know the details of the affair. And she needed to know the extent of Gareth's treachery with that tart. For a tiny part of her heart hung on to the hope that perhaps Abigail had thrown herself at him. It wouldn't diminish the hurt of his betrayal, but if she had been chasing him then Tina could see him not as a predator but as a weak man. It was an important distinction when you were facing the destruction of everything you had held dear to you your entire life. She had been unable to talk to anyone about this: it was one humiliation too far. Prison, well, she had squared the circle of that: gambling was an addiction and addictions were illnesses and illnesses deserved sympathy.

God damn him and Abigail and Charlie, who'd been the architect of Tina finding out. OK, she hadn't dragged her to see Gareth's infidelity in action – she could've dealt with that if she'd never met Abigail. Because she could've hated her, despised her, had she known nothing of her. She would've forever been the other woman rather than a friend. Charlie had been the one playing Little Miss Worthy to cover up her own insecurities. With her softly spoken simpering suggestions of beating loneliness. That had been why she'd gone to the prisoners' wives group. If she'd stuck it out, she would never have had this double dose of deceit. The pain shot through her again and there was bile in her throat. Possessed and obsessed, her usually clear mind was clouded: what should she do? How was she going to recover? She felt sick as she was pulled this way and that.

Tina checked her watch. Just a few minutes to go until Abigail finished. Just a few minutes to decide how she would handle this. A few minutes until … She knew now what to do: she would follow her home, insist on going inside and hold her to account. She would be unable to shake her off then or run or slam the door on her. Somehow, she felt Abigail would give her the truth. Perhaps it would be because she was a woman who had broken the sacred bonds of friendship. It was Tina's best chance to find out.

When Gareth had rung, she'd been tempted to tell the voice that no, she wouldn't accept the call from the inmate of Her Majesty's Prison Swansea. Abigail was just a friend, he knew Tina would act like this if she'd known about her, that's why he hadn't told her. He begged forgiveness over and over, he'd claimed he had deliberately arranged for them to visit on the same day so he could introduce them. His credit ran out after a few minutes. He hadn't even given her the opportunity to speak. She'd known in her gut he'd been lying.

A letter had come too, a sheet of cheap prison-issue A5 lined writing paper, this time saying she was the wife of his friend, the one he'd mentioned. By which Tina understood he meant the ex-con who'd arranged the phone drop. Total crap – Andrew had never been near a prison in his life, she'd rung him and checked. How dare Gareth think she was that stupid. A tear stain had wrinkled his signature. She suspected he'd spat on it instead. She didn't believe him. Because not once had he asked how she was feeling. He was sorry he'd been found out: he'd fucked up, royally, mixing up their visitors' forms. She would prove to him now that she wasn't the gullible simpleton he saw her as. How he had treated her their entire marriage, she saw that now. He had controlled her in every aspect of their lives. He had chosen their home and decor, he had said there was no need for her to work, he had encouraged her to spend her time at spas and in shops and by obeying him, she had been rewarded with clothes and jewellery and cars. Was he up to no good then? Probably. Why else would he have insisted on a private school for Darcy away from her friends, knowing she wouldn't hear bad words about him. And he had blackmailed Tina into covering up for him. He knew that whatever happened next, she would still protect them. In spite of everything.

At 5.33 p.m., Abigail stepped out of Classy Cutz, looking around her, probably for me, Tina thought. Beneath the murky humid sky, she was drawn and pale – that dark dye did nothing for her. Tina was seeing through bitter eyes, she knew that, because she was her rival now, and she keenly sought out her chips and bumps, wanting to hate her. Those too-large hips and sagging small breasts, he'd had them and he'd impregnated her with his vile seed ... Yet the anticipated thrill, the longing to rip her to pieces, wasn't there. Instead Tina was horrified when she felt pity: this child-hungry woman who had been so desperate for a baby that she was prepared to do anything to have one. She couldn't let in so much as a chink of sympathy. Think of Darcy, think of her having to share a father with a bastard sibling. Tina fought to stop herself throwing up, gripping the metal support of the shelter. This was how low he'd pushed her.

Abigail put her head down and walked quickly, hugging the facades of the row of shops, turning left out of sight. Tina darted across to keep up and pursued her, hanging back if Abigail stopped to check the road, then dashing forward when she was back on the move. Her keys were jangling in her hand, it couldn't be far, and it wasn't. Hers was a grotty flat-roofed two-storey mid-link home where the brick was broken up by filthy white panelling. There was a broken gate and an overgrown lawn and one of the windows was boarded up. Tina wanted to think this was all Abigail deserved. But she was choking on it as if her mind was rebelling. There was no time for that: Tina raced ahead and stuck her foot in the door as Abigail tried to slam it shut behind her. Pushing it back, Tina thrust herself in, catching Abigail completely unawares. She gasped, clutched her chest, her eyes were wide, she was stepping away as Tina stood firm, panting, nostrils flaring ready to ... do what?

'No!' Abigail whimpered, afraid, cowering even.

Tina felt a shot of dominance inside of her. And she suddenly realised that this was how Gareth behaved for kicks. It didn't feel intoxicating, though – it was overwhelming and wrong.

'I ... I'm not going to hurt you.' Tina had whispered it. Where the hell had her resolve gone? She shrank into her shoes. 'I just need to know ... about you and him.'

'I'm sorry,' Abigail cried, 'I didn't know. I didn't know.' She was panicking, up against the greasy cream and gold striped wallpaper of the hallway. 'I've ended it. I ended it there and then. When I saw you in the prison.

He tried to stop me seeing who was making the noise, he held my wrists and yanked me into him.'

There were faint patches of bruises on her arms.

'But a guard saw, he grabbed him and I turned round just as you were being led out. I knew it was you. He was taken away and I tried to chase after you but you'd gone. I'd never do anything to hurt you.'

'Am I supposed to be grateful?' Tina said, her face a grid of lines and contorted muscles.

'No. NO.'

This moment, Tina had dreamed of it: the things she was going to say, the punishment she was going to inflict. But there was an emptiness of spirit, a hole in her soul, a crashing inside of her as her beams collapsed.

'We need to talk.'

Abigail nodded, still wary. Tina closed the door silently and looked around the living space. It was like her own but worse: a making-the-best-of-the-dampness which clung like shadows of cancer. A stained carpet. A threadbare sofa missing an arm and a deckchair. A thud and a shout came from next door.

'Come into the kitchen.'

They sat at a wobbly table, laying bare their agony with twisting hands and haunted eyes.

'What do you want to know? I'll tell you anything, everything ...'

'I don't know where to start.' Landmines were everywhere so she chose safety first. 'You changed your hair.'

'He said I looked like mutton blonde.' The floor may as well have exploded. Was this her setting out her stall as a victim? Abigail's eyes, though, were dull and lifeless. Tina had never been criticised by Gareth for her appearance. But he hadn't had to. She had always wanted to please him.

'Did you always do as he asked?' Tina saw the sliver of metal in the knife of her words.

'He pressured me into things. The mobile. I had to meet this screw in a car park in the dark.'

No wonder he'd never asked again for Tina to do it. 'You had a choice. I refused.'

'He's made me look after money. Money they don't know about. It was his insurance.'

'Oh, you stupid—'

'Whore? You can't call me worse than he did.'

Tina dipped her head. This was so hard to take: she'd never seen this side of him. Although now she remembered the glint of violence in that visit when he'd told her about what he'd called 'emergency money'. It hurt her so much she lashed out.

'Did you know about me? Did you know I was his wife? Is that why you became my friend? Was it a sick game or did you just have some kind of twisted need to get inside my head?'

'I didn't know it was you. Not until last week. Honest to God, Tina. I'm so ashamed of myself.'

'Didn't you think the details were all too similar? His name? His circumstances?'

'You and me hardly talked about … our men. You only ever called him Gareth, I knew him as Eddy. He only ever talked about you as 'the ex-wife' or Chrissy … I didn't know your surname was Edwards. We made a pact, remember, not to talk about it?'

Tina believed her. She had been using her maiden name of Dooley since she'd moved here, just in case. And the last time she'd been called Chrissy or Christina was back in high school - he'd deliberately used that name to cover his tracks.

'But what about the wedding photo in my house? You saw that.'

'It was twenty-odd years ago. He doesn't look like that any more.'

He wasn't the same man either. He'd become greedy. Entitled.

'I'm sorry,' she said. 'And I'm terrified. He messaged me last night. Threatened to implicate me because of the money.'

The phone. He'd called *her*. Not Tina. Her blood ran cold then hot. Tina had been the virgin, Abigail the whore.

'Where is the money? Where did it come from?'

'It's in the salon. He never said where it came from. But he didn't deny it wasn't from the fraud.' Why else would he hide it? 'All of this,' she said, 'that's what I meant when I told you I'd done things I was ashamed of.'

'But you stayed with him. Did you think a baby should be brought into the world with him as the father? Did you think he was going to leave me?'

'I know.' Abigail gave a soft shrug. 'He said he would leave when he was out. I never thought it'd happen, not really. I just wanted a child.'

Tina looked at her with disgust. 'Just because you want something doesn't mean you have to have it.' Shame was all over Abigail's face. It was cruel to heap on more but Tina wanted her to feel the torture she was feeling. 'You miscarried. When?'

'Just before he went inside.' Abigail was talking to her lap, her shoulders hunched.

Tina shut her eyes in pain. He'd fathered a child around Christmas time when he had been crying into the early hours on Tina's shoulder about how Darcy must never know about it if he went down. She'd thought he loved them so much. It was becoming clear he loved only himself. Pity for Abigail began to trickle back in. She turned her back on it.

'Did he stay here then?' Tina swept her eyes around the room to show her disgust.

'Are you mad?' Abigail shot her down. Tina took it because it was becoming clear who the real villain in all of this was.

When Abigail spoke again it was quieter and contained. 'Hotels. When he was here on business. And then a rented flat in the marina. He set it all up.'

'Of course. When he'd been working so hard. For me and Darcy.' Tina laughed scornfully. 'How did you meet then?'

'Two years ago. I'd just left my husband. I was at a casino with a friend. He bought us drinks.'

'Ever the gambler.' Tina puffed through her cheeks and then rubbed her eyes. She hadn't had the result she'd been after. She just wanted him to suffer now. Abigail was broken.

'Do you know something? I wanted to hate you. I thought I did. But look at the fucking state of us. Both of us living in squalor because of him. He's got it easy in there. Meals provided, no bills, no worry. He'll come out and carry on having learned nothing. He's sent the pair of us to the brink of madness, he's used us both.' Tina stood up, feeling clearer. Calm and still. 'And I think we should make sure he gets his just desserts, don't you?'

Abigail rose to her feet. 'If you'll let me help … I'd like nothing more than to nail the bastard.'

Tina hesitated. She had to know something else because it had been churning away in the background ever since she'd seen Gareth kissing Abigail. 'Was it you? Who rang Sunshine FM? Were you Gail?'

Abigail nodded. 'Were you listening?'

'It could've been me talking that night. I was exactly like you, lonely and desperate, not seeing the truth, blinkered by love and fear and denial. The advice, to get out and build a life, well, if it hadn't been for that I'd never have met you. There've been times when I wish I hadn't, believe me. But if I hadn't … I'd be worse off than now, I'd have no one to turn to.'

So, yes, you can help me nail the bastard, Tina thought, because Abigail had once helped Tina. She would forgive Abigail eventually. But Gareth? Never.

37

Delme had woken up knowing yet again he was going to do it.

Yes, he might have opened the cupboard; yes, he might have taken out his porridge and yes, he had even poured some out into a bowl and gone through the motions of adding milk and microwaving it. He'd even taken a spoonful and held it to his mouth but that was as far as he'd got. He was going to sin and there was no point fighting it.

Because the urge inside of him for junk food wasn't some temporary whim that he could ride out with slow breathing or a shower. It had been there every day for more than a fortnight since the morning he'd left Charlie's and walked out of his way to the twenty-four-hour greasy spoon and sat down at 5 a.m. to a mega brekkie of five sausages, ten rashers of bacon, four rounds of toast, four fried eggs, with chips and beans. The satisfaction had been fleeting: the grease on his lips had lasted longer. And so it had continued, forgetting the self-disgust each night as he lay there bloated and lethargic from another binge, needing to confirm to himself he wasn't worthy of anything better. Feel dirty, eat dirty, and on and on. He'd put some weight back on and lost some fitness and definition on his body. Hopeless, that's what he was, as if the healthy eating and the exercise had been in vain. Because it didn't change who he was deep down: not good enough.

He was a disappointment of a brother and son, a fair-weather friend, a professional loser and unsuitable boyfriend material. All right, he hadn't expected Charlie to ditch Jonny and come running to him – it'd only be a rebound thing if that had happened; he was wise enough to know she'd be leaping out of the frying pan and into the fire minus factor fifty. That wasn't her. And had she even looked as if she was going to do it, he'd have got the oven gloves on because he didn't want to be burned either. Yet he wished she had at least chucked him a bone. Or a crumb, that would even have done.

She'd been really grateful to him last week, in a two-minute exchange while he made her coffee at Cheer on the Pier, that thanks to him, she'd finally had the guts to finish it with Jonny. Delme had been one hundred per cent right about him and he'd helped her see the light, she'd said, and he was chuffed he'd made a difference. To see her finally free of that idiot was amazing – it was what she deserved. And even better for her that he had gone AWOL for his final show after Charlie had turned the tables on him – it wasn't just revenge, it was justice. But while it was embarrassing to admit he was hurt because there hadn't been a flicker of recognition of anything they'd shared that night in her house: it was as if she'd turned off the gas. Not a 'Let's see what happens …' or a 'I don't want to get your hopes up …' or even a hint that they'd even had any intimacy or agreed on the fifty-day deadline, which was now down to thirty-three.

Of course, she didn't owe him anything. He was just

bitterly disappointed – it was selfish of him, he knew that. Perhaps she had never really been into him at all. Perhaps they had clung to each other when they'd needed somebody at that specific moment – they'd been there for a reason – and now that reason was gone. But it didn't stop it hurting. Especially as she had come out of the other side, he'd seen it in her determined eyes, to focus on work and herself. Especially as he felt as if he'd failed. Ultimately, he felt that no matter what he had been through by changing jobs and lifestyle, he hadn't cleared the last hurdle. He thought he'd proved to himself he had substance. Apparently he hadn't. And so the constant murmur in his head was self-perpetuating sabotage and when you worked in a cafe and the food was free, what was going to stop his daily nosh of fry up, baguette, chips and cake?

Not even on his days off, like today, when he had the chance to go clean did the voice go away. It was louder than ever, offering a filling of comfort and cream when he felt so empty. Particularly so this morning because today was the day he'd find out if he'd qualified as a lifeguard. Whereas during the course, he'd been dead set on passing, now he felt numb to it. He almost hoped he'd cocked it up because he'd know what to do with that. If he hadn't, then it would be a reminder of a moment in time, of once when he'd had the guts to try to change. It had been about Sam too and the pressure to see him, because he'd run out of excuses, would make him bounce off at the wrong angle like a rubber ball.

His porridge abandoned, he'd left his flat to walk away from himself. At first he'd tried to convince himself he was looking for the places that showed he belonged, to make him reconnect. To stir within himself all of the things that meant something to him.

To feel the pride of being a Swansea Jack, the nickname for natives so called after a black retriever who'd rescued twenty-seven people from the docks and riverbanks in the 1930s. To tap into the 'pretty, shitty city' from the cult film *Twin Town* about two brothers who took drugs and stole cars. To feel Dylan Thomas's poetry, to see Bonnie Tyler's big hair and hear her even bigger voice. To taste the tubs of cockles at the market, to ride on a pedalo swan on Singleton boating lake, to watch the RNLI Mumbles raft race, to pay respects on the anniversary of the Mumbles lifeboat disaster of 1947 when all the crew perished on a shout. But nothing had touched him. The wagon had gone on without him.

Now, he was following his feet on the streets of Swansea, on his way for a dish of self-destruction. Here, finally, on St Helen's Road, did he feel something amid curry houses and students, rented flats and offices. It was an area which buzzed with colour and life, spices and noise. There were pockets of deprivation, he could see them in the drawn and torn curtains in windows and in the burst rubbish bags spilling onto the pavement, with violence and theft in the headlines. It would all change because the city centre was earmarked for a huge redevelopment. The strategists said it was underperforming compared to Cardiff and so it'd been earmarked for green spaces and retail and leisure builds. He just hoped the character of the place wasn't lost, the character he could feel in his fingerprints which started twitching when he saw Joe's Ice Cream up ahead.

The powder-blue art deco-style parlour, one of a chain set up by the Cascarini family in the last century, was as much part of the fabric of Swansea as it was in Delme's life. It was where he and Sam would come as kids for a swirling sundae with nuts and strawberry sauce with Mam and Dad and later for a cone when they were teenagers. Sometimes when they were older, they would dare each other to have as many scoops as their stomachs could take before declaring one or the other the winner. One day, he had always vowed, one day he would bring Sam back here. But only if he had redeemed himself. It seemed that was all gone.

He hesitated at the door to check his phone to see if he'd had any missed calls or emails. But still nothing. Still nothing. Waiting had never happened to him before. It was alien to him. Instant gratification had been his thing – and he had learnt there was no pleasure in abstinence. The pain he felt around Charlie was unpleasant – he was afraid he wore it in her company as obviously as a sequinned dress. It was unbearable and he'd taken to tying his pinny low around his waist in a restraining order on his groin. Otherwise it'd be 'Here's your coffee with a side of hard-on'.

He felt his skin prickling and then his saliva glands tingling as a woman inside attacked a creation of vanilla ice cream and red sauce topped with a strawberry. Which looked like a nipple. That was it, he was going in and he was ordering one for himself, promising he'd be good later, and sitting down, imagining his tongue licking a peak of sweet joy ... The decadence thrilled him too – ice cream for breakfast, it was the stuff of dreams – it had been for him and Sam and that made him feel bitter, he needed the sweet of the sundae coming at him to counter-act it. He shut his eyes as he took his first mouthful. He played with it at first with his tongue, until the edge was taken off the cold, and then the creaminess of whatever it was in this secret recipe of theirs melted into him and he heard himself groan.

'Maybe you need to get a room?' said a breathy voice.

Instantly he knew it was her. Fflur was sliding into the seat opposite him. She looked like Jessica Rabbit, all flashing green eyes, tumbling red hair and cleavage and hips, and his heart missed a beat. This was terrible timing. He was a soft target and he hoped she didn't sense it.

'Fflur,' he said, flattening himself out.

'I was passing, outside. I just popped out for some bits.' She lived locally. He should've known to avoid the area when he was in such a state. 'I saw you making love to that ice cream and thought I ought to remind you children are present.'

She gave him a lazy smile which, combined with her loaded words, told him she was going straight for his achilles heel. Or rather, his dick. They'd had massive sexual chemistry, right from the off, sleeping together from the first night they met at a bar and at every oppor-tunity for two years. When they were apart, their mes-sages were sexy. Her imagination and curiosity had taken him places he had never been to. And it was crazy mad love. He never knew what was coming next. Everything they did was with passion, including the arguments and the storming off and the breaking plates, which was her doing. It had been an addiction of sorts: she knew how far she could push him and then she'd push some more, making him feel as if he was about to fall off a very high ledge and then she'd swoop in and pull him back and tell him she would die for him.

Until he had reached a new level of love, which felt as if he was submerged inside of her and he wanted to be with her permanently, every night and every morning, sharing a home and creating a future. That was when she'd stepped away, aloof, and it had driven him insane, making him want her even more, and she would dip her toe back into him, not often, but just enough to keep him hanging in there hoping she would come round.

He'd realised she was toxic for him. He had to remind himself of that as he gulped, drawn in by her eyes.

'Not in work?' he asked as a drip of his sundae ran down his thumb. He used a serviette rather than his tongue to wipe it up – she was that dangerous.

She shook her head and there was something about the way she dipped her chin and then reached for a sachet of sugar on the table as if she needed a prop.

'I've been trying to get hold of you, Del.' She twisted the tube too tightly and it ripped, trailing granules of brown demerara down like an egg timer. He had stopped answering her calls and texts because he wanted to extricate himself from her. Then she lifted her face to his and he saw a different person. No, no, no, he could feel himself sinking and wondering what harm could there be in chatting to her?

'What's up?' He hadn't ever seen her like this. He didn't want to see her like this. A kind of love still remained in the way it did when your time with someone who had meant something was up.

'I've been signed off for a few weeks.' She cleared her

throat self-consciously which made Delme sit forward. This wasn't her at all. She was a trooper. Nurses had to be to get through those hours and what they saw, especially in accident and emergency. Fflur had never come in upset by anything; she'd either say her shift had been 'the usual' or dish out some gallows humour.

'How come?'

'Oh, they say I've got PTSD.' She rolled her eyes and sighed.

He pushed his ice cream away. That was some beef. 'What happened?'

'A patient came in, he'd been in a crash. He survived but his little boy died. He said he'd wished he'd gone instead of him.' She said it dispassionately, staring out the window. Fflur was always bouncing: to see her so lacklustre told him how devastated she was.

'Shit. That's awful.'

'I don't know why it affected me.' She looked back at him with a shrug.

'Of course it would. I can't think of anything worse.'

'No, no. Stuff like that happens all the time.'

'So what was different?'

'Little Tyler, he was only four. He'd gone out to McDonald's for a treat. He never went home. I dunno, it kind of hit me that I'd made a mistake.' Her eyes fell to her lap.

'Did you? But you're one of the best there is.'

'No, not at work. That I'd been wasting my time for so long and life, it's precious. That I'd made a mistake ...' she said, looking up at him, 'with you.'

Oh. God.

'I've fucked up. I let you go. I didn't realise what I had

until you'd gone.' She was big pleading eyes now and he hated this feeling that he had the power to make it all right.

He had to swerve it. He didn't know what to think. He'd have jumped at the chance a few months ago. Then he'd distanced himself from her. Now he was confused. 'Are you having counselling?'

'Yep.'

'Good. How long you off for?'

'Until the flashbacks stop and the night sweats and the fear because I can't go back in like this ...' She was trembling now and that was all it took for him to get up, answer the call and move to her side of the table and put his arms around her. Her hair, soft and smelling of strawberries, her body folding into his, so familiar and yet not as he'd known. For she was gripping him and crying; there hadn't been this before when everything between them had been on a line of tension, whether that was sexual or emotional. When games had been played.

Her knuckles were white, he noticed, such was the intensity of her hold. She felt different; this felt different. And there wasn't just sympathy for her inside of him – there was an echo of that feeling he'd had when he'd wanted to move things on.

'Oh Del, I'm such a mess.' She sniffed into him and squeezed him tighter.

If he could fix her he would and he was about to tell her when he felt his phone vibrating.

'I've got to take this,' he said, apologetically, picking up, holding his breath and hearing the news which he accepted with thanks but not much else. He couldn't process it here and now, and he was sighing.

'What is it?' Fflur was rubbing his back, understanding of old the pitch of his breath. That was what could be his, theirs ...

'I've er ... I've qualified as a lifeguard.' He still didn't believe it.

'Lifeguard?' she said, bewildered.

'Yeah. Because of Sam.'

'Oh, right! Oh, I see! It makes sense ...' she said, looking serious until she gave him a nudge. 'I thought you were looking more buff than normal.'

Well, he had been.

'You're so funny, Del, you've just got this spirit, you're irrepressible! So unpredictable!'

There it was – she was speaking the truth about him and he may as well not fight it any more.

'Well, do you fancy celebrating? Come on,' she said, pulling him up and along with her. 'I can drown my sorrows and you can save me!'

She was laughing and he was feeling dizzy. This was what they always used to do – never mind it being just 11 a.m. on a Tuesday. They'd turned things upside down, they always had. Del and Fflur did what they want, when they wanted to. Rules weren't for them. His chest was pumping as he saw what they could be. How easy it would be to fall back into it. Into her. They could mend each other, she had virtually said she was ready to make a commitment to him. That was cause for celebration. Not the sacrifice he'd been hell-bent on, denying himself and curtailing his spontaneous side. With her, he'd be able to have it all. Life was for living, he decided, as they stood up as one, drunk already on their excitement, arguing about where to go first.

'Oh, who cares!' Fflur said, nuzzling against his chest, 'Let's just see where we end up!'

'I've missed you,' he said, feeling his face bob up from under the water, free to breathe again and ready to take in huge gulps of air.

38

'Taking us to the lunchtime news, it's Fleetwood Mac with *Little Lies* ...'

~

It had been the most manic fortnight of Charlie's life. Like waking up from a nightmare, she knew dumping Jonny could've left her looking back in horror, traumatised by the ordeal, battered and bruised from the car crash of the relationship. Instead, having talked it out to Katie from Crymlyn Bog, she found she was overwhelmingly thankful that she was free.

The last few months had been the making of her – without this move and all its challenges, she would never have realised what a survivor she was. She felt fine, there was no need for Mum and Dad to visit or for an emergency visit from Zoe or Libby. Besides, Gen was on hand as self-appointed soother-in-chief. Not that Charlie needed it; save a few tears every now and again, which were mostly of relief, she had hardly cried at all.

'You're on a wee high,' Gen had said today over Saturday morning croissants and coffee in the garden. 'I remember feeling the same when I left with Claudia. But you might have a wobble once you've come out the other side, when it's safe to do so. I know I did.'

'I've had so many wobbles the last couple of years though that it's like I've used them all up. It's like I can't be doing with it any more.'

Gen had given her a wise smile across the fuchsia wrought-iron table. 'Oh, there's always room for more. Particularly if another man comes along. And don't say there'll never be a man in your life again ...'

Charlie didn't want to go there. It was too confusing. 'Did you meet anyone else?'

'Oh yes. Plenty.' Her blue eyes twinkled. 'But I'm between men at the moment. I like to have a rest every now and again!'

Charlie didn't blame her. Jonny had been exhausting, that she was prepared to admit. Thank God that era was over. Instinctively, she knew she'd never hear from him again – a criminal would be a fool to return to the scene of a crime. Or in other words, a bully was clued up enough to know when he was beaten. Jonny was canny enough to disappear to try to salvage something of his tattered reputation. Zoe had filled her in on the fallout: not only did he miss his final show, he also didn't appear at his leaving do. And like all best friends, Libby revealed she'd never liked him – that's why she'd encouraged her to leave London in the first place. That was all in the past. Charlie felt nothing for him – she simply wiped him from her mind, knowing she'd wasted enough on him. Her energy was being poured into the Party on the Pier.

With a month to go, it was beginning to come together – she was putting in twelve-hour days to contact big wigs, councillors and community groups as well as being the go-between for the department heads at the station. Just when she'd solved one issue, another would crop up but she was grateful for the focus. This was about keeping her job because there was no trampoline to cushion her fall. But it reflected her new-found sense of self: she had parameters and boundaries, which suited the organised side of her, but within those, she could be creative.

That's not to say she was in cruise control. Because there were two things concerning her.

First, Delme. Where the hell did she start to unravel *that*?

She could protest to herself until she was blue in the face that she didn't have feelings for him yet she just had to see the top of his head as she walked past the cafe and she'd burst. The night he'd said he fancied her had been all sorts of crazy: had Jonny not called, she would've kissed him ... probably. While her gut was loud and clear with everything else, it was on hold about him. She didn't know what to do: it felt wrong to keep him waiting or to give him false hope. She was in no position to enter a new relationship. And most of all, he wanted commitment. Big style. What if it wasn't the real thing? What if she found out her desire for him was actually just a platonic thing? She didn't want to hurt him – he was vulnerable too. And so she zipped herself up in his company, making sure she gave him no signals, keeping it to just good friends. She resigned herself to doing nothing. Unlike her second problem – Tina.

Charlie's texts to her had gone unanswered. Then earlier this week she'd found out from Priti in sales, who'd been moved to cover for Tina, that she wasn't ill but had taken holiday to tackle a personal issue. When she returned to work on Monday, Priti would stay as office manager while Tina became Sian's PA. It was all so sudden. Charlie had dithered about messaging her because Tina hadn't replied to her earlier messages. But she gave it one last try yesterday, sending her love and offering her a chat if she wanted one. Charlie hadn't been prepared for Tina's response: 'I don't want your "helpful" advice. Your interference and do-gooding have caused quite enough damage already.' What did it even mean? Of course, Charlie had wrestled with Tina's text which had accused her of meddling – did she interfere? But people came to her didn't they? Or maybe she'd got too big for her boots – did she deserve a dressing down? Last night, she had decided to leave things be. But come this morning, Charlie couldn't help it – she was desperately worried. This wasn't the Tina she knew. Even so, as she set off to seek her out, hoping for an explanation, Charlie prepared herself for a door slamming in her face. If she could, she'd make amends. She just couldn't give up on her.

Where would she find her? It could only be in Townhill.

Designer-dressed Tina may have appeared far too posh to be living in one of Wales's most deprived areas. Her husband was big in Dubai, after all. But Charlie remembered her boarding the number twelve bus, the Townhill circular, the evening of the Night Ride. There was that man too who'd turned up at Sunshine FM and asked for a Tina from Townhill. And being the anorak she was, she'd checked the day Tina had said she was going to Heathrow to meet Gareth in Charlie's first week in Swansea and there had been massive delays on the trains, which would've made it impossible for her to see him, have lunch and return in a few hours. Once a traffic geek, always a traffic geek.

She may be putting two and two together and coming up with five. Even so she needed to eliminate this vast estate, she thought, as she puffed up Constitution Hill, Swansea's steepest incline. The area was every bit as people said: rough round the edges, with pebbledash houses stacked in lines and on top of each other and a fair few mattresses in front gardens. It put her on edge: if she found her here, what if she went ballistic? But Charlie refused to believe Tina was capable of that. Tina had stuck her neck out for her, warning her she needed to up her game to stay at Sunshine FM. And she had always been there for a reassuring word right from day one. If Charlie had got it wrong, she'd grab some humble pie or at least a sausage roll at the bakery she'd passed on her way up. It wouldn't be a wasted journey anyway because she wanted to see the view from Pantycelyn Road that people raved about.

Reaching the top, Charlie stuck her hands on her hips to catch her breath only to lose it straight away. The whole of Swansea lay beneath her in a dazzling smile of sea and sand. There was the ferry terminal and the docks, the golden crescent of the bay, the blocks and shops of the city centre and the curve of Mumbles. A beautiful band of green lay between Townhill and the hustle below, which was a haven for wildlife and plants as well as parkland for kids and families. Apparently, Wales's most famous writer of hymns was called William Williams Pantycelyn. If this road was named after him she could see why because it was like being as high up as heaven.

Tina had said this was a good place to think. And so

Charlie did, working out how to find her. For over an hour, she went from shop to shop asking for her, and the people were genuinely keen to help, shouting out the back if they didn't know. But blank followed blank – until her last stop at a hairdresser's. The woman admitted she knew her but she was cagey until something about her rich voice made Charlie wonder. And then she saw she was drinking tea from a Bring Me Sunshine mug. She couldn't possibly be … Gail, could she? The lady gasped and once Charlie had explained, she picked up her phone to call Tina. Waiting for the verdict, Charlie crossed her fingers in her pockets, and the nod came with directions, a thanks for her help on the phone-in and a good luck. Luck? Charlie had had her fair share of it today, she thought, now fearing she'd run out.

Tina was there at her weathered door waiting for her. But it was a person she didn't recognise. Her hair was scraped into a ponytail, her eyes were heavily bagged and she was wearing a T-shirt and leggings.

'Thanks for letting me pop by,' Charlie said as she tried to hide her shock at the run-down flat which was so far away from the lavish mansion they all assumed she'd lived in.

Tina sighed and beckoned her in. 'I don't want a row.'

'No, course. I'm just worried. I'll go if you want. Just say.'

Tina said nothing and led her through the tatty lounge out into the kitchen where the radio was tuned in to Sunshine FM. They hovered, staring warily at each other, until the introduction of Fleetwood Mac's *Little Lies* and Tina dropped her head and walked into the garden.

'Oh!' Charlie said at the unexpected riot of colour and

scent of flowers, 'this is lovely.' It was like a cottage garden with blooming pink, red and yellow roses, speckled apricot foxgloves at the back, lavender, lofty purple delphiniums and a herb patch with basil and rosemary. 'And you grow your own!' There were tomatoes turning red, heaps of tiny cucumbers and beds of lettuces in a greenhouse.

Tina remained silent and knelt to pull out a weed in the soil. Charlie had no idea how long she'd be welcome so she went for it.

'Tina, look, I'm sorry. I'm sorry I hurt you, I'm sorry. I don't know why, I feel like I've failed you. I don't need you to forgive me, I just want you to know, can I help?' Charlie braced herself in case this was the oxygen to Tina's flame.

But she crumbled down onto the border wall. It wasn't what Charlie had been expecting. Tentatively, she lowered herself to the warm paving stones and began.

'I don't know what's up but … I've been through a few things myself.'

Tina was pensive and Charlie knew she had one shot. She launched into her story: her charmed life, falling for Jonny, how it all crashed down, losing her voice and her job, how Jonny trapped her and nurtured her insecurities, how she'd finally got rid of him and she hadn't looked back … 'And after all of that, I've realised I've been seeking approval from people my whole life when I should only be seeking it from myself.'

Tina began to nod and her eyes lifted to Charlie's as if something had registered. 'That's the trouble. I've let myself down very badly. Very, very badly. I took it out on you, I blamed you and I'm sorry.'

Charlie took no pleasure in hearing that.

'The caller, Gail, the one you met ... when you said you'd thought once it could've been me ringing in ... well, it might as well have been. Because the same man reduced us both to this state.'

'How do you mean?'

'We met at a support group after her call, after I'd heard your advice. We got on very easily, became friends. Then, I ... I've been lying about my husband. He's not in Dubai. He's in Swansea Prison for fraud.'

'Oh, Tina.' This was worse than anything Charlie had imagined.

'We lost everything. We used to have everything. He fiddled the books. He said he had a gambling problem, that's why he needed the money. I supported him, blah, blah, blah,' she spat, her veins running with anger. 'But it turns out he's just greedy. He'd been supporting our lifestyle plus another woman's, she even carried his baby for a while before she miscarried. She was so desperate for kids, you see, her marriage had broken up because of the endless cycle of trying, conceiving and losing her babies. Gareth was stashing away money to set up home with her when he came out.'

Charlie let out a groan. She could now guess who. 'With Gail?'

'Yes. But she found some documents in with it, a home in Spain. Which she knew nothing about.'

'No!'

'Yes! And that man who turned up at work, he was her ex-husband, trying to tell me the truth. But I refused to believe it. I only realised when Gareth mixed up our visiting forms, double-booking us and I saw her with him. It turns out he was having us both on. We were his puppets. He told her he was going to leave me. So I understand how you feel about being controlled and then feeling a fraud. The same thing's happened to me.'

'It must've been so hard on you, pretending.'

'The worst. Watching what I say, who I talk to, using my maiden name. I had to leave Cardiff because of the shame. I had to move here to be closer to him.'

'So how do you feel now?'

'Awful. Stupid. Foolish. But better for telling you,' she conceded. 'I'm not surprised you clicked something was up. It was always going to be you that realised. And I don't mean what I said about you interfering, I was just looking for someone to blame.'

'It's OK. I know how it feels to be so scared you invent a world for yourself to keep you safe. So what will you do? What about the money?'

'Don't worry. Abigail and I have sorted that out.'

What did she mean? The phone rang inside.

'Let me get that and I'll explain. Get us some coffee too.'

But when she did return, she held nothing but her head in her hands.

'What is it?'

'My daughter!' she cried. 'She's at Swansea Station.'

'That's good though, isn't it?'

'She has no idea about any of this.' Tina was white and frightened. 'We kept it from her.'

Oh, Jesus Christ. 'How did she not find out?'

'Darcy's at uni, her life is in Leeds. The friends she has either don't know or are too well brought up to say anything. She went to a private school outside of Cardiff so her circle wasn't local. I never wanted to keep it from her but Gareth forced me to – my family's my world.

I did it, convincing myself I was protecting her. The timing of it made it seem possible – six months, so he spent Christmas with us and then away he went. He'd be in and out without her having to know.'

'Hang on, where does Darcy think you both live?'

'She thinks we downsized to Swansea. We said we'd had a bit of financial trouble. I said I was renting here until Gareth was home from Dubai when we would find a place in the countryside to do up.' Her forehead cracked in agony. 'This is going to break her, seeing me live in ... this shithole. She's on her way in a cab now. She's going to hate me. What am I going to tell her?'

Charlie had to do something but this felt too massive even for her. Yet the sight of Tina's panic was so upsetting. Charlie got up and followed her into the lounge where Tina stood at the window checking for the taxi.

'What am I going to do?' Tina pleaded.

There was nothing for it. 'You're going to have to tell her the truth.'

'But ... no ... how? I can't.'

'Listen, Tina, protection is one thing but no good ever comes of deceiving someone or pulling the wool over their eyes. I was brought up in such bliss I had no idea what the world was like. I thought nothing would go wrong in my life because it had all gone like clockwork. Then when Jonny ... did what he did ... it was such a shock I zoned out. Withdrew. And it's taken me years to recover. Darcy is an adult. She needs to know what kind of woman you are, how you tried to stop her from finding out but her father ... She should know who he is and what's he like. The truth hurts but lies are worse.'

'What if she's so upset she blames me?'

'She might be cross, yes, but she'll understand once she's had time to think. If she's anything like you—'

'Oh, she is, everyone says that.'

'Then she'll know you only acted out of love. And it's important she sees you standing up for yourself so if she ever finds herself in the same situation ...'

'Oh, I couldn't bear her to live through what I have,' Tina said. 'It's going to hurt her though, so much. But I suppose it's going to be even more painful when he buggers off to Spain.'

Charlie let it all sink in. She had tried her best. And there was the sound of an engine pulling up and a girl with a backpack was getting out of a car.

Slowly, Tina reached for her wedding ring and slid it off. 'I had to pawn my showy one. I won't be going to buy it back.'

'You're stronger than anyone I've ever met,' Charlie said, going to the door, opening up and slipping out as the girl, Tina's double, with shiny brown hair, checked the address with confusion. It was horrific to see. The words 'surely Mum isn't living here' might as well have been written in a thought bubble above her head. Then came the split-second rush of joy in her eyes when she saw Tina and the crumple of tears because it didn't make sense and the stabbing realisation that something had gone very wrong.

Charlie turned away as the rucksack hit the ground, as mother embraced daughter, as old wounds were reopened and new ones were inflicted. But she knew even when the sobbing broke out that, eventually, Tina would heal her daughter and herself.

39

Tina drank in Gareth's grateful green eyes.

'You came,' he said as she reached him in the prison visiting area.

'Yes,' she breathed, having finally agreed to see him, having finally worked it all out in her head and heart. Because no matter what anyone else thought, however else they reacted at Gareth's treachery and her pain, it had been Tina who had had to wrestle with her feelings and decide how she was going to live from now on.

'I'll make it up to you, Tina, I swear.'

'There's no need,' she said softly.

'Oh, Tina! My angel!' His shoulders relaxed and he exhaled with relief. 'Thank God, I knew you'd come round.'

He went to kiss her but she gave him the swerve and slid down into her seat. Gareth nodded, understanding his punishment would be to be deprived of physical contact. 'It won't be long now, I'll be out soon, next month. Us, back together.'

This was just what she'd expected: he was arrogant enough to make a play for forgiveness at what he saw as a misunderstanding but she knew was betrayal. His last two letters, which she hadn't replied to, had stated his case once again and if she'd come to see him, he could explain. She had been determined to let him fester; to never respond to him personally again, going through a solicitor. But after Darcy's distress, Tina wanted him to know the damage he'd caused.

She let him believe his own version of events, his own reality, for a split second as she unwound her summery scarf and placed it in her lap. His eyes swept across the bare skin above the scooped neckline of her T-shirt and to her face again as he murmured his appreciation. 'So beautiful,' he said, touching his own throat.

She eyed him in his denim shirt: the one for so-called 'best'. Clearly he thought Tina was too stupid to decode that this was his uniform for her days rather than for his mistress. She focused on the orange of the bib instead – this was who he was. Scum.

'Brains too, don't forget,' Tina smiled.

'Of course, love.' He held up his hands and then crossed them over his heart. It was an almost sincere grovel.

'So what you been up to?' Gareth said, leaning towards her, placing his hand palm-down on the table, inching his fingers towards her. Tina felt herself recoil just a fraction – it reminded her what she was here to do. She shrugged slightly to say, 'Not much, this and that'. Then having disarmed him, she went for it.

'Telling Darcy the truth about you.'

'What?' His sallow cheeks went white.

'You heard. She knows everything. That's why I'm here. She never wants to speak to you again. She asked me to tell you in person.'

He sank his head into his hands and then decided he'd give it one last go.

'She knows you lied to her?' he sneered.

'Darcy understands why I didn't want her to know what a waste of space her father was. She's fine, by the way, thanks for asking, fine, now at least. It was very tough for her to find out you're not just a criminal and an adulterer, but a criminal who isn't interested in rehabilitation. It was crushing for me but for a daughter it's far worse, because fathers are supposed to be heroes. And what on earth is heroic about a man who steals, lies, gambles, carries on with another woman and gets her pregnant and uses her to stash ill-gotten gains? You can see why Darcy thinks she wasn't enough of an incentive for you to stick on the straight and narrow. Don't worry though, I've more than enough love for her.'

'I hope it pays the bills for you, love,' he snarled. 'And—'

But she was done with listening to him. It was time to get her revenge.

Tina bolted out of her chair, tipping it over, sending it clattering down and waved at a prison officer who came immediately to her side. Gareth froze as the room went silent.

'Officer,' she said, loud and clear, 'this man has a mobile phone somewhere inside the prison.'

'You bitch.'

She smiled at Gareth with glee because she wasn't finished.

'And he's also hidden some of the fraud money on a premises in Townhill to reclaim when he gets out ... which will be a bit later than he expected now, I'd think.'

She turned her back on him and heard a fist thump the table and then a voice informing him he was being arrested and he didn't have to say anything ...

Tina was euphoric: she felt as if she'd thrown off a heavy coat and that she was walking on air. She didn't know what her future held, where she would live from now on because she couldn't stay in her flat knowing it would be her permanent home. But she had friends, a higher salary as Sian's PA and she didn't have to live a lie any more. Her job was far from safe but fingers crossed, she'd keep it because whoever took over would need a secretary. If the worst happened, she'd at least have a reference from this century. Best of all though, Darcy was coping and the pair of them were working out the foundations of their new relationship. Darcy had wanted to support her mother – it was a sign she was no longer that little girl in pigtails who thought a kiss made everything better. Her grown-up daughter understood survival depended on far more than that – and it was a relief for Tina to know Darcy was resilient. She'd said she'd been waiting for something to go wrong in her life because it had been too charmed – well, having a dad banged up didn't just meet that but exceeded it. Secrets, Darcy had said, were OK when you were dealing with a kid but she was an adult and she should've been told right from the start. It was one of the vows they'd promised to keep: to be open with each other, no matter what. Today certainly called for a celebration – where else would Tina go but to Cheer on the Pier for a coffee?

'You look pleased with yourself!' Merri said, looking oddly merry as she banged the beans into the silver machine.

'So do you!' Tina gasped, eyeing her new look. Gone were the clothes in black, replaced by a stripy white and daffodil-yellow sailor dress and purple DM boots. She was jigging from side to side, too, at one of DJ Disgo's dance tracks which was playing on the radio behind her and then she did jazz hands as she presented a latte. 'There's an aubergine on my coffee. I haven't had aubergine for quite some time!'

Merri fluttered her eyelashes coquettishly.

'Oh, but I see you have!'

'Might've done.' Merri winked, before moving on to the next customer, leaving Tina to wonder who the mystery man was. Good on her! she thought, spotting Charlie at a window seat. It was the first time in ages Tina had seen her in here – fair play to Charlie, the Party on the Pier had consumed her lately, chaining her to her desk or sending her out for meetings and then she had the show to prepare and appear on.

Tina went over and as she did she noticed Charlie was scowling across the cafe so Tina followed her eyes and saw Del giving a very attractive woman a hug before she left. Oh dear – was Charlie jealous? Or perhaps she was tired and feeling sorry for herself? She went over to find out.

'What's up?' Tina asked, hesitating before she joined her because Charlie might want to be alone. 'Monday blues?'

'Stuff,' Charlie sighed, raising her eyes to the heavens, deep in her own thoughts, before realising Tina was hovering. 'Have a seat,' she said, coming to. 'Forget me, I'm just having a moment.'

'Everything OK?' Tina said, setting down her drink and handbag and taking in the summery scene on the beach. The school holidays were under way, August started tomorrow, and the bay was bustling with body-boards, sandcastles, paddlers and rock poolers.

Charlie waggled her head as if to say she was 'so-so'. But she didn't want to discuss it. 'What have you been up to then?'

'Oh, not much,' Tina said, coyly, before she unleashed a huge smile. 'Just taking my revenge.'

Charlie jumped to attention in her seat and Tina filled her in, which made her soar all over again. It proved to be infectious, putting a bounce back in Charlie's mood, and they began to compare notes about controlling men.

'It's like the blinkers come off and you can suddenly see things for yourself again,' Charlie said.

'And you'd rather be alone for the rest of your life than live another day under their perverse regime.'

'It's just occurred to me, and I don't think she'll mind me saying, but my landlady, Gen, she's been through the same kind of thing with a bloke like Gareth. Maybe you could—'

'I'd love to get to know her,' Tina said. Before today she would never have been so brave. But things had altered.

'Oh, you'll love her, she'll be up for that. I'll introduce you. She's so easy-going ... It's like you said, when we did the Night Ride, relationships should be straightforward and easy.'

That evening seemed like a long time ago, yet it was only six weeks ago. The naivety of her! But then Gareth hadn't always been in charge – it had been simpler in the days when they'd had nothing. The change in him had come when he'd started to make money and it had turned his head.

'Who's easy?' Del said as he plonked himself down beside them with a bowl of steaming lasagne and half a loaf of bread. Tina noticed Charlie stiffen slightly. It was odd seeing as Del and her seemed to share a special chemistry ...

'Friendships. Relationships. They should be easy,' Tina said. 'That's what we were talking about.'

'Oh, yeah, deffo,' Del said, gooey-eyed at the oozing spoon of meat and stretchy cheese heading towards his mouth. 'Who can be doing with the drama, eh?' He shut his eyes, emptied his spoon extravagantly and then groaned. 'Cowing lush. Now if Merri wasn't off the market, I'd marry her for her lasagne.'

'Merri's off the market?' Charlie squeaked in spite of her composure. 'That's fab! Who is it then?'

'My lips are sealed,' he said, tapping his nose, getting it all wrong as if he was drunk on lasagne. 'I'm not telling you about Claudia either!'

'What? Is she with someone now too? Oh, about time!' Charlie sang.

'Stop! You won't get it out of me!' Del cried. 'Torture me all you like but I'm saying nothing!'

Tina found herself laughing out loud. 'Oh, this is nice,' she said, 'us getting together.'

'Yeah, it is!' Del beamed, shiny-eyed at Tina. 'It's been a while.'

But then he looked pointedly at Charlie and Tina saw her jaw jutting out, taking exception to him. So he'd noticed she hadn't been in the cafe too.

'I've been busy,' Charlie said, defensively, crossing her arms and aiming her elbows at him.

'Haven't we all?' Del's voice was dripping with sarcasm.

'I can see you've been busy.' There was a frosty edge to Charlie's tone.

My God, she was alluding to the sexy redhead who'd been draped over him when Tina arrived. Tina clenched her bum she was so uncomfortable.

'Yeah, well, Fflur is just helping me through a few things.' He shrugged and shovelled in another mouthful. 'And she needs me at the moment.'

'Oh, good,' Charlie said, grimacing with a forced smile before she nodded at his lunch.

This was painful. Tina felt very awkward watching them – they had forgotten she was there. Or maybe they just didn't care. The pair of them seemed to have been waiting for this opportunity, like it had been building in both of them, and now they had it, they were going to go for it.

'Now hang on. I'm just having a break from the healthy eating, that's all. Now that I've qualified as a lifeguard. Thanks very much for asking.'

Something between them shifted. Del looked genuinely hurt and Charlie looked genuinely crestfallen.

Oh, it was wrong for Tina to be observing this ... this tango of two people who obviously had feelings for each other, but hadn't worked out what to do with them. Yet she couldn't tear herself away. If she did, she might interrupt their tentative dance to solve the issues standing between them.

'Shit. Sorry,' Charlie said, her body thawing, leaning forward, offering her palms to him. 'That's amazing, well done. I'm really pleased for you.'

Del immediately softened. He laid down his spoon and pushed his bowl away. 'Cheers, mush.'

'You must be so chuffed!'

'Yeah.' He didn't sound it though. 'I am, yeah,' he repeated as if to convince himself. He'd dipped his eyes and was ruffling his hair.

Charlie was straining her neck to one side to get him to look up at her. 'It's brilliant news, Delme.'

He looked up from under his eyelashes, paused and then exhaled, relaxing completely into himself with a dashing grin which Charlie seemed to drink up.

'So … how did it go with your brother then?' she asked excitedly. 'I bet he was bloody thrilled to see you!'

Tina didn't know what this had to do with anything but judging by Del's immediate slump, it was obviously important, maybe even critical.

'I haven't seen him yet.' Del spoke quietly as if it hurt him to talk. 'Too … busy.'

Too difficult more like, Tina sensed, without knowing why.

'Oh … right … well, there's no rush. If it's because you … don't want to go alone, I can come with you, I meant it when I said I would.' Charlie's eyes were pleading to help him.

He sized up her offer and Tina started to pray the stars would align so the two of them would resolve whatever it was that stood in the way of them. Whether that was a friendship or something more, and it should be something more, such was the bond between them. For crying out loud, she wanted to say, life is too short to be miserable! How often did two people click so beautifully? Even in conflict they seemed to share a passionate rhythm. And that conflict had been over in a flash. Come on, she willed them, sort this out …

'Thanks for the offer but … uh … Fflur's going to come,' he said eventually, not meeting Charlie's wincing eyes. 'She's just been a bit tied up. A few things going on. We're going this Sunday … or next.'

Charlie nodded in defeat.

'OK, of course,' she said in a small voice.

Tina sagged all over as all hope stood down; they'd come so near yet had ended up so far. She didn't know what to do – her instinct was to reach out to both of them, to try to heal whatever this pain was about his brother. Whatever she could say though, whatever advice she could give, it wouldn't fix them. Besides, what did she know about relationships? Without understanding the circumstances she could end up sounding as cheesy as a slice of Caerphilly. Perhaps she just needed to tell them she hoped everything would work out OK. That would at least show she was there if they needed someone. The words began to form on her tongue and as she looked up to speak she saw Charlie packing her bag and Del getting up to go back to work.

'It'll all work itself out, you know,' Tina said into their no man's land, hoping her reassurance would hit home if not now then later.

But Del and Charlie had turned their backs to one another – and all that was between them now were muttered goodbyes falling into the cracks of a cold silent wasteland. Tina felt ridiculous as an ache hit her throat as if she was going to cry. Why was she so affected for heaven's sake? There was her sadness that the two of them were missing out on their something special together. More than that though, she guessed this was the low that followed a high, compounded by the disappointing realisation that despite her lifelong-held belief, love didn't conquer all, after all.

40

In Del's doorway, Charlie solemnly handed over his hoodie as if it was a rugby ball made of glass.

He took it reverentially, almost bowing his head at the neatly folded and, by the sniff of it, freshly laundered bundle. As peace offerings went, the return of a long-sleeved Nike running jacket in size XL wasn't your usual gift to make amends. But it was almost biblical for them. She could've easily dropped it in a carrier bag at Cheer on the Pier any day of the working week, after all. But by coming here, out of her way on a Sunday morning, Charlie was trying to restore cordial relations after another fortnight of awkward half-hearted hellos and weak waves across the cafe. More than that, it was a reminder of the night they'd shared a bed, when he'd left it at hers, a reminder that there was something unspoken which took courage to face, and a nod to what his fitness had represented. A nudge that he'd since gone off the tracks, much like their friendship.

'OK?' she asked, raising her eyebrows, asking if he wanted to try to be mates again. Self-consciously, she pushed back a spring of hair and tried to tuck it into her loose side ponytail, which gave her an excuse to break eye contact.

He made the most of it and stared at her, taking in her heart-shaped face dotted with beads of moisture and pink from the warm walk over here from the city centre, her freckles which could've been sprinkled on her like she was a cappuccino, the flutter of her doe-like eyelashes, her rosy full lips and the soft down at the curve of her cheek. Oh God, maybe they couldn't be friends, not really. Not after they'd both confessed they had non-platonic downstairs feelings for each other.

'Yep.' Of course. Forever. In spite of it all, he'd always want to try to be mates with her.

'We can talk about it if you want?' she muttered, looking up, the electricity of it plugging right into him, 'You know, I mean I'm fine about it all but if you …'

'Oh, no need. I haven't given it a thought, to be honest,' he lied.

'No. Me neither.' She was lying too. But what was the point? There were people who had the whole right time, right place thing going on. While they had the place bit right, it was wrong time-wise. As simple as that. Elvis had left the building. In their case, the bus had left the depot. They both nodded and smiled and examined the ceiling and the floor until they settled on each other again.

'So … can I come in then?' Charlie said, gingerly.

'Oh, right. Yes. Yes!' He was an idiot. He smacked his forehead with his fingers. When people came over the done thing was to invite them in. 'Ha! I've seen yours so I suppose you can see mine!' Oh God. He had just unintentionally done the worst, most cringiest double entendre. 'Not that I meant it like that … because we … I meant where we live, our houses. Well, your house, my flat …' He trailed off as she walked in deliberately looking anywhere but at him. He wanted to bite his fist in mortification. So he did behind her back. He performed a quick scan of the kitchen-diner-lounge to see if there was anything shaming to see in amongst heaps of dirty shorts, abandoned exercise mags and bits of paper. Then he saw Fflur's lipstick from yesterday on the worktop and he quickly covered it with his hand and rolled it off the counter and put it in a drawer. He didn't want her jumping to any conclusions.

He hadn't had time to check for incriminating evidence before Charlie'd arrived – he had been busy when she'd texted, he'd only seen her message twenty minutes ago and his armpits had been the priority. His hair was still wet from the shower and the towel he'd used was … where? Great. Thrown over the back of the sofa, probably giving off student damp smells. He leapt across to swipe it off and chucked it in the washing machine.

'God, it's gorgeous here!' Charlie said from the balcony bay which overlooked bobbing yachts and boats winking in the sunshine.

'Open the doors if you like,' he said. Blimey, he had doors that opened: he really had so much to offer a woman.

'It feels like I'm on holiday! On the riviera!' she called from outside. 'We should sit out here, soak it all up!'

The trouble was he had to be somewhere. He'd been distracted by it with her turning up here – the task ahead of him landed with a thud in his stomach. His hesitation drew her back inside and she spotted his packed bag on the table.

'Oh, sorry. You've got plans. Off anywhere nice?'

'Yeah, to see Sam,' he said, not feeling able to smile because of the nerves. 'Finally getting round to it.'

'Amazing, that's brilliant,' Charlie said, her face taken over by an encouraging smile.

'Yeah, I hope so.'

'Right, I'll be off then,' she said, moving towards the door. 'I'll leave you to it.'

'I'll come with you, actually,' he said, picking up his stuff, shutting the doors, searching for his trainers, almost leaving the flat before remembering he had something in the freezer he had to take.

'What's that?' Charlie asked as he emerged into the corridor with a thermal cooler which he tucked into his rucksack.

'Just some ice cream. Joe's. I got him some tubs, it's his favourite.'

'Ah! That's thoughtful. Get you! You're so prepared!'

'I know, did it all yesterday. Got him some felt tips, fancy ones, and a rugby ball. Usually when I pack for something I do it last minute. Honest to God, I once turned up in Goa with two pairs of pants and five jumpers.'

Charlie's laugh echoed off the walls of the stairway as they trotted down to the foyer and he forgot his fear when he saw her reach for a shiny silver bike resting against the wall.

'Nice wheels! I thought you'd walked.' He was impressed.

'I got it off Gumtree last week,' she said, tapping the handlebar. 'I ended up doing the Night Ride and loved it so much that I thought I'd join. It's fun. I go straight from work and then cycle home. They're a good bunch, a bit eccentric some of them but then it's only strangers you think of as normal until you get to know them, right?'

Del laughed. 'I was going to get the bus to Caswell but I think I'll ride too! My bike's in the storeroom.'

'Cool! I'll wait for you,' Charlie said, as he went into the back for his bike. 'Got a pump if you're a bit flat.'

Weirdly Del felt his heart racing at the prospect of the change in his plan from catching the bus to cycling. Or was it because he was with Charlie? Never mind that, he thought, squeezing his dusty tyres – he needed a top-up. Once that was done, Charlie and Del stepped out into the glorious bone-warming sunshine and mounted their saddles. While they fiddled with their helmets, Charlie sighed, smiled up at the sky and chit-chatted about the sea air and the weather. Which, it turned out, was all a precursor for what she really wanted to know.

'Are you meeting Fflur there then?' She spoke evenly as if she was making polite conversation. But what a question. He flicked his eyes towards her but she was adjusting her chin strap.

'She's not very well.' He didn't build on that – Charlie had been a bit touchy when he'd mentioned her before. He wasn't kidding himself she was jealous, it was more that Charlie knew how badly Fflur'd treated him and he looked weak, sort of, seeing her again. He would've felt the same if she'd let Jonny back into her life. But Fflur had changed, she was more vulnerable, less gung-ho – altogether more human. And she wasn't pushing for physical comfort either; he didn't know where it was going or if it was going anywhere but he still loved her. They'd decided not to rush into anything, a decision that had made them both laugh because they'd never thought they'd be capable of that, and what would be, would be. Her recovery from her trauma was so-so, one step forward and two back kind of thing. When she'd come to see him yesterday, she'd said she'd go with him, but he could tell she wasn't up to it. And if it didn't go well, then he'd offload on her and it might affect her. He'd made the choice for her – and really, he should grow a pair. He was thirty-five and he didn't need someone to hold his hand ...

'She offered to go with you though so that's what counts,' Charlie said, pulling up beside him. 'You wouldn't be here if it hadn't been for that.'

That was very generous of Charlie. But really, if he was going to be honest, it had nothing to do with Fflur. He wouldn't be on his way to see Sam if it hadn't been for Charlie! She'd set this all off by turning up here in March, making him challenge what he was doing with his life, inspiring him to make a change: she had been the one to tell him to look at what Sam could do, not what he couldn't. And then two weeks ago when Charlie had showed her disappointment that he hadn't yet been to see him once he'd passed his lifeguard course – that had been the definitive spur to action. Last Sunday he'd been with Rhian so that left today ... and so he'd cleared it all with Mam and Dad and Rhian and Becky and then sent a text to Sam to say he was coming and he'd replied with a string of smiley faces and Del knew once that had happened he would go no matter what.

So no, it wasn't down to Fflur. It was all Charlie's doing. But he couldn't say it to Charlie because he had no right to lay it on her: she'd been through enough emotional stuff with her ex. He didn't want to put this her way in case she saw it as manipulation or meaningful. Because he didn't want to complicate things, not when she had come out the other side and found happiness. That was enough to calm him, to put all of that aside and to focus on the ride along Swansea Bay's sweeping six-mile curve of beach, cycle path, green spaces, walkers and joggers.

By the time they got to Mumbles, there was only a mile and a half to go to get to Caswell. Del pulled up just by the roundabout at Newton Road to give Charlie the chance to say goodbye but instead she overtook him and carried on up the hill, turning left onto Langland Road. Both puffing and panting, with thighs screaming as they stood to dig deep, they went up and up and then just when they couldn't take it any more, as their chins hit their chests, the crest turned into a dip and they free-wheeled down Caswell Road to the bay.

Wordlessly, Charlie followed him all the way to Eden House.

'You don't have to do this,' Del said, as they locked up their bikes and crunched up the gravel of the driveway together. He'd had six months to prepare for this, since he'd last seen Sam. Plus nearly twelve years. It didn't stop the shaky breaths though.

'I'm not doing anything,' she smiled as they entered the building. 'I'll just wait for you. There's a family room, look, it says there.'

She squeezed his hand and then disappeared, leaving him alone at the foot of the stairs. He thought of her bravery and her resolve and it spurred him up two steps at a time. Right, come on, Del, you've got to do this, he thought, as he reached Sam's floor and then his corridor, where the door was ajar and he could see a signed poster of the captain of the Welsh rugby team on his wall.

He stopped, feeling a wave of emotion. This was it. Was he going to wipe-out? Was he hell. He rode it all the way down the hall and with a knock and into Sam's flat, calling his name, and standing there as his brother looked up and gave him a huge grin.

'Bro!' Del cried, holding out his arms. It was like being kids again as Sam came at him in a red Wales rugby shirt not knowing his strength, Del tensing his tummy muscles and his legs as their bodies collided, squashing the breath out of their chests. Sam had put a bit of weight on since January – it was a chin-wobbler moment: he'd noticed it because it had been so long since he'd seen him.

'Where've you been? You've been ages,' Sam said, slapping him on the back with giant's hands. He said it with such innocence that Del could've cried.

'Got held up, son.' He heard himself on the edge of tears. He had to stop it before he wept. Pity, he wasn't having any of it, never again. Clearing his throat, he managed it. 'I'm really sorry. Just had a few things to sort out, you know?'

'Yeah, bro,' Sam said, simply, before he stopped to examine Del's wave tattoo as he always had done and then led him to the sofa where he put his arm around Del's shoulders unselfconsciously. The telly was on and there was a flash of legs and mud.

'What you watching?' He knew what he was watching. It was the DVD that the parents of Sam's mate Tim, the ones he'd met before when he'd come up to the unit, had given them.

'Rugby. My favourite. Look! Look at this try!'

Del forgot it all then – this was what they'd always

done together, chilling out with the sport on, shouting at the ref, cheering the try over the line. It was timeless, this bond between them, he could see it now, he could feel it in his heart.

'We've won! Wales have won!' Sam cried as if this was happening live, not that he'd seen this clip over and over until he knew the words of the commentary which he began to recite.

'We have, Sam,' Del said as his brother leapt on him in celebration. 'We always do.'

Sam pulled away and shook his head. 'We don't! We've gone to shit since I stopped playing.'

Del burst out laughing. 'We can fix that, if you'd like?'

'Maybe,' Sam said, shrugging. It was too open a concept for him – it was a reminder of how rusty Del was at this. Nuance was confusing to him: he had to make sure he was straightforward. 'I've brought you some stuff,' he said, getting up to get his bag. 'A ball. We could have a throw later if you wanted?'

'Yeah?' His eyes were bursting but then his face dropped. Fuck, what had Del done? What if he'd let him down? What if he'd ballsed it up because Sam could see he was trying so hard and it was coming over as clumsy? This boded badly for the future, his doubt whispered, you've come in here and within two minutes ruined it yet again. What hope do you have for a new start with him, eh?

'I can't today. Art club later.'

His fear shrivelled instantly – it was a pardon, that's for sure.

'Cool. You might need these then ...' He took out the pens and chucked them at him.

Sam missed and Del cursed his own stupidity: why

did he have to go and do that? He wasn't who he was, Del raged, Sam couldn't catch anything these days except a cold. But, thank God, Sam wasn't bothered because he was so excited about the gift. He simply picked up the pack and turned them around and around examining them at every angle with undiluted childlike joy.

Focus on what he can do, he heard Charlie saying to him.

'What you working on in art club?' Because that was something he could do.

'A picture for Mam.'

He remembered the one Sam had drawn of himself with Del. The one that had crushed him when he was in a bad place in January and the way he'd discarded it because it had hurt him so deeply.

'Oh, she'll love it. Like I love mine,' he said, now realising it. 'I haven't had it framed yet but I will.'

'Yeah?' Sam said, delighted.

'Maybe we can do an exhibition here of your work?' Was that too much, too keen? Del waited and prayed he'd got it right.

'We're doing one soon. In a place in Swansea.'

'Amazing!' And not just because it meant Del was on the right track with what Sam was capable of but because anyone putting on a display of their work had balls the size of beanbags. That took guts.

'Oh, one last thing,' Del said, remembering the ice cream, 'you better put this away before it melts.'

Sam's jaw dropped and he ripped the carton off him like he was in a tackle.

'Got them especially from Joe's. Remember? When we'd go with Mam and Dad for sundaes?'

Sam looked at him blankly. 'I don't always … because of this.' He tapped his head. Del waited for the blow to his heart – of course, the nurses had said way back that his memory would be affected. But Sam didn't look sad.

'Tell me what we'd have,' he said, as if Del had the key to the treasure.

'You, a cherry one with a flake and nuts, me, vanilla with strawberry sauce. And a flake because I had to copy you … you were my hero.'

Sam giggled as he opened his freezer compartment and carefully stacked the tubs away.

'In fact, you still are.'

He wasn't expecting any reaction. He was just happy to have said it because it was true: Del was seeing his brother as he was, not as he had been. He'd overcome so much and was still going. Sam walked back to Del and looked serious for a moment.

'Have you got a girlfriend?' he asked.

Del laughed. 'Nope. I'm useless with women.' He felt a pang that he couldn't discuss his feelings for Charlie with his big brother. It was too abstract, too vague. 'Have you?'

Sam shook his head and he was lost in thought for a moment.

'Rhian is my daughter,' he said, matter of factly. 'Her mum was my girlfriend. I remember that. I love Rhian so much.'

There we go, Del thought, he hadn't forgotten everything. He may be reciting what he'd been told or he might have looked in the recesses of his mind and found it tucked away. But it didn't matter when love remained.

'My chalkboard says she's coming later. You better go,'

Sam announced without awkwardness. Del understood social niceties weren't his strong point – ha, like me, he thought, but at least Sam had an excuse. He wasn't offended, it was refreshing to get straight to the point.

'No problem. I'll see you next week, yeah? Or sooner? It's up to you.'

'I'll have to check my diary.'

It made Del snort. Here Sam was, with a busy life, happy and fulfilled, and Del was the one who had to get cracking on what happened next. Sam came at him again but this time it was a bear hug but a gentle one as if he was Paddington.

'Bye,' he said simply, waving at the threshold of his flat.

'Bye, bro.' Del's heart was filled with … what? He'd expected this morning would leave him heavy but instead he was light and buzzing, chuffed to bits and the most positive he'd felt in years. It was redemption, that's what it was. Skipping down the stairs, he went to find Charlie in the family room. And he did a double-take when he saw Charlie deep in conversation with Mam and Dad while Rhian was marvelling at her hair and plaiting corn rows on the top of her head. They were all here! All his favourites!

'How did it go?' Charlie asked amidst them as if she'd been part of the family forever.

'Good,' he said, emphatically. 'I'll tell you later. Do you mind if I just nip to speak to one of the guys here? I've had this idea for a while and I wasn't sure it'd work but coming here makes it seem possible. I want to see if I can set up a beach day for the residents. Bit of surfing, I've seen it online, you can get custom-made boards with harnesses and seats. Hold a rugby tournament, maybe, too.' Because that was what he was going to do, he'd decided.

Stay at Cheer on the Pier and set up a surf school for people with disabilities. There were a few around the UK but none in Wales. It'd combine his love of action and adventure with his newly discovered sensible side. Maybe he'd be able to leave the cafe if he made a success of it …

'And Rhian, next time we're at the hut, I'll join you for a sea swim!'

'No way!' Rhian said, chuffed to bits.

His mother beamed at him with eyes which threatened to spill happy tears. But she kept it together and asked if Charlie would like to come for Sunday lunch once her, Dad and Rhian had been up to see Sam, perhaps? Sam wasn't coming because he was making his own with Tim. God bless him. Charlie was looking at Del with raised eyebrows as if he was kingmaker: she was checking it was OK with him. If only it was that simple: this was a biggie. Meeting the parents before any move had been made. They hadn't been allowed anywhere near Fflur when she came on the scene – he had to make sure she wouldn't run a mile when they produced the baby photos.

But Charlie was different. And he needed to make it up to Mam.

'Yeah, awesome, Mam,' he said – then to Charlie, 'As long as you don't nick all the roasties. Because my mam's are world-beaters!'

By the smile on his mother's face, it was as if he'd just proposed to Charlie there and then. But it was just lunch. And that was good enough.

41

'The above-temperatures for this time of year are coming to an end, folks. It wouldn't be the August bank holiday weekend if we didn't have heavy rain, stormy seas and 60 mph winds heading for South Wales. Mumbles Head is expected to bear the brunt so brace yourselves. Now, back to Sian for *Home Time* …'

Charlie stepped off the bus and watched with pride as it pulled away.

Up close, it looked fantastic and the impact remained as it continued its journey around Mumbles. The bright yellow sunshine, with red love-heart emoji eyes and streaking rays plastered on both sides and the back of the bus, was shining like a beacon, giving the real beating sun a bit of competition. Charlie could see heads turning all the way up the prom.

She couldn't have asked for more. The livery, which read 'Find Your Crush on the Bus at Party on the Pier', had been adopted by every vehicle on the Mumbles routes in a sponsorship deal from a local hi-tech company. It had been covered by the local press and had even trended on Twitter in Swansea under the hashtag

#lovebus. Facebook was going mad for it too with threads of confessions of who fancied whom on their commute.

Tickets were selling like hot Welshcakes – more than half of the five hundred on sale for twenty-five pounds and included a welcome cocktail, canapés and live entertainment, had gone. The departments involved reckoned walk-ups would make it a sell-out on the night.

Charlie bloody hoped so, she thought as she walked up the pier and into the shadow of the huge marquee that had been erected. The bash was two days away. The venue was yet to be tarted up so it looked like a field hospital. The stage was halfway there and the furniture was stacked waiting but the decor wouldn't be arriving until Saturday morning. Merri would be working through the next two nights to get the canapés ready. Colin and the technicians had to set up the sound system. The pop-up food stalls were yet to be constructed, the afternoon procession was one long nightmare of juggling participants, there was an online poll to set up to ask which charities should benefit from the proceeds and health and safety was a total headache of cable covers and wire trip hazards. At least it hadn't been Delme in charge! And she still hadn't worked out what she was going to wear! Luckily, Libby was coming down to help her choose from a few options she had to meet the beach party theme, combining her visit with picking up her wedding lingerie. Charlie had asked Zoe but she hadn't replied. There was no time to worry about that though: Zoe had probably fallen in love again! Or she was just busy – Charlie knew the feeling. Wasn't she consumed by work? The flutter in her stomach as she entered Sunshine FM agreed with her.

Tina had given her a moment yesterday in work to

say Sian was making the final recommendations to head office for whoever was chosen as the new boss. She didn't say anything else and Charlie wouldn't have dreamed of asking her, but her eyes had communicated it was crunch time for everyone. The latest listener figures were due any day – that would have an impact too, as would the efforts of the teams behind each show to make themselves a standout identity. Whispers were going around that some of the weekend DJs had upped their game with inventive formats which were destined for weekdays. Charlie had certainly noticed a change in tempo, with outside broadcasts at community events and more upbeat playlists alongside the classic Welsh artists that the older generation loved. Sunshine FM had become an altogether different place to work as a result. It felt more dynamic, particularly during the pre-show brainstorming meetings between Joanie, Roy and Charlie. They'd been busting their collective rude bits lately.

At her desk, Charlie found an envelope marked 'Confidential' with her name on it. This was mysterious, she thought, as she pulled out a newspaper article from the *Evening Post*.

It was about a man who'd appeared in court charged with offences under the Proceeds of Crime Act. His name had been circled: Gareth Edwards. And Tina's handwriting beneath said 'Hell hath no fury like two women scorned'. It was brilliant work! She rang her straight away.

'We both went forward to the police. Abigail has been questioned but they reckon the CPS won't bother with it because she'd been forced to smuggle the phone and hide the money under duress.'

'That's great news.'

'Oh, and the divorce is under way! I can't thank you enough, Charlie. Without you ... Listen, I'm going to start telling people about Gareth and what happened. Not in any big announcement way but just as I go along. What do you think? Because I trust your opinion.'

'I reckon you know your own mind best of all, Tina. And I've got your back.'

'Oh, I know, Charlie. And I've got yours.'

Charlie couldn't help but read into that: was Tina saying her job was safe? Or did she mean it affectionately? Then she corrected herself. What was it she'd said to Tina about self-approval ... that was what mattered and Charlie was closing in on it.

'By the way, do you need any veg? I've got cucumbers coming out of my ears!'

'Yes, please! But don't let Merri hear that or she'll start putting suggestive emojis on your cappuccino!'

Talking of which, a coffee appeared under Charlie's nose.

'I'll bring some in tomorrow for you and Gen,' Tina said, 'and if you're still OK to donate—'

'Sorted already. I bought some this morning. It's such a fab idea.'

Tina was organising a collection of rice and pasta, toiletries and tinned veg to donate to a foodbank.

'Well, I wanted to redress the balance,' Tina said. 'That whole thing about Gareth committing a so-called "victimless" white-collar crime ... Now I'm not under his spell any more I can see him as the vermin he is. Society suffers.'

'From Delme, on the house,' Joanie said, nodding at the cup on Charlie's desk when she was off the phone.

She peeked under the lid to see a four-leaf clover on the foam of her latte. He was wishing her good luck – he knew that was the only thing on her mind. What was on her heart though was a different matter: Delme Noble. It didn't signify anything but she'd seen his flat and met his family, sat down over a roast with them, got to see him in his own environment and she'd liked it very much. But it was an extraordinarily intimate thing to have been part of when they were only friends. It hadn't escaped her notice either that the deadline he'd mentioned when he'd stayed over was almost up. When he'd asked her if she'd consider seeing him as someone more than a mate. She doubted he even remembered that – so much had happened to him since then. He was solid, back on an even keel, having had a wobble in between. Visiting Sam had made him grow up overnight. She didn't want to rock his boat – and Fflur was clearly still on the scene. She'd seen some girly stuff in his flat when she'd visited, a cardi in amongst some clothes and a lipstick on the side, which was bound to be hers. Did it mean they were an item again? Or almost one? Charlie continually reminded herself it wasn't her business – she'd given up the right to know his personal stuff when she'd told him she couldn't promise him anything. She did it again now and caught Joanie smiling – no! Mooning romantically over her coffee cup.

'What did you get?'

'Dancing ladies!'

'What does that mean?' Charlie said.

Joanie smirked. Charlie narrowed her eyes at her across the table. There was something else going on, she could tell.

'All will be revealed!' was all she'd say.

The 4 p.m. *Home Time* jingle began and Sian's voice announced the news and weather.

'Right, here comes Roy. Roy! Let's do this. Party on the Pier recap then we'll talk tonight's show.

'First up,' Charlie said, 'is Specs Appeal and Mr Bookworm. Have we got them confirmed?'

'Tick,' Joanie crowed. 'As are Geek in Glasses and Zombie Girl, Looks Like Frank Sinatra and Liza Minelli Lady, and Bearded Man and Hipster Chick, which takes us to four couples.'

'Fab. I can't wait for that bit, that's what the night is all about.' Charlie hugged herself at the prospect of the finale when a procession of lovebirds who'd met on board through the *Evening Mumbles* show would play a game of 'Mr & Mrs', during which they'd have to show how well they knew each other, competing for the title of Crush on the Bus of the Year.

Sucking the hair of his beard on his top lip, Roy wasn't looking quite as thrilled though. 'Have you seen the forecast? They say there's a chance it'll miss us by a whisker but there's a big storm on its way.'

On cue, the newsreader was introducing the weather and they all listened aghast.

'It's not ... the Pembrokeshire Dangler is it?' Joanie cried.

'The what?' Charlie gasped.

'It's when showers in the Irish Sea turn furious and dump their load.'

Charlie shuddered.

'The dangler, ladies,' Roy said sternly, 'is a winter phenomena. You're not taking this seriously.'

'I've never been more serious about anything in my

entire life, Roy,' Charlie said. 'There's not much we can do though if it hits us. The party either happens or it's cancelled. There's no middle ground. We can't exactly shift venues and move everything like that,' she said, clicking her fingers. 'We have to keep going as if it's going ahead.'

'I agree. Positive vibes all the way from me,' Joanie said.

'All right. Count me in,' Roy said. 'I'm an old grump at the moment. This review is getting me down.'

'But you're so experienced! They won't get rid of you!' Charlie said.

'I'm a dinosaur, that's what I am. And a kid would get half my wages.'

Shit. No one was safe. 'That's why we have to nail this!' Charlie said.

'Agreed,' Roy said, 'So tonight …'

'What you thinking?' Joanie said.

'The big push. Not just for Saturday night. But for our place on this station.' He gave the table a whack with his fist. 'No one knows how long we've got left; we've had a good six months building up *Evening Mumbles*. I think we can say we've been the first to give it a bit of welly. Crush on the Bus and Bring Me Sunshine have lasted longer than any previous formats in years, well, since I've been on the show. But we can't rest on our laurels. We have to treat tonight and the night after that and the night after that as if it's our last show.'

'Yes, sir,' Joanie said.

'Definitely,' Charlie agreed. 'And I've been working on a few ideas for the future. I hadn't told you because I didn't feel I was up to it.'

Joanie and Roy swapped 'what was she on about' faces.

'You two, without you, I'd never have made it past the

first night. You've been incredible.'

The pair of them shook their heads.

'No, no, listen, you have. You believed in me when I didn't.'

'We kind of had no choice,' Joanie laughed, winking.

'That is so true!' Charlie said, knowing that underneath Joanie loved her back.

'Now you listen,' Roy said at his most gruff, 'I don't want to hear any more about it. You've earned your place here and we're a team, us three.'

Charlie and Joanie had a little simper at their boss giving them some praise.

'But don't go soft,' he warned them. 'Now about those ideas, come on, let's be having them.'

It was the happiest working day of Charlie's life. She was about to start gushing all over again when Roy lifted an eyebrow. So she found her secret notepad, the one she'd spent idle moments scribbling down thoughts and details at random in – at random! – about tune-in triggers, capturing and connecting with listeners, brand building and tailored adverts. The 'zoo' format introduced by Steve Wright was becoming old hat – what would come next? Online radio was taking off. Should we stream on the internet? Did Sunshine FM need an app? What about a Christmas confessions slot called Deck the Halls With Boughs of Sorry? A Christmas singles night called Mingle All the Way? Make our station fun, happy and local: stand-up slots, musical talent showcases, vinyl sessions, a day in the life of Mumbles characters, appeals for good causes ...

This was the list she'd never dared to dream she would share. With pride, Charlie drew breath to start the next bulletin of her career.

42

'So here's your host for the Party on the Pier! The one and only ...'

⟨~⟩

It was a miracle! The storm had somehow held off as if health and safety Brian had ordered a directive for it to stay away.

At least that's what it had looked like every time Charlie had seen him peering at the horizon through polycarbonate goggles and muttering into his walkie-talkie. Whatever was responsible, she simply accepted it as good fortune, and payback for everyone's hard work.

It had been muggy all day – the clouds had sat heavily on the green sea, flattening it down so everything was eerily still. This was the calm before tonight's show, which Charlie had been not just getting on the road since breakfast but driving it all the way.

Now as the early evening turned sticky and sultry, she was getting changed in the loos at work in her first moment to reflect on how things had gone.

It had been so far, so brilliant: the afternoon procession of vintage open-top buses had carried Cubs and Brownies, sports clubs and charities, plus lifeboatmen and women, reflecting the vibrancy of Mumbles. People had flocked to watch and soak up the atmosphere, which smelt of candyfloss thanks to the temporary fairground on the prom. There'd been a buzz behind the scenes too, where Charlie had spent most of her day, performing a non-stop juggling act of dressing the marquee, setting up food stalls, arranging tables and ticking things off her list.

Physically, she was tired. Charlie could see it in the mirror as she put on her face: she'd barely had a bite to eat, her throat was dry from all the talking and her cheeks were pink. But she'd get through the Party on the Pier with a second wind, which was beginning to stir inside. Her outfit pepped her up too – she'd gone for the hula girl look with a black body attached to a yellow grass skirt and red, purple and orange flowery garlands on her wrists, around her neck and on top of her hair that she was wearing loose. Not bad, she thought, giving her skirt a swish, as long as everyone else was going along with the beach party theme. A rush of heat hit her all over – this was the doubt she'd been batting off all day. It seemed to know she was alone. She let it have its moment. If she'd learned nothing else this last six months it was that she could overcome it: channel it into something more power-ful, regard it as adrenalin and use the moment to cross-check herself. With that, her determination knocked the negatives for six. She was Charlie Bold! she told herself as she stepped out of the radio station onto the pier. While it was a long way from being dark, dusk was falling and her glow matched the strings of sunshine-yellow bulbs that she'd hung between the railings earlier in the day. But it was nothing compared to how she felt when she entered the marquee: her spirits went full wattage.

Yes, she had been part of the makeover crew but where it had been empty and static, now just five minutes after the doors had opened, it was alive with music, laughter, delicious smells and smile upon smile. The guests had really gone to town, or rather the beach, with their outfits. Board shorts and wet suits were teamed with dickie bows, there were lifeguards, hat-tipping Aussie hunks and *Baywatch* babes, sailors, men and women in sarongs, Neptunes, two crabs, a shark and a squid. The bar was a raffia-roofed Hawaiian tiki hut which featured tropical potted plants provided by the local garden centre. One food stall was serving chips in small buckets, Joe's Ice Cream was selling cones off an old-fashioned bike and the greengrocer was doing brisk trade with tropical fruit kebabs. There were beach umbrellas and pink flamingoes everywhere: large ones on the tables and small ones in cocktails.

A net bulging with hundreds of Sunshine FM beach balls covered the ceiling – when the disco began, they'd be released from on high. And helium balloons of sunshines with love-heart eyes shone brilliantly here and there wafting to and fro as if they were warming up to boogie.

It couldn't get better than that, surely?

Except there waving at her were her mum and dad with Libby, who was sporting a scuba mask and flippers.

'You came!' she shouted at her parents, who she'd invited but hadn't expected to make the trip, let alone look the part. Charlie grabbed them in a group hug and then stepped back to admire their costumes. Dad was a comedy bearded Captain Birdseye and Mum was a fisherwoman in yellow mac and sou'wester and a necklace of plastic trout. She felt delirious with the hilarity of it all.

'We're booked in a B&B; we got some right funny looks when we left to walk over,' Mum said.

'Isn't it obvious I'm Captain Birdseye?' Dad said with a withering shake of his head. 'It could've been worse. The fancy-dress shop had some idiot trying on a foam fishfinger!'

'I can't believe you're here!'

''Til Monday so don't you go spoiling our fun, you go off and do what you've got to do,' Mum said.

'There's someone else you've got to see,' Libby said, looking back at the ladies' loos and pointing at a scarlet-lipped woman with the glossiest black bob and bangs – waddling towards her in a *Finding Nemo* onesie.

'Zoe!' Charlie squealed so excitedly she was lucky she didn't pop a tonsil. Her reaction wasn't just out of glee at seeing her old friend but because of the surprise of her appearance. She'd either put on loads of weight or she was ...

'Yes, breaking news, babe. I'm up the duff.'

'What? When? Oh, wow!' Her voice was husky with surprise and emotion.

'I see you've turned into Bonnie Tyler!' she cackled. 'I'm five months gone. The love of my life turned out to be a piece of shit. I had to get signed off because I had that pukey thing Kate Middleton had so I was in and out of hospital. Then I had to move back in with my mum. Sorry I went off radar for a bit.'

'No wonder! Why didn't you say anything?'

'Because it was about time I looked after myself. You know, not lay my problems at your feet like I always did. Oh hang about, I need to go for a wee again,' she said, unzipping herself and revealing a cleavage the size of two watermelons. 'Bad planning on my part for wearing this. Oh, and before I forget – baby brain is the pits, let me tell you – apparently Jonny made it to Exeter ... but he turned up drunk on his first shift and got the elbow!'

Charlie sniggered but quickly all she felt was pity. That life was done and dusted.

She spun round, thinking she would burst with happiness. And she began to when she clapped eyes on a pair of heads smooching at the DJ decks belonging to Merri and DJ Disgo who were in matching blue and white striped Victorian bathers. What the hell? So that was what the foam emojis had all been about!

Charlie was bubbling over – and then she was overflowing because walking towards her were two pirates ... two friends she knew so well – but clearly not well enough because Claudia and Joanie were holding hands and looking besotted with each other. This couldn't be happening – it was all too surreal. Taking a second to make sure she wasn't in a parallel universe didn't help much. Bus conductors walking around with ticket machines for the raffle and unicycling Night Riders in snorkels made her feel even dizzier. But she fit right in with her impression of a fish opening and closing her gob. It was real! And it was bloody lovely!

'I'd like you to meet my crush on the bus,' Joanie said coyly, beneath a face-painted moustache.

'So you know I said I'd never been in love ...' Claudia said, over her beard which tumbled down her New Romantic black buttoned jacket. 'This kind of explains it. I was barking up the wrong tree!'

Charlie couldn't speak she was so amazed. All she could do was applaud.

Gen appeared carrying a tray of cocktails with Tina – the pair of them were in ship ahoy uniforms with jaunty white caps, shift dresses decorated with mini anchors and red heels. They looked impossibly glamorous with styled and set hair as if they were in a 1940s swing band.

'Look what Gen made!' Tina said, giving Charlie a twirl. 'I feel like the belle of the ball!'

She looked it too … but she had competition. Charlie's guts dropped at the sight across the marquee of a foxy redhead, who was wiggling as she walked with her hands threaded through the arms of two men Charlie recognised. Dressed as the Littlest Mermaid complete with lilac bandeau bra and a skin-tight green skirt made of scaly sequins, Fflur was being supported by Delme and Rodney. Charlie's jealousy felt as naked as Fflur's toned midriff. Quickly, she concentrated on doing the opposite of what she really thought with a wave in their direction. Fflur tossed her thick mane as if she was a film star and Rodney saluted with an orange hand inside his fishfinger costume – he was the idiot Dad had seen in the fancy-dress shop. Delme was the only one who came over and he did so with an over-the-top smoothy swagger in keeping with his garish pink Hawaiian shirt, shorts and flip-flops.

'I know, I know, lush aren't I?' he said to her, pretending to push back a crowd of admirers. It was a bit off seeing as he had turned up with that trophy on his arm. Rodney meanwhile was gawping at Joanie and Claudia as if it was Christmas. 'Tonight's the night, then.'

'It sure is,' Charlie said, knowing he was referring to the event but unable to stop herself thinking of the fifty-day deadline which was hours away. It was irrelevant now, of course. He'd brought Fflur as his plus one – and considering the scale of the night and the people who'd be here and witness it, it was a grand statement. They were obviously back on. Charlie was crushed: if only he could've waited to do this. It was all a bit 'flaunting it' in her eyes. Yet, there was no anger, more a sense of defeat because she couldn't complain. She hadn't told him her feelings; in fact she hadn't even admitted them to herself. Standing here now, they began to bud in her heart, all brave now that the chance to confess had gone. Come on, Charlie, she told herself, love was no good at paying the bills. The only guarantee if you jumped from one bloke to the next was a twisted ankle and she'd had one of those thanks to him already. Work was what she needed to focus on now, she said firmly in her head. Not how handsome he was with his brown curls and smooth tanned skin, which, maddeningly, looked even more gorgeous next to the pink of his get-up.

'I need to talk to you later,' he said, just as a hush fell under canvas.

For Sian was up on stage, praising the community and Sunshine FM for what was going to be a fantastic night and she was introducing Charlie as 'your compère'.

The feverish excitement within her frothed over sending her racing up the steps to start the live broadcast which would be on air for the next two hours. Roy, who was already in position at the mixing desk in a white peaked Popeye cap, was joined by Joanie but only after she'd kissed Claudia goodbye as if she was leaving the country to go to war. The *Evening Mumbles* music began, Joanie was counting her in, three-two-one, and then it was all systems go as Charlie went to shout a 'Welcome everyone to Party on the Pier!'.

Except her voice had turned to sandpaper. She tried again, tensing her diaphragm to deliver it with force but it ended in an extended croak. The faces around her were slowly realising she couldn't talk. That heat she'd felt earlier prickled again, her forehead was beading with sweat and her vision went funny as if she was looking into the back of a spoon. It was all gurning flamingoes and leering sea creatures.

No, this couldn't be happening, not now at her big moment. She tried again but her throat burned and she felt needles when she tried to swallow.

The colour drained from her eyes when she realised she was going to have to surrender. The injustice brought tears to her eyes: she'd overcome losing her voice here at Sunshine FM. But now when she was willing, she was still unable. So much for redemption, hard work and atonement.

Charlie looked across the crowd for help. There was Ivor Mone in a dishevelled dinner jacket with red-wine stains on his shirt, holding down some poor woman from sales on his lap. Ed Walker hadn't bothered to come and DJ Disgo was gazing at Merri as if they were on their own island paradise. Then she clapped eyes on the one person who was capable – and offering – to do it. Grateful the show would go on and desperate to shake the dizziness, she nodded and in a split second he was by her side, taking her microphone.

Sian stepped forward, understanding what was happening. 'Change of plan! So without further ado, here's your host for the Party on the Pier, the one and only Delme Noble!'

'Are you ready to rumble, Mumbles?' Delme cried. A

small cheer went up but it wasn't enough for him. 'I said, ARE YOU READY TO RUMBLE, MUMBLES?'

A roar went up as he pumped the air.

'Strap yourselves in, people, put on your shades. It's *Evening Mumbles* and tonight we'll be showing you … a whole lotta love! Get ready! Get steady! Let's gooooo!'

Joanie was on it and before he'd even finished his intro the guitar riff of Led Zeppelin's *Whole Lotta Love* was shaking the speakers as the crowd went wild.

He was a genius. He was a life saver, and not just in the saving lives at sea department. With the last of her energy, Charlie threw her arms around him before her legs turned weak. Within a few minutes, he'd carried her to the St John Ambulance tent where he gave her the tortured look of being torn between wanting to stay to help her but being needed back on stage. Charlie wouldn't have any of it – she ordered him away as her eyes slammed shut. The next thing she knew, she woke up on a camp bed with her mother patting her hand.

'Oh, Mum!' Charlie whispered, feeling her neck glands throbbing, her head aching and her teeth chattering.

'Don't talk! It's fine. Your boss, Sian's been in and said you were a trooper. And Delme's done you proud. Listen!' Mum said, as the muffled boom of his lilting accent went up and down in the background. A dose of paracetamol and a blanket later, he was by her side, flapping with concern.

'You were amazing!' she said through a mouth of gravel.

'You were robbed,' he said, shaking his head. 'I'm so sorry. How are you feeling?'

'Boiling cold, freezing hot. But so grateful. You saved me again.' This damsel in Hawaiian dress.

'Hardly. You did all the work, I got all the glory. We're a team,' he said, dabbing her rosy face with a wet flannel. He understood. He always had. 'Let me take you home, we're done here.' He held up a door key which Gen had given him so he could.

'Mum says she'll do it.'

'She's on the dance floor with your old man. I don't want a late night. I'm taking Rhian and Sam to Langland Bay tomorrow.'

'What about Fflur?' Charlie whispered.

'She's cool about it. Don't worry.'

Oh God, that was even worse – his girlfriend was actually really nice.

And with that, he was helping her up and holding her steady with muscular arms and filling her in on the night as they walked down the pier, the whoops and music swallowed by the waves. '"Mr & Mrs" was a hit,' Del said, filling her in. 'Mr Bookworm and Specs Appeal won. And then he only went and got down on one knee at the end. She said yes!'

'A Crush on the Bus wedding! Do you reckon we can broadcast from it?' she said, as he hailed a cab.

'Would you switch that brain off,' he said, as he put his arm around her shoulder. The motion of the journey made her nod off and he had to rouse her when they pulled up at her house. Inside, he hurried her upstairs, plumping pillows and turning the lights on low before he gathered water and painkillers for the night, giving her the chance to get into an old nightie. Her bed had never felt so good.

'All right, then?' he said, smoothing the duvet, and then his thighs, his lovely firm thighs, and rubbing his hands, his soft but capable hands. She was slipping into a light-headed daze, imagining she was in a feathered nest, so settled and finally warm.

'Need anything else … or?'

'Huh?'

'Shall I shoot?'

He wanted to go. Of course he did – who in their right mind would stay longer than was necessary in the company of a sweaty, shivering ill person.

'Yes, course. I just need to sleep.' She couldn't stop a huge ugly yawn. What must she look like? And this was the second time he'd seen her in a mess in nightwear.

'Whatever it was you wanted to tell me—'

'It can wait. It's nothing important. I just want you to get better.'

He gave her arm a squeeze. A compassionate friend-ly-with-concern squeeze which said she was no match for Fflur. She saw on her bedside clock it was approaching midnight. The deadline was nigh. The deadline was meaningless. Whatever they'd had had hitched a ride and gone. He was her mate. And actually that was OK. Heart-breaking but survivable. There'd been so much love tonight to make up for that, what with Mum and Dad, Libby and Zoe, Merri and DJ Disgo, Tina and Gen and Joanie and Claudia. Their happiness was what mattered.

Delme retreated to the door.

'I'll ring you tomorrow,' she said, as brightly as she could muster which only made her sound like an adolescent boy whose voice was breaking.

'Don't worry. Your parents are here. Enjoy them. I'll see you soon.'

She nodded and shut her eyes, not wanting to see him leave, hoping insanely that he'd change his mind and insist on lying beside her all night. She heard the door close on the house and her heart. And she burrowed herself into her comfort zone so deeply she wouldn't come up for air until Sunday lunchtime.

43

Half past eight on a Friday night and Delme was done in.

He hadn't had a day off this week because it was the final push of the summer holidays and Merri needed all hands on deck. His evenings had been spent applying to the RNLI for a job next year and researching how to go about setting up a surf-therapy school, including training and shadowing another outfit in Cornwall. His head was full of emails he had to write and replies he had to send. But admin wasn't his forte. Put him in front of a group of people and he could wing it but sitting down to type those words down was too big a hurdle tonight.

He shut his laptop and sprawled his naked top half over the kitchen table. Obviously he elbowed his bowl of cold chicken noodle soup and it slopped over the lip and pooled into his lap. Still a clumsy fool even if he was more fulfilled than he'd ever been. Apart from the Charlie thing. That was still unresolved. Massively. And it would forever be that way.

The fifty-day deadline he'd been counting down had passed unnoticed by her. OK, he didn't want to be all Hollywood about it – he hadn't exactly been mooning about beneath a huge ticking clock, sighing at the thought of her. Well, not much anyway. But he had hoped she'd have acknowledged it either on the night or afterwards. Then again, if he was going to give someone bad news wouldn't he try to dodge it too? He'd alluded to it, hadn't he, when he'd said he'd wanted to have a word with her just before she'd gone on stage.

He hadn't rehearsed it, he wasn't that 'new and improved', but he'd known what it was he'd wanted to tell her: he still had feelings for her. Big ones, bigger than he'd ever had for someone before, that he couldn't suppress. His love for Fflur was a fondness you had for someone who had once meant something: to his relief, Fflur felt the same; she'd admitted she hadn't wanted to come to see Sam because she was worried he'd take it as a sign she wanted to be back in his life for good. People who had been together often fell back into it when shit happened – it was human nature to seek comfort. They'd remained friends, and Rodney's fiancée had pulled out of going to the party so Del had offered Fflur the ticket as a gesture. He hadn't expected her to come but having told her about Charlie, she'd said she'd come to make him tell her. If he didn't, she would.

It turned out to be a good thing he hadn't said any of this to Charlie – it might've looked as if he wanted the night to be about him rather than her success. The kind of thing Jonny would've done.

And he didn't think himself that important. Definitely not more important than everything that had consumed her – the Party on the Pier, falling ill and having her parents and friends around. She'd said she'd ring the next day but she hadn't. He'd checked on the grapevine she was on the mend – she was and his ego had to face facts that he couldn't blame her silence on, God forbid, a coma.

As he rubbed his lap with a tea towel, he realised he had to let go. Churning it all around wasn't going to get him anywhere. It was staring him in the eyeballs: they just weren't meant to be. He had to accept it, move on – put her down as a person who'd inspired change, who'd come into his life for that purpose but nothing more, full stop.

Perhaps she was actually pig sick that she hadn't been able to present the show. He'd have been gutted too if he'd been her. But she wasn't the spiteful type. It could of course be total disappointment in herself: she'd put so much pressure on her own shoulders in the build-up that anything short of an Oscar would've left her wanting.

Bamboozled and confused, he shook it all off. He was too tired to untangle it – he had to clear up this shithole of a kitchen then he'd go to bed.

He switched on the radio for company – and then immediately regretted it. Sunshine FM was the station, *Evening Mumbles* was the show. And Charlie's voice, which was even sexier with huskiness, was nattering away.

So she was well enough to be back at work. That made it even worse. He had kept an eye out for her in Cheer on the Pier but he'd had no sightings, not even today when presumably she'd have been at work and could've popped in for a coffee.

He allowed himself a few seconds of her company and then went to the sink windowsill to turn it off. But, wait a minute! What was she on about?

'As I said earlier, it's my last night on *Evening Mumbles*

so it's a special show with the top ten of my favourite bits from my time here ...'

Her last night? She was leaving? Delme's hands groped for the worktop to steady himself. Charlie was leaving. It hit him hard in the guts and he winced as he tried to work out how it had come to this. The feedback from the party had been great, thousands of pounds had been raised for charity. And yet ... Charlie wasn't staying. Had she lost her job in the review? Or was she walking?

His head dipped as he guessed it was more likely she was going of her own choosing – she felt she had done what she'd come to do: to face up to her past, prove she wasn't a fraud and that was enough. And that meant he was surplus to requirements. Delme lifted his face to look out at the sky which was the colour of agony: purple bruises and red sores, orange flames and blood. It was pretty close to how he was feeling. He had lost her. He, Delme Noble, once a swordsman who had grabbed life by the balls. Now he'd been punched in them because he'd lost his bloody bottle. Anger and frustration surged through him and he smacked the sink. Except he couldn't even do that properly – his finger had caught on the edge of the tap and it was killing him. He was pathetic ...

'We've come to my number one. I'll say goodbye now because I might go on a bit. My producer's on standby to cut me off if I do ...'

Del wanted to think horrible things about her but he couldn't. He could hear the emotion catching in the way she spoke and he imagined her face up close to the microphone, holding her headphones tightly against her ears, as if she was in the same room as all her listeners.

'I just want to say a huge thanks to you all for listening

and for joining in and making me so proud to have been a part of your evenings ...'

Oh God, this was making him want to cry. He was going to miss her so much. Charlie Bold would forever be the one that got away.

'I've spent a lot of time giving out advice and hearing problems, well, I hope you don't mind but there's something I want to get off my chest ... so here goes ... Crush on the Bus. It's been the best ride of my life. I came up with it in panic, when I turned up here and couldn't get the words out. But it grew into something amazing, we've got our first Crush on the Bus wedding, after all! That's not why it matters so much to me though ...'

Delme's index finger hovered over the off button. Could he turn her off? Was a clean break the way to do this? Yet something kept him hooked.

'You see ... I've had a crush on the bus since the first day I got here ...'

Oh, fucking great. This was just marvellous – she was about to rip open his chest, pull out his heart, then not just ride over it but reverse back on it too for good measure.

'I know, I should've said something before, what good is it saying it now when I'm going? But then again can one journey with somebody technically be a crush on the bus? I wasn't sure but then I thought, what the hell, it is whatever I want it to be ...'

One journey? One bloody journey? And there he was tormenting himself about a deep connection he thought he'd had with her over six months. And for God's sake, she was sounding as if she was all about spontaneity!

'Because I only sat beside him once ...'

He'd never thought of her as a one-night-stand type, fair do's, he wasn't going to judge her if she had or she hadn't, but you had to be unhinged if you fell in love that quickly.

'I didn't know it at the time and I don't think he did either but that for me was the start of the most amazing friendship of my life. More than that, a love that I've never felt before. A racing of my pulse when I see him but a sense of calm at the same time ...'

Yep, he thought, bitterly nodding in agreement at the radio. That was exactly how she made him feel too.

'It doesn't make sense – it never has done. We're total opposites. We have nothing in common ...'

'I know,' he whispered, taking shuddery breaths of sadness.

'It was a Monday in March. After my first ever show ...'

Charlie's first show ... he racked his brains ... Oh, he'd caught the bus with her. She was going to resign. He remembered it now, she was going to the city centre, he went too, he was going to go to Wind Street, then she told him not to but he went anyway because he'd been upset about Sam. God, it felt so long ago and he felt the relief that he wasn't in that bad place any more. Although this spot wasn't so great at the moment ... unless ... No, he didn't dare believe it. Don't go getting your hopes up, it'll hurt all over again. Even so, he was gripped.

'He got me through it. He somehow managed to cope with being thrown onto live radio without a script and save my bacon because I'd been panicking ...'

Oh! Was it him? No, no, he couldn't go there. He needed to hear her say his name before he'd believe it.

'I hadn't meant to get this job, you see. But I'm so glad

I did. I wanted him to be my sidekick but circumstances … anyway. The point is I met someone who made me think about the way I'd been living my life and who gave me the strength to face up to some things I didn't want to confront …'

It had to be him, that was what she'd done for him. He touched the radio with his fingertips.

'That was a wonderful thing to happen. And I have to be content with that because I only have myself to blame. I should've seized the day and told him, but I didn't, I was scared and there were things I had to do … So thank you, Delme Noble, for doing that for me.'

'It's me! It's me!' he sang, hopping on one foot then the next as euphoria took over. His heart was leaping and he had the most ridiculous grin. 'It really is me!' he said again, running around the kitchen, nearly slipping on a clammy noodle.

'But it doesn't matter now anyway as he's back with his ex …'

'What?' he said, stopping dead, his excitement turning to horror.

'It wasn't meant to be for me but that doesn't mean it has to be the story for you. Guys, if you're ever in the same situation then don't be like me and end up crying into your cocoa – go for it and seize the day. So that's it from me and I'm off for a ride on the number 2A for old time's sake—'

Delme smacked off the radio. He had to go and find her. What if she was leaving tonight or first thing tomorrow? What if he missed this chance? He ran to the door and almost dashed off until he remembered he needed shoes. He found five but no matching ones.

He didn't care – so he put on a trainer and a moccasin and then realised he was only wearing boxers. Damp noodley ones. So he threw his drawers open and found a pair of shorts and a T-shirt and chucked them on, only realising when the door had slammed on him that his shorts were back to front and his T-shirt was inside out. And his keys ... he'd left them inside. There was a spare at his neighbour's but her car wasn't in her space and he did a kind of jig in one direction and then the other before deciding his fate.

'Fuck it!' he cried. If he didn't go now he'd miss her bus pulling in at the bus station. So he ran and ran through the shiny marina full of Friday night diners, past the deep dark basin of the docks, across the streaming traffic of Oystermouth Road, up along the big Tesco, the deserted Quadrant shopping centre and up to the glass doors of the bus station. He'd run so fast he felt like he was going to throw up so he bent over, heaving and panting, looking up every now and again to see which bus was pulling up until hallelujah, he saw her face looking out of the exact same seat they'd sat on all those months ago. She looked sad but accepting, as if it was her fate.

He walked up to the bus and as soon as the doors opened, he pushed past the people trying to get off, apologising profusely, he had to get to her, you see. Funnily enough no one argued with him: that had to be his outfit. He looked cuckoo – and he felt it, hysterical with joy and then befuddled by her getting the wrong end of the stick, not to mention the fact she was leaving – LEAVING! – and then she was there, standing up, holding onto her bag, not seeing him, looking at her feet until ... their eyes met, her mouth opened wide and as he waved like an idiot she began to smile a big goofy grin and then she began to laugh when she saw his feet. They were inches away from one another in the aisle ... And then he was suddenly the most nervous he'd ever been in his life.

'What do you look like?' Charlie said, her eyes shining.

'To be fair, mush, this is your fault,' he said. 'You could've given me some warning. You know how much I like to have lots of notice about things.'

'Oh, get over yourself,' Charlie said. 'You need to live a little.'

They swapped a deliciously smug snort, so pleased they were with their teasing. Then Del realised he had something urgent to tell her.

'I'm not with her,' he flapped. 'I'm not with Fflur.' He stared at her intently – this was the most important thing he'd ever said to her.

'No?' Charlie's voice ended on a note so high it almost hurt his ears.

'No!' he boomed.

'Does that mean ...' she whispered.

'Yes,' he whispered back.

For a few seconds they looked at each other in disbelief. Then came the frisson as they wondered who was going to make the first move.

The answer was both of them, stepping into each other: as it always had been, meeting in the middle. Their mouths met tenderly and then hungrily as they finally connected as one. Delme had never experienced such bliss. A rev of the engine beneath their feet then a beep of the horn brought them to their senses and they peeled away from each other as passengers wolf-whistled them off the bus.

'Shall we go back to yours?' Delme asked once their blushing had subsided, after a bashful wander going-nowhere-special that had taken them to the foot of Swansea Castle, which was lit up the colour of amber. Like her beautiful eyes. Oh God, he fancied her like mad ...

'Blimey, that's a bit forward isn't it?' Charlie said, with faux shock, pulling him in for another kiss.

'It's just ... I can't bear to be apart from you – and because I've locked myself out.' He bent down to nuzzle her neck and then pulled her hair free from its ponytail, wanting to get lost in its glorious softness.

'Some things don't change!' she said, running her hands through his curls and across his shoulders which took him to heaven. Momentarily.

'Except everything will,' he said, suddenly gloomy, falling off cloud nine onto cloud zero, realising he wasn't alone with his fair maiden in the grounds of the twelfth-century fortress which had held off sieges, rebellion and the Blitz but not the developers of office blocks which dwarfed the crumbling ruins. 'You're leaving. Why didn't you tell me?'

'The job offers came in this afternoon just before I went on air.'

A drunken shout and then hyena laughter came right on cue in a cruel reminder that love might not conquer all when the reality of Wind Street with its Nando's and bars, NCP car park and boozers was around the corner.

'Offers?' he squeaked. That was it, then.

'Ridiculous, I know. Word's got round, radio's a small place.'

'No, no! You're amazing. You deserve this. You showed them – and yourself.'

'Thanks, Delme, that means so much. So ...' She was breaking it to him gently, he saw the regret in her eyes. 'I had to pick one on the spot. I made my mind up there and then. That's because of you.'

His tummy flipped at the compliment then flopped at what she meant. 'Great. So just when this happens you decide you're going to live dangerously and I'll lose you and it's all my fault.'

'Delme, listen. It's not so bad.'

'Isn't it?' he sighed, as the blue lights of an ambulance approached. He may as well flag it down for open-heart surgery.

'Not necessarily,' Charlie said, holding his face in her hands. 'It depends on how you look at it.'

'Really?' He couldn't see a way through a long-distance relationship. Not when he had made peace with himself and Sam.

'Just think of it as an adventure!'

'Adventure? Since when did you like adventure?'

'A magical mystery tour then.'

'Can I get a return just in case?' he asked, weakly.

'Are you playing it safe, Delme Noble?' Charlie challenged him with narrowed eyes.

'Me? The original party animal? The wild child? The Welsh warrior?' he blustered. Then he became serious because what else had this summer been about? 'I am. Yes.'

She bit her lip and nodded slowly at him. 'Well, that makes two of us.'

And then Charlie's mouth twitched into a secretive smile.

'Eh?' What did she mean? Suddenly he had an inkling it wasn't going to be as drastic as he'd thought.

'I'll explain on the walk home,' she said, as their foreheads touched and then their bodies followed until they were pressed together so tightly there was no light between them.

And as he closed his eyes and her perfect lips found his, he felt as if the sun wasn't going down on them but only just coming up.

Ten days later

Epilogue

'It's time ... welcome to the all-new breakfast show ...
with your favourite DJ Charlie Bold!'

❧

The digital clock flicked to 6.58 a.m. Charlie whispered the final run-through under her breath, but
the patter she had put together wasn't written down on a
script nor a cue card. It was in her head and in her heart
because this was what she had always dreamed of: hosting
her own radio station breakfast show. And what better
timing than just after the start of the new school year
when she could equip herself with fresh notepads and
pens. September the tenth, a new term, a new beginning
created for her and by her with a trusted team of pros.
Well, apart from one ...

The nerves she felt rattled up and down her spine as
if she was a xylophone but instead of being crippled by
them, she was dancing along to the tune with confidence.

Ten days, no, ten years of wanting, this was Charlie's
moment to step out into the sun. She had loved *Evening
Mumbles*, it was where she had learned to be herself again.
But there was a literal meaning too. While she would
be getting up in darkness throughout the winter to start

work, she would be able to seize the rest of the day too.

Good things come to those who wait, people had said to her. She accepted their well wishes but inside she disagreed because that wasn't the whole story. Good things came to those who worked hard, who didn't just lay their ghosts to rest but put them to bed forever. It hadn't landed in her lap after all. Although Ivor Mone disagreed. He'd slung the accusation at her after he'd been called in by Sian, who'd been promoted to the position of station controller the day of Charlie's last *Evening Mumbles* show. Sian's thorough and inventive review for a 'Smarter Sunshine FM' meant his tenure as the host of *Morning Mumbles* was over because Charlie was taking the helm. He'd been offered the weekday 4 a.m. to 7 a.m. graveyard slot instead. Muttering 'bloody women', he'd walked though when his victim at Party on the Pier made groping allegations which prompted several more women to come forward. That wasn't the only good news though. Hours later, Charlie's second job offer had come from Orbital FM – Stig Costello had heard of her success and suggested she might want to apply for lead traffic presenter on breakfast. They were having a shake-up after Jonny Kay's departure. How wonderful to be asked! she'd said and Stig had fussed and gushed, asking her when she'd like to start. But instantly she'd decided that she wanted to stay in Swansea, thank you very much, she was very happy to be a big fish in a small pond rather than London roadkill.

It wasn't just Charlie who'd benefitted from the revamp. Ed Walker had taken early retirement when *Mumbles Matters* had been axed, paving the way for Disgo Colin to do three hours of pop anthems, chat and quizzes on *Mumbles Mash-Up*. It meant he could pick up Merri's daughter from school as well as build his kiddies disco business on the side. Sian had raided her contacts book and come up with a formidable female ex-MP for *Mumbles Matinée*, the afternoon debate show, and a respected newspaper editor she knew for *Home Time*. As for *Evening Mumbles*, Sian had wished Charlie could do that too because it had been such a success but breakfast had to come first – that was how the station would define itself. Crush on the Bus and Bring Me Sunshine would still be part of Charlie's gig. As for *Evening Mumbles*, Sian was prepared to take a gamble by hiring a twenty-something woman who had glowing references from university, hospital radio and an internet station, where she'd learned her trade over the last two years. Charlie had already decided she would mentor her.

The effect of this new blood pumping through Sunshine FM had been incredible already: advertising had reported a surge of interest with companies in negotiation to sponsor the weather, sport and outside broadcasts. And you could feel it in the building, in the clip-clop of heels strutting along the corridors, the off-the-hook ring of phones and in the scramble when Merri arrived with her new venture, deliveries from Cheer on the Pier's Coffee Club. Speaking of which, where was hers? She took a time check: it was 6.59 a.m.

'Where is he?' Joanie hissed into Charlie's headphones, tapping her watch at her in the control room through the glass window.

'He'll be here, don't you worry!' Charlie said, not at all concerned.

'If you say so,' Roy said, but with a wry smile because he was one hundred per cent behind the changes.

Just then, Delme flew through the studio door with two coffees in his hands. He preferred to go old school with a pick-up – and he wanted to make sure Merri's new member of staff was settling in because he still felt guilty for handing in his notice with nine days' notice.

He'd slept on it, that night, after their first kiss on the bus, when Charlie had told him she was staying at Sunshine FM but on one condition: that he would be her co-presenter. Sian had suggested it after he'd proved again he could think on his feet. She hadn't forgotten how much the listeners had loved him when he'd made his unintended debut with Charlie in March. And then when he'd covered two hours off the hoof at the Party on the Pier, she'd known he simply had to get back behind the microphone.

Delme had tried to last until morning but he'd woken Charlie excitedly at 4 a.m., telling her it was a yes! He could still do part-time lifeguarding in the summer and he was absolutely committed to his surf-school too. The way he was, two hours of DJ work wasn't work at all – he'd have plenty of energy for the rest of his day. When she complained about the time and couldn't he have waited until morning, he'd told her he was just getting her used to the early starts.

They'd only been together since that Friday night but already Charlie was head over heels. In lust at least. But it was more than that – oh, so much more. They laughed non-stop, they had fun doing nothing and they'd taken to quiet nights in, cooking or watching telly. Last night, while they were eating spag bol, he'd told her he already loved her. She didn't panic because she felt free with him. When she'd replied she could see herself telling him the same sooner rather than later, he'd taken the piss. 'Stop! I'll die of the romance of it all!' But he knew just as she did that this was for good because they both had the same values even if they were from different planets. The upshot was they each brought out the best and tamed the worst in each other. Charlie felt braver with him by her side and Delme felt more stable. It was also lovely to dip into the other's world: he loved a cuddle on the sofa, she loved a sudden announcement of dinner out. Everyone was delighted for them. Especially Libby because she could take the credit for giving Charlie the right advice when it mattered: good things did happen if you let them ... and they were happening right now.

'Sorry! Sorry!' Delme said, jumping into the seat beside Charlie, 'Couldn't find my shoes.'

'There's a surprise!' she laughed, wanting to kiss him all over but refraining in the interests of professionalism. She'd sneak one later when Joanie and Roy left the room.

'No snogging!' Joanie shouted. 'The cameras are streaming us live, remember?'

Bugger. And that had been Charlie's idea too. Never mind. She could wait. They had already decided they'd go back to bed after the show – 'we could even have a nap,' Charlie had suggested cheekily – before Delme went to see the mental health team at Sam's place who were advising him on the kinds of issues he'd face when he launched his surf-therapy school. It would work, that was for sure: Charlie had met his brother for the first time yesterday and while he'd been elbowing Delme with 'oi, oi' when she'd been introduced as his girlfriend, he'd forgotten it as soon as he remembered they were going in the waves.

While Delme was out, she was going house-hunting with Claudia and Joanie. Not for them because Joanie had already moved in with Claudia, they were that together. But for Charlie, who wanted to buy her own flat in Mumbles. There was only so much spontaneity she could cope with. Tina had meant to be going with her but had pulled out because she was meeting Abigail – they were mending their friendship, why should they suffer because of Gareth? – to celebrate the fact that public enemy number one had been relocated to a new prison with a much longer stretch inside after he'd harassed them both.

When Charlie moved, Tina was going to leapfrog into her old room – her and Gen had become big mates and they were besides themselves with glee at the thought of living together. They had never had the chance to do it when they were young, having gone straight from home into marriage. This was their time, they'd concluded, and they were going to have a ball. As well as grow their own veg.

Charlie went to switch off her phone just as a message came through. She had a big smile. Talk of the devil, Tina was sending good luck – plus an 'I knew all along you'd be good together!'.

'So, what have you got then?' Charlie asked as she lifted the lid on her coffee to inspect her foam emoji. Her fingers were trembling but she suspected it was because of him, not the seconds heading towards 7 a.m.

'A sunshine!' Delme said.

'Me too!'

'Well, I make that happy bloody days, don't you?'

'A reminder to watch your language,' Roy said over the cans.

'Yeah, yeah, course, mate. Charlie, I got you a toastie too.' He handed over a squashed package from his shorts pocket.

'Ah! Thanks!' She peeked inside. 'Ham!'

'I know. It's like I'm psychic. So … what's coming up then, mush?' Delme said as if it had just occurred to him that he was about to go on the radio.

'It's fine. You don't need to know,' Charlie said. 'Just do what you do.'

'OK,' he said looking completely unperturbed.

It made Charlie's head rush – she was in awe of his ability to take things in his stride. For her, she was steadying her breath now as the jingle sounded out 7 a.m. But it was OK. This was healthy, this meant she would do her best. Because she was where she'd always meant to be. The promo announced it was time and Joanie nodded at her to go …

'Wakey, wakey, Mumbles!' Charlie cried, 'This is Sunny Side Up on Sunshine FM. I'm Charlie Bold …'

'And I'm Delme Noble. We're here to give you some morning glory! To put the nuts in your crunchy corn-flakes! And to get your bacon – or veggie substitute – sizzling!'

'Yes,' Charlie continued, 'We've got so much coming up for you today and every weekday between seven and ten – think of us as your happy, chatty station with the best music and guests to get you going. So whether you're heading into or coming home from work or on the school run, we'll be here to keep you company. We'll have competitions galore, you'll meet Mumbles's everyday heroes, we'll do tide times, surfing forecasts, you name it, we'll do it. Standby for all of that. It's the news and weather next, but first, we start off as we mean to go on ... here's Katrina and the Waves and *Walking On Sunshine*!'

Acknowledgements

Oh, sunshine! It's the bringer of joy, just like these people who make up Team Sunshine ...

My agent Lizzy Kremer always gets the first mention because she is The Boss Lady. Every bit of contact I have with her is like basking in the sun – under her direction, my writing grows and blossoms. (There's the occasional bit of sweating too but that's entirely of my own making.) Vision, insight, patience and belief – and talk about astute, she has it all. Kremer, I adore you.

Clare Hey, publishing director at Orion and my sublime editor. I absolutely love working with her. Chey, you untangle the knots and know exactly what I want to say, which is pretty bloody genius. It's a total delight to be in your gang.

Same goes for my Orion lovelies – Lauren Woosey, Jennifer Breslin, Olivia Barber, Jen Wilson, Andrew Taylor, Mark Stay – plus everyone at David Higham Associates. I appreciate everything you do.

My copy-editor Kate Shearman for pointing out my stupidity, plot holes, spelling errors and for enquiring very politely what the word 'flubber' meant. I'd only made it up. Don't hold your breath for it to be included in the dictionary.

Artist Robyn Neild – again you brought the picture in my head to life. Another fantastic cover, thank you so much.

One very important person is next: Charlotte Morgan, radio supremo, who checked the jargon – thank you so very much for your time and support. Diolch! Not forgetting Laura Waters too, from Public Sector Prisons Wales, who helped me with a couple of queries. Any mistakes are mine.

Mel at Griffin Books in Penarth, for championing me – it's an honour to be in your window and on your front table.

Big love to the pro reviewers, particularly Anne Cater, Clare Frost, Natasha Harding and Isabelle Broom, a fabulous author too, for all your incredible support.

And to all you bloggers, NetGalley readers, Amazon reviewers, Goodreads bookworms, you lot do it for the love of books and let me tell you, your support is utterly humbling and amazing and you're the best.

Author mates, you're a hug of laughs, encouragement and inspiration. Milly Johnson, Lucy Diamond, Cathy Bramley, Heidi Swain, Amanda Jennings, Miranda Dickinson and all the Swans – Jill Mansell, Rosie Walsh, Veronica Henry, Cally Taylor, Kate Riordan, Katherine Webb, Emylia Hall … I'm amazed to be in your company.

Twitter, you make me hoot. Radio 5 Live, you're always on and you always will be.

My friends are the best. Especially Ceri and the Babas, who are my dream commune squad.

My husband, son, cat and dog, they're all Cardiff City fans so they're appalled this book is set in Swansea. Not sorry though because the Mumbles is one beautiful place. Anyway, you're my sunshine and I love you.

And finally, my readers – without you, I wouldn't be doing this and it's so lovely when you get in touch. Thank you so so much. I'm on Twitter and Instagram @LauraJaneKemp and have a Facebook page called Laura Kemp Books – please, please, keep in touch.

Sometimes all it takes to make the world a better place
is a small act of kindness …

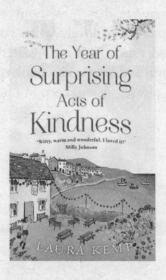

The Year of
Surprising
Acts of
Kindness

'Witty, warm and wonderful. I loved it!'
Milly Johnson

LAURA KEMP

When Ceri Price arrives in the small seaside village in West Wales, she
only means to stay for a couple of nights – long enough to scatter her
mother's ashes, and then go back to her life as a successful make-up
entrepreneur.

But when a case of mistaken identities means she lands a job as the
barmaid in the local pub, she unexpectedly finds friendship, and
perhaps a chance at love. And when the plans for a new housing estate
put the local woodland under threat, she fears the way of life here
could disappear.

Then mysterious acts of kindness – strings of bunting, a new signpost,
pots of paint to spruce up the seafront houses – start bringing new life
to the village. But who is behind these surprising gifts, and can a little
kindness change all their lives?

'A truly wonderful and heartwarming read'
Heidi Swain

'An adorable life-affirming book'
Rowan Coleman

Available in paperback and ebook now